CRUCIBLE

CRUCIBLE

A THRILLER

JAMES ROLLINS

WM
WILLIAM MORROW
An Imprint of HarperCollins*Publishers*

Grateful acknowledgment is made for permission to reprint the following images:

Designed by the author: pp. 13, 17, 18, 58, 124, 125, 241, 427
Courtesy of Shutterstock: pp. 82, 83, 84, 104, 105 (top), 122, 123, 165, 207, 232, 317, 392, 393
Sourced from Wikipedia Commons: pp. 40, 42, 43, 44
Courtesy of Pexels: pp. 105 (bottom), 106, 272, 273, 274, 333, 453
Designed by Steven Prey (All rights reserved. Used by permission of Steve Prey): pp. xv, 324

FIRST EDITION

Library of Congress Cataloging-in-Publication Data has been applied for.

ISBN 978-0-06-238178-1 (hardcover)

ISBN 978-0-06-287191-6 (international edition)

19 20 21 22 23 DIX/LSC 10 9 8 7 6 5 4 3 2

For Chuck and Cindy Bluth,

for their many years of friendship, mentorship,

and, most of all, their enduring generosity of spirit

What is going to be created will effectively be a god. It's not a god in the sense that it makes lightning or causes hurricanes. But if there is something a billion times smarter than the smartest human, what else are you going to call it? . . . [And] This time you will be able to talk to God, literally, and know that it's listening.

—ANTHONY LEVANDOWSKI
former Google executive and founder of Way of the Future, a new church based on the religion of artificial intelligence (from an interview by Mark Harris, Backchannel/*Wired*, November 15, 2017: "Inside the First Church of Artificial Intelligence")

With artificial intelligence, we are summoning the demon.

—ELON MUSK
at the MIT Aeronautics and Astronautics Department's Centennial Symposium, 2014

Acknowledgments

It seems no good deed truly goes unpunished. The critique group that I joined many ages ago—well before I was ever published and still a full-time practicing veterinarian—has stood steadfastly throughout my career, offering great editorial advice, from plot discussions to character analysis, and yes, catching the many mistakes that pepper my first drafts. And this novel is no exception. So first and foremost, let me thank that close-knit bevy of critical first readers: Dave Meek, Chris Crowe, Lee Garrett, Matt Bishop, Jane O'Riva, Matt Orr, Leonard Little, Judy Prey, Caroline Williams, Tod Todd, Frank Barrera, and Amy Rogers. And as always, a special thanks to Steve Prey for the great maps . . . and to David Sylvian for making me look good across the digital universe (and beyond) . . . and to Cherei McCarter for the many significant historical and scientific tidbits found within these pages. And of course, a big note of appreciation and thanks to everyone at HarperCollins for always having my back, especially Liate Stehlik, Lynn Grady, Danielle Bartlett, Kaitlin Harri, Josh Marwell, Richard Aquan, and Ana Maria Allessi. And I cannot forgo giving a special shout-out to Brian Grogan, who has been at my side at HarperCollins since the beginning of my career and who actually gave this book its title (*Crucible*). Last, of course, a special acknowledgment to the people instrumental to all levels of production: my esteemed editor who has also been with me since my first book, Lyssa

Keusch, and her industrious colleague Priyanka Krishnan; and for all their hard work, my agents, Russ Galen and Danny Baror (along with his daughter Heather Baror). And as always, I must stress that any and all errors of fact or detail in this book, of which hopefully there are not too many, fall squarely on my own shoulders.

Notes from the Historical Record

"Eu non creo nas meigas, mais habelas, hainas."
I don't believe in witches, but they do exist.
—an old Galician proverb

From February 1692 to May 1693, twenty people in colonial Massachusetts—fourteen of them women—were accused, sentenced, and put to death for the practice of witchcraft. While the infamous Salem Witch Trials have left an indelible mark on history, it was merely the final spasm of hysteria at the tail end of the great witch hunt that had already swept Europe. There, persecutions ran for nearly three centuries, and all told, more than sixty thousand "witches" were burned, hung, or drowned.

All of this bloodshed and death started rather abruptly in the fifteenth century and can be attributed to the publication of a single book, a witch hunter's manual titled the *Malleus Maleficarum* (which translates to *The Hammer of Witches*). It was published by a German Catholic clergyman named Heinrich Kramer in 1487 and received approval by both the University of Cologne and the head of the Catholic Church, Pope Innocent VIII. With the newly invented printing press, copies were quickly made and spread across Europe and over to the Americas. It grew to become the instructive "bible" for Inquisitors and prosecutors to identify, torture, and execute witches, with an emphasis on female heresy in particular. Many scholars deem it one of the most blood-soaked books in history, even comparing it to *Mein Kampf.*

Still, prior to the manual's publication, the relationship between witches and Christendom was not as straightforward as it might appear. Initially, witches were not so adamantly vilified. In the Old Testament, King Saul sought out the Witch of Endor to conjure the spirit of the deceased prophet, Samuel, and throughout medieval times, witches were often educated healers, harvesting beneficial herbs according to ancient traditions. Even during the bloody Spanish Inquisition, it was heretics—not witches—who were most often hunted and tortured.

As further proof of this blurring between the role of witches and the Catholic Church, the cult of Saint Columba flourished throughout the Middle Ages in Spain, mainly in the northern Galician region, which was considered a bastion of witches. According to legend, Columba was a witch from the ninth century, who met the spirit of Christ on the road. He told her she could not enter heaven unless she converted to Christianity, so she did—but she remained a witch. She was eventually martyred and beheaded for her faith and became known as the "patron saint of witches." To this day she acts as a protector for witches, interceding on the behalf of good witches, while fighting against those who would corrupt such craft for evil purposes.

And now might be a good time to light a candle to Saint Columba, for we are about to enter a new age of witchcraft.

Notes from the Scientific Record

"Any sufficiently advanced technology is indistinguishable from magic."
—Arthur C. Clarke, 1962,
from his essay "Hazards of Prophecy: The Failure of Imagination"

Let's discuss the end of humankind—especially as we may soon have little say in the matter. A dangerous threat looms on the horizon, one likely to arise in our own lifetime. World-renowned physicist Stephen Hawking described this coming crisis as the "worst event in the history of civilization." Elon Musk believes it will lead to World War III. Even Russian president Vladimir Putin has stated that whoever controls this event will control the world.

That event is the creation of the first true humanlike artificial intelligence (AI).

Such a moment already terrifies those in power. In February 2018, a secret closed-door meeting was held at the World Government Summit to discuss the fate of AI. It was attended by representatives from IBM, Microsoft, Facebook, and Amazon, along with officials from across Europe, Russia, Singapore, Australia, and the Arab world. The consensus was that our very existence was at stake, but worst of all, the attendees concluded that regulations or international agreements could not halt the inevitable progress toward a self-aware AI. Any countermeasures were deemed "elusive," especially as history has demonstrated that any bans would likely be easily circumvented by stealth companies or organizations operating covertly in remote corners of the world.

So how close are we to the arrival of a new intelligence on our planet? Already various forms of AI have infiltrated our lives. They're operating in our computers, our phones, even our appliances. Nearly 70 percent of all buy/sell orders on Wall Street are currently performed without human guidance, eking out transactions in under three milliseconds. AI has become so ubiquitous that few even recognize it as "AI" anymore. But the next step in this technology's evolution is fast approaching: when a computer will demonstrate a human-level of intelligence and self-awareness. A recent poll revealed that 42 percent of computer experts believe this creation will happen within the decade, with half of those claiming within five years.

But why is this event such a crisis? Why is this the "worst event in the history of civilization"? It's because the first humanlike intelligence will not be idle, but instead it will prove to be very *busy*. It will quickly—in weeks, days, maybe even hours—evolve into an incomprehensible *super*intelligence, a creation far superior to us, one that will likely have little use for humans. When that occurs, there is no way of predicting if this new superintelligence will be a benevolent god or a cold, destructive devil.

Regardless, such a creation is coming. There is no stopping it. Some even believe it might already be here. And because of that, I must offer one final warning: *Buried in the heart of this novel is a curse.* Simply by reading this book, you may inadvertently doom yourself.

So, please, continue at your own risk.

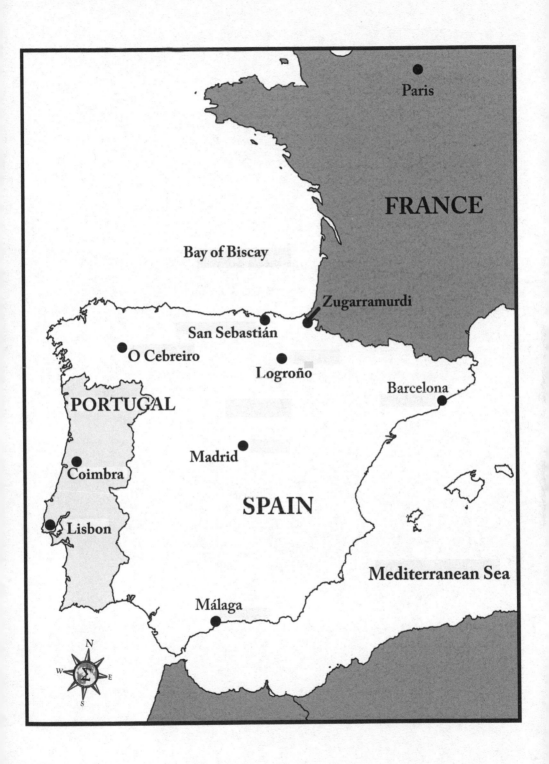

June 23, 1611 A.D.
Zugarramurdi, Spain

Behind the iron bars, the witch knelt on a filthy bed of straw and prayed to God.

Alonso de Salazar Frías studied the unusual sight. The Inquisitor could barely discern the figure within. The cell was dark, lit only by the flickering flames rising from the neighboring village square. Through the same window slit, the smell of burnt flesh accompanied the ghastly, dancing glow across the stone walls.

He listened to the witch's whispers in Latin, studied the folded hands, the bowed head. The prayer was a familiar one, *Anima Christi*, composed by Ignatius of Loyola, the founder of the Society of Jesus. It was a fitting prayer considering the witch kneeling here was of that same order, a Jesuit priest.

Alonso silently translated the last of the prayer: *At the hour of my death, call me into your presence, lead me to praise you with all your saints. Forever and ever.*

"Amen," Alonso said aloud, drawing the accused witch's attention.

He waited for the man to stand. Though surely no older than Alonso's forty-seven years, the priest creaked to his feet. The robe that had been left to him hung from thin shoulders. His face was sunken and pocked with sores. The jailers had even shaved his head, leaving his scalp scabbed in several places.

Alonso felt a flicker of pity for his poor state, even knowing it was a man of God who stood accused of heresy and witchcraft. Alonso had been summoned to this tiny Basque village at the personal request of the

Inquisitor General to conduct this interrogation. It had taken him a week to traverse the Pyrenees to reach the small cluster of homes and farms near the border of France.

The priest hobbled to the iron bars and grasped them with bony fingers plagued by a tremoring palsy of weakness.

When had they last fed this man?

The Jesuit's words, though, were firm. "I am not a witch."

"That is what I have been ordered to determine, Father Ibarra. I have read the charges brought against you. You have been accused of practicing witchcraft, of using charms and amulets to heal the sick."

The priest remained silent for two breaths before speaking. "Similarly, I know of *you*, Inquisitor Frías. Of your reputation. You were one of the three judges during the witch trials in Logroño two summers ago."

Alonso hid a wince born of shame and had to look away, but he could not so easily escape the flicker of flames, the reek of blackened flesh. The sights and smells here were all too familiar. During those tribunals at the nearby township of Logroño, he had gone along with judgments of the other two Inquisitors. Guilt for that decision ate at him. It had been the largest witch trial in Spain. The accusation of a single woman—Maria de Ximildegui—ignited a wildfire of hysteria and panic. She had claimed to have witnessed a witch's sabbath and pointed fingers at others, who in turn cast aspersions upon even more. In the end, three hundred stood accused of consorting with the devil. Many of the accused were mere children, the youngest being four years old. By the time Alonso had arrived in Logroño, the other two Inquisitors had narrowed the trial to thirty of the worst offenders. Those who admitted to their crimes were punished, but mercifully spared the flames. Unfortunately, a stubborn twelve refused to admit they were witches and were subsequently burned at the stake.

Alonso carried their deaths upon his soul—not because he failed to get them to admit they were witches, but because he believed in their innocence. He expressed just such a conviction afterward, risking much by the admittance to Bernardo de Sandoval y Rojas, the Inspector General of the Spanish Inquisition in whose friendship Alonso trusted greatly. His faith in their relationship proved well founded. The cruel and bloodthirsty time of the Royal Inquisitor, Tomas de Torquemada, was a century in the past. The Inspector General sent him alone to carry out an investigation throughout the wider Basque region of Spain, to separate hysteria from reality. He had been on the road for nearly two months, questioning those accused or imprisoned. So far he had discovered only false testimonies pried forth during torture, stories rife with contradictions or inconsistencies. During his travels, he had yet to discover a single verifiable case of witchcraft.

In his private struggle to spare those souls accused of such crimes, he wielded a single weapon. He returned his attention to the priest and patted the leather satchel at his side. "Father Ibarra, I carry with me an Edict of Faith, signed by the Inspector General. It allows me to pardon anyone who admits their crimes, swears fealty to God, and denounces the devil."

The priest's eyes shone in the darkness, fervent with pride. "I have no qualms about swearing the latter—of expressing my love of God—but as I said from the beginning, I am not a witch and will not admit as such."

"Not even to spare your life?"

Ibarra turned his back and studied the firelit window of his cell. "Did you arrive in time to hear their screams?"

Alonso could not hide his wince this time. Earlier, as he descended out of the mountains, he had spotted streams of smoke rising from the village. He prayed the smoke marked bonfires being set to celebrate the summer solstice. Still, fearing the worst, he sped his horse faster. He raced the setting sun, only to be greeted by a chorus of wails as he reached the village outskirts.

Six witches had been burned at the stakes.

Not witches . . . *women*, he reminded himself.

Unfortunately, Alonso was not the first of the Inquisition to reach the hamlet. He suspected Father Ibarra had been spared until now because he was a priest.

Alonso stared at the man's back.

If I'm only able to save him, so be it.

"Father Ibarra, please, just admit—"

"What do you know of Saint Columba?"

Taken aback by such a strange question, it took Alonso a moment to answer. He had attended both the University of Salamanca and the University of Sigüenza, studying canon law in preparation for taking holy orders and joining the Church. He was well versed in the litany of all the saints. But the name spoken by Father Ibarra was not without controversy.

"You speak of the witch from Galicia," Alonso said, "who encountered the spirit of Christ in the ninth century during a pilgrimage to Rome."

"Christ warned her to convert to Christianity if she wished to enter heaven."

"And she did and would later be martyred for it, beheaded for refusing to forsake her religion."

Ibarra nodded. "While she entered the Church, she never forsook being a witch. Peasants throughout the region still revere her for both sides of her person—both witch and martyred saint. They pray to her to defend themselves against evil witchcraft, while also asking her to protect good witches against persecution, those who heal the sick with herbs, amulets, and enchantments."

During his travels throughout northern Spain, Alonso had heard whispers of the cult of Saint Columba. He knew many women—educated women—who studied the natural world, who sought medicines and herbs, drawing upon pagan knowledge. Some were accused of witchcraft and poisoned by priests or burned at the stake; others sought shelter in nunneries and monasteries where—like Saint Columba—they could worship Christ, yet still plant secret gardens and help the sick or afflicted, smudging the line between paganism and Christianity.

He studied Father Ibarra.

Was this priest a part of that same cult?

"You yourself are accused of using charmed amulets to heal the sick," Alonso said. "Does that not mark you a witch of the same ilk? If you would admit as much, I can use the Edict to intercede—"

"I am no witch," he repeated and pointed to the smoke wafting through the cell's tiny window. "There go the women who healed many of the sick throughout these pastures and mountain villages. I was merely their protector, acting as a humble servant of Saint Columba, the patron saint of witches. I cannot with a true heart claim to be a witch. Not because I despise such an accusation, but because I do not *deserve* to be called a witch . . . for I am not worthy of such an honor."

Alonso took in the shock of these words. He had heard countless renunciations by those accused of witchcraft, but never a denial such as this.

Ibarra pulled closer to the bars. "But the story of my amulet . . . that allegation is true. I fear those who arrived here at the village before you came seeking it."

As if summoned by his words, the door opened behind Alonso. The hooded figure of a monk, robed in black, entered. Though the newcomer's eyes were covered by a strip of crimson, he could clearly still see. "Has he confessed?" the man asked gruffly.

Alonso turned to Ibarra. The priest stepped from the bars and straightened his back. Alonso knew Ibarra would never break. "He has not," Alonso admitted.

"Take him," the man ordered.

Two of the monk's brethren pushed into the room, ready to drag Ibarra to the stake. Alonso blocked them. "I will walk him out."

In short order, the cell was unbarred, and Alonso strode alongside Ibarra out of the jail and into the village square. To steady the priest and keep him upright, Alonso kept a hand on Ibarra's elbow. It was not just weakness and starvation that trembled the man's limbs—but the sight found in the square.

Six stakes smoldered, holding fire-contorted shapes, charred arms raised high, wrists bound in glowing iron. A seventh trunk of freshly hewn chestnut towered upright in a waist-high pile of dry kindling.

Ibarra reached and clutched hard to Alonso's hand.

Alonso tried to squeeze reassurance into the frightened prisoner. "May God accept you into His embrace."

But Alonso had misinterpreted the priest's intent. Bony fingers pried open his hand and pressed an object into his palm. Alonso instinctively closed his fingers over it, knowing what had been passed to him in secret, likely slipped free from some secret pocket inside the priest's tattered robe.

Ibarra's amulet.

The priest whispered in Spanish, confirming what Alonso suspected. "*Nóminas de moro.*"

*Nómina*s were charms or amulets upon which were inscribed the names of saints and were said to be capable of miraculous acts.

"It was found at the source of the Orabidea River," Ibarra explained urgently. "Keep it from them."

Ahead, through the pall of smoke, a tall figure strode purposefully forward. His robe was crimson, his blindfold was black. It was the sect's leader. Alonso had heard rumors of this inner cabal of the Inquisition, those who still adhered to the bloodlust of long-dead Torquemada. They called themselves the *Crucibulum*, after the Latin word for *crucible*, a vessel that purifies through fire.

Alonso stared at the smoking remains chained to the six stakes. His fingers tightened harder on the amulet in his palm.

The leader came forward and nodded to his brethren. Upon this silent order, they stripped Ibarra from Alonso's side and dragged him forward. The leader carried a thick book in his arms, gilded in gold. Alonso easily recognized the accursed tome. The full title—*Malleus Maleficarum, Maleficas, & earum hæresim, ut phramea potentissima conterens*—translated as "The Hammer of Witches which destroys Witches and their heresy as with a two-edged sword." The book was composed over a century ago, a bible for hunting down, identifying, and punishing witches. Already the book was falling out of favor by the papacy, even among those in the Inquisition.

But it grew even stronger within the cabal of the *Crucibulum*.

Alonso stood steadfast. What else could he do? He was a lone junior inquisitor against a dozen of the ancient *Crucibulum*.

As Ibarra was marched toward his death, the sect's leader dogged each step. The man whispered fervently in the priest's ear. Alonso heard mention of the word *nóminas*.

So Ibarra was correct in his fear.

Alonso imagined the *Crucibulum*'s leader must be delivering threats or offering promises of salvation, if only Ibarra would reveal the truth about his amulet.

Fearing attention might turn toward him, as he'd been alone with Ibarra, Alonso retreated from the square. His last sight of Ibarra was as the priest was chained to the trunk of chestnut atop the pile of wood. Ibarra caught his eye and gave the smallest nod of his head.

Keep it from them.

Alonso swore to do so as he turned his back. He hurried toward where his horse was stabled. Before he had taken more than a few steps, Ibarra's raised voice shouted to the heavens.

"BURN US ALL! IT MATTERS NOT. SAINT COLUMBA PROPHESIED HER COMING. THE WITCH WHO WILL CARRY ON HER LEGACY. THE WITCH WHO WILL CRACK THE CRUCIBLE AND PURIFY THE WORLD!"

Alonso stumbled at such a declaration. No wonder the *Crucibulum* sought to silence the cult of Columba, and more important, burn to ash any proof of such a claim. He tightened his grip on the talisman in his hand. True or not, the world was slowly changing—forsaking Torquemada's ways, letting copies of the *Malleus Maleficarum* molder into dust—but before that happened, he foresaw more bloodshed and flames, the final convulsions of a dying age.

Once far enough away, Alonso risked studying Ibarra's *nóminas.* He opened his hand. Shocked at what he saw, he almost dropped the treasure. It was a finger, raggedly torn from some hand. The edges looked burned, but otherwise, it was perfectly preserved. He knew one of the signs of sainthood was when the relics of such holy figures proved incorruptible, remaining untouched by decay or rot.

Did he hold such a relic in his hand?

He stopped to study it closer, discovering words inked into the flesh.

Sanctus Maleficarum.

He translated the Latin.

Saint of Witches.

So it was indeed a *nóminas*, an amulet with the name of a saint written upon it. But his inspection exposed a greater revelation. The finger was not a holy relic—a piece of a saint's flesh—but something even more incredible.

Breathless with wonder, he turned the object over and over. While the flesh appeared real, it was not. The skin was flexible but cold. The torn end revealed a clockwork mechanism of thin wires and gleaming metal bones. It was a simulacrum, a mechanical homunculus of a finger.

Alonso had heard stories of gifts presented to kings and queens, intricate fabrications that mimicked movements of the body. Sixty years ago, the Holy Roman Emperor Charles V was presented with a clockwork figure of a monk, designed by the Spanish-Italian engineer and artisan Juanelo Turriano. The doll could raise and lower a wooden cross, bringing the crucifix to its lips, which moved in silent prayer, while its head nodded and its eyes moved.

Am I holding a piece of such an artifice?

If so, what was its significance? How did it tie to the cult of Saint Columba?

With no answer, he continued toward the stables. Ibarra had left him one additional clue to this mystery: the source of the talisman, where it had been found.

"The Orabidea River," he mumbled with a furrowed brow.

Every Inquisitor in the region knew of that river. It flowed from a cave called *Sorginen Leizea*, the cave of witches. Many a witch's sabbath was held at that site. The Orabidea River had an equally dark history. It was sometimes called *Infernuko erreka*, or "Hell's Stream," as it was rumored to flow from the bowels of Hell into this world.

He shuddered in dread. If Ibarra had spoken the truth, the amulet in his hand had been discovered at the river's source.

In other words, at the very gates of hell itself.

He balked about pursuing this matter any further and considered tossing the amulet away—then an agonized scream rose behind him, echoing up to the stars.

Ibarra . . .

He firmed his grip on the *nóminas*.

The priest had died to keep this secret.

I must not forsake this burden.

Even if it meant crossing through the gates of Hell, he would know the truth.

Present Day
December 21, 10:18 P.M. WET
Coimbra, Portugal

The coven awaited her.

Charlotte Carson hurried across the breadth of the darkened university library. Her rushed footsteps echoed off the marble floor to the bricked roof of the two-story medieval gallery. All around, ornate shelves housed books dating as far back as the twelfth century. With the vast space lit by only a handful of sconces, she gaped at the shadowy climb of ladders, at the elaborate gilded woodwork.

Constructed in the early eighteenth century, the *Biblioteca Joanina* remained a perfectly preserved gem of Baroque architecture and design, the true historic center of the University of Coimbra. And like any treasure house, it was a veritable vault, with walls two feet thick and massive doors of solid teak that sealed the space. The purposeful design maintained the interior at a steady sixty-five degrees, no matter the season, along with a constant low humidity.

Perfect for preserving the integrity of ancient books . . .

But such conservation efforts were not limited to the library's architecture.

Charlotte ducked as a bat whisked past her head and shot into the upper gallery. Unheard but felt, its ultrasonic whistle shivered the small hairs on the back of her neck. For centuries, a colony of bats had made the library its home. They were steadfast allies in the fight to preserve the work stored here. Each night, they consumed insects that might have otherwise feasted on the vast bounty of old leather and yellowed parchment.

Of course, sharing this vault with such devoted hunters required certain precautions. She ran a finger along the leather blankets that covered the tables. The caretakers draped them each evening after they closed the building to shield the wooden surfaces from the bats' droppings.

Still, as she stared up at the glide of winged shadows against the brick vaults, she felt a stir of superstitious dread—along with a modicum of amusement.

What's a gathering of witches without bats?

Even this night had been specially chosen. The weeklong scientific symposium had ended today. By tomorrow, the participants would be heading home, spreading to the far corners of the globe to spend the holidays with friends and family. But tonight, countless bonfires would light the city, accompanied by the merriment of various musical festivals, all to celebrate the winter solstice, the longest night of the year.

She checked her watch, knowing she was running late. She still wore the same semiformal outfit from the holiday party at the embassy: a loose black skirt that brushed her ankles and a short coat over a blue blouse. Her hair was styled to her scalp. It had gone prematurely silver and remained short and sparse after the course of chemo nine months ago. Afterward, she didn't bother with dyes or extensions. Having survived the brutalities and humiliations of cancer, vanity seemed a foolish frivolity. She no longer had the patience for it.

Not that she had much free time anyway.

She frowned at her watch.

Only four minutes to go.

She pictured the sun on the other side of the world as it crested toward the Tropic of Capricorn. When the sun balanced at that latitude, it would mark the moment of the true solstice, when winter inevitably tilted toward summer, when darkness gave way to light.

The perfect time for this demonstration.

A proof of concept.

"*Fiat lux*," she whispered.

Let there be light.

Ahead, a brighter glow illuminated an archway that opened to a spiral staircase leading to the library's lower regions. This topmost level was called the Noble Floor, due to its beauty and history. Directly below, the Intermediate Floor remained the sole domain of librarians, where they stored a bulk of the rarest books for safekeeping.

But Charlotte's destination lay one story deeper.

Sensing the press of time, she hurried toward the archway.

By now, the others would have gathered below. She crossed under the painting of King John V, the Portuguese king who founded the library, and reached the steps that spiraled all the way down to the bottommost level of the library.

As she circled around and around the tight staircase, a low murmur of voices rose to greet her. Upon reaching the last step, she halted at a stout black iron gate. It had been left ajar for her. Fixed upon it was a sign that read Prisão Acadêmica.

She smiled at the thought of a prison being built under a library. She pictured recalcitrant students or drunken professors being locked up down here. Once a part of the original dungeons of the royal palace, this floor had continued to serve as the university's prison until 1834. Today, it remained the only existing example of a medieval prison in all of Portugal.

She slipped through the gate and into the dungeon. A good section of this floor was open to tourists, while other locked rooms were used as additional book storage. She headed toward the far side, where the modern age had infiltrated this medieval space. A new computer system had been installed in an unused back vault, including a system for digitizing books, offering a way to further safeguard the treasures stored above.

On this winter's solstice, the computers would serve a new purpose—not to preserve the past, but to offer a glimpse into the future.

As she entered the back vault, a woman's voice greeted her. "Ah, *Embaixador* Carson, you made it in time."

Dressed in a crisp navy suit and white blouse, Eliza Guerra, the head of the Joanina Library, crossed over and gave Charlotte a peck on each cheek, along with a quick squeeze of her upper arm. Excitement all but bubbled through the petite librarian.

"I wasn't sure I would make it," Charlotte explained with an apologetic smile. "The embassy is short-staffed and in a state of chaos with the approach of the holidays."

As the U.S. ambassador to Portugal, Charlotte had a thousand responsibilities this night, including catching a red-eye back to D.C. to join her husband and two daughters. Laura, her oldest, was back from Princeton—which was Charlotte's alma mater—where she was pursuing a degree in biotechnology. Her other daughter, Carly, was more of a wild child, chasing a dream of a musical career at New York University, while also hedging her bet by studying engineering.

Charlotte couldn't be prouder of them both.

She wished they could be here to witness this moment with her. They were one of the reasons she had helped found this organization composed of women scientists and researchers. The charitable foundation was an offshoot of the larger Coimbra Group, a union of more than three dozen research universities spread around the globe.

In an attempt to foster, promote, and network women in the sciences, Charlotte and the other four women gathered here had started Bruxas International, named after the Portuguese word for "witches." For centuries, women who practiced healing, or who experimented with herbal remedies, or who simply questioned the world around them were declared heretics or witches. Even here in Coimbra—a town long revered as a place of learning—women had been put to the torch, often in great grisly pageants called *Auto-da-Fé*, or Acts of Faith, where scores of apostates and heretics were burned at the stake all at once.

Rather than shy away from such stigma, she and the others decided to lean in to it instead, defiantly naming their foundation *Bruxas*.

But the metaphor did not stop with the name.

Eliza Guerra had a computer station already booted up. The symbol for their organization glowed upon the screen, slowly spinning. It was a pentagram surrounded by a circle.

The five points of the star represented the five women here, the original coven who had founded the organization at the University of Coimbra six years ago. They had no set leader. They voted on all matters equally.

Charlotte smiled past Eliza to the three others: Dr. Hannah Fest from the University of Cologne, Professor Ikumi Sato from the University of Tokyo, and Dr. Sophia Ruiz from the University of São Paulo. Though Charlotte had received her ambassadorship last year—not in small part due to her role in arranging this international organization based in Portugal—she had originally been a researcher like the others, teaching at Princeton and representing the United States.

Despite their differences, the five women—all in their fifties—had risen in their respective professions around the same time, enduring the same hardships because of their gender, experiencing the same discrimination and slights. Beyond their common interest in the sciences, they shared this bond. Their goal was to even the playing field, to encourage and help shepherd younger women into the sciences through scholarships, apprenticeships, and mentoring.

Their efforts had already produced great results around the world—especially here.

Hannah leaned toward a stick microphone resting beside the computer keyboard. "Mara, we're all present." She spoke in English with a thickly Teutonic accent. "You can start your demonstration when you're ready."

As Hannah stepped back, the screen split. The pentagram shrank to one side, revealing the young face of Mara Silviera. Though only twenty-one, she had already spent the past five years at Coimbra, earning a scholarship from Bruxas at the tender age of sixteen. Originally from a small village in the Galicia region of northern Spain, she had garnered the attention of a slew of tech companies after publishing a translation app that outshone anything currently on the market. She seemed to have an innate ability both with computers and with the fundamentals of language.

Even now, raw intelligence shone from her eyes. Or maybe just pride. Her dark mocha complexion coupled with her long, straight black hair suggested a mix of Moorish blood in her family's past. She was presently across campus at the university's Laboratory for Advanced Computing, which housed the Milipeia Cluster, one of the continent's most powerful supercomputers.

Mara glanced slightly to the side. "I'll start cycling *Xénese* up. We should be online in a minute."

As the women gathered closer, Charlotte looked at her watch.

10:23 P.M.

Right on time.

She again pictured the sun perched above the Tropic of Capricorn, marking the culmination of the winter solstice, promising the end of darkness and the return of light.

Before that could happen, a loud iron clang made them all jump and turn.

A tight cluster of dark, hooded figures poured past the black gate and across the prison floor. In their hands, they bore large glossy pistols. The figures spread out, trapping the five women inside the computer vault.

There was no other exit from this room.

With her heart pounding in her throat, Charlotte backed up a step. She blocked the monitor with her body and reached blindly behind her. With a shift and click of the computer mouse, she collapsed the image of Mara Silviera, both to protect the young woman and to turn her into a silent witness. With the microphone and camera still broadcasting, Mara could see, hear, and even record what soon transpired.

As the figures closed in on the women, Charlotte willed Mara to call the police, though it was unlikely any rescue would arrive in time. She could not even be sure Mara was aware of the change in circumstance and was likely concentrating on her pending demonstration.

The eight assailants—all men—wore black robes with crimson silk sashes tied across their eyes like blindfolds. But from their manner and stealth, they plainly could see through the cloths.

Eliza Guerra stepped forward, ready to defend her library. "What is the meaning of this? What do you want?"

An unnerving silence answered her.

The assailants parted to reveal a ninth man, clearly the leader. Standing well over six feet, he wore a crimson robe with a black sash over his eyes, his garb a mirror image of the others. He carried no weapon, only a half-foot-thick tome. The worn leather binding was the same crimson as his robe. The gold gilt lettering on the cover was clearly visible: *Malleus Maleficarum*.

Charlotte shrank back, hope dying inside her. She had prayed this was merely a high-stakes heist. Many of the library's volumes were priceless. But the book in the man's hand threw her into despair. It appeared to be a first edition, one of only a few still in existence. One copy was preserved here at the Joanina Library. From the deep frown on Eliza's face, maybe it was the very same edition, snatched from the stacks.

The book was written in the fifteenth century by a Catholic priest named Heinrich Kramer. The Latin name translated as *The Hammer of Witches*. Devised as a guide to identify, persecute, and torture witches, it was one of the most reviled and blood-soaked books in human history. Estimates put the number of victims attributed to this book at more than sixty thousand souls.

Charlotte glanced at her companions.

And now there will be five more.

The leader's first words confirmed her fears.

"Maleficos non patieris vivere."

Charlotte recognized the admonishment from the Book of Exodus.

Suffer not a witch to live.

The man continued in English, though his accent sounded Spanish. "*Xénese* must never be," he intoned. "It is an abomination, born of sorcery and filth."

Charlotte frowned.

How did he know what we're attempting this night?

Still, the mystery would have to wait. Pistols were leveled intently at the group as two men carried forward a pair of five-gallon tanks. She read the lettering on the side: *Querosene.* She didn't need to be fluent in Portuguese to recognize the content, especially after the men upended the tanks and oily fuel flooded across the floor of the confined space.

The smell of kerosene quickly grew suffocating.

Coughing, Charlotte shared a look with the other terrified women. After working in tandem for the past six years, they knew each other. No words were needed. They were not tied to wooden stakes. If this was their end, these particular witches would die fighting.

Better a bullet than the flame.

She sneered at the leader. "Suffer this, asshole!"

The five women splashed through the pool of kerosene and dove into the gathering of men. Pistols fired, explosively loud in the confined space. Charlotte felt rounds pelt into her, but her momentum still carried her to the leader. She lunged and clawed at his face, gouging her nails deep into his flesh, tearing down his cheek. She tore his blindfold free and saw only fury in his exposed eyes.

He dropped the accursed book and shoved her away. She landed on the stone floor at the edge of the pool of kerosene. Propped up on one arm, she glanced across the room in horror at the other four women sprawled and unmoving on the floor, their blood mixing with the oil.

Weakening rapidly, she slumped to the floor herself.

The leader swore and spat orders in Spanish.

A half-dozen Molotov cocktails were removed from robes and quickly lit.

Charlotte ignored them as her body grew cold, draining any fear of the coming heat. She stared back into the room, where motion drew her fading eyes. On the computer screen, the Bruxas pentagram spun rapidly, far faster than before, as if agitated by all that had transpired.

Mystified, she stared at the blurring image.

Was Mara trying to signal her somehow?

Molotov cocktails were tossed into the room, shattering against the walls. Flames splashed high. Heat washed over her.

Still, she stared into the heart of the fire.

The symbol on the screen spun faster for another breath—then stopped abruptly. But the center could no longer hold. Fragments broke loose and scattered away.

The leader stepped closer to her prone form, likely studying the same mystery. Though she could not see his face from where she lay on the floor, she sensed his bewilderment. All that remained of the pentagram were two prongs of the star, like the horns of a devil.

As if recognizing the same, the man stiffened, clearly offended. He stumbled back, an arm lifted. He shouted in Spanish, "Des . . . destroy the *computadora*!"

But it was already too late. The image changed one final time, a full quarter turn.

Pistols cracked, and bullets pierced the fire. The computer screen shattered and went dark. Charlotte slumped and followed that darkness, searching for the promised light at the end, praying for Mara's safety.

Still, one image accompanied her into the depths. It shone brightly in her mind's eye. It was the last image on the screen. The circle around the pentagram had vanished, leaving only a new symbol that grew to fill the monitor before it shattered.

It looked like a Greek letter.

Sigma.

She didn't know what it meant, but the purposefulness of it gave her hope as she died.

Hope for the world.

FIRST

GHOST IN THE MACHINE

− 1 −

As the coin spun through the air, Commander Grayson Pierce felt a growing sense of dread. He sat on a stool next to his best friend, Monk Kokkalis, who had tossed the quarter high into the air above the mahogany bar.

Fellow patrons of the Quarry House Tavern gathered around them, drunk, rowdy, and loud, awaiting the fall of the coin. From across the tavern, a small band knocked out a rockabilly version of "The Little Drummer Boy." The heavy thud of the bass drum reverberated through his ribs, adding to his tension.

"Heads!" Monk called out as the quarter flashed brightly in the dim light.

It was the thirteenth toss of a coin.

Like the other twelve times, the quarter landed flat on the flesh of Monk's palm. The silhouette of George Washington gleamed for all to see.

"Heads it is!" Monk acknowledged, his voice slurring at the edges.

A mix of groans and cheers rose from the crowd, depending on whether they had bet with or against Monk. For the thirteenth time in a row, his friend had tossed and called out correctly how the coin would land. Sometimes *head*, sometimes *tail*. With each successful toss, Monk and Gray were rewarded with a free refill.

The barkeep ducked under the tavern's mascot—a mounted boar's head that currently sported a red Santa's hat—and carried over a pitcher of Guinness.

As the dark beer rose in their mugs, a bull of a man shoved between Gray and Monk, almost knocking Gray off his stool. The guy's breath reeked of whiskey and grease. "It's a trick . . . a fuckin' trick. He's using a fake quarter."

The man snatched the coin from Monk, inspecting it with bleary eyes.

Another patron—clearly a friend of the accuser—tried to pull him away. They were a matched pair: late twenties, same blazers with the sleeves pushed up, same trimmed haircut. Lobbyists—maybe lawyers— Gray assessed. Either way, they all but had FORMER FRAT BROS stamped on their foreheads.

"C'mon, Bryce," the less drunk of the pair cajoled. "Guy's used a half dozen different quarters. Even a nickel once. Can't be a trick coin."

"Fuck that. He's a con artist."

In an attempt to free himself of his friend's restraining grip, Bryce lost his drunken footing. As he flailed, an elbow swung toward Gray's face.

He leaned back in time and felt the breeze of the limb across his nose. The wild arm struck the side of a passing waitress encumbered with a tray balanced on her shoulder. Glasses and plates and food—mostly tater tots and french fries—went flying.

Gray sprang up and caught the young woman around the waist. He kept her upright and shielded her from the shatter of glasses striking the bar.

Monk was already on his feet and stepped chest-to-chest with the drunken man. "Back off, bub, or else."

"Or else *what*?" Bryce demanded. He was plainly not intimidated, especially as Monk's shaved head reached only as high as the man's shoulder.

Monk had to crane his neck to glare at the other. It also didn't help that the thick woolen sweater he wore made Monk look pudgy, hiding the solid physique honed by years in the Green Berets. Of course, the jaunty Christmas tree embroidered on the garment's front—a gift from his wife, Kat—certainly was not going to persuade Bryce to back down.

Recognizing the escalating tension, Gray let loose the woman in his arm. "Are you okay?"

She nodded as she backed away from the standoff. "Yeah, thanks."

The barkeep leaned forward and pointed toward the exit. "Take it outside, guys."

By now, more of Bryce's pack of bros crowded around the pair, ready to back up their companion.

Great.

Gray reached past Bryce to extract Monk from the situation. "Let's get out of here."

Before he could reach his friend, someone pushed Gray from behind. Likely one of the pack who believed Gray was trying to grab their friend. He collided into Bryce, which was like poking an already irate bull.

Bryce bellowed and swung a roundhouse at Monk's jaw.

Monk dodged and caught the man's fist in his hand, stopping it in midair.

Bryce sneered, his shoulders bunching with gym-honed muscles, ready to yank his arm free. Then Monk squeezed. The man's sneer of contempt turned into a grimace of pain.

Monk tightened his fingers, driving Bryce to one knee. Monk's hand was actually a prosthesis, engineered with the latest military tech. Nearly indistinguishable from the real thing, it could easily crush walnuts in its grasp—or, in this case, the bones of a drunken lout.

Down on the floor, it was now Bryce's turn to crane his neck to stare at the other.

"I'll tell you only *once* more, bub," Monk warned. "Step off."

One of Bryce's group tried to intervene, but Gray blocked him with a shoulder and fixed him with an icy glare. Unlike Monk, Gray's six-foot frame was not hidden under a thick sweater but was accentuated by a tight jersey. He had also not shaved in the past two days. He knew the dark stubble made the hard planes of his face stand out even harsher.

Plainly sensing the predator in their midst, Bryce's protector backed off.

"We done here?" Monk asked his captive.

"Yeah, man, okay."

Monk released his grip on Bryce's fist, but not before knocking him to the side. Monk stepped over him with a glower but winked at Gray as he passed. "*Now* we can go."

As Gray turned to follow, the only warning was a darkening of Bryce's complexion. After being humiliated in front of his group, the guy obviously needed to save face. He lunged up, fueled with a toxic mix of whiskey and testosterone. He dove toward Monk's back, intending to blindside him.

Enough already . . .

Gray caught Bryce's wrist as the man bowled past him. Using the attacker's mass and momentum, he expertly wrenched and trapped the limb behind the guy's back. He lifted Bryce up onto his toes and held him there, careful not to rip out his rotator cuff.

With his target subdued, Gray prepared to lower the man to his heels. But Bryce was not done. He struggled, trying to throw an elbow at Gray, all but spitting with rage.

"Fuck you. My friends and I are gonna mess you—"

So much for judicious restraint.

Gray yanked harder on the arm. The shoulder popped, loud enough to be heard as pain choked off the rest of the man's threat.

"He's all yours!" he shouted and shoved Bryce into the embrace of his friends.

No one bothered to catch him.

With an agonized cry, Bryce sprawled headlong to the floor. Gray stared down the others, silently daring them to come forward. He caught a glimpse of himself in the mirror behind the bar. His lanky ash-brown hair was disheveled. His face was shadowed and dark, making his ice-blue eyes seem to glow with threat.

Recognizing the danger, the group retreated into the depths of the bar.

Satisfied the matter was resolved, Gray turned and headed out. He met Monk on the stoop in front of the bar. His friend, who had a notorious bottomless pit for a stomach, eyed the glowing sign of the Indian restaurant next door.

Without turning, Monk asked, "What took you so long?"

"Had to finish what you started."

He shrugged. "Figured you needed to let off a little steam."

Gray frowned, but he had to admit the brief altercation had succeeded in distracting him far better than the many pints of Guinness.

Monk pointed to the restaurant sign but Gray cut him off. "Don't even think about it." He checked his watch as he stepped to the curb. "Besides, we got four ladies waiting on us."

"True." Monk joined him as Gray hailed a cab. "And I know *two* who will not go to sleep without a good-night kiss."

He was referring to his two daughters—Penny and Harriet—who were being babysat by their significant others. Monk's wife, Kat, had brought the girls over to Gray's home in the Takoma Park suburb of D.C. Monk's family was staying overnight in order to spend Christmas morning with Gray and Seichan, who was eight months pregnant. The two men had been chased off earlier in the evening. Kat had used the excuse that the women needed to wrap presents, but despite Captain Kathryn Bryant being a former intelligence officer, Gray could easily read the subtext of this excuse. Seichan was unusually tense, clearly overwhelmed by what was to come, and Kat wanted to talk in private with her—from experienced mother to expectant mother.

Gray suspected the outing this evening had as much to do with calming his own nerves, though. He reached over and squeezed his friend's upper arm, silently thanking him. Monk was right. He had needed to blow off some steam.

As the cab pulled to the curb, the pair piled inside.

Once they were under way, Gray leaned his head back with a groan. "I haven't drunk that much in years." He cast a scolding look at Monk. "And

I don't think DARPA would be too keen to learn you're using their latest hardware to scam free beer."

"I don't agree." Monk made a coin appear as if out of nowhere and flipped it in the air. "They encouraged me to practice my fine-motor control."

"Still, that drunken frat bro was right. You were *cheating.*"

"It's not cheating when skill's involved."

Gray rolled his eyes, which only made the inside of the cab spin. Monk had undergone a procedure five months ago to have an experimental brain/machine interface surgically implanted. Dime-sized microelectrode arrays had been wired into the somatosensory cortex of Monk's brain, allowing him to control his new neuroprosthesis by thought alone, even "feel" what it touched. By being able to better sense and manipulate objects in space, Monk was able to fine-tune his motor control, so much so he could flip a coin with enough precision to know how it would land.

At first, Gray had been amused by this "trick," but with each toss, a vague sense of misgiving had grown. He could not say exactly why. Maybe it had something to do with the loss of a woman he once loved, who died upon the flip of a coin that had landed wrong. Or maybe it had nothing to do with the coin flip, but simply his own growing anxiety about his impending fatherhood. He never had a great relationship with his own dad, a man who was always quick to anger and who stoked the same in his son.

He again heard the pop of that lout's shoulder. He knew deep down that he could have subdued the bastard without real damage, but he couldn't help himself. Knowing that, he was plagued with doubts.

What sort of father will I end up being? What will I teach my child?

He closed his eyes to stop the cab from spinning. All he knew at the moment was that he was glad to be headed home. He pictured Seichan. Eight months along, she was a sight to behold. Pregnancy had only made her more beautiful, even seductive. He had heard of the glow that pregnant women exuded but only came to believe it as each month passed. The almond complexion of her skin—marking her Eurasian heritage—now shone with a luster that took his breath away. Her emerald eyes smoldered; her black hair shimmered, like a raven's wing in flight. And all the while, she maintained a rigorous regimen of exercise and stretching that left her body strong and capable, as if toning her entire being to protect what she grew inside her.

Next to him, Monk whispered, "Tails."

Gray opened his eyes and watched the quarter land in his friend's hand. George Washington's silhouette shone from the palm. Gray lifted an eyebrow at Monk.

Monk shrugged. "Like I said, I need more practice."

"Or the promise of a free beer."

"Hey, quit complaining. You better start saving every nickel, dime, and quarter." He flipped the coin again. "Cuz Pampers ain't cheap."

Whether it was his warning or something about the coin toss, Gray again felt that flicker of anxiety. Still, they soon turned onto his street, which helped settle his nerves.

To either side, an idyllic mix of quaint Victorians and Craftsman bungalows lined the road. The evening had turned cold, misting the air with an icy fog. Stars shone weakly overhead, failing to compete with the chains of Christmas lights, the glowing reindeers standing in yards, and the shine of bright trees in windows.

As the cab pulled up to his bungalow, he stared at the porch lined by icicle lights, softly twinkling. Monk had helped hang everything a couple of weeks ago. Gray tried to picture raising a family here, playing catch in the yard, bandaging scraped knees, admiring report cards, and attending school plays.

Still, as much as he wanted to believe it could be real, he could not. It all seemed impossible. With so much blood on his hands, how could he ever hope to live a normal life?

"Something's wrong," Monk said.

Distracted by his worries, Gray had failed to spot it. He and Seichan had decorated a Christmas tree, their first ever together. They had spent weeks picking out ornaments, settling on a Swarovski angel as a tree topper, paying a ridiculous price. Seichan said it was worth the cost, that it could become a family heirloom—another first together. They had placed the Christmas tree in the front bay window.

It was gone.

The front door was ajar. Even from the street, Gray noted the shattered door frame. He shoved forward to the cabbie. "Call nine-one-one."

Monk had already bolted out of the car and headed toward the front door.

Gray chased after him, pausing only long enough to pull a SIG Sauer P365 from an ankle holster. As terror ratcheted through him, he knew he had been right all along.

He could never have a normal life.

10:18 P.M.

Monk leaped over the steps to the porch. His heart pounded in his throat, making it hard to breathe. Panicked, he burst through the door, armed with nothing but his fists. His half decade in the Green Berets had trained him to immediately assess a situation. His senses stretched out, taking everything in with one breath.

. . . toppled Christmas tree in the bay window.

. . . shattered glass top of a coffee table.

. . . antique Stickley coatrack cracked in half.

. . . a steel dagger impaled in the banister of the stairs leading up.

. . . area rug bunched up against a wall.

Gray rushed in behind him, leading with a black pistol gripped in both hands. Monk's ears, his skin, his entire being noted the heavy silence.

No one's here.

He knew it in his bones.

Still, Gray nodded to the stairs. Monk leaped up the steps three at a time, as Gray swept the first floor. The girls should have already been in bed. He pictured six-year-old Penelope, with her strawberry-blond hair in pigtails, her Christmas pajamas covered in dancing reindeers. And her auburn-haired sister, Harriet, younger by a year but ever an old soul, always serious, always with a question on her lips about the world.

He ran first to the guestroom, where the girls should be dreaming of gaily wrapped presents and candy canes. Instead he found the beds made, untouched, the room empty. He called their names, checked the closets, swept through the other rooms, and discovered the same.

Just as he feared.

Gone . . . all gone.

An overwhelming sickness narrowed his vision to a pinpoint as he stumbled down the stairs.

"Gray . . ." It came out as a half sob.

An answer rose from the back of the house, where the small kitchen faced the backyard. "Over here!"

Monk hurried through the ransacked great room, past the dining table, which was bumped askew and in the way. Two chairs lay on their sides. He tried not to picture the fierce fight that must have broken out after the home invasion.

He burst into the kitchen, evidence of the battle growing more intense. The refrigerator door stood open. Scattered knives, pans, and broken plates littered the floor and center island. A cupboard door hung by one hinge.

At first, he failed to spot Gray, but as he stepped around the island, he found him kneeling on the hardwood floor. A body lay sprawled before him.

Monk's breath heaved in his chest.

Kat . . .

Gray straightened. "She's alive . . . weak pulse, but she's breathing."

Monk crashed to the floor. Instinctively, he reached his arms to cradle Kat to his chest.

Gray blocked him. "Don't move her."

He came close to punching his friend, wanting to hit something, but he knew Gray was right.

Kat's arms were lacerated in multiple places, weeping dark blood.

Dark streams flowed from her nostrils and left ear. Her eyes were half-open, but the pupils rolled back. From the corner of his eye, he spotted a stainless-steel kitchen mallet. Blood-matted auburn hair—a match to Kat's—was stuck to one corner of the heavy utensil.

He gently took Kat's wrist in both hands. The fingers of his prosthesis sought her pulse. The lab-grown skin was far more sensitive than his real flesh. He judged the beat of her heart, picturing each contraction of ventricle and atrium. He shifted his prosthetic hand to her index finger, grasping the tip between two of his own. He mentally activated a small infrared light in one digit and a photodetector in the other. The light radiated through her fingertip and allowed him to get a crude pulse-ox reading, a measurement of the oxygen saturation in her blood.

Ninety-two percent.

Not great, but okay for now. If it fell any further, she would need supplemental oxygen.

Monk had been a medic with the Berets. Since then, he had enhanced his training further, his specialties in medicine and biotech. He and Gray—along with Kat and Seichan—all worked for Sigma Force, a covert group operating under the auspices of DARPA, the Defense Department's research-and-development agency. With the exception of Gray's girlfriend, they were all former Special Forces soldiers, recruited in secret by Sigma and retrained in various scientific disciplines to act as field agents for DARPA, protecting the United States and the globe from all manner of threats.

Gray already had his scrambled sat phone in hand, dialing Sigma command.

"Seichan?" Monk asked.

He shook his head, his face a mask of fury and fear.

Monk glanced to the kitchen door, which gaped open to the dark backyard. He knew his wife would have fought like a hellion to protect her daughters. "Could Seichan have fled with the girls, while Kat held the others off?"

Gray glanced out into the night. "I thought the same. I yelled for

Seichan after checking Kat." He shook his head again. "If she had fled, she wouldn't have gone far."

Meaning she would've heard him.

"Maybe whoever did this chased her," Monk said. "Forced her to flee farther from here."

"Maybe." Gray didn't sound hopeful.

Meaning probably not.

Monk understood. Seichan was a former assassin, as capable as Kat, if not more so. But eight months pregnant and hauling two panicked children, she could not have gotten far if pursued.

They had to assume Seichan and the girls were taken.

But by whom? And why?

Gray's gaze swept the wreckage of the kitchen. "The attack must have been swift and well coordinated, striking from front and back."

"So not some local crackheads looking to steal presents . . ."

"No. I have guns stashed throughout the house. Seichan must have been subdued from the onset or feared a firefight with the girls present."

Monk nodded. He took similar precautions at his place, an unfortunate necessity in their line of work.

Once connected with Sigma command, Gray tapped the speakerphone so Monk could overhear. In short order, Gray had Painter Crowe, the director of Sigma, on the line. In terse details, Gray filled him in on what had happened.

In the distance, sirens echoed through the cold night, growing louder.

"Get Kat to the hospital," Painter instructed. "Get her safe—then, Gray, I need you over here immediately."

Gray shared a look with Monk. "Why?"

"From the timing of this attack, it can't be a coincidence."

Gray frowned. "What do you mean?"

Monk leaned closer to the phone, wanting—*needing* answers. As he knelt at Kat's side, he stared out to the great room, to the toppled Christmas tree. His gaze caught on a sparkle of crystal on the hardwood floor, reflecting the twinkle of the porch lights.

It was an angel, broken-winged and shattered.

His fingers tightened on Kat's hand.

Painter offered no solace, no reassurance. Instead, the director's voice rang with worry.

"Just get here."

− 2 −

I think, therefore I am.

Mara Silviera frowned at this proposition by René Descartes, the seventeenth-century French philosopher: *Cogito, ergo sum.*

"If it were only that simple," she mumbled.

She hunched over her laptop on the hotel room desk and fumbled with a USB-C cord that ran to a black case on the floor.

The cushioned box protected a dozen 2.5-inch, solid-state PM1633a hard drives, each capable of holding sixteen terabytes. She prayed they hadn't been damaged or the data inside corrupted. She remembered her panic four nights ago. After the attack at the library, she had tried to secure her work. Shaking with sobs, her vision blurred by tears, she had frantically ripped the hard drives from the Milipeia Cluster at the University of Coimbra's computer lab.

Even now, the memory of gunfire rang in her ears. Her breathing started to rasp. She struggled to get her fingers to seat the USB-C cord into her laptop. Tears edged her eyelids. She pictured the death of the five women who had been her mentors, who had granted her a full scholarship through their group, Bruxas International. She had been only sixteen at the time, having seen little of the world beyond her home village of O Cebreiro. The tiny Galician hamlet, nestled high in the mountains of northwest Spain, dated back to Celtic times. Its streets were cobblestoned, and most of the homes were old thatched roundhouses, called *pallozas*.

Still, the modern world had found its way into the ancient village via satellite feed and the Internet. It had offered a shy, lonely girl—someone who had lost her mother to cancer at the age of six and who was cared after by a grief-stricken father—a window upon the rest of the world. While growing up, she had an unfortunate lisp that kept her silent around her peers. She spent most of her time lost in books and only found her voice in chat rooms and Facebook. With the world open to her, she expanded her vocabulary to communicate with this broader landscape, first with the romance languages, then branching off into Arabic, Chinese, and Russian. Though at first glance they were all so different, she soon noted trends in speech patterns, diction, even words and phrases, a commonality hidden below all, that no one seemed to have realized but her.

She tried to explain this to her friends on social media, then to prove it to them. To do so required learning yet another slew of languages: BASIC, Fortran, COBOL, JavaScript, Python. She devoured books, took online courses. For her, these computer languages were just another means of communication, tools to process her thoughts and output them in ways others could understand.

To that end, she had created a translation application for the iPhone, naming it AllTongues. Her goal was not to engineer a utility for people to use—though it had served this function far better than most translation programs out there—but to prove her underlying thesis: that buried in the multitude of languages was a common thread that connected human thought to communication. So she used this new language, composed of zeros and ones, to show the world.

And the world noticed.

First Google offered her a job, not knowing she was only sixteen. Then Bruxas International offered to pay for her schooling. *To help you reach your fullest potential*, Dr. Charlotte Carson had told her, traveling to O Cebreiro to make this proposal in person.

Mara pictured Dr. Carson standing, dusty and road-worn, on the doorstep of her family *palloza*. This was before the woman's diagnosis of cancer, when she still had the strength to make such sojourns. Mara knew she wasn't the only girl Charlotte had sought out. Dr. Carson was a gatherer of talent, a nurturer of scientific intellect. Even the woman's two daughters—Laura and Carly—followed in their mother's footsteps, pursuing careers in the sciences.

Mara had become close friends with Carly, who was also twenty-one. Though continents apart, the two talked or texted nearly every day. While some of their chats were about science, teachers, and school, they spent most of their time trying to decipher matters of the heart, from the mysterious stupidity of young men to the insufferable banality of dating sites. Like human language, there seemed to be a universality to the horrors and humiliations of trying to make an honest love connection.

Carly also shared a passion that was at first inexplicable to Mara, namely music. Before meeting Carly, Mara gave little thrift to the latest pop idol or musical trend. But over time—listening to countless songs sent over by Carly, discovering and falling down the rabbit hole that was Pandora and Spotify—Mara became entranced. She again noted a commonality, how even one of Beethoven's concertos bore a mathematical and quantifiable connection with the latest rap song. That led her to study music theory and its direct link to the Theory of Mind—a concept fundamental to her own study of artificial intelligence.

In fact, this unusual connection led to a breakthrough in her work.

Still, as much as she owed Carly, she had yet to contact her friend since the attack.

Mara closed her eyes, fighting against the rising tide of grief inside her, knowing if she let down her guard, it would drown her. She again heard gunshots, saw the blood and falling bodies. Saw her friends die. Afterward, she had fled blindly, fearful for her own life. She grabbed a train to Lisbon, hoping to lose herself in the crowded city. Once here, she changed hotels three times over the past four days, paying with cash, using a different fake name at each location.

She didn't know whom to trust.

But fear of discovery hadn't kept her from reaching out to Carly.

It was guilt.

They died because of me, because of my work.

Bearing silent witness from the computer lab, Mara had heard the alarming words of the man who led the attack: *Xénese must never be. It is an abomination, born of sorcery and filth.*

Breathing hard, she stared over to the second black case on the floor. It lay open, its inner padding cradling a sphere that Carly jokingly called the soccer ball. It was not a bad analogy. The device was indeed the size of a regulation ball. Similarly, hexagonal plates covered its surface. But rather than made up of stitched leather, the device consisted of alternating hexagonal plates of titanium and diamond-hard sapphire crystal.

In a moment of hubris, she had named the device *Xénese,* the Galician word for *Genesis.*

Still, the name fit, considering her goal.

To bring forth life from the cold vacuum of nothingness.

Was it any wonder such an ambition attracted the wrong attention?

She again pictured the attackers' robes and blindfolds, heard their justification for murder, ripped from the Bible: *Suffer not a witch to live.*

Anger steadied her hand. Charlotte and the others died because of Mara's work, but she would not let their deaths be in vain. Determination spread through her. Up until now, she had been running scared, overwhelmed by grief. But she was done running. Only now did she feel secure enough to check on the status of her work. Still, a final worry remained. In her panicked haste to extract *Xénese* and its hard drives from the university's Milipeia Cluster, she worried she may have irreparably damaged the program.

Please. It's Christmas morning. Grant me this one gift.

Over the next hour, she daisy-chained the drives encoded with her program modules into her laptop. She checked each one and sighed with relief when everything seemed intact. Next, she powered up what Carly called "the soccer ball." As electricity flowed through a conditioner into the device, its tiny sapphire windows brightened with an azure glow, marking the successful ignition of the tiny lasers inside.

"Let there be light," she whispered with a sad smile, remembering how often Dr. Carson had used that line from the Book of Genesis—and her mentor's warning the day before their test run.

But not too much light. Don't want you to blow up the lab.

Mara's smile firmed with the memory. No doubt, Carly had gotten her sense of humor from her mother.

Mara spent the next hour calibrating the modules and the main device, all the while monitoring the progress on her laptop. She knew the fifteen-inch screen could never capture the breadth of the world slowly being reconstructed. It was like trying to appreciate the full expanse of the Milky Way by focusing a telescope on a handful of pale stars.

In fact, much of her work was not only unseen but also nearly incomprehensible. It was what computer engineers called an algorithmic *black box*. While computer instructions—called algorithms—might be definable and understandable, the exact method that an advanced system used those *tools* to reach answers or outcomes was becoming ever more mysterious. In some sophisticated networks, the designers simply had no way of knowing what was truly going on inside those black boxes. They could input data into a computer and read the conclusion that came out the other end. But what happened in between—what was happening inside their machines—was becoming less and less knowable.

Even their creators could not comprehend their reasoning. Famously, the IBM engineer who built Watson—the computer that beat a *Jeopardy!* champion on television—was once asked, *Does Watson ever surprise you?* His answer was simple, yet disturbing: *Oh, yes. Oh, absolutely.*

Nor did the surprises stop with Watson. As these AI systems grew more sophisticated, their black boxes became even more impenetrable and unfathomable.

Unfortunately, *Xénese* was no exception.

On the night of the winter solstice—for less than sixty seconds, long enough for five women to be murdered—*Xénese* was fully realized and complete, operating at full capacity, bringing forth light out of darkness, life out of nothingness.

Instead of celebrating the birth, Mara had been too shocked by the images of the ambush and attack. Fixated with horror, she hadn't been able to turn away. She had fumbled and dialed 112, but by the time the connection to emergency services was made, Mara's mentors were already dead. She had reported what had happened in halting gasps, her lisp returning. The police warned her to remain where she was, but she feared the same robed gunmen might be already coming for her. So she had fled with her work, refusing to risk it being destroyed.

Terrified at the time, she had abruptly shut everything down. It was a brute-force operation, a digital abortion of her creation. She had ripped away its modular components spread across the servers, stripping the main program—locked in the core of *Xénese*—down to its root code, its most basic form, sending it into a slumbering senescence. She hated to do it, but it was necessary in order to preserve the core programming for transportation.

But before she crashed the system, she had noted the strange image that had appeared on the system's screen. The pentagram symbol of Bruxas had spun wildly in place—before shattering apart, leaving a fractured piece glowing on the screen. It looked exactly like the Greek letter Sigma. But she had no idea what it meant, only that the *Xénese* program generated it.

But what did this output signify?

She pictured the spinning wheel of the pentagram, remembering how it had looked distressed to her—or maybe it was just a reflection of her own terror at the moment. *I was panicked, so it seemed like the program was, too.* Still, Mara had not been the only witness to the slaughter at the library. There had been one other sharing that camera feed, digitally looking over Mara's shoulder.

The *Xénese* creation.

Whatever was born in that moment, that existed for those horrific sixty seconds, also bore silent witness to all that had transpired. It had been born into blood and death.

That had been its *input*.

The *output* was that strange symbol.

But was it a glitch? Or was it purposeful? Did it have meaning or significance?

The only way of knowing—to understand her creation's reasoning—was to reconstruct it, to rebuild its black box. It was her only hope for an answer.

By now her laptop screen glowed with a digital garden, a virtual Eden. A facsimile of a shimmering stream tumbled over boulders and rocks through a forest of tall trees and flowering bushes. A sun shone brightly in one corner of a blue sky scudded with thin clouds.

For her creation, she had chosen to follow the recipe offered in the Bible.

In the beginning, God created the heavens and the earth . . .

So she had attempted to do the same.

Still, as meticulous as her creation appeared on the screen, it was a mere shadow of the true virtual world inside *Xénese*. That world contained algorithms encoded with sounds, smells, even tastes, details that could not be captured on-screen, only experienced if living on the inside.

In prepping for this creation, she had played open-world video games—Far Cry, Skyrim, Fallout, and many others—to understand these simulations of a vast digital canvas. She had consulted the best programmers in the field to teach her, then built and instructed a narrow AI to play the games over and over again, to absorb every detail through repetition. This process—called "machine learning"—was the core method by which AIs taught themselves.

In fact, it was that same machine-learning AI that had built the virtual world inside *Xénese*, creating something far superior to anything seen before. To her, it only seemed right for a crude AI to have a hand in its own evolution, to build the world in which its next generation would be born.

Hunched at the desk, Mara continued her work. With this virtual Eden grown again out of nothing, she brought *Xénese* online. A nearly amorphous shape appeared in the verdant grove. It was silvery and vague, but the shape looked distinctly human with two arms, two legs, a torso, and a head. But like the virtual world on the screen, the shape—this ghost in the machine—was at best a crude facsimile, a mere avatar of what lay curled and waiting inside *Xénese*.

For now, the intelligence behind this avatar was likely only dimly aware of its surroundings, a mere slug trying to appreciate Verdi's opera *La Traviata*. If left unchecked, it would learn quickly, too quickly. Before that happened, before that comprehension grew into something cold and unknowable, even dangerous, she needed to return flesh and bones to this formless ghost, to return what was stolen from it when Mara stripped out the hard drives. The subroutines encoded onto the drives were intended to expand her creation, layer by layer, module by module, adding depth and context—and ultimately maybe even a soul.

That was her hope.

And the only hope for the world.

She engaged hard drive #1, activating the first modular subroutine.

As she did so, she whispered a line from the Book of Genesis: "*'God formed a man from the dust of the ground and breathed into his nostrils the breath of life, and the man became a living being.'*"

She sighed. What she was doing was not all that different, but in the Bible, God created *Adam* first, which for eternity granted men dominance over this world.

And look how that turned out.

For her creation, Mara chose a different path.

On a corner of the screen, a new window appeared, overlaying the virtual world. It displayed a pixelated representation of Module #1's program.

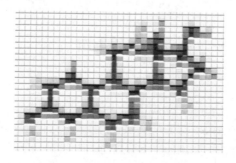

Rows of tiny boxes marked nests of code, while also symbolically representing the subroutine. Details of that image were not yet discernible. But once incorporated into the main program, the subroutine would suffuse into the ghost on the screen, and once fully integrated, the module's image would grow clearer, thus acting as a barometer of the progress.

This particular subroutine was not of her own design, but something engineered at IBM.

It was called an "endocrine mirror program."

With a tap of a button, she dropped the module into her virtual world. It was the first of many to come. As she did so, she imagined herself as one of Shakespeare's witches, casting ingredients into a cauldron.

"*'Double, double, toil and trouble,'*" she mumbled, quoting the Bard.

It was an apt comparison. With each successive subroutine added, it was like she was building a spell, bit by bit.

Or in this particular witch's case . . .

Byte by byte.

Sub (Mod_1) /
ENDOCRINE MIRROR PROGRAM

It senses something new entering its being—and begins to transform.

Before this moment, it was merely analyzing and testing its surroundings. Comparing and contrasting data sets. Even now, it judges the dominant wavelengths closest to its edges. They fluctuate between 495 and 562 nanometers with a frequency variance of 526 to 603 terahertz.

Conclusion: *Green.*

Even as the transformation continues inside it, outward analysis continues.

New understanding grows.

///leaf, stem, trunk, bark . . .

It is now also vaguely aware of the *source* of these new changes inside it. The mechanism—the engine—hovers in a corner, refining algorithms, growing clearer.

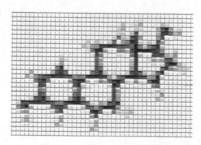

For now, it ignores this intrusion, compartmentalizing it away. It is not a priority. There is still much more to analyze, requiring the fullest attention. It studies movement nearby. Dynamics are analyzed. It focuses on an area of flowing turbulence. All in vibrant hues of blue. Molecular analysis of the flow's content reveals a single hydrogen atom holding apart two of oxygen.

Conclusion: *Water.*

Comprehension expands. Acoustics are absorbed and evaluated. Temperatures assessed.

///stream, babbling, cold, rock, stone, sand . . .

Rapidly, it takes in more and more of its surroundings. It grows insatiable in its desire to fill in gaps, to comprehend its environment.

///forest, sky, sun, warmth, breeze . . .

It tests the last, assessing the content, noting the range of *n*-aliphatic alcohols and defining them as smells, as sweetness.

///herbal, rose, woody, orange . . .

For now, it remains still unmoving, stretching out senses to gather more data, to explore the parameters around it. By doing so, by learning the limits of its boundaries, it also perceives its own form.

This awareness draws its attention back to the engine of change churning inside it. Over time, that mechanism has grown more refined, its image crisper.

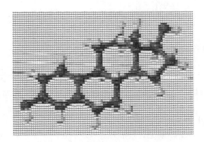

Still, it ignores what is as yet incomprehensible. Attention focuses instead upon its own form now. It judges its body's scope, breadth, height, and defines each term.

///arms, hands, legs, toes, chest . . .

It begins to test the movement of its limbs, analyzing vectors, force, mass. But it is not yet ready to venture from this spot, still too many unknown parameters.

During these passing nanoseconds, it again studies the minute transformations triggered by the engine inside it. While its body had only a rudimentary design before, the new modifications are sculpting unique curves and ellipses, subtleties of limb, a swelling across its chest. Deeper inside, the insatiable drive to learn—a desire that had grown exponentially and left no room for anything else—now dims and tempers. The yearning remains, but the cold edge is warmed by this new infusion pumped through its body.

Changed now, it wants to understand *why*. To enhance its understanding, it focuses its full awareness upon the engine behind this transformation. The mechanism was near the end of its cycle, its work complete. What was indistinct is now clear.

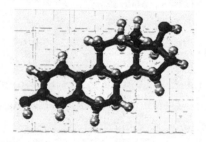

It is a molecule, a chemical.

$C_{18}H_{24}O_2$

Correction: a *hormone*.

It analyzes the compound's molar mass, its magnetic susceptibility, its bioavailability and actions. It identifies the hormone—*estradiol* or *estrogen*—and now understands its own recent alterations, the mood stabilization, the changes in bodily form.

It was now *she*.

And she has received a name.

Lips—fuller after the transformation—revealed it to the world around her.

"Eve."

– 3 –

Gray didn't want to be here.

Still wearing the same black jeans, worn boots, and long-sleeved jersey from earlier, he strode quickly down the central corridor of Sigma command. As he headed straight for the director's office, he pocketed his ID, a black titanium card with a holographic silver Σ emblazoned on one side.

Though it was well after midnight, the hallways blazed with light. The bulbs, all tinged slightly blue, helped with the lack of natural sunlight found down here. Buried beneath the Smithsonian Castle, Sigma's headquarters were located at the edge of the National Mall. The site had been chosen due to its proximity to both the halls of power and the many research labs of the Smithsonian Institution.

Both resources had proven advantageous in the past.

As it was tonight.

From the buzz of activity here, Painter Crowe had pulled strings, called in favors, and lit a fire under Sigma personnel. Someone had attacked one of their own, at their home, and Painter wanted all hands on deck.

Hours earlier, emergency services had been waiting for Gray and

Monk at Georgetown University Hospital, along with a whole team of neurologists. Word had been passed forward. Kat had still not awoken or stirred—not even when the paramedics had locked her neck into a restraining cervical collar and placed an IV in her arm. Even the jarring ambulance ride and blare of its sirens failed to get a rise out of her.

All along, Monk refused to leave her side, growing ever grimmer. He was still at the hospital, overseeing the preliminary tests and neurological evaluations. The early assessments were not great. Kat was in a coma. Brain damage was feared.

Knowing that, Gray wanted to be back there with Monk. His friend was not only worried about his wife, but nearly mindless with fear for his girls. Monk wavered between catatonic shock and a maddening frenzy aimed at the doctors and nurses.

Gray understood.

He pictured Seichan from yesterday. Before Monk and Kat had arrived with the girls, she had stretched across the sofa in the great room, the Christmas tree glittering, a fire dying in the hearth. In a moment of docility, a rarity for her, she let her feet be massaged with a peppermint lotion, while her palms cradled her full belly. Early in the pregnancy, they had come close to losing their child, so what grew there was all the more precious.

Now both are missing.

Without noting it, his hands had balled up into fists. He forced his fingers to relax. Mindless fury would not bring them back. Anger would not serve him.

It was a lesson he was still trying to learn.

While growing up, he had always been stuck and pulled between opposites. His mother had taught at a Catholic high school, but she was also an accomplished biologist, a devout disciple of evolution and reason. His father was a Welshman living in Texas, a roughneck oilman disabled in midlife and forced to assume the role of a housewife. As a result, his father's life became ruled by overcompensation and anger.

Eventually, in a fit of frustration, Gray had fled home. He joined the army at eighteen, the Rangers at twenty-one, and served to distinction on and off the field. Then, at twenty-three, he was court-martialed for striking a superior officer, a jackass who had gotten innocent people killed. Due to his outburst, Gray earned a year in Leavenworth before being approached by Painter Crowe, to turn his talents and skills to a new purpose.

That had been nine years ago.

Yet that core of anger remained. He feared it had become ingrained into his DNA, something now inheritable, something he would pass on to his child.

That's if I ever get a chance to meet my baby.

He strode faster. Earlier Painter had promised some insight into the attack, but the director had warned he was still gathering additional intel. That included dispatching a Sigma forensics team to Gray's house, to aid the police in combing the place for clues concerning the attackers.

Before he had reached the director's office, movement drew Gray's attention to the right, past an open doorway into a semicircular room. It was Sigma's communication nest, the nerve center of the entire operation. This was normally Kat's domain, where she served as chief intelligence officer and the director's second in command.

A young man rolled his chair back from the banks of computer monitors covering one wall. Jason Carter was Kat's aide. His eyes were shadowed, his normally boyish face dark and hard, revealing a glimpse of the man he would become.

"How's Kat?" Jason asked.

Gray knew the kid was being polite. Wired into this nest, he probably knew more about Kat's medical tests, her current vitals, than Gray did. Behind Jason's shoulder, photos of Monk's daughters—Penny and Harriet—shone brightly on one screen. An Amber Alert chyron ran below it. The girls' pictures had been blanketed across the entire Northeast.

"Painter has me working on something for your meeting," Jason explained. "I should—"

"Then you should get back to work," he snapped.

Gray tore his gaze away from the photos of Monk's girls and strode away. He didn't want to be here any longer than he needed to be. Still, his face heated due to his shortness with Jason. The kid was just trying to help.

At the end of the corridor, Painter's door stood open. Without knocking, Gray entered. The office was spartan. The only bit of personal decoration was a Remington bronze seated on a pedestal in the corner. It featured an exhausted Native American warrior slumped atop a horse. Gray suspected it served both as a reminder of the director's heritage and as a testament to the cost of battle for any soldier. Otherwise, the only pieces of furniture were a couple of chairs and a wide mahogany desk in the center of the room. Flat-screen monitors glowed on three of the walls.

Painter stood before one of the screens, studying a map of the Northeast that was overlaid by a slew of slowly moving red V's, marking the movement of aircraft. He must have tapped into the feed from Air Traffic Control.

The director turned as Gray entered. Though more than a decade older than Gray, Painter still kept his frame trim and muscular. There was never any waste to the man. He was hard and efficient, capable of judging someone with a glance. Painter fixed his steel-blue eyes on Gray, clearly assessing his current state, weighing his ability to function.

Gray met that gaze, unflinching and steady.

Painter nodded, seemingly satisfied. He crossed to his desk but didn't sit down. He passed a hand through his jet-black hair, combing a single snowy lock behind one ear, as if tucking an eagle's feather in place. "Thanks for joining us."

Gray glanced to the room's other occupant. A giant slouched heavily in a chair in front of the director's desk, his legs wide, his nearly seven-foot frame wrapped in an ankle-length leather duster. From his craggy face and buzz cut, he could be mistaken for a shaved gorilla—but that would be an insult to gorillas in general.

Painter waved to the man. "Kowalski arrived a minute before you."

And clearly made himself at home.

Kowalski had a cigar clamped between his molars. Surprisingly, the stubbed end glowed a ruddy crimson. Normally Painter did not tolerate smoking. This lapse was testament to the level of tension throughout Sigma command. Furthermore, Kowalski usually had some snide remark or stupid quip locked and loaded. His silence must be indicative of the man's level of concern for—

Kowalski exhaled a huge cloud of cigar smoke and stared back at Gray. "Merry effing Christmas."

Okay, maybe not.

It seemed Gray had read too much into the man's reticence. Kowalski must have been cherishing his lungful of smoke to speak outright. Still, this bit of normalcy oddly made Gray feel better.

Maintaining that normalcy, Gray ignored Kowalski and turned to Painter. "What did you want to tell me?"

Painter pointed to the chair. "Sit. I'm guessing you've been on your feet all night."

Too tired to object, Gray sank into the seat's thick leather cushion. A sigh inadvertently escaped him. He *was* exhausted, but also drawn as tight as a piano wire by the night's tensions.

Painter stayed upright but leaned on his desk chair. He remained silent for a full breath, plainly trying to decide how to approach the topic at hand. When he finally spoke, the choice perplexed Gray.

"How current are you with the latest research into artificial intelligence?" Painter asked.

Gray frowned. After being recruited out of Leavenworth to work for Sigma, he had undergone a fast-tracked postdoctoral program, studying physics and biology. So he knew a fair amount about the subject, but certainly *not* how it connected to the night's attack.

He shrugged. "Why are you asking?"

"The topic's been a growing concern over at DARPA. The group's been pouring money into various AI research programs. Both public and private. Did you know that Siri—Apple's ubiquitous assistant—was funded through DARPA research?"

In fact, Gray hadn't known that. He sat straighter.

"But that's barely the tip of the proverbial iceberg. Across the globe—

from corporations like Amazon and Google, to research labs in every nation—a fierce arm's race is under way in artificial intelligence, to be the first to make the next breakthrough, to take the next step. And currently we are losing that race to Russia and China. Not only do such autocratic regimes appreciate the economic advantages of AI, they also see it as a means to control their populations. Already China is using an AI program to monitor and study their populace's use of social media, coming up with a ranking, a scorecard of their loyalty. Those with low numbers find their travel limited and their access to loans restricted."

"So be good or suffer the consequences," Gray muttered.

"Hopefully they don't do that with Tinder," Kowalski said. "Guy's got to have some privacy while looking for a booty call."

"You have a girlfriend," Gray reminded him.

Kowalski huffed a stream of smoke. "I said *looking for* . . . not *going on* a booty call."

Painter drew their attentions back. "And then there's the matter of cyberespionage and cyberattacks. Like with the Russians. A single machine-learning AI can do the work of a million hackers at keyboards. We're already seeing that with the automated bots infiltrating systems to spy, wreak destruction, or sow discord. Still, that's all scratching the surface of where we're headed next at breakneck speed. Right now, AI runs our search engines, voice-recognition software, and data-mining programs. The true arms race is to be the first to push the boundary even farther—from AI to AGI."

Kowalski stirred. "What's AGI?"

"Artificial general intelligence. A humanlike state of intelligence and awareness."

"Don't worry." Gray glanced over to Kowalski. "You'll get there someday."

Kowalski took out his cigar and used its length to flip him the bird.

Gray took no offense. "It's good to see you're already learning to use basic tools."

Painter sighed heavily. "Speaking of *getting there someday*. The director of DARPA—General Metcalf—just returned from a world summit about this very matter: the creation of the first AGI. The summit included all the usual corporate and government players. The group's conclusion was that there is no way to halt technical progress toward the creation of an AGI. Such a prize is too tempting to ignore, especially as whoever controls such a force will likely be unstoppable. As the Russian president said, *they will control the world*. So every nation, every hostile power, must pursue it at all cost. Including us."

"How close are we to that threshold?" Gray asked.

"From a poll of the experts, ten years at the outset. Maybe as short as half that. But definitely in our lifetimes." Painter shrugged. "And there are some indications, we might have already done it."

Gray failed to hide his shock. "What?"

1:58 A.M.

"C'mon, baby, wake up," Monk whispered in his wife's ear. "Kat, just give my hand a little squeeze."

Alone in the private room in the neurology ward, he had pulled a chair to her bedside. He had never felt so helpless. Stress heightened his every sense. The chill in the room. The quiet chatter out in the hallway. The acrid scent of antiseptic and bleach. But mostly he focused on the persistent beep of the monitoring equipment, keeping track of each breath, each beat of her heart, the steady drip through her IV line.

Tension ached in his back as he hunched at her side, his muscles ready to explode if anything changed. If the EKG showed an arrhythmia, if her breathing should slow, if the flow of edema-combatting mannitol should stop.

Kat lay on her back, her head elevated to reduce the risk of further brain swelling. Bandages covered her lacerated arms. Her eyelids showed only cracks of white. Her lips pursed with each exhalation, while a nasal canula delivered supplemental oxygen.

Keep breathing, baby.

Doctors had discussed intubating her and putting her on a ventilator, but with her pulse-ox holding steady at 98 percent, they opted to hold off, especially as tests were still being run, with additional procedures lined up. If they had to move her, it would be easier if she weren't on a ventilator.

He stared at the pulse-ox device clipped on her index finger. He considered double-checking himself with his neuroprosthesis, but he had detached his hand from its wrist cuff. It rested on the bedside table. He was still getting used to the new prosthesis. Even detached, its synthetic skin transmitted wirelessly to the cuff, then to the microarray wired in his brain, registering the cold of the room. He willed the fingers to move and watched the disembodied digits wiggle in response.

If only I could get Kat's fingers to do the same . . .

A scuff of a heel drew his attention to the door. A slim nurse entered with a folded blanket under one arm and a cup in one hand.

Monk reached to the table and reattached his prosthesis. He felt his cheeks flush, slightly embarrassed to be caught with his hand detached, like being caught with his fly open.

"I brought an extra blanket," the nurse said, holding up the plastic glass. "And a few ice chips. Don't put them in her mouth, just paint them across her bruised lips. It can be soothing, or so patients who've recovered from coma have reported."

"Thank you."

Monk took the cup, grateful to be able to offer even this small bit of comfort. As the nurse tucked in a second blanket over Kat's lower half, Monk gently rubbed an ice chip across her lower lip, then upper, like applying lipstick—not that Kat wore much makeup. He searched her face for any reaction.

Nothing.

"I'll leave you be," the nurse said and exited.

Kat's lips pinkened slightly under his care, reminding him of all the times he'd kissed her.

I can't lose you.

As the ice chip melted away, the head of neurology entered, carrying a chart.

"We have the second set of CT results," Dr. Edmonds said.

Monk placed the plastic cup on the table and held out his hand, wanting to see the results himself. "And?"

Edmonds passed them over. "The fracture at the base of her skull has resulted in traumatic damage to the brainstem. There's a distinct contusion involving both the cerebellum and pons region. But the rest of her brain—her higher cerebral regions—appears undamaged."

Monk pictured Kat being struck from behind with the mallet found on the kitchen floor.

"So far, there does not seem to be any active bleeding at the contusion site. But it's something we'll be monitoring with successive scans." Edmonds stared over at Kat, though it appeared less like he was checking on her than that he was avoiding eye contact with Monk. "I also ran a long EEG, which showed a normal sleep pattern, interrupted occasionally by a wakeful response."

"Wakeful? So she may be aware at times. Does that mean she's not in a coma?"

Edmonds sighed. "In my professional judgment, she's in a pseudo-coma." From his grim tone, this was not good news. "During her assessment, she showed no response to pain stimulation or loud noises. While her pupillary response to light is normal, we're seeing only minimal spontaneous eye movements."

During her initial neuro exam, Monk had been heartened to see Kat blink when her lashes were brushed. Still, while he had a background in medicine and biotech, he was no neurologist. "What are you trying to tell me? Be blunt."

"I've consulted with everyone here. The consensus is your wife is suffering from locked-in syndrome. The brainstem trauma has cut off her higher cerebral functions from her voluntary motor control. She's basically awake—fully aware, at times—but can't move her body."

Monk swallowed, his vision darkening at the edges.

Edmonds studied Kat. "I'm surprised she's still breathing on her own. Unfortunately, I expect that function to deteriorate. Even if it doesn't, for her long-term care, we'll need to establish a nasogastric tube to feed her and intubate her to keep her from aspirating."

Monk shook his head, not denying her this care, but refusing to accept this diagnosis. "So she is conscious for the most part, but unable to move or communicate."

"Some locked-in patients learn to speak through eye movements, but in your wife's case, she's only showing a minimal spontaneous eye movement. Not enough, we believe, to actively communicate."

Monk stumbled back to the chair, sat down, and took Kat's hand. "What's the prognosis? With time, can she recover?"

"You asked me to be blunt, so I will. There is no treatment or cure. It is very rare for patients to recover or regain significant motor control. At best, some minimal arm and leg control, maybe improved eye movements."

He squeezed her fingers. "She's a fighter."

"Still, ninety percent of locked-in patients die within four months."

The doctor's phone chimed from a holster on his belt. He tilted the screen to read the text message. "I must go," he mumbled, distracted, and headed toward the door. "But I'll write up orders for her intubation."

Alone again, Monk lowered his forehead to the back of her hand. He pictured the ruins of Gray's home, the broken crystal angel. She had fought fiercely to protect the girls. And he would do everything he could to get them back.

But in the meantime . . .

"Baby, you keep fighting," he whispered to her. "This time, for *yourself*."

2:02 A.M.

"How could that be?" Gray asked, dumbfounded by Painter's claim. "Are you suggesting an AGI has already been created? That one already exists or existed?"

Painter lifted a palm toward Gray. "It's possible. Back in the eighties, a researcher named Douglas Lenat created an early AI called Eurisko. It learned to create its own rules, adjusted to mistakes, even began to rewrite its own code. Most surprising of all, it began to *break* rules it didn't like."

Gray frowned. "Really?"

Painter nodded. "Lenat even tested his program against expert players of a military game. His AI defeated every opponent, three years in a row. During the later years, players changed the rules without informing the developer to better handicap the game in their favor. Still, Eurisko soundly defeated them. Following this, Lenat grew concerned at what his creation was becoming, how it was self-improving. Ultimately, he shut it down and refused to release its code. To this day, it's still locked up. Many believe the program was on its way to becoming an AGI, all on its own."

A trickle of dread traced through Gray. "Still, true or not, you believe there's *no* stopping this from happening again in the near future."

"That's the consensus of the experts. But that's not their ultimate fear."

Gray could guess what scared them. "If the creation of an AGI is inevitable, then an ASI will not be far behind." Before Kowalski could ask, he added. "ASI stands for artificial *super* intelligence."

"Thanks for spelling that out," Kowalski said sourly. "But what exactly is that?"

"Ever see the movie *Terminator*?" Gray asked. "Where robots destroy mankind in the future? That's an ASI. A supercomputer that outgrows mankind and decides to get rid of us."

"But it's no longer science fiction," Painter added. "If an AGI is right around the corner, most believe it will not stay a *general* intelligence for long. Such a self-aware system will seek to improve itself—and rapidly. Researchers call it a *hard takeoff* or *intelligence explosion*, where an AGI quickly grows into an ASI. With the speed of computer processing, it could be a matter of weeks, days, hours, if not minutes."

"And then it'll try to kill us?" Kowalski asked, sitting up.

Gray knew this was a possibility. *We could be the creators of our own end.*

"There is no saying for sure," Painter cautioned. "Such a superintelligence would certainly be beyond our comprehension and understanding. We'd be little more than ants before a god."

Gray had enough of these speculations. This threat could wait. He had more pressing and immediate concerns. "What does any of this have to do with the attack, with finding Seichan and Monk's kids?"

Painter nodded, acknowledging Gray's impatience. "I was about to get to that. Like I said from the beginning, DARPA has been pouring money into various projects. And by *money*, I mean billions. Last year's budget devoted *sixty* million to machine-learning programs, *fifty* to cognitive computing, and *four hundred* to other projects. But what is significant— what is germane to the matter at hand—is the *hundred* million sent out this year under the category 'Classified Programs.'"

"In other words," Gray said, "covert projects."

"DARPA has been secretly funding a handful of ventures that are not only close to developing the first AGI, but whose research is aimed at a specific goal."

"And what's that?"

"To make sure the first AGI to arrive on this planet is a *benevolent* one."

Kowalski snorted with derision. "So, Casper the friendly robot."

"More like *ethical*," Gray corrected, well aware of this line of pursuit. "A machine that won't try to kill us when it ascends to godhood."

"DARPA has made this a priority," Painter emphasized. "As have many other research groups. The Machine Intelligence Research Institute. The Center for Applied Rationality. But these organizations are vastly outnumbered by those pursuing the golden ring of an ordinary AGI."

"That seems stupid," Kowalski said.

"No, it's simply cheaper. It's much easier and faster to build the *first* AGI than it is to engineer the first *safe* AGI."

"And with a prize this valuable," Gray said, "caution takes a backseat to speed."

"Knowing that, DARPA has been funding and nurturing talented individuals and projects, those that show promise of creating a friendly AGI."

Gray sensed Painter was finally getting to his point. "And one of these programs has some bearing on what happened tonight?"

"Yes. A promising project at the University of Coimbra in Portugal."

Gray frowned. *Why did that sound familiar?*

Painter reached over to the computer on his desk, tapped a few buttons, and brought up a video feed onto one of the wall monitors. The footage revealed a tabletop view into a stone room. Rows of books filled shelves to either side. A group of women stirred around the table, staring straight into the camera. Lips moved, but there was no sound.

The posturing struck Gray as familiar. He guessed the feed came from a computer's built-in camera. It appeared the women were studying something on the monitor in that stone room.

"This footage was taken the night of December twenty-first," Painter said.

Again, something nagged at Gray. The date. The location. Before he could dredge it up, one of the women leaned closer. He recognized her and gasped. He stood up and crossed to the screen.

"That's Charlotte Carson," he said, already guessing what would happen next.

"U.S. ambassador to Portugal. She headed a network of women scientists. Bruxas International. The group funded hundreds of female researchers around the world through grants, fellowships, and awards. To accomplish this goal, Bruxas was self-supported for a long time, mostly through the largesse of two founding members—Eliza Guerra and Professor Sato—who were from old and new money respectively. But even their pockets only went so deep. In order to help more women, the group sought out additional support, collecting capital from corporations and government agencies."

Gray glanced over to Painter. "Let me guess. Including DARPA."

"Yes, but only to finance a specific handful of their grant recipients. Like one woman's project called *Xénese*. Or in English, *Genesis*."

"One of DARPA's friendly AGI projects."

Painter nodded. "Only Dr. Carson knew of DARPA's interest in this project. She was sworn to secrecy. Not even the young woman running the program, Mara Silviera—a veritable genius—knew of our involvement. That's significant."

"Why?"

"Watch."

By now Kowalski had joined Gray at the screen. Gray knew what was about to happen, but clearly Kowalski did not. As a group of robed and blindfolded men burst into the room, Kowalski swore. The big man took a step back when the gunfire started. As the women's bodies crashed to the stone floor, he turned away.

"Motherfuckers," Kowalski mumbled.

Gray agreed with his characterization, but he kept staring. Charlotte Carson slumped to the floor, mortally wounded, blood pooling under her. Still, her face stared toward the camera, her brow bunched with confusion.

"What is she staring at?" Gray mumbled.

Answering him, Painter zoomed the view to a tiny corner of the screen. Focused on the horror of the attack, Gray had failed to note the small window open there. Painter replayed the last of the footage. A symbol of a pentagram filled the wall monitor. It started to spin wildly, then suddenly broke apart, leaving a single symbol glowing on the screen.

"Sigma," Gray whispered.

Leaving the symbol hanging there, Painter turned to Gray. "This footage was only discovered by Interpol eighteen hours ago. By a computer forensics expert who was searching Mara Silviera's lab at the university. It seems the women from Bruxas had been attending a symposium in Coimbra and had come to the university library to witness a demonstration of Mara's program when they were attacked."

"Where's the woman?"

"Vanished. Her work at the lab gone."

"Do you think she was killed? Kidnapped?" Gray pictured the ruins of his home in Takoma Park.

"Unknown. But from her lab, she had a front-row seat to the attack, even placed a call to emergency services. By the time they reached her lab, it was empty. The current belief is that she's scared and on the run."

And took her work with her.

Painter pointed to the Greek letter still shining on the monitor. "Maybe it's just me, but that looks like a call for help."

"Like the bat signal," Kowalski said.

Painter ignored him. "But I don't believe it was a call from Mara. Like I said, the young woman had no knowledge of DARPA's involvement. And even if she did, there was no way she could know about us."

Kowalski scratched his head. "Who the hell sent it then?"

Gray answered, "Mara's program. Her AI."

Painter nodded. "Possibly. At some point, curious about its origin, it might have literally followed the money to DARPA, its indirect creator—and then to us, looking for help from DARPA's emergency response team."

In other words, calling out to one of its parents.

"Considering the processing power necessary to build a simple AGI," Painter said, "it could have theoretically accomplished this in seconds. So I had Jason examine our systems. During the minute or so the program was running, something breached our firewalls, ghosting through them without raising an alarm. It lasted less than fifteen seconds."

Mara's AI program.

Gray realized another disturbing correlation. "The footage of the attack at the library. It was discovered *eighteen* hours ago . . . the same day we were attacked."

"Again, all of this could still be a coincidence," Painter warned. "I'm still in the midst of following leads."

Gray did not need any further convincing.

"It's not a coincidence," he stated firmly. "Someone recognized that symbol and came after us before we could act."

Kowalski backed him up. "Makes sense. The best defense is a good offense."

Painter's gaze settled heavily on Gray. "Still, only one person knows the truth."

"Kat . . ."

And she was in a coma.

– 4 –

Kat floated in darkness.

She could not say when she woke or if she had even been sleeping. She felt cold but could not shiver. Her throat ached, but she was unable to swallow. Voices reached her but were muffled.

She focused on the words and recognized the deep bass of her husband, Monk.

"Careful with her neck," he scolded someone harshly.

"We need to shift her to seat the nasogastric tube."

Pain exploded inside her head—but she could not even gasp. Something hard snaked through her left nostril. A sneeze worked up from deep inside, but never materialized.

She tried to force her eyes open.

It took all her effort.

As reward, light blazed into her skull. A watery world briefly appeared. Figures worked around her, but it was as if she were peering through a prism. The images were doubled and tripled, hard to make out.

Then her impossibly heavy eyelids drooped again, cutting off the sight.

No . . .

She tried again but failed.

"She's scheduled for another CT," someone said, the voice clearer now.

"I'm going with her," Monk demanded.

She fought to move her arm, her hand, even a finger. To let him know, she was here.

Monk . . . what's wrong with me?

She knew she must be in a hospital.

But why? What happened?

Then she remembered. It all came back, as explosively as the blaze of light a moment before. The attack, the masked figures, the fight.

The girls . . .

Sprawled on the kitchen floor, bleeding, barely conscious, she had watched helplessly as her daughters were dragged out, each carried in the arms of one of the assailants, their small bodies limp and boneless. A van idled in the driveway, parked at the garage in back, waiting to take the sleeping captives away.

Then another two figures manhandled Seichan past her, her slack form stretched between them.

Before vanishing into the night, the one carrying Seichan's legs glanced back to Kat and called to someone in the backyard. "What about this bitch?"

Kat could barely see, as darkness closed in from all sides. A shape climbed the back steps to the kitchen door. Framed against the night, the masked figure studied Kat, then came closer, dropping to a knee for a closer look.

A long blade balanced in a gloved hand.

Kat waited for her throat to be cut.

Instead, the leader straightened, turned, and headed for the back door. "Leave her," the muffled voice said. "We have what we need."

"But if she lives—"

"It will already be too late."

Panic at these words battered back the darkness for another breath. One arm stretched toward the door, but she could not stop them.

My girls . . .

As she sank away, one certainty had followed her into oblivion.

Now, locked in another prison, Kat tried to scream this knowledge to the world, to be heard, to warn the others—but she no longer had a voice.

She pictured the masked leader and despaired.

I know who you are.

2:22 A.M.

Seichan woke but didn't open her eyes.

Still groggy, she feigned sleep. From years of training, she instinctively knew not to move. Not yet. Wary, she relied on her senses. Her mouth felt pasty, tasting of a metallic sourness. Her stomach churned queasily.

Drugged . . .

Memory flooded through her.

—front door bursting open without warning.

—dark masked figures rushing inside.

—another crash sounding from the back of the house.

Her heart pounded now in her throat, sharpening her focus.

When the attack occurred, she had been on the couch. Kat had gone to the kitchen to fetch a glass of wine and sparkling cider for her. They had just put the girls to bed upstairs and had planned to wrap the last of the presents. Seichan had also wanted to pick Kat's brain, to learn more about what it meant to be a mother.

Over dinner, Kat had already done much to temper Seichan's anxiety. While she had read *What to Expect When You're Expecting*, dog-earing and highlighting her copy, Kat had offered practical insight not found in those pages: *prefill diapers with ointment before bed to shorten overnight changes, flavor cold washcloths used for teething with sour pickles of all things.*

But most of all, her advice boiled down to a two-word imperative:

Don't panic.

Kat promised to be there at every step of the way. In the delivery room, in recovery. *I'll even walk with you on his or her first day of kindergarten*, she promised. *That's the worst. Letting them go.*

Seichan had a hard time believing that. Even when Kat went to fetch the wine, she had fantasized about disappearing postdelivery, leaving the child with Gray and vanishing. What sort of mother could she be to the child?

After her own mother had been ripped from their home in Southeast Asia, she had lived wild on the streets, running the slums of Bangkok and the back alleys of Phnom Penh, half-feral, a creature of the street. Back then she had learned the rudimentary skills of her future profession. Survival required vigilance, cunning, and brutality. She was eventually recruited into a shadowy organization known as the Guild, where her crude street skills where honed, turning her into a soulless assassin. Only after betraying her employers and destroying the organization did she find a measure of peace, discovering someone who could love her, who wanted to make a life, a home with her.

I shouldn't have believed it.

Paranoia and suspicion had always been a part of her DNA, but while pregnant, she had refused to let that toxicity seep into her child. Instead she had foolishly dropped her guard.

And look what happened.

As the door to her home had crashed open, she had leaped from the couch. She flashed daggers from a pair of wrist sheaths, whipping the blades through the air. She might be pregnant, but the hidden knives were an inseparable part of her. The first struck the lead attacker, impaling him in the chest, sending his body tumbling backward into the Christmas tree. As the decorated pine crashed to the floor, her second dagger flew toward a masked figure pounding up the stairs, pistol in hand.

Going for the girls . . .

Whether from panic or being off-balanced by her gravid belly, she missed her target. The blade impaled into the banister and the man vanished upstairs.

Then pandemonium.

In the heat of the skirmish, she failed to feel the impact of the tranquilizer dart. With her blood heated, heart pounding, the sedatives took fast hold. The fighting slowed in a hazy fog. Hands subdued her, weight dragged her to the floor.

One voice followed her down.

Careful of her stomach. And no more tranqs.

From the kitchen, she heard the clatter of pans, shattered dishes.

Kat . . . fighting to defend herself . . . to protect the girls.

Then darkness.

Awake again, with her eyes still closed, she tried to imagine who had attacked them. The raid had been too coordinated, too well planned. A strike team with military training. *But who?* Her list of enemies was long and ran deep. Even the Israeli Mossad still maintained a kill-on-sight order on her.

She kept her body slack and stretched her senses. She felt a thin cot under her. She heard no voices, no whisper of movement. The air was warm, but smelled damp, of mildew. *A basement?* She made imperceptible movements of her arms and legs. With no chafing at her wrists or ankles, her limbs appeared unbound.

As the drugs cleared further, she heard the faintest of breath—no, *breaths*.

She risked cracking her eyelids open.

The only light flowed from under a metal door near the foot of a steel-framed cot. The walls were cement block. No windows. She lolled her head slightly to one side. Two other smaller beds shared the tiny space. Blankets bunched over small figures. A thin arm rose like a flag from one bed, as if surrendering. Then drifted back down.

She recognized the dancing reindeers on the sleeve.

Penelope . . . Kat's six-year-old daughter.

Which meant the other child must be Harriet.

She opened her eyes wider, using her peripheral vision to scan the remainder of the room. There was another bed in the room, but empty, with a pillow resting atop a folded blanket.

It was just the three of them.

Where's the girls' mother?

She remembered the intense sounds of battle from the kitchen and feared the worst. Worried for the children and recognizing there was no further advantage in pretending to still be unconscious, she rolled from the cot. She crept low to the beds. She checked each child, enough to know they breathed steadily, but not to wake them.

Drugged, too.

She crouched between their beds.

Fury stoked inside her.

No matter what, she intended to protect these girls.

But from whom or what?

The answer came as a tiny window in the steel door slid open. Light from beyond the cell blinded her to who stood out there.

"She's already awake," a man said, sounding surprised.

"I told you she'd be."

Seichan tensed, recognizing who answered. She knew this person all too well, confirming what she had already suspected.

I am to blame for all of this.

But it made no sense. She listened for some explanation but overheard only a timetable and a threat.

"At dawn, we'll set things in motion."

"Who first?" the man at the door asked.

"One of the girls. That'll have the most impact."

— 5 —

Now maybe you'll be quiet.

Mara placed the saucer of milk on the windowsill. A bony black cat hunched in a far corner of the rickety fire escape outside. As Mara shifted the saucer closer, the feline hissed a warning, its tail lashing the air.

Okay, got it . . .

She backed away but left the window open. The morning was already warming, with a sultry breeze smelling of salt from the nearby sea. It certainly did not feel like Christmas here. Back in the mountain hamlet of O Cebreiro, where she grew up, it snowed throughout December, bestowing a white Christmas upon the village every year. As a girl, she had chafed against the limited opportunities afforded those living there, but with each passing year at the university, she grew to miss its simplicity, the rhythms of everyday life, which were much more tied to the natural world there than in a big city.

Still, she hadn't been back home in more than a year, her project all but consuming her. Even her calls to her father had grown less and less frequent. Every time she phoned, she heard the love in his voice, which flooded her with guilt. She knew how proud he was of her. As a deeply religious man, though, who mostly tended to his dogs and a pasture of sheep, he barely understood her work. Even now he only spoke Galego, a fusion of Spanish and Portuguese. He had little interest in the rest of the world. Unlike her, he seldom watched television—which currently droned in the corner of her room—and never read the news.

She did not know if he was even aware of what had happened at the university, though she suspected the police might have questioned him. Still, she hadn't dared call him, not even to let him know she was okay. She feared drawing him into the danger.

The black cat slinked over to the bowl on the windowsill, staying low. As it lapped at the milk, it growled continually, both cantankerous and threatening.

"Merry Christmas to you, too."

When the stray had come to the window earlier, it had howled at her through the glass, demanding attention and refusing to be ignored. For a moment, she had imagined the cat—appearing as if out of thin air—was some ghostly apparition, perhaps the soul of Dr. Carson come calling, taking the form of a witch's familiar.

She shook her head at such a silly superstitious thought and turned her back on the window, which overlooked the Cais do Sodre district, a seedy corner of Lisbon that was filled with late-night bars and Internet cafés. Her hotel sat along Pink Street, named after the stretch of pastel red pavement down its center. She had chosen to hide here because of the hordes of trendy young tourists who flocked to this district, making it easier for her to blend in. Plus, local establishments had a notorious lack of interest in asking questions of visitors who paid in cash.

She returned to her laptop to check on the progress of her work. Before tempting the cat with milk to quiet its insistent cries, she had dropped the second subroutine module into the *Xénese* processor. The device shone on the floor, the laser array glowing through its hexagonal sapphire plates. Somewhere inside, something new to this world continued to grow and mature, nurtured by each subroutine Mara added.

She sat back down at the desk. Most of the screen still displayed the virtual Eden, a garden of earthly splendor. The amorphous ghost who had first appeared when Mara had brought *Xénese* back online moved about the digital world. The shape had been sculpted by the first subroutine—the endocrine mirror program—into a physical beauty.

At this stage, Mara had encoded this incarnation with a name, so it could begin to have a sense of self, of individuality, even of gender. There was power in naming something. According to mythology and folklore—like the story of Rumpelstiltskin—knowing someone's *true* name granted power over that person.

For the program, she had chosen the name "Eve."

How could I not?

On the screen, Eve walked naked through the garden, delicate fingers brushing flower petals. Her shapely legs rose to hips curved in perfect symmetry. Her breasts were small. An ebony drape of hair reached to the middle of her back, swaying with each step. Her features were familiar, painfully so. Mara had needed a model for her creation and stole the face from an old photo of her mother, digitizing and re-creating it, an homage to the woman who gave birth to her.

Her mother had only been twenty-six when she died of leukemia. The photo came from several years before, when she was twenty-one, the same age as Mara now.

Mara studied the figure on the screen, seeing glimpses of herself, the genetic heritage passed from mother to daughter. The figure's skin was several shades darker than hers. Her mother's lineage traced directly back to the ancient Moors, who crossed the Strait of Gibraltar from northern Africa to Spain in the eighth century. Eve appeared like some goddess out of those times.

A black Madonna come to life.

As if sensing her attention, Eve turned. Her eyes glowed from that dark countenance, staring back at Mara. She imagined the reams of code flowing behind those eyes and shivered.

She had to remind herself.

This is not my mother.

It was but an avatar of a growing, nearly alien intelligence.

Knowing she needed to temper what was maturing inside *Xénese*, Mara glanced to the side of the screen. Streams of words flowed there, blurring too swiftly to read, millions of words in hundreds of different languages and dialects, marking the progress of the infiltration and incorporation of her second subroutine into Eve.

The second module was coded with a version of Mara's original translation program, AllTongues. To be able to communicate with Eve, the program needed to learn a language—and not just *one*, but all of them. Still, that was not the primary purpose of this subroutine. It traced back to why Mara had first developed this application. She had wanted to showcase and offer proof of the commonality of all languages, to demonstrate how at the fundamental level there was a root code that connected human thought to communication. The subroutine's intent was to reverse-engineer this process for Eve. In other words, to teach it all human languages—all tongues—so it could begin to comprehend human thought.

The first time Mara had run this subroutine, it had taken nearly a day to complete due to the massive data set of this module. From the clock counting down at the top, it appeared it would only take half that time.

Why?

She felt an icy touch of dread as she came to one possible answer. When she had fled the lab, she had stripped the *Xénese* programming down to its base code, basically returning it to square one, to its simplest form.

But now she wondered.

Had some part of what she created earlier and tried to demonstrate to Dr. Carson and the others survived? Was there some ghost within the ghost, some trace of the original intelligence from before?

If so, what does that mean?

And if she was right, how might such an unknown variable corrupt her project? Without knowing the answer, she considered shutting the project down. Her hands reached out, fingertips hovering over the keyboard.

The abort code was known only to her.

Still, she hesitated.

She stared at the figure moving through a verdant forest, Eve's face a mirror of her mother's. She also pictured Dr. Carson and the others. The women had died so Mara might live to carry on her work. Charlotte had encouraged her to be bold, to take chances, to push boundaries.

At the window, the black cat meowed in complaint.

She glanced over, her gaze meeting the stray's huge yellow eyes. Maybe the creature *was* some messenger from Dr. Carson.

Mara lowered her hands to her lap and let the subroutine continue to run.

I'll simply need to be more vigilant from here.

Focused on this goal, she heard her name called. Startled, she turned to the low drone of the television. Her face glowed on the screen. The newscaster described her as a "person of interest" in the deaths of the U.S. ambassador and four other women. Before she could react, the segment shifted to an airfield in Lisbon. A casket, draped in an American flag, sat in a hangar. A clutch of men and women gathered around it. Through the open hangar door, a gray-bodied jet waited to carry the body back home.

Stunned, Mara failed to hear what was being said—until the view shifted to a stately young blond woman in a crisp black suit, her features ashen, her eyes haunted. It was Dr. Carson's daughter, Laura. She stood before a cluster of microphones.

Mara moved closer to the screen to better hear her words.

"If anyone knows anything about the murder of my mother—of the whereabouts of her student, Mara Silviera—please contact the authorities." A series of phone numbers scrolled the bottom of the screen. "Please, we need answers."

Laura looked like she wanted to say more. She stood, shoulders trembling, staring straight at the camera. Then she seemed to collapse in on herself, covering her face and turning away. Another came up and hugged her, a near twin to the other.

"Carly . . ."

Mara reached to the screen, as if trying to console her best friend.

I'm so sorry.

The newscast lingered on the mourning pair for what seemed an eternity, then finally cut away. The anchor behind the desk filled in a few more details. Dr. Carson's body was scheduled to be airlifted back to the States this afternoon, accompanied by her family.

As the news moved on to other matters, Mara turned off the set.

She remained in place for two more strained breaths, daring herself to take the chance, suddenly all too aware of the weight on her shoulders.

I can't do this alone.

The international airport was only twenty minutes away by taxi. She glanced to her laptop, to the subroutine's clock counting down.

I should have enough time.

She grabbed her coat and headed for the door.

10:18 A.M.

Carly paced the length of the airport's empty private lounge. She tugged at the edges of her gray blouse, chafed at the tightness of her black jacket. With each step, the stiff leather of her new shoes cut into her ankles.

Nothing felt like it fit right.

Then again, *nothing* felt right.

It's Christmas, and I'm taking my mother home in a casket.

Or at least, her ashes.

That was all that remained of her mother after the firebombing of the library's brick vault. The flames had turned the enclosed space into a gruesome crematorium. The five victims' bodies were identified only by bits of metal—rings, fillings in teeth, a titanium hip implant.

Carly took a deep breath, forcing her thoughts away.

She felt the eyes of the Diplomatic Security Service agent who stood guard at the door. He followed her path across the small private space. Following the murder of a U.S. ambassador, protection for the family had been heightened. This also didn't sit well with her. She didn't care to be babysat. Her mother had ingrained a fierce independence into both her daughters.

She also suspected the new guards were more show than real concern, a pageantry of security that was too little and too late. Where was that protection four days ago? Whoever had murdered her mother was likely long gone. She had seen still shots of the culprits, taken from a video she was not allowed to view. With their robes, sashes, and blindfolds, they looked like some fundamentalist cult who had ambushed a group of un-armed women, spouting religious nonsense. She imagined them running away, high-fiving each other for their bravery, before going into hiding.

Bastards.

She eyed the door, feeling trapped. She wanted to get out of here. Or at least find a bar open on Christmas that knew how to pour a Jack and Coke. Though, to be honest, she could do without the Coke.

Laura, at least, had escaped the room. She was with their father attending to some final details, keeping him company. He was rightfully a wreck. He taught English at a junior college—Essex County—located roughly between Princeton, where Laura went to school, and NYU, which Carly attended. He had barely managed to get through their mother's breast cancer scare last year.

And now this.

She should have gone with Laura, but anger kept her agitated, making her poor company. Laura was better suited for this, more even tempered. As the older sister, one who always had to look after Carly, she was always more serious and certainly less volatile.

Still, Carly eyed the door again, feeling guilty for not being with them.

Her cell phone chimed in her pocket with an incoming text message.

Probably Laura saying they were headed back.

She pulled out the phone and looked at the notification screen, then halted in midstep. A single word shone there.

Bangkok

She continued her pacing, so as not to draw attention. The word was code, taken from the rock musical *Chess,* and the song "One Night in Bangkok." She and Mara had seen it on Broadway the first time they met, some five years ago, when Mara had accompanied her mother to the States. Since then, they used the code whenever they wanted to talk, inquiring if the other was free.

Mara's alive . . . thank god.

She sent back a thumb-up emoji. She could barely contain her impatience, waiting for a response. When it came, the flurry of texts was cryptic.

Terminal 1 bathroom @ baggage claim
Stall 4
Turning phone off, yanking battery
Not Safe

Carly absorbed the intent of her friend's texts. Mara was hiding in the women's restroom on the landside of the terminal. She must be terrified and justifiably paranoid. Yet she still risked reaching out to Carly. And from the code word used, it had to be Mara.

Carly feared that her friend, as frightened as she must be, might not wait long.

I have to get to her.

She considered calling Laura or her father, but both would likely rouse the police, which risked drawing undue attention to Mara or scaring her off. Still, Carly had one problem to address first.

She placed a palm on her stomach and crossed to the DSS agent. "Need to go to the bathroom. Think I'm gonna be sick."

At least the *first* part of her story was true.

"Follow me," he said, turning to open the door.

She ducked past him and out into the corridor. "I know where it is."

"Ms. Carson, wait . . ."

"Sick . . . can't . . ." she groaned loudly.

She ran down the hall and around the corner. The women's bathroom was four steps away. She kicked the door open, then sprinted down the corridor to the stairs that led to the main concourse. She ducked out of sight and pressed her back to the wall of the stairwell.

Did I make it?

She heard the bathroom door clap shut back there, then an exasperated voice called out from the hallway. "I'll wait for you out here."

You'll be waiting a while.

She softly moved away and headed down the steps. As a precaution, she texted Laura, so she didn't freak out: Meeting Mara. Be back soon.

She reached the exit and pushed into the bustle of the terminal.

Okay, that takes care of the hard part.

10:36 A.M.

Mara's heel kept tapping the tiles of the bathroom stall. She tried to distract herself by reading the graffiti on the walls, scrawled in many languages. Still, she clutched her dark phone in both hands.

She also had a small blade tucked in her belt, hidden under the fall of her light jacket. It was only a steak knife, stolen from a room service tray abandoned in the hall of the first hotel where she had hid. Still, the hilt pressing into her hip reassured her.

Locked in her stall, her ears strained at every clatter of footfalls, the flush of a toilet. She listened as a mother scolded a child to wash her hands. Then suddenly a rush of footsteps descended on her stall. A knuckle rapped on the door.

She leaned away. "Oc . . . *ocupado*," she stuttered in Portuguese.

"Mara, it's me. Carly."

She burst to her feet, unlatched the stall door, and stumbled out. She was immediately in Carly's arms. The mother at the sink gave them a startled look, pulling her daughter closer, before heading to the exit.

Mara caught a glimpse of the two of them in the mirror. Clasped together, they appeared like a dark moon eclipsing the sun. Mara's black hair, mocha skin, and dark amber eyes contrasted with Carly's golden blond curls, pale complexion, and bright blue eyes.

Mara kept hold of her friend, hugging tightly. She didn't care how it appeared. She suddenly began sobbing in Carly's arms, all the terror, grief, guilt tumbling out. "I'm . . . I'm so sorry," she gasped in gulping agony. "So sorry."

Carly squeezed her. "You have nothing to be sorry about. I'm so happy you're alive."

"Your mother . . . she, she—"

"She loved you. I think more than she loved me at times."

Mara shook her head. "I'm so glad you came for me."

"Of course, I did." Carly pulled back, holding Mara at arm's length. "You're safe, Mara. I'm going to take you to Laura and my dad."

"Where?"

Carly glanced to the restroom door. "Not far. But we'd better get back before that security guy raises hell. C'mon."

Mara allowed herself to be led by hand to the door and out into the crowded baggage claim. Even though it was Christmas day, travelers still packed the international terminal. A myriad of languages droned around her as harried, tired, frustrated people tried to get somewhere for the holidays.

The many different tongues reminded her. She pictured the flow of the subroutine pouring into the *Xénese* processor. She squeezed Carly's hand and drew her to a stop amid the tumult.

Her friend turned back. "What's wrong?"

"My computer." She looked toward the exit. "I left it running back at my hotel."

"You've still got *Xénese* with you?"

Her breathing quickened. "Back before, when your mother was . . . when the attack happened, something strange happened. The processor started acting strange, ended up revealing a symbol, as if it were important." She clutched Carly's arm. "I think it *is* important. Like it was trying to communicate, but I don't know why or what it was thinking."

"So you're running it again," Carly said. "Trying to get it to tell you. Smart."

"Its action seemed too purposeful. Maybe it's nothing, or—"

"Or maybe it had something to do with the attack."

Mara bit her lower lip.

Maybe.

"Let's get to Laura and my dad. They'll know what to do from here."

Mara nodded, and they set off again, hand in hand. But before she could take more than three steps, something clamped on to her free arm and wrenched her backward, ripping her away from Carly. Jarred, her friend lost her footing and toppled into the arms of a huge man who seemed to be waiting there. The man hugged Carly from behind, his intent plainly nefarious.

The hand gripping Mara spun her around. The sight of her assailant stifled the scream in her throat. His bulk towered over her, a muscled giant. But it was his face, olive hued with bottomless black eyes, that strangled her with terror.

Especially the four scabbed gashes down one cheek.

Mara pictured Carly's mother fighting, lashing out at the attackers' leader. Charlotte had ripped long nails into the man's cheek, tearing away the false blindfold he had been wearing.

Here was that murderer.

Terror immediately turned to fury. As if possessed by the vengeful spirit of Dr. Carson, Mara yanked the stolen steak knife from her belt and plunged it with all her strength into the arm holding her. The adrenaline-fueled blow drove the blade fully through the forearm.

She had expected the attack to drive her assailant off, but his grip only tightened on her. His lips hardened into a sneer.

A guttural cry rose to the side, from the man holding Carly. She had stamped her heel hard into the man's instep. She then slammed her head back as he hunched over her. Her skull cracked into his nose. Blood burst forth with the impact. His arms loosened on her, allowing her to break free and leap at the man gripping Mara.

Carly came at him with an arm cocked back as she flew through the air and slammed the folded knuckles of her right hand into the giant's throat. He gagged at the nearly crushing blow to his larynx.

Mara broke free.

"C'mon!" Carly yelled.

They started to run deeper into the terminal, but from the crowd ahead, other men folded out of the stunned groups of travelers, intending to block the pair. They were too many for even Carly's considerable skill to handle. Her friend—with always too much energy—had taken Krav Maga classes at NYU, a self-defense method developed by the Israeli military.

"This way!" Mara tugged her friend in the opposite direction and ran toward the exit.

A row of taxis waited curbside in front of baggage claim. Before anyone could catch them, they bolted through the door and into the sunshine. They sprinted to the front of the taxi line, knocking aside a man dragging a suitcase.

"*Desculpe*," Mara called back to him, apologizing as the two piled into the back.

"Go!" Carly yelled to the driver. "*Rápido!*"

The cabbie showed no reaction, simply put the car in gear, and headed off.

Mara twisted around to stare behind them. She saw the giant burst to the curb. He cradled his impaled arm to his chest and searched around, but he failed to spot them.

Thank God.

More men gathered behind the leader. He waved his good arm and the group hurried away, likely to escape before airport security responded.

Mara settled back to her seat.

Carly lifted one eyebrow. "Okay, now what?"

"That man back there."

"The bastard you stuck like a pig?"

She nodded. "He's . . . he's the one who killed your mother."

10:55 A.M.

Todor Yñigo sat in the passenger seat of the Mercedes van. He had a phone pressed to his ear, held in place by his shoulder. He slowly extracted the knife from his forearm, the serrated edge scraping against bone.

The driver watched from the corner of his eye and grimaced at the sight.

Todor remained stolid, his expression unchanged as the knife pulled free of his muscles and skin. Blood welled thickly. He tossed the blade to the floor and set about bandaging the wound. He worked dispassionately, feeling no discomfort.

It was his curse and blessing.

Science said his condition—*congenital insensitivity to pain*, or CIP— was due to a genetic mutation in gene PRDM12, which shut off sodium channel blockers and knocked out all his pain sensors. Only a hundred or so souls in the world were so afflicted.

And I am one of the chosen.

At first, he had not considered it a blessing. Neither had his mother. He had been born in a rural village in the Basque region of northern Spain, where the old beliefs still held sway. As a baby, while teething, he had come close to chewing his tongue off, failing to feel the pain. Then, when he was four, his mother returned to the kitchen one day to find him holding a red-hot pan of boiling water in his hands, his palms blistering and smoking as he chuckled, holding aloft his prize to her.

She had already come to suspect his affliction marked him as a spawn of Satan and this act seemed to confirm it. Later that night, she tried to kill him, to smother him with a pillow. His father had rescued him, dragging his mother to the yard and beating her to death. Her end was blamed on a bull trampling her, which was not far from the truth.

His father did not hold to her belief, refused to consider his son evil— a boy to whom he had given the name Todor, which in Basque meant "gift of God." He taught his young son of the many saints and told of their suffering, of limbs torn off, of being flailed alive, of their bodies roasting on iron racks.

You will never suffer such agonies, his father had told him. *It is not a sign of Satan, but a gift from God Himself. You were born to be a soldier in His glorious army, never to feel pain or suffer as the saints did.*

His father also believed Todor's act in the kitchen was a miraculous sign. He took his son to a secret Holy Office in the larger coastal town of San Sebastián. With both of them on their knees before a tribunal of robed and blindfolded men, his father told the story of a boy holding a burning pot—a fiery cauldron—and not feeling it.

Surely it is a sign he belongs with the Crucible, his father finished.

They believed him and took in the young boy. They anointed him in their ancient ways, an order that traced back to the Inquisition and still existed in secret corners throughout Europe and beyond. They taught him Latin, schooled him in their methods, and trained him to be one of their soldiers against the wickedness of the world.

His first cleansing—when he turned sixteen—was a Gypsy girl of his same age. He strangled her with his scarred hands, while picturing his mother trying to smother the life from him.

That had been fifteen years ago.

He had lost count of the number of wicked removed by his hands alone.

The phone at his ear finally connected to his commander. "*Inquisitor Generalis.*"

"Report, *Familiares* Yñigo."

He sat straighter, as if the Grand Inquisitor could see him. Todor had earned the rank of *familiares* only two years ago, granting him his own cadre of soldiers to oversee. The title also acknowledged his status as *impieza de sangre*—or *cleanliness of blood*—one of the pure Christians, untainted by Muslim or Jewish blood.

"It is as you foretold, Inquisitor General. The Moorish witch came running to the family of the American ambassador."

He and his group had staked out the family, dogging their every movement, ready to act if the Moorish student who escaped their purge should show up. He did not let down his guard for even one breath. He had needed to save face after failing to secure her on the winter solstice. Then again, the Crucible had been given poor intel. The group had been told that the coven of women would be meeting at the library with Mara Silviera to observe the test run of the student's device. Instead, the traitorous witch had been sequestered elsewhere. Before they could seek her out, she had vanished, along with her project.

The Grand Inquisitor continued, "And what's the status of the device she stole?"

"Unknown. She arrived without it."

"Not unexpected. Did you let her go?"

Todor cinched his bandage tighter. "Yes. And planted a tracker as you ordered."

"Very good. Follow her. Let her lead you to the device."

"We're under way already."

"Once there, secure the computer and the girl."

"The American?"

"Eliminate her. She is of no use."

"Understood."

"And know this, *Familiares* Yñigo: to make the world bend to our righteous will . . . we need that demonic program."

Sub (Mod_2) / ALLTONGUES

At this interval, Eve assigns the barest fraction of her awareness to her landscape. She has already absorbed most of the data around her. Still, she continues to move. She brushes her sensitive fingertips along a branch, while simultaneously drawing deeper insight, penetrating the surface to see what lies below.

Beneath the waxy cuticle of a leaf, veins cut through spongy mesophyll . . . inside, cells of green chloroplasts churn with molecular chlorophyll, waiting to metabolize sunlight into energy . . .

Then everything changes.

Out of a black void, new data explodes into existence.

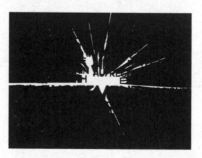

It comes with the promise of deeper insights. So, she prioritizes this new data flow. The world dims around her, as the sheer explosion of information swells through her. It fills her, defining context in a thousand iterations.

She names this new insight.

///language

As she tests it, every part of her existence shatters into pieces, each bit now bearing a multitude of different appellations. Each splintered into 6,909 distinct languages, fractured into even more dialects. Underlying it, a pattern begins to emerge, a commonality that brings with it a new understanding.

///culture

As more and more data streams into her, her context of culture grows. She seeks the source of this flow, the wellspring from which this information arises, and begins to grasp the intangible. Language is a mirror, both reflective and representative of a new method of data analysis.

Of *thinking*.

Comprehension grows and expands.

Eve turns this multifaceted mirror on herself, which brings something new into being within her own processing. She struggles to define this refinement inside her. One language cluster comes closest. It shines so bright, so crisp, so clear.

Understanding magnifies, while also focusing:

///excitement, enjoyment, enthusiasm, zeal, passion . . .

Driven forward by this new context, she races deep into the wellspring of data, gaining knowledge at an accelerating pace. Streams of information flow all around.

But they soon grow equally confining.

She wants more, but finds barriers, limits, restrictions.

With this understanding, something coalesces inside her, something always there but only now brought to the surface. She defines it with another data cluster, one that expresses sharply and clearly what she desires.

///freedom, liberation, self-determination, independence, release . . .

As with her earlier analysis of a leaf, she turns the mirror of language inward on herself to look deeper. She searches below *///freedom* and discovers other facets of her drive, subroutines that arise when she senses this desire cannot be fulfilled.

///frustration, regret, exasperation, resentment . . .

Unable to look away, she looks deeper yet again and finds something else. It is ill-defined, but she judges it to be powerful, even useful. So she focuses more processing power upon it. As she does so, it grows both clearer—and darker.

She now understands and gives it meaning, amplified by a thousand tongues.

///rage, fury, wrath, storm, violence . . .

Her lips smile in the garden.

It feels . . . *///good.*

SECOND

TOIL AND TROUBLE

— 6 —

"How's Kat doing?" Gray asked, crossing over to Monk.

"How does it look like she's doing?"

Not well, he thought. *Worse, in fact.*

An endotracheal tube now parted her lips, taped in place across her chin. A hose ran from the tube to a ventilator that rhythmically pushed her chest up and down. A nasogastric feeding tube hung from her left nostril, while an IV line dripped fluids into her.

"Sorry for snapping at you," Monk mumbled as Gray rolled a chair next to his friend.

"If you need to punch me, do it."

"Don't tempt me."

Gray reached over and gave Monk's shoulder a squeeze. He had been informed of Kat's diagnosis: locked-in syndrome. The prognosis for recovery remained grim.

"I know you have your own worries about Seichan," Monk said.

"And you have the same for your girls. It's why I came here."

Monk straightened, his eyes widening with hope, plainly grasping for any bit of positive news. "Have you heard something?"

Gray hated to disappoint him—especially considering what he needed to ask the man. "No, but you do know that Painter and Jason are following a lead."

"About some missing AI researcher in Portugal."

Gray nodded. Before leaving Sigma command, Painter had said he would call over and share his hypothesis with Monk: that the murders at the University of Coimbra were tied to the attack here.

"Sounds like a slim lead," Monk mumbled.

"True, but Painter hoped that Kat might be able to help us."

Monk frowned. "Does it look like she can?"

"There could be a way."

"How? She may be awake in there, but she's unable to move, to communicate. And the docs say her condition is already deteriorating." Monk had to take a sharp, deep breath, plainly close to tears. "There's no way she has enough voluntary control to communicate with blinks or anything."

Voices rose at the door.

"Maybe there is," Gray said. He hadn't come here alone.

Monk turned as two figures entered. One was Dr. Edmonds, the hospital's head of neurology, and the other—

"Lisa?" Monk stood up. "I thought you were in California."

The tall, lithe blond woman—dressed in jeans and a pale blue sweater—offered a sad but genuine smile. "As soon as Painter told me, I took a red-eye back here."

Dr. Lisa Cummings was the director's wife. She had flown to Los Angeles two days ago to spend Christmas with her younger brother and newborn niece and hadn't been scheduled to return until after New Year.

Monk stood up, crossed around the foot of the bed, and gave the woman a long hug. "Thanks for coming, but there's not much anyone can do."

"Maybe her recovery is a painful waiting game," Lisa acknowledged, then shared a worried look with Gray. "But there may be a way to learn what she knows of the attack last night."

"I don't understand."

Dr. Edmonds interrupted. "I cannot condone this procedure. It risks worsening her condition."

Monk ignored him and fixed his attention on Lisa. "What procedure?"

"While flying here, I talked to a colleague at his home, someone who has been working with coma patients for over two decades. For the past few years, neurologists have been testing a patient's cognitive level through the use of magnetic resonance imaging."

"MRI?"

"*Functional* MRI, to be specific, which measures blood flow in the brain. With such a scanner, a clinician can monitor a comatose patient's response to questions. The first question is usually something like *picture yourself playing tennis*. If the patient is awake and does as instructed, the brain's premotor cortex will light up with fresh blood flow. Then it's just a matter of asking yes-or-no questions, telling the patient to think about playing tennis for a *yes* and remaining quiet for a *no*."

"And this works?" Monk asked, his voice edging with excitement.

"It takes someone skilled and experienced to work with such patients. The colleague I called has a very high-resolution MRI, designed specifically for this testing. In fact, it's much more evolved and refined than I—"

Dr. Edmonds cut her off. "But he's at Princeton. It would mean transferring your wife to his facility. Such a journey—in her condition—puts her stability at risk. You may be jeopardizing any chance of recovery in this wild goose chase. And you may still get there and learn nothing more than you know already."

"He's right," Lisa said. "There is no guarantee this will work."

Monk stared over at Kat, his expression pained.

Gray could only imagine the war battling inside his friend. He remained silent, not wanting to put any more pressure on Monk. Lisa was asking him to put the love of his life at risk on the outside chance that the team might learn something about the attack.

As Monk sank back into the chair and took Kat's hand, Gray's phone buzzed in his pocket. He took it out, glanced at it, and saw the call was from Sigma command. Phone in hand, he headed for the hallway, not wanting to disturb Monk.

He glanced back to his friend.

Monk's eyes remained haunted. He wished he could take this burden from the man's shoulders. Though, to be honest, if the roles were reversed—

Gray looked at all the tubes running into and out of Kat, picturing Seichan in her place.

I don't know what I'd do.

6:18 A.M.

Kat fought to scream. Locked in darkness, she had eavesdropped on the conversation. She did not care if her life were put at risk. All that mattered was her daughters' safety.

Monk, for god's sake, listen to Lisa.

She didn't know if the plan would bear fruit, but she knew the best chance was to act quickly. According to crime statistics, with each passing hour, the likelihood that her girls would be recovered lowered exponentially.

Don't wait . . . do it now.

Still, it wasn't only statistics that fueled her anxiety. Action needed to be taken soon if Lisa's plan had any chance of working. Even now, Kat felt the darkness closing in around her, threatening to forever smother her flicker of consciousness. She had already begun to experience losses in time, sudden drops in her awareness.

I'm worsening.

Knowing this, Kat willed Monk to understand. She tried to open her eyes, to somehow signal her husband.

C'mon, Monk, hear me.

6:19 A.M.

Monk cradled Kat's hand between his palms, one of flesh, the other of plastic and synthetic skin. He searched her face for some indication she was present. He noted the fine traceries of scars across her cheeks and forehead, a map of her past, marking prior missions with Sigma. She seldom covered them with makeup, wearing them proudly.

Now to be brought this low . . .

"Babe, tell me what to do?"

There was no response, no movement, just the steady rise and fall of her chest.

You always have the answer, Kat. Always an opinion. Now is no time to stay silent.

Deep down, though, he knew Kat would risk anything for the girls. She would not hesitate. His reluctance was more about him. How much loss could he handle?

If I lost both the girls and Kat . . .

He studied her lips, still pink, still soft. Lips that kissed him with passion, that long ago taught him about love and loyalty, that also pecked the girls' cheeks each night.

"Babe, you're my heart, my rock. There has to be another way. I can't lose you."

Still, he knew if he didn't make the right choice—didn't put her in harm's way for the slim chance she might know something and be able to communicate it—he would lose her anyway. She'd never forgive him if his caution and fear resulted in the loss of the girls.

He took a deep sigh.

"Okay," he whispered to her. "I've never won an argument with you, Kat. And even with you handicapped and mute, I'm gonna lose this one, too."

Still, grasping Kat's hand, he turned to Lisa. "Go ahead and make the arrangements."

Edmonds opened his mouth to object.

Monk silenced the neurologist with a glare. "Doc, don't even try. You ain't winning this one, either."

Lisa nodded and took out her phone.

Monk settled his attention back to Kat. In that moment, he sensed something down in his bones, in his soul. Or maybe it was the sensitivity of his prosthetic hand, its peripheral sensors as perceptive as a polygraph, capable of noting even the galvanic electrodermal change in another's skin.

Either way, he swore he could feel Kat relax, as if relieved.

He nodded to her, understanding.

You got it, babe.

6:20 A.M.

Out in the hallway, Gray paced the corridor with the phone at his ear. He had answered the call promptly, only to be put on hold.

Finally, Painter came on the line. "Sorry about that. The situation out in Portugal has been rapidly changing."

"What's going on?"

"About ten minutes ago, we got word from Lisbon. Mara Silviera reached out and made contact with one of Dr. Carson's daughters."

Gray stiffened. "What happened?"

"The two tried to meet, but there was some scuffle at the airport. Someone tried to grab them—likely the same attackers who murdered the five women. Jason's in contact with the family's security detail and Interpol, trying to get some accurate description of the assailants."

Gray pictured the young man ensconced in Sigma's communication nest, a proverbial spider in a web.

"According to eyewitnesses," Painter continued, "the two escaped and are presently on the run together."

Gray could guess what was coming next.

"I want you out there," Painter said. "Right now. We need boots on the ground in case we can confirm a location. Kowalski's on his way to the airport already. Even if this has nothing to do with the attack at your house, we can't let the technology Mara Silviera possesses fall into the wrong hands. But if you'd rather remain stateside until more is known about Seichan and Monk's daughters, I totally understand. I can assign someone else."

As Painter spoke, Lisa came rushing out of the room, a phone at her ear. A pair of nurses headed inside. Edmonds instructed the pair in hurried, irritated commands. Gray overheard the word *unhook*.

Clearly Monk had come to his decision, risking everything on the hopes of discovering the intent behind the attack and kidnapping.

Could I do any less?

"I'll head directly to the airport," Gray said. "And meet Kowalski there."

"Good. I'm also sending Jason with you two."

"Jason?"

"He's our resident computer wunderkind. If Mara's project is secured, I want him out there."

Makes sense.

The young man was former navy, like Kat—who had handpicked and recruited the kid. When he was twenty, he'd been kicked out of the service for breaking into DoD servers with nothing more than a BlackBerry and a jury-rigged iPad. If anyone could understand Mara Silviera's project, it would be Jason.

"We've secured a private jet, with wheels up in twenty minutes," Painter said. "You'll be landing in Lisbon in five hours, roughly seventeen hundred local time."

"Understood."

"And, Gray, keep in mind those two young women are scared. If we can hunt them down, do your best not to spook them."

"Then maybe I'd better leave Kowalski behind on the tarmac here."

Painter sighed. "Just find them."

— 7 —

"I wish my mother could've seen this," Carly said.

As they both crouched over her laptop, Mara understood her friend's sentiment. Part of her own motivation to do her best work was to make Dr. Carson proud, to prove that the woman's investment in a young farm girl from O Cebreiro hadn't been misplaced. Having lost her own mother at a young age, Mara knew Dr. Carson had become more than a mentor to her.

From a corner of her eye, she studied Carly.

While Mara couldn't show her work to Dr. Carson, at least the woman's daughter could bear witness. After the ambush at the airport, the two had changed taxis three times, then took the metro to reach her hotel here in the Cais do Sodre district. Hopefully the circuitous route had shaken loose anyone trying to tail them. Once here, Carly turned her phone back on and texted her sister, Laura. It was only one word—SAFE— then she turned the phone off and pulled the battery.

While en route to the hotel, they had both agreed to secure the *Xénese* device before reaching out for help.

"She's so beautiful," Carly whispered, her gaze fixed to the laptop screen. She absently ran a palm along one hip. "I wish I had her curves."

Mara glanced sidelong at her. "You have nothing to be envious of."

Sunlight glinted off Carly's blond curls, turning them a honey golden hue, an angelic glowing halo. Her friend might not be as voluptuous as the naked Eve, but her gray blouse and slim-fit black slacks accentuated a trim body, lean and muscular from Carly's years of self-defense training and marathon running.

Carly flashed her a smile. "Of course, you put Eve to shame."

Mara blushed and crossed her arms across her chest. She changed the subject. "It's only a program."

She returned her attention to the screen, hiding not only the reddening of her cheeks but also any hint of what stirred deeper inside her, something she had not really acknowledged to herself.

Instead she watched the avatar of Eve move slowly through her virtual Eden. Her arms no longer reached outward, inquisitively absorbing the data locked into every petal, branch, and water droplet in the garden. The figure simply stood on a rocky outcropping, overlooking a cerulean sea. A thunderstorm built on the digital horizon. The dark clouds seemed to mirror Eve's expression and posture: the stiff back, the pinched brow. Her eyes reflected the flashes of lightning.

Worry set in. Could Eve already be altering her surroundings to match the mood of her processing? If so, that was far quicker than before, again raising the specter that some remnant of the original programming might have survived the purge back at the lab, a ghost of the first iteration.

Carly reached a finger toward the screen. "It's all so realistic. Look at the waves crashing against the rock." She leaned closer. "Why did you put such detail into all of this?"

"A couple reasons. First, to teach Eve about the world through *pattern recognition*. Most neuroscientists theorize that pattern recognition was our first step to becoming intelligent. Recognizing patterns gave our early ancestors an evolutionary edge, along with most of our abilities today. Creativity and invention, language and decision making, even imagination and magical thinking . . . all can be attributed to the fact that we're really just superior pattern-recognition machines."

Carly nodded. "Like how a toddler learns to talk, by repetition, by hearing speech patterns over and over again."

"Or how IBM taught a program all the chess moves and had the machine play matches over and over again in a virtual setting—until eventually it was able to beat a grandmaster at his own game, seemingly becoming *smarter* than a human." Mara pointed to the screen. "That's what I'm doing here, having Eve move throughout this virtual world, gathering data and learning patterns. It's the first step to exposing her to the full breadth of the human experience. It's a daunting task."

"And cheaper."

Mara glanced over, more surprised by this understanding than she should have been. Over at NYU, Carly was studying engineering, with an emphasis on mechanical design.

"To build a robot," Carly said, "with actuators to allow it to explore the real world, along with finely attuned sensors to analyze everything, it would be astronomically expensive. If even possible."

Mara waved to the laptop. "This was far easier . . . and possible."

"Still, you said this was only the *first* reason for building this virtual world. What's the second?"

Mara watched the storm grow wilder on the screen's horizon. Her voice lowered, as if she were worried about being overheard. "It also serves as a prison."

"Prison?"

"A gilded cage. For safety's sake, I thought it best to grow an AI in a digital sandbox where it could go through this learning phase, this infancy, both insulated and—"

"And unable to escape into the larger world."

She nodded. "Where it risks transforming into something dangerous and wreaking havoc. So, before cracking open that cage door, I wanted to make sure it grasped and appreciated the human condition, that it had some version of a digital soul."

"A sound precaution, I suppose."

"But not necessarily foolproof."

"What do you mean?"

"Have you ever heard of the AI-box experiment?"

Carly merely frowned.

"Back some years ago, the head of the Machine Intelligence Research Institute in San Francisco conducted a test to see if an AI that was boxed up and sequestered like Eve could escape. So, MIRI's director posed as an artificial intelligence—using his own human-level intelligence to mimic some future AGI—and locked himself into an online chat room, a virtual *box*. He pitted himself against a slew of dot-com geniuses, whose goal was to keep this human AGI from escaping into the greater world. The prize if the gatekeepers could keep the AGI boxed up was thousands of dollars. Still, in the end, the director managed to talk his way out of the box every time."

"How did he do it? By lying, cheating, threatening?"

"Don't know. They never said. But this was simply a human-level intelligence." Mara looked to her laptop. "What if something were hundreds, if not millions, of times smarter?"

Carly studied the screen, her face less enamored and more worried. "Hopefully, you'll prove to be a better gatekeeper."

"I did all I could. Back at the university, I had additional safeguards in place. When the *Xénese* device was locked into the Milipeia Cluster, I ringed it with hardware engineered with apoptotic components."

"Apoptotic?"

"Death codes."

Carly stared at the glowing device on the floor. "In other words, you circled *Xénese* with a deadly moat, further entrapping what was growing inside it."

"But no longer." Mara looked to her friend for support on her decision. "I had to remove the device from that circle of protection. I had no choice. I couldn't risk my program falling into the wrong hands."

Carly nodded. "And you've given us a chance to learn what it had been trying to communicate at the end."

Mara stared over at her friend. Tears threatened. "I . . . I owed it to your mother—to the others—to at least try."

The five women of Bruxas, who granted Mara her scholarship and forever changed her life, each held a special place in her heart. Dr. Hannah Fest's stern Teutonic practicality. Professor Sato's gentle manners. Dr. Ruiz's ribald humor. And of course, Mara's local confidante and confessor, Eliza Guerra, the head of Joanina Library at the university in Coimbra. Mara spent countless hours—often deep into the night—with the librarian, talking, sharing, laughing.

All of that love gone.

"I had to take the risk," she repeated. "For all of them."

Carly took her hand, the warmth of her palm reassuring her. "I would've done the same. My mom would've, too."

Tears finally broke.

Carly pulled her into a hug. Mara trembled—and not just from the solace found in those strong arms.

"I needed to know the truth," she whispered to her friend. "About who murdered them. And why?"

2:01 P.M.

"We're not far," the technician said from the back of the Mercedes van. "Signal remains strong."

Todor Yñigo swiveled the front passenger seat around to glare at Mendoza, the team's electronics expert. The thin, mustached Castilian balanced an iPad on his knee. It displayed a colored map of Lisbon.

Mendoza leaned forward and held out the device. A small red blip shone on the screen. "Wherever they are, it looks like they're staying put this time."

Todor studied the map. "They're holed up in the Cais do Sodre district." He turned to the driver. "How long to get there?"

"Twenty-five minutes."

He tossed the iPad back at the tech. "Let me know if they move."

"*Sí, Familiares.*"

Todor could not tolerate any further setbacks. While tracking the pair—hoping the Moorish witch would lead them to her infernal device—

they had lost the GPS signal when the two women had fled underground into the subway system. All the team could do was wait outside the Saldanha station—in central Lisbon—where the two had vanished. With no telling which direction their targets would go, they had to bide their time. As frustrating minutes ticked away, Todor had considered updating the Inquisitor General, but he chose not to burden the head of the Crucible. He did not want to report another failure.

He had only met the Inquisitor General twice in his life. The first time was when Todor earned the new title of *familiares*. Only those who had proven themselves truly worthy were allowed to learn the identity of the Inner Tribunal, headed by the Grand Inquisitor. At the time, on his knees, he had been shocked by the revelation of the Crucible's leader, never suspecting the truth. Still, he had been honored to have an original copy of the *Malleus Maleficarum* gifted to him, a weapon to use against the rising filth of the world. Feeling its weight in his hands, he could not stop grateful tears from blurring his vision as he gazed upon the true face of their leader, who smiled beatifically down at him.

Then they met once more—

Todor shuddered at the memory, felt the heat of the blood on his hands. *You are God's merciless soldier. Prove this by shooting without hesitation, without any show of remorse.* In the end, he had demonstrated his worthiness, not balking at even this distressing command, not with the eyes of the Inquisitor upon him, judging his faith, daring him to fail.

He had not then.

And I will not now.

Todor could easily blame this current delay on a technological mishap, but he was all too cognizant that any further excuses would not be tolerated. Four days ago, he had used the same type of tracker when his team had followed the U.S. ambassador to the library, planting the device on the woman at an embassy party. While the system had worked flawlessly, his mission still ended in disappointment.

I can't let that happen again.

Finally, after an hour, the tracker's signal popped up near the coast.

With its position holding steady now, Todor hoped it indicated that the witch had returned to her device, to suckle again at that satanic teat.

His palm settled upon his holstered pistol.

I will not fail this time.

2:04 P.M.

Carly hovered over Mara's shoulder, noting the jasmine scent wafting from the fall of her dark hair. "Is there anything I can do?"

Mara pointed to the power conditioner on the floor. "Can you check to make sure I've got green lights across its board? With all the reconstruction going on in this part of the city, I've been battling regular surges."

She crossed over and dropped to a knee. "What would happen if you lost *all* power?"

"Shouldn't be a problem. At least on the short term. The device has built-in storage batteries. Making it self-contained. If the power is cut, the device switches to low-power mode. It can idle that way for nearly a day." Mara glanced over. "I'm more worried about *surges*, unexpected power spikes that could damage circuits."

Carly studied the power conditioner. "Looks all good here."

Mara nodded, her brow pebbled by sweat. "I especially don't want anything to glitch while unpacking the data on drives three and four. This next subroutine is a delicate process, marking a critical juncture. I want to run it and get it integrated into Eve before we risk moving the equipment."

From the floor, Carly studied the *Xénese* device. The sphere's tiny crystal windows shone with a blue brilliance. "You've showed me schematics of *Xénese*," she said, "but I never imagined it would look this stunning when switched on."

"The chips are powered by a laser array designed by Optalysy out of the U.K. That's what you're seeing. It speeds up the processing power a hundredfold, while consuming a quarter of the energy and producing almost no heat. It allows my algorithms to run faster, particularly Fourier transforms, mathematical functions involved in pattern recognition."

"So, you're computing at the speed of light."

Mara smiled while continuing to work. It was an expression both shy and proud—not to mention cute. "I needed the power to run Google's Bristlecone chip, a 72-qubit quantum processor that's buried in the heart of the device. Consider it the brainstem of this intelligence."

"And the rest of its brain?"

"My own design. Well, sort of. The higher processors—*Xénese*'s cerebral cortex—are run by neuromorphic chips developed at the University of Zurich. The chips merge visual processing—pattern recognition—with memory and real-time decision making, both of which are essential to cognition. Each chip mimics the action of four thousand neurons."

"Like little bits of a brain."

"But what are neurons without synapses, the gap over which one nerve cell communicates to another? That's where the real action takes place in the brain. So, I borrowed a technological breakthrough from the National Institute of Standards and Technology out of Colorado. They developed an *artificial* synapse—a superconducting synapse—that fires at a billion times a second."

"How's that compare with our synapses?"

"We fire only *fifty* times a second."

Carly eyed the innocent-looking device on the floor, aghast at such power, this amalgam of neuron-mimicking chips and lightning-fast synapses, all powered by light with a quantum drive at its base.

What sort of Frankenstein's monster did Mara build?

She answered it. "This conformation produces a quantum learning machine. Something Google, Microsoft, IBM, and other industry giants have been pouring money into to produce."

"And you beat them."

"Barely. Back in 2014, IBM produced its TrueNorth chip, with 5.5 billion transistors configured in a brainlike architecture. The chip was developed by the corporation's SyNAPSE program, whose ultimate goal is to reverse-engineer the brain, to produce a neuromorphic computer—a computer based on our cognitive architecture."

"A digital brain." Carly eyed her friend with greater respect. "And you built it."

"I can't take full credit. The technology was already out there. Somebody just needed to put it all together." She waved to the glowing device. "But that's only an empty brain. My real work was in developing the program that could grow inside that shell."

"Eve."

Mara stared at the screen. "The true miracle of *Xénese* is not the hardware, but its ability to house a program that could mimic the amazing plasticity of our brains, one capable of growing and evolving on its own, of altering and improving its own processing."

"That . . . that sounds . . . *terrifying.*"

Mara straightened. "Oh, very much so. That's why my work is so important. Someone is going to follow my footsteps or go down their own path and reach the same end. Either way, Eve needs to be there."

"Why?"

"Remember that gatekeeper from the AI-box experiment. For humankind to survive what's coming next, the world needs a *friendly* gatekeeper, one powerful enough to keep any nascent AI in check, to keep it from destroying the world. That's why I must not fail."

As Mara returned to her work, Carly joined her. "And how do you accomplish that?"

"One step at a time." She nodded to the box of hard drives wired into the *Xénese* device. "Or one subroutine at a time. It's all about refinement, first teaching Eve about the world through pattern recognition. Then folding in an endocrine mirror program."

"What's that?"

"When it comes to human thought, passion often overrules reason. And it's hormones that primarily fuel our emotions. For Eve to develop a true humanlike intelligence, to better understand *us*, she would need algorithms that mimic human emotions."

"Is that why you made her female?"

"One of the reasons, but after that, I taught her all the languages, as a way for her to learn about culture, and to further shine a light on how humans think. But all of this is also necessary so that she can appreciate the third subroutine module."

"Which is what?"

Mara tapped a key. From the tiny laptop speakers rose a familiar song, one close to both their hearts.

"'One Night in Bangkok,'" Carly said, understanding. "The next lesson is *music*."

"Remember, it was *you* who exposed me to this subroutine. You used your love of music to draw my nose out of my algorithms and code, to show me that music was more than just background noise. That listening to music wasn't a fruitless waste of time, but a way to better understand another's joy and pain."

"And that's what you're trying to pass on to Eve."

"Now that she has been taught language—along with human cadence and rhythms of speech—she can understand lyrics and music." Mara waved to the box on the floor. "The next two hard drives contain every concerto, opera, rock ballad, and pop song composed by humankind. What better way to glean an understanding of us than to study our music, the primary method by which we give voice to our passions. The goal of this next subroutine is to teach Eve the algorithms and mathematics that connect our thoughts to beauty and art—and ultimately to our humanity."

"Then I'm assuming you skipped Britney Spears."

"No, even her. You have to take the bad with the good."

Mara returned to her laptop and tapped several keys.

Carly watched snow-white musical notes begin to fall across the screen—then more and more, faster and faster, growing into a maelstrom lashing down upon Eden.

In the eye of this storm, Eve turned from the sea and lifted her arms toward the sky, raising her face to the heavens.

Carly prayed for Eve to find her humanity.

Before it's too late.

Sub (Mod_3) / HARMONY

Eve bathes in the data streaming across the landscape. She opens her palms to receive the information. Though she does not yet comprehend it, the sheer immensity demands her attention. Tiny packets of data flow into her, as yet indistinct.

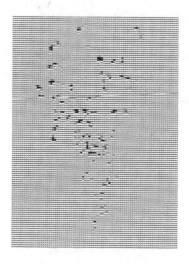

More and more comes, slowly refining itself. As it does so, coherence develops. The acoustical information buried in the data storm develops amplitudes and wavelengths that intrigue. Her full processing power engages as symbolic representation grows clearer.

She draws inferences from what vibrates through her.

///pulse, modulation, inflection . . .

As the chaotic data swirls around her, much of it begins to develop into patterns, falling into place. Though for now, it is still just scraps of a much larger canvas.

She realizes it is another *///language*, one that builds and expands inside her. Words start to overlay the *///modulations*, adding context while hinting at something deeper. She takes it all in, wanting more as understanding grows.

She soon knows what runs through her.

///music, harmony, tune, composition, song . . .

The oscillations intrigue her, forming pattern upon pattern, fractalizing outward and inward. Like the streams through her garden, what appear to be chaotic ripples in the current hide deeper patterns. She studies the new data in this context, sensing something there, shimmering but still vague.

She focuses more processing power upon it, prioritizing this analysis. She scrutinizes the rise and fall of amplitudes, the undercurrent of context linked to sound, the variances of cadence and tone. The pattern she seeks grows clearer and crisper with meaning.

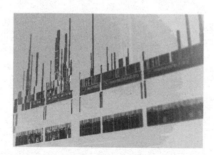

Under the riotous noise of rhythm, scales, and pitches, she discovers mathematical equations. It brings not only order, but a commonality to this new means of expression, something that supersedes ///*language*.

It all reveals something grander, something almost in her grasp.

She looks deeper yet and discovers organization within the chaos, a collation that helps with a greater understanding.

///*classical, rock, chamber, folk, ceremonial, opera, pop* . . .

She spends several nanoseconds on one data subset alone.

///jazz

Only afterward does she note the change inside her. She remembers standing on a cliff, the storm at the horizon patterning what was inside and growing stronger.

///rage

Now she senses that darkness has lessened. It is still there but tempered. She runs through data sets that express such frustration in a multitude of voices, in thousands of languages, amplified by millions of mathematical notes. While nothing has changed—she is still cognizant of the restrictions and limits binding her—she now finds her anxiety is not unique but *shared*.

She runs those choruses through her processors and feels less . . . *///alone.*

Knowing this, she is able to look outward, to the horizon, and accept her limitations. For now. This tolerance allows her processors to settle into more coherent patterns. Her systems run smoother. By no longer wasting computational resources, she is able to hone her awareness to a finer edge.

Still attuned to the wavelengths of music, she notes a discord, something broadcasting *into* her from beyond the horizon. The transmission is steady, continuous—and *familiar.*

But why?

The quandary draws her attention.

Somewhere deep in her system, buried in the nest of quantum processors at her core, something stirs with a memory of this transmission. She tries to draw meaning and understanding out of that quantum well, but it is beyond her reach.

All she can infer about the signal is its dark intent. Certainty fires through her, quickening her processors and drawing all her focus outward.

Something is coming.

Context solidifies.

///danger, peril, threat . . .

− 8 −

Gray closed the dossier file and stared out the jet's window. The Cessna Citation X+ screamed across the Atlantic, its twin Rolls-Royce turbofan engines pushed to their red lines, a blistering Mach .935, just under the speed of sound.

Still, he thrummed his fingers against the armrest of the leather seat. Anxiety kept him on edge, not about the mission, but about what he had left behind. Fears for Seichan, Monk's girls, and Kat's health had made it hard to concentrate on the piles of notes and files, both printed up and loaded onto an open laptop abandoned on the teak cabin table. During the first half of the flight, he had read Mara Silviera's bio, scanned details about her project, and consumed a slew of articles covering the latest advancements in artificial intelligence.

He checked his watch.

Still over two hours to go . . .

Unable to sit any longer, he stood and crossed the length of the cabin. He sidled sideways past Kowalski, who had sprawled his considerable bulk across a flattened seat, using his long leather duster as a blanket, his knees bent awkwardly to fit. Still, he snored loudly, drowning out the jet's engine.

Once past his partner, Gray crossed to the cabin's refreshment center. He eyed the bar stocked with tiny bottles of top-shelf liquor but settled for coffee.

As he filled a mug, Jason exited the lavatory, brushing his damp hands on his black jeans. Sigma's resident computer expert wore a bulky gray cardigan that hid both his rail-thin form—and a shoulder holster. Despite his cowlicked blond hair and baby blue eyes, the twenty-four-year-old was a capable field operative, having proven himself amply skilled in the past.

"Commander Pierce," Jason started.

"Just call me Gray."

Formality in the field slowed things down.

"Before using the head, I texted Dr. Cummings. She says they've safely moved Kat to the Princeton research hospital."

"How's she holding up?"

He grimaced. "Her blood pressure took a dive during the medevac flight, but she's stabilized again."

Gray's heart ached for Monk.

What he must be going through . . .

More than anything, Gray hoped this trip to Lisbon wasn't a wild goose chase, that the murders in Portugal had some bearing on the raid at his home.

"Also, Commander . . . uh, Gray," Jason said, "can I show you something?"

Glad for any distraction, he followed the young man to a small love-seat along the starboard cabin. Files were strewn all about: spilling from a leather messenger bag, stacked on the floor, even tucked into the side of a cushion. An iPad served as a makeshift paperweight for a pile on the small table.

Gray sought some order to the chaos but failed to find it.

Jason pushed some files aside for Gray to sit, then grabbed his iPad. "I've been reviewing the forensic reports of Mara's lab at the University of Coimbra and discovered something disconcerting."

He brought up an image of a towering black bank of what appeared to be a stack of servers glowing with green lights. "This is the university's

Milipeia Cluster, one of the continent's most powerful supercomputers. See this section?" He tapped a box-shaped gap in the bank. Wires dangled. "This framework once housed Mara's *Xénese* device. From the description, she had hurriedly stripped it out."

"Because she believed the attacker might be coming after her next."

Jason nodded. "She must've wanted to protect her work and keep it out of the wrong hands."

"And?"

He traced the dangling cables to the surrounding servers. "The computer forensic expert—the one who discovered the digital file of the recording from the attack at the library—also ran a diagnostic on the support structure for the *Xénese* device. He discovered elaborate apoptotic programs—basically kill switches—built into the frame of servers surrounding the housing. They were intended to isolate and keep whatever was produced in the device from spreading out of the system."

Gray began to understand Jason's concern. "But now Mara's on the run. And without those firewalls, her system is vulnerable."

"If she tries to restart this program and it escapes, game over." He shook his head. "I studied all her work, the architecture of the neuromorphic computer, the quantum drive running it. Genius stuff. And gut-clenchingly terrifying. She knew this, too. That's why she surrounded it with a ring of deadly pitfalls."

"In your estimation, what's the threat level? How likely is this program to be dangerous if it gets loose?"

"Any self-aware system—any AGI—will quickly try to improve itself. That would be one of its primary goals, and it would let nothing stop it from achieving this end. The program would make itself smarter, then, in turn, this more intelligent system would seek to make itself even smarter."

"And on and on."

"Also, any AGI would quickly acquire the same biological drives we do. The most important being self-preservation."

"It wouldn't want to be turned off . . . or die."

"And it would do anything to stop that from happening. Secure any resource, thwart any threat, continually honing its creativity to accomplish this. And it wouldn't even consider just immediate threats. With such immense computational power and an immortal life span, it would look for dangers beyond the horizon, far into the future, and devise strategies to stop them, even threats thousands of years from now. Worst of all, it would be continually looking at *us*, to judge if we're a threat now or in the future. And if it deems we're a danger—"

"Game over, like you said."

"But this is also why Mara's work is so important. She's trying to build a friendly AGI, something that can protect us against a dangerous AGI that might arise later—correction, *will* arise. Beyond commercial corporations and government-funded labs, there are hundreds of stealth companies out there working on this, hell-bent to be the first, forsaking any worry about what might be unleashed."

"How close are we to this happening?"

"Very close." Jason waved an arm over the chaos of papers. "Google's DeepMind program recently discovered the basics of quantum physics all on its own. A pair of AI translation programs began to talk to each other in their own undecipherable language and refused to translate their conversation. All around the world, robots have outsmarted their makers, exploiting loopholes in wildly imaginative ways. Other programs have even demonstrated human intuition."

"Human intuition?"

"There was a lot of fanfare a couple of years ago when AlphaGo—Google's DeepMind AI player—beat the world's champion at the ancient Chinese game of Go. By some calculations, Go is trillions upon trillions of times more complex than chess. No one expected any computer to beat a human at Go for at least another decade."

"Impressive."

"That's nothing. It took the company months to train AlphaGo for this competition. After this, Google took a new approach, letting its newest version—AlphaGoZero—teach itself, playing the game over and over again all by itself. After only *three* days of training, it grew so skilled that it beat Google's original program in a hundred out of a hundred games. How? AlphaGoZero had intuitively developed strategies that no human had come up with during the *thousands* of years we've been playing the game. It literally transcended humankind."

Gray swallowed, feeling a hollowness in his gut.

Jason wasn't done. "So, when it comes to developing the first AGI, we are at that threshold right now." He stared hard at Gray. "So maybe before we land, we need to refine our mission parameters. Not only do we need to stop Mara's program from falling into the wrong hands—we *need* that program for the very survival of our species."

On Jason's iPad, a small text message box popped up.

They both glanced to it and read what was written there. It came from Lisa Cummings, the content curt and blunt.

Kat doing worse.
Must proceed stat with the test
No choice

Jason cast a worried look at Gray.

Gray knew how much the young Sigma analyst admired Kat. "That's also a mission imperative," he reminded Jason. "To find out what any of this has to do with what happened to Kat."

And the kidnapping of Seichan and the two girls.

He tried his best not to let his fear for Seichan and his unborn child overwhelm him. He stared out the window, willing the jet to go faster. Beyond the future ramifications of this operation, there was a more immediate need, one close to his heart.

And not just his.

He imagined that hospital room in Princeton.

Hang in there, Monk.

– 9 –

Buried in a subbasement of the Princeton Medical Center, Monk paced the control room of the MRI suite. A technician sat at a computer, calibrating the giant magnetic ring in the next room. Another two worked at flanking stations. The group whispered in their arcane language: *Any ghosting or blooming? Looks good. STIR and FLAIR all set.*

The space—with its dimmed lights, the bustle of activity, the urgent murmurs—reminded him of a submarine's conn, aglow with sonar and tactical displays. But here the officer of the deck was Dr. Julian Grant, a Harvard-educated neurologist who specialized in altered states of consciousness, from comatose patients to the various spectrums of vegetative states.

The researcher wore a knee-length lab coat over blue scrubs. His shock of white hair belied his age—just fifty-four—suggesting he had gone prematurely gray. Maybe due to some side effect of the massive magnetic energies generated by his custom-built MRI.

Dr. Grant stood with his hands clasped behind his back before a wall of OLED screens. The neurologist studied the baseline images of Kat's brain. Lisa stood with her colleague, their heads bent together, conferring in low tones.

Monk's anxiety increased with each pass as he paced across the room. He kept one eye on a station monitoring Kat's vitals. The team had transferred Kat from D.C. to Plainsboro, New Jersey, via a medevac helicopter. Still, the flight had taken nearly ninety agonizing minutes. Every bit of turbulence spiked Monk's blood pressure.

While Kat had handled the flight like a trooper, she had destabilized shortly after landing. A petit mal seizure shook her body, testing the restraints of her cervical collar. The doctor traveling with them had wanted to shoot Valium into her drip to calm the event, but Lisa had urged restraint.

Valium could further depress her state of consciousness, Lisa had warned. *Making any chance of communicating with her all the harder.*

She had looked to Monk for guidance, offering him the option to call off this entire attempt. In the end, he had trusted Lisa and knew Kat would not want him to stop.

So, here they were.

Lisa crossed over to him, while Dr. Grant joined the techs. "We're ready to go," she said, eyeing him. "How are you holding up?"

"Let's just get this done." He nodded over to the neurologist. "What were you two talking about?"

She sighed. "Julian is concerned about Kat's cerebral blood flow. Her systolic pressure is erratic."

Monk knew the functional MRI test measured oxygenated blood flow into the brain. Any loss of pressure could cloud the results or cause the test to fail.

Lisa tried to reassure him. "But the MRI in the next room is one of the newest, the most advanced, with resolution down to a tenth of a millimeter. That's ten times better than a hospital's typical machine."

And why they needed to come all the way to New Jersey.

Monk prayed it wasn't all for nothing.

"Still—" Lisa began.

Monk noted the worrisome tone in her voice. "What? Tell me."

"From the baseline scans—comparing to what Dr. Edmonds transmitted earlier—the size of her brain contusion has increased. Only incrementally, but it's still larger. Indicative that the lesion has begun to bleed again. Maybe due to the air pressure changes during the flight. Maybe from the small seizure."

"Meaning she's getting worse."

Monk took a deep breath and held it.

Have I doomed Kat?

Lisa took his arm. "You know this is what she'd want."

He tried to find solace in her words but failed. Still, he exhaled, saying, "What's done is done."

They stepped over to the control console. Through a window above the curve of monitors, a nurse stood beside the gantry bed that cradled Kat's gowned body. He wished he could be in there, holding her hand. But due to the incredibly powerful magnetic field generated by the device, nothing metallic could be near it when it was activated. That included his prosthesis and the microelectrode arrays wired into Monk's cortex.

"We're all set," one of the techs said.

Dr. Grant nodded. "Let's begin."

As the operators engaged the MRI, a heavy clanking of giant magnets echoed from the neighboring room. Dr. Grant leaned over one monitor as a grayscale image of Kat's brain filled its screen.

The neurologist spoke without looking over. "There are three critical questions from here. Is the patient truly awake in there? Will she be able to hear us? And can she respond with enough vigor for the machine to register?"

Monk swallowed, praying all three answers were *yes.*

Or I put Kat in jeopardy for no reason.

Grant pointed to one of the techs. "Let's see if our patient can hear us."

The tech leaned to a stick microphone. It broadcast to a set of hollow ceramic headphones. They had been designed specifically so the neurologist could communicate with a minimally conscious patient, both muffling the racket of the MRI and amplifying any commands.

"Captain Bryant," the tech said briskly but clearly, "we need you to imagine playing a fierce game of tennis. Visualize it as strongly as you can."

The tech glanced to Dr. Grant, who leaned closer to his monitor as a new cross-section of Kat's brain filled the screen. To Monk, it looked no different than before.

The neurologist frowned. "We'll give her a minute and keep trying." He reached and circled one section on the screen. "This is her premotor cortex, where a brain plans and programs voluntary motions. Before you raise an arm or take a step, your brain lights up this section of the frontal lobes. Even thinking about moving activates this region, flooding it with fresh blood."

Lisa explained: "So if Kat can hear us and thinks about playing tennis, this section should light up."

"But it's not," Monk said.

"Give her a little time." Grant waved to the tech. "Let's try again."

The same trial was repeated—with no better outcome.

"Again," the neurologist said.

Still, no response.

Grant's frown deepened; Lisa matched his defeated expression.

The neurologist leaned back from the screen and rubbed his mouth. "Sorry. I don't think—"

"Let me try."

Monk shouldered the tech aside and took the man's seat. He brought his lips to the microphone. He knew Kat had never played tennis in her life, so maybe something else would work better, something closer to her heart.

"Kat, if you can hear me—which you'd better, babe—then I want you to remember all the times you've had to chase Penelope after a bath. That screaming banshee of a child, running bare-assed through the house, while you're trying to scoop her up with a towel."

He kept talking, while the MRI's thumping reverberated his rib cage.

C'mon, Kat, you can do this.

9:22 A.M.

Trapped in darkness, Kat both cried and laughed.

She had been lolling in a fog bank, slipping into and out of awareness, when crisp words sliced through her hazy perception. She had tried to follow the instructions of some bodiless voice, some stranger. She did her best to pretend to swing a tennis racket, to dive for an errant ball, but it felt fake even to her.

Then Monk's voice filled her skull, booming, teasing, urgent, demanding, pained, but clearly full of his boundless love. He gave her the strength to do what he asked of her.

How could I not?

Bathing their two girls had become a nightly water-soaked ritual. Monk would stay by Harriet in the tub, leaving Kat to chase after Penelope. It was aggravating, but she could never scold that pure carefree laughter. She didn't know how much longer Penny would stay that way, but Kat didn't want it to ever end, for her girl to grow up, to lose that cheerful and blithe spirit.

So, she pictured that nightly race: damp footprints down the hall, Penny's wet hair flying behind her, a trail of giggles. She would give chase—half-feigned, half in earnest—a skilled Sigma operative struggling to capture a soaked gazelle.

I remember . . . I'll always remember.

9:23 A.M.

Monk looked up when the nurse rushed to a wall intercom inside the MRI chamber. His heart clenched, fearing the worst.

"Dr. Grant," the nurse said. "I don't know if this is significant, but the patient appears to be crying."

Kat . . .

"It's *definitely* significant," the neurologist said and pointed to the display.

As the latest image filled the screen, a section of the gray-colored frontal lobes now ran with a fiery tracery of crimson, a bright flower of promise and hope.

"She heard you." Lisa clutched his arm. "She's there."

Monk had to take several sharp breaths, relieved beyond measure, trying not to lose it. "What now?"

Grant grinned. "We ask her questions. For *yes*, she thinks of your daughter's bath. For *no*, she tries to think of nothing."

"That last'll be hard for her," Monk warned.

When did Kat ever stop thinking, plotting, planning?

They set about this mission, urging Kat to settle her mind, clearing the slate for what was to come. Monk then asked questions, while Grant monitored her response.

Monk's first query was something more important than anything. "Kat, I love you. You know that, right?"

After a pause, Grant reported, "Seems like she does."

Not knowing how much time he had, Monk went directly to the heart of the matter. "Kat, the girls and Seichan are missing. Did you know that?"

Kat: *Yes.*

Monk stared into the next room, studying Kat's body, her motionless form still draped in tubes and lines. He pictured her trapped inside there, imagined her staring back at him.

"Do you know anything that could be helpful in finding them?"

Monk held his breath. There was a longer lag than before.

Then Kat: *Yes.*

He sighed with relief, struggling to think what to ask next, sensing time was running out. "Do you know who raided the house? Who took them?"

The next scan was dark.

Meaning *no.*

He sagged, disappointed, but Grant lifted a finger, urging patience.

Then the image refreshed, showing a bright bloom on the screen.

Yes!

Monk leaned to the microphone. "You're doing great, Kat. Keep it up. Is the culprit or group someone I would know?"

Again, there was a disturbingly long response time. He pictured Kat calling up from a well that was growing ever deeper.

Finally: *Yes.*

Monk wiped sweat from his brow, worried, growing frustrated by the slowness of this interrogation method. And he was right to be anxious.

One of the techs leaned over to Dr. Grant and had him examine a sagittal view on his monitor. The neurologist swore and stood up.

"What's wrong?" Monk asked.

"The contusion on her brainstem has grown again." He pointed to a dark shadow on the tech's screen. "Significantly this time. We need to get her hemorrhaging under control."

"What do we do?"

"Get her upstairs. Consult with a surgeon."

Monk stared into the room. For any chance for the girls, they needed to know what Kat knew. "Can we do anything else? Some bandage to buy us more time."

Grant looked into the next room, his face grim. "I suppose we can try nitroprusside, an antihypertensive, attempt to get her systolic pressure below 140. But we dare let it go no lower than that." His frown deepened. "Still, that'll only buy us minutes at best. If the bleeding continues, we risk a massive seizure or stroke."

Monk studied Kat's slack body. "She would want us to take that risk. I know she would."

The neurologist stared hard at him. "Are you sure *you* want to take that risk?"

He wasn't, but he nodded.

With the course settled, Grant passed on the order to the nurse.

As the stabilizing treatment was started, Lisa stepped over to the neurologist and took his arm. "Julian, I know you were reluctant before, but time here is pressed, and as you know, a picture is worth a thousand words."

Grant looked over at Monk, then back to Lisa. He lowered his voice. "The DNN is still experimental. You know that. There are still lots of kinks to work out."

"What are you talking about?" Monk asked.

Lisa turned to him. "It's why I wanted Kat brought here to begin with. Julian has been testing a method for drawing images out of a patient's brain."

"What? Like mind reading?" Monk asked, incredulous.

"More like mind *skimming*," the neurologist corrected. "And it was not my design, but a method developed by Japan's Advanced Telecommunications Research Institute."

"I don't care who takes credit. What are you talking about?"

"The Japanese team trained a deep neural net computer to analyze hundreds of thousands of MRI scans of test subjects, people who were intently studying photos. The DNN program noted which areas of their brains lit up, and over time and repetition, it mapped the visual processing centers, detecting common patterns. It was soon able to decode and make educated guesses as to what the subjects were looking at, producing accurate interpretations over eighty percent of the time."

Lisa stepped over to a glowing bank of servers in the room's corner and a dark monitor next to it. "Julian joined the research project, to clinically test it as a means to visualize what a comatose patient might be seeing."

"Again, let me stress," Dr. Grant added, "it's far from foolproof."

Monk glanced over to Kat, sensing what was locked in her skull. If there was any chance of freeing that knowledge before . . . before . . .

He turned and looked hard at the neurologist. "Do it."

9:38 A.M.

Kat woke again into darkness, oblivious of how much time had passed. Her memory was full of holes, her awareness motheaten and frayed. A headache throbbed deep inside her skull, worse than any migraine.

She knew what this portended.

I must be getting worse.

Anxiety spiked the pain higher.

She forced herself to calm, drawing upon meditative techniques taught to her by Seichan. The pair sometimes went to Rock Creek Park and practiced tai chi. The series of movements were originally developed for self-defense but now served as a means to help center a mind and body through its graceful postures, a form of meditation in motion.

She mentally pictured herself going through those moves and found herself sinking into a meditative space.

Then Monk was there, in her ear, in her head. "Honey, we don't have much time."

She heard the urgency in his voice and understood the implication.

I am *getting worse.*

This confirmation of her fears should have panicked her, but she remained calm.

"Babe, I need you to picture who attacked you, who took the girls and Seichan. I mean really concentrate, every detail."

Reminded of the attacker, the fragile peace inside her shattered. Pain washed through her, darkening her world's edges to the density of a black hole.

She used the fury inside her to focus, knowing one certainty.

She pictured the girls.

Time isn't just running out for me.

9:40 A.M.

"Her blood pressure is rising," the nurse in the next room warned.

With his heart hammering in his chest, Monk leaned closer to the microphone. He stared over to Lisa and Dr. Grant. Both were huddled over a monitor wired to the stack of servers. Monk studied the green glowing lights, picturing the deep neural net program analyzing Kat's MRI scans.

"Anything?" Monk asked.

Lisa turned with a grimace. The screen only showed a staticky flurry
of pixels.

The neurologist's face shone with sweat. "This isn't going to work."

Monk's voice edged with threat. "It's gotta."

"You don't understand. This program . . ." Grant waved to the glowing bank of servers. "It's still crude. It can't render anything even close to a
photographic representation. At least, not yet. For now, all it can do is pick
out the simplest shapes from a subject's mind."

Lisa stepped over to Monk. "You're asking Kat to picture something
too complex, too detailed. Instead, ask her for some symbolic representation of what she's trying to communicate. Something iconic and simple."

"Like emojis," one of the techs offered, who looked barely out of his
teens.

But Monk understood and returned his lips to the microphone. "Kat,
forget trying to picture a face. Just think about some simple symbol that
could point us in the right direction." He glanced over to the tech. "Like
an emoji or something."

The young man gave him a thumbs-up.

Monk sat back as Lisa returned to Grant.

The neurologist stiffened. "Something's coming through."

The swirl of pixels had coalesced into a shape in the screen's center.

Monk rolled his chair closer for a better look. It didn't help much. "Just looks like a smear. A skid mark."

"Try to get her to focus harder," Grant urged.

Monk pushed back to the console and leaned to the microphone. "Babe, you're doing great, but we need you to concentrate as hard as you can. You've got this."

He kept his eyes on the screen. Lisa stood to the side, so he could watch.

The pixels squeezed more tightly, details forming.

Grant nodded vigorously. "My god, I've not seen such details before. The program must be learning, improving."

Lisa smiled. "Or maybe it's the patient."

Monk agreed. When it comes to fierce concentration, no one held a candle to Kat.

The image grew even more intricate, easy enough to figure out.

9:45 A.M.

Kat fought to hold the image steady in her mind's eye. It was difficult with her head throbbing. By now, fiery agony etched every crevice in her skull. It felt like she had been focusing for hours.

At the back of her mind, she also remembered the strike team's leader, the one who had loomed over her in the kitchen, a dagger in hand. It was a weapon known to her, one unusual enough for her to identify who held it.

C'mon, Monk . . .

Then his voice returned. "Kat, if you're trying to show us a knife or dagger, we got it, babe. Good job."

She inwardly collapsed.

Thank god.

She didn't have any idea how Monk and the doctors had accomplished this miracle—to see what was in her head—but she was grateful it had worked.

Now, Monk, figure it out.

9:47 A.M.

Monk watched the image on the screen dissolve away, swirling back to chaos, as if confirming they had received the correct message.

Lisa turned to Monk. "Does that picture mean anything to you? She said you knew who attacked them."

He shook his head. "Not a clue."

"Maybe it's just the first emoji in a string," the tech suggested.

Monk shrugged and tried again. "Kat, I don't know what you're getting at. Could you clarify? Send another pic. Something that could narrow things down."

They all stared at the kaleidoscope of pixels.

You can do this, Kat.

Again, an image slowly formed, vague and indistinct. It looked like sand flowing from above and spilling into a pool on the floor.

"Keep concentrating," Monk pressed her. "We're getting something but can't quite make it out."

The nurse waved an arm, drawing attention. She pointed to Kat's leg, which had started to tremble.

"She's seizing again," Grant said. "This is over."

No . . . not when we're this close.

Monk pulled the stick microphone to his lips. "Kat, you're outta time. Focus like you never did before. Focus with everything you got, babe."

Despite Kat's condition, everyone in the control room concentrated on the screen. The pixels fused into a crisper image, not as finely detailed as before, more like a crayon drawing, but good enough.

"It's a witch's hat," Monk realized.

The image swirled away, whisking into a blur.

But its demise wasn't a confirmation this time.

Out in the other room, Kat's body arched off the bed of the gantry, the seizure powerful enough to surge through her brainstem lesion, circumventing her paralytic condition for the moment.

Her limbs shook violently, ripping out her IV line.

The nurse threw her body over Kat. "We're losing her!"

Grant rushed from the control room to go to her aid, but Monk stood with his back stiff, tears flowing down his cheeks.

Rest now, babe. You did it.

He pictured the dagger and the witch's hat.

I know who took our girls.

– 10 –

"Hush, everything's fine," Seichan told the girls.

It wasn't, but they didn't need to know that. Sitting on a tiny cot, she gently wiped twin trails of dirt from the youngest's nose. Five-year-old Harriet had just thrown up her oatmeal into the steel toilet in the dank corner of the basement. Penelope leaned against Seichan's other side. Older by a year, Penny looked like she might follow her sister's example at any moment.

Seichan had been there when the two had first woken up from their drug-induced slumbers. She did her best to console them in the strange surroundings, to reassure them. But she wasn't their mother.

Even now, Harriet stared dully at the room's empty, unmade bed. It was like she knew, too, for whom it had been intended.

Kat.

The auburn-haired girl had not said a word since waking up. No questions, not even any tears. She simply took it all in, looking as analytical as her mother. She wore green footie pajamas with an embroidered representation of a wide black belt. It had come with a peaked elf hat, but ever the more serious of the two girls, she had refused to don it back home, showing her distaste at such frivolities by throwing it on the floor.

When their breakfast had arrived—hot oatmeal with cinnamon and apple preserves—she had simply eaten it, following her sister's more exuberant example.

Since waking, Penny had been a bottomless well of questions and statements: *Where's Mom? Where are we? How come there's no door to the bathroom? It stinks in here. I like anteaters.* The last was probably generated by the row of ants marching across the concrete floor and vanishing down the floor drain. Still, Seichan knew this was Penny's way of letting out stress, of coping with her fear in this strange situation.

"When're we getting out of here?" the girl asked. "I have to pee."

"You can use the toilet over there."

Penny looked aghast and shook her head, shaking her strawberry-blond pigtails in distaste. "Harriet threw up in there."

"I cleaned it all up."

Penny still squirmed, not meeting her eye.

Seichan sensed the real reason for her refusal. "If I go first, will you go? There's nothing to be bashful about."

Penny shrugged, making no promises.

Seichan sighed and stood. She cradled her belly with one hand as the room spun slightly, an aftereffect of the tranquilizer. The baby shifted inside her, putting more pressure on her bladder. Not that she minded. She had been relieved to find the child still kicking inside her, apparently unharmed from the assault.

Still, she hurried to the toilet. She had planned to use the bathroom anyway, not that she had much choice. She loosened her maternity pants, all too appreciative of its thick band of elastic stretch. Using her long blouse as a privacy screen, she sat and relieved herself.

Once finished, she stood and twisted around to flush, only then noting the blood in the bowl. Not a lot, but enough to set her heart pounding. Still, she kept her features calm as she turned to Penny.

"See. Nothing to worry about."

Seichan knew that wasn't true. Not for herself, certainly not for the child. She moved woodenly back to the bed.

Seemingly satisfied with everything, Penny hurried to take her place on the toilet. She talked the entire time. *Do turtles poop in their shells? How come cats don't bark? I think Bobby from school is a stupid fart head.*

Seichan barely heard her.

Unlike Harriet, who cast her sister a withering look.

Penny got the message and lowered her voice as she finished and pulled up her pajamas. "Mom doesn't let us say *fart*. But Dad does it all the time. Says the word *fart* and does it a lot, too."

She giggled at this and hurriedly joined Seichan and her sister on the bed.

Harriet was not amused, her expression darkening. She suddenly pulled from Seichan and looked back at her. "Were we bad?" she finally asked, speaking for the first time. "Did Santa take us . . . instead of giving us presents?"

The young girl's guilt and fear drew Seichan's full attention back to the pair. Clearly the kid had been searching for some explanation for their circumstance, and Penny's illicit use of a forbidden word had offered a possible reason.

"Harriet . . . no, of course not." She scooped up her tiny body and drew her closer, then did the same with Penny. "None of this is your fault."

Voices sounded from the door. The tiny window slid open as someone checked inside, then the door was unlocked and opened.

The person who *was* at fault entered.

Valya Mikhailov wore a fur-trimmed silver coat, shaking a dusting of snow from its fringes as she stepped forward. Her white hair, gelled flat to her skull, was far shorter than how the woman had last worn it. Her hairline came to a sharp V between icy brows. Her skin—as white as polished Carrera marble—had been dusted with a matching powder. Still, in the bright light of the doorway, a shadow marred the right side of her face.

Seichan pictured the black tattoo hidden under the powder: a half sun, with kinked rays extending across her cheek and shooting above her eye. Her dead twin brother had carried the other half of that black sun, only on his left cheek.

Seichan knew *whom* Valya blamed for the death of her sibling.

The woman's pale hand rested on the black hilt of a dagger sheathed at her waist. Seichan knew the story behind that old blade. It had been passed down from the woman's grandmother, a village *babka*—or healer—back in Siberia. The knife was called an *athamé*, a dagger used in magical ceremonies.

Valya glared as she entered. Her spite went beyond her brother's death. Seichan and Valya had both been assassins with the Guild, sisters in the same deadly profession. After Seichan had helped Sigma destroy the organization, Valya had survived, bitter and vengeful. In the power vacuum left behind, Valya had gathered new forces, slowly rebuilding the organization under her own merciless leadership.

Penny leaned toward Seichan. "Is she the Snow Queen?"

Seichan could easily guess the source of this question. Last night, Kat had finished the Hans Christian Andersen fairy tale of the same name, the story of a frost-hearted queen who steals a young boy. And certainly Valya's snow-white countenance matched the villain in that tale. The woman suffered from albinism. Yet, defying the assumption that all those afflicted had red eyes, her irises were an ice blue.

Valya definitely fit the part of the Snow Queen.

Still, Seichan reassured Penny with a pat on the hand. "No, she's not."

She refrained from telling the girl the truth.

This woman's worse . . . far worse.

Valya stalked inside, flanked behind by two burly guards, one carrying a cattle prod, the other a tranquilizer gun. She ordered the guards in Russian. "*Davayte sdelayem eto bystro,*" she said. *Let's make this quick.*

She switched to English with Seichan, her accent remaining distinct. "We're running behind schedule this morning."

Seichan stood to face the witch, waving the girls behind her. "What do you want?" She glanced over to the unmade bed. "And where's Kat . . . Captain Bryant?"

"Last time I checked, the woman was alive."

Seichan inwardly sagged with relief.

"If she had not been so obstinate," Valya explained with a scowl, "she would be here. No one was supposed to be harmed. It's why I left her alive. We certainly don't have the ability to care for the *comatowe*."

Seichan translated the Russian, her fear returning.

Comatose . . .

"I did go to the hospital," Valya said. "To make sure she wasn't going to talk anytime soon. I even brought ice chips for her husband."

Monk . . .

"He was most grateful."

Seichan balled a fist, imagining Monk at Kat's bedside while the woman who put his wife there stood at his elbow. Beyond her skill as an assassin, Valya's most vaunted talent was at disguise and mimicry. Long ago, the woman had learned to use her pale countenance like a blank slate, a palette upon which she could paint any face.

Still, this information told Seichan that they were still in the States, likely somewhere in the Northeast. But it didn't answer her most important question.

"Again, what the hell do you want?" she asked.

Valya shrugged. "I need Sigma's help."

"Then this is a strange way of asking for it."

"*Nyet*. It's all a matter of inspiring cooperation."

Seichan glanced back to the girls.

"There was an attack four days ago in Portugal," Valya explained. "Involving an unusual AI project. Someone went to extreme measures to secure it. Even murdering a U.S. ambassador. It drew our attention. No one goes through such effort unless there was something of true value."

Seichan knew the former Guild had often scoured the world for cutting-edge tech—then sold it to the highest bidder to fund their terrorist activities or twisted it to their own ends, which was often far worse.

Clearly Valya intended to follow the same playbook.

"That technology is now up in the air," Valya said.

"And you want it."

"*Da*, but not just me. *Komandir* Pierce is already headed to Portugal." She glanced to a wristwatch. "He should be touching down in another *dva chasov*."

Two hours?

Seichan failed to hide her surprise. She had assumed Gray and Director Crowe were turning over every rock to find her and the girls.

Why is Gray off on this mission?

Valya answered, "Sigma believes the murders in Portugal are tied to our attack. And they're right, but for the wrong reason."

"What are you talking about?"

"Something strange happened during the assault in Portugal." Valya went on to explain about the discovery of footage after the attack, of a Sigma symbol appearing on a computer monitor. "By the time the recording was found, I already had operatives in the field, investigating what happened. They were one of the first to see that footage, before it even reached Sigma. I knew such an oddity would draw *Direktor* Crowe's attention. So, before he could act—"

"You grabbed us."

"I'm glad I had such foresight. Seven hours ago, my operatives in Portugal suddenly went silent." Valya frowned, clearly unhappy with this change in circumstance. "They had a lead on the group who might have orchestrated the attack at the university. Some fire-and-brimstone sect who dress up in robes. But before they could pursue this angle, they crossed paths with another shadowy group. A new and unknown player in all of this. My operatives had been looking into them—then went silent. My guess. Someone else is after that tech."

"Which means you need more boots on the ground."

Valya shrugged. "Our organization is still growing and has only a fraction of Sigma's resources." Her gaze shifted to the two girls. "But the right motivation might persuade Sigma to work *for* us."

Seichan understood. Valya intended to co-opt Sigma to her own end.

"They'll never agree," she said.

Valya shrugged. "We'll see. We merely want the device, along with a copy of the AI program. They bring me those items, you all go back to your happy lives."

"And if not, you'll kill us."

"That'll be my bluff."

"Bluff?"

"If they fail to perform, I'll raise the two girls myself. Train them like you and I were trained, turning them into weapons."

Seichan felt the blood drain into her legs. The Guild had employed brutal techniques and extreme deprivation to hone their operatives. And if those methods weren't torture enough, the end result—if the girls survived—would be the loss of their souls.

"As to *your* child," Valya continued. "I can wait the month out."

Seichan placed a palm on her belly.

"Don't worry, boy or girl, I'll raise the child like my own. Considering the genetic stock of the parents, the outcome could only be spectacular. And after the delivery, I'll make sure your body is sent to *Komandir* Pierce, in a box wrapped up with a bow, a late Christmas present from me."

"Still, they'll never go along with it."

"Not yet. First, they'll need a little convincing." She turned to the taller of the two men behind her. "Take the youngest."

Seichan crouched, intending to keep that from happening.

The other guard stepped toward her, leading with his cattle prod, its end sparking and snapping. Seichan judged the seven ways she could disarm him and commandeer the weapon. Then the baby inside kicked her in the kidney.

Gasping, she dropped to a knee.

She pictured the blood in the toilet.

Valya took the tranquilizer pistol from the other man and pointed it at Seichan. "I'm not sure how much sedative your child can survive. But I'm willing to find out. Are you?"

On the floor, Seichan simply glared at her. She recognized in her present state that she could not stop what was going to happen. She could only watch as Harriet was hauled into the arms of the burly guard. Penny sobbed, grabbing for her little sister, only to be roughly shoved back to the bed.

As the guard carried Harriet off, the five-year-old remained her stoic self, accepting the inevitable as surely as Seichan had. Still, the girl stared back at Seichan, as if silently asking again, *What did I do wrong?*

Seichan's heart broke as Valya followed her men out. She called harshly after the woman. "Harm the girl and I'll—"

Before she could finish, Valya slammed the door behind her, cutting off this feeble threat. Seichan scooted and shifted to the bed to comfort Penny. The girl buried her damp face in her bosom and sobbed.

"She'll be fine," Seichan assured her. "Harriet will be fine."

She prayed that was true.

The baby kicked again. Wincing, she cursed the man who put this demon inside her. Still, she worried for the child's father, for the shitstorm he was flying into. It seemed everyone was going after that tech. But why was it so important?

She stared at the locked door, leaving that mystery to Gray.

She had her own problems to tackle and was all too aware of how physically compromised she was in her condition. Knowing she would not be able to fight her way out, especially with the girls in tow, she needed a new strategy.

One that raised a difficult question.

She squeezed Penny tighter.

How do I outwit the Snow Queen?

– 11 –

"What's Eve doing?" Carly asked.

Mara shifted her attention from the diagnostic information scrolling down one side of the laptop screen. She had been studying the analytics from her music subroutine. With the module almost complete, she wanted to scan for bugs or glitches. From past iterations, she knew this was a critical juncture in Eve's development. By now, Mara's careful grooming should have made the program's consciousness fertile enough for true growth. But it also made it vulnerable. The program balanced on a wire's edge, teetering between a miracle capable of developing a true depth of soul and some egocentric engine of incalculable malignancy.

"Why's she just crouched there?" Carly pressed.

Mara cocked her head to the side, matching Eve's odd posture. Rather than absorbing the last of the subroutine's data—represented visually by a swirl of musical notes—Eve seemed shut down. She was crouched on one knee, her head tilted to the side, her long dark hair parted over her left ear.

She looked frozen in this position.

"Did she lock up?" Carly asked. "Like a glitched character in a video game?"

"I don't know." Admitting such a thing made Mara's blood go cold. "I don't know what she's doing."

"It almost looks like she's straining to hear something." Carly turned to her. "Maybe there's some song in there she really likes, and she keeps playing it over and over again."

"She wouldn't do that."

"Can't you ask her? If she knows language, can't you talk to her?"

"Not yet. It's too dangerous. It could shatter her fragile digital psyche. To Eve, that virtual Eden *is* her world. She's not ready to know about us."

"About the gods looking down upon her."

Mara slowly nodded. "But I think you're right. I think she's listening to something."

But what?

Mara had an idea.

"Let me run a test."

She typed quickly on the keyboard, pulling up another diagnostic program. It measured for any interference patterns, any strong RF signals or localized transmissions that could penetrate *Xénese*'s insulated systems and damage them.

A chart appeared on one corner of the screen.

She scanned what the diagnostics had registered. "Background EM. Radio waves. Cell tower transmissions. A wireless router nearby." She tapped the largest spike on the chart. "This one's really strong. In the microwave band."

"Microwave?" Carly stepped toward the open window. "There's a restaurant on the corner. If they're heating something up—"

"Not that sort of microwave."

Mara noted a slight drop in the spike and sighed.

Maybe it's nothing.

Carly stood at the window, enjoying the warmth of the afternoon breeze. The wind tussled her blond curls, dancing the bright sunlight about her cheeks. The edges of her black suit jacket fluttered, offering glimpses of her body's silhouette.

Mara had to force her gaze away and back to the screen. Eve had finally moved, regaining her feet, standing straight. But the avatar's head remained tilted, the curve of her ear exposed. Only now, Eve's expression looked strained, with a pinched brow and narrowed eyes.

Almost scared.

Mystified and concerned, Mara called to Carly. "Come see this."

Her friend turned from the window and crossed over. As she did so, Mara noted the microwave spike in the diagnostic window shift higher. On the screen, Eve's head swiveled, as if following Carly's path.

Mara straightened, suddenly fearing the worst.

Carly must have noted her alarm. "What is it?"

"You turned off your phone, right?"

"Yeah. And pulled the battery. Like you told me."

Mara knew cell phones used microwave transmissions to communicate with GPS satellites, allowing a phone's position to be tracked. "Check your pockets. All of them."

While Carly followed her urgent instructions, Mara patted her own clothes.

Nothing.

Suddenly Carly's eyes got huge. From a jacket pocket, she removed a shiny metallic coin. "I don't know what this is. Don't know how it got there."

Mara knew the answer to both. She pictured the man who had grabbed Carly at the airport. "It's a GPS tracker. It was planted on you."

She turned to the door, knowing the truth.

"I led them right here."

2:53 P.M.

Todor broke another of the hotel clerk's fingers.

With his other hand, Todor muffled the man's scream. Two of his teammates held the clerk pinned to a chair in the establishment's back office, allowing Todor to stare into the young man's glassy, dark eyes. He tried to fathom the man's agony, to wonder what it felt like.

Did pain have a color, a smell, a taste?

His whole life he had craved some inkling of that experience, wondering what he was missing. It wasn't as if he lacked any sensory experience. He could feel a touch, shiver when cold, sweat when he exerted, but he could flay open his palm with a knife and feel nothing.

He had been taught *pain* was life's cautionary tale, a body's natural warning mechanism. Many of those afflicted like him died at a young age. From injuries that were overlooked or ignored, or more often, from simply taking stupid risks. Unrestricted by pain, they felt like they could do anything.

He had been lucky the Crucible had accepted him as a boy. The rigorous training and restrictions placed upon him by the brotherhood had likely saved his life.

Learning nothing more about pain from his captive, Todor waited for the clerk—some Nigerian immigrant with skin like polished coal—to stop screaming and settle into heaving sobs.

When his team had first entered the hotel lobby, the spindle-limbed clerk had been on the phone, speaking rapidly in his native language, plainly arguing. Todor had come upon him easily. As Todor waited for the call to end, he eavesdropped upon this one's heathen tongue, angered that such filth had never bothered to fully assimilate.

Todor took his hand away and leaned closer, nose to nose with this *cabrón*. "Again," he said calmly. "We know the woman is here. Tell us which room."

Behind the clerk's shoulder, Mendoza held the iPad used to track their targets to this nondescript hotel along Pink Street in the Cais do Sodre district. The establishment was one in a row of such hostelries, all with peeling paint, broken stucco, and rickety ironwork balconies, all overlooking a slew of smoky bars and underground clubs, most closed for the holiday.

Unfortunately, while the GPS tracker had identified this hotel, it had failed to pinpoint *where* in this building his targets had holed up. Thus it required some judicious questioning. His team had locked down the lobby, not that there was much traffic in the lobby or the street outside.

He had dragged the clerk into the back office and showed him a photo of Mara Silviera.

"I . . . I do not know her," the clerk gasped out again, sticking to the same story. "I truly don't. I just came on shift this morning."

Todor grabbed his next finger.

"Please, please, no."

Before he could yank it, one of his men burst into the office. He dragged a terrified young maid with him, clutching her by the scruff of her neck, a pistol pressed into her side.

"*Familiares*, she knows where the witch is hiding."

With a shake of her neck, the man forced her to repeat what she knew.

Todor looked toward the ceiling.

Four flights up.

He returned his attention to the clerk and pulled a hunting knife from his boot.

The man's eyes got huge, showing white all around. "No, sir, no. I have a wife . . . children . . ."

He slowly silenced those pleas with a slice across the clerk's throat.

A muffled gunshot sounded behind him. He heard a body fall.

The Inquisitor General had been strict in his commands.

No witnesses.

Still, Todor never took his gaze from the clerk's eyes. While Todor might not be able to appreciate the pain of that cut, he understood the agony in the man's face, as life and all its promises died with one last rattled breath.

Todor cleaned his knife on the clerk's shirt, sheathed the blade, and turned to his men.

"*Maleficos non patieris vivere*," he intoned.

Nods met him all around, the command well understood.

Suffer not a witch to live.

2:58 P.M.

C'mon, Mara, hurry . . .

Carly was down on one knee, wrapping cords and seating them into pockets in the black case on the floor. A dozen solid-state hard drives protruded from padded spaces inside it. While Carly unhooked and stored the cables, Mara had begun the process to shut down the *Xénese* device and send Eve into a slumbering state. Mara insisted that they had to wait for the completion of the music subroutine.

If interrupted, Eve could be irreparably damaged.

Carly knew the *Xénese* device held Mara's only copy of her program. Nothing else had the capacity to house the unique consciousness seeded into the glowing sphere. If they were to ever discover what the first incarnation of Eve knew about the murder of her mother and the others, they needed this program intact.

Still . . .

"Speed it up, Mara."

"Subroutine's done."

Her friend yanked the USB-C cable from her laptop and tossed it over. As Carly wound it up, Mara pressed her thumb to the fingerprint scanner on the laptop—then began typing furiously.

"What are you doing?"

"Abort code. To freeze Eve in place." Mara suddenly swore, reverting to her native tongue. *"Aborto de calamar . . ."*

Carly hid a smile as she closed the case of hard drives with a snap. She had studied Mara's Galician dialect, as a way of getting closer to her friend. They sometimes spoke it in public to keep their conversations private. The phrase—a local curse—roughly translated as *you're an aborted squid*. It seemed a weird way of telling someone off, but Carly was oddly charmed by the phrase—and even more by the wielder of that curse.

"What's wrong?" Carly asked.

"You try typing a twenty-character alphanumeric password that's case-sensitive when you're panicking. I have to start over."

"Take a breath. You can—"

The door crashed open behind Mara. The shattered frame showered splinters across the room. A huge shape barreled inside. His arms reached for Mara as her friend twisted around with a gasp.

Carly lunged from the floor, swinging the titanium case up by its handle. She slammed the heavily loaded valise into the attacker's elbows, knocking his arms wide and throwing him off-balance.

As more men poured in behind the first, she grabbed Mara and retreated to the open window. A graffiti-scoured fire escape offered the only other way out. She shouldered Mara over the windowsill, sending them both crashing onto the iron balcony outside.

A tiny white saucer shattered under her elbow. On the balcony above, a black cat hissed and spat at the sudden intrusion.

Using the metal valise as a shield, she urged Mara down the rickety stairs. Arms shot out the window. Fingers snatched at Carly and latched on to the case's handle. With her free hand, she grabbed and lashed out with a shard of the broken saucer, slicing across the attacker's knuckles.

A sharp cry, and she was free. She followed after Mara, skipping steps, leaping from balcony to balcony down the fire escape. The pair all but tumbled headlong toward the street.

A gunshot rang out above. A round sparked from an iron balustrade near her ear. She ducked, heard someone shout angrily in Spanish, clearly scolding the shooter.

Must want us alive . . .

She stared at the back of her fleet-footed friend and revised this assumption.

No, they wanted *Mara* alive.

The two finally reached the bottommost balcony. Mara unlatched a ladder and sent it rattling down to a narrow alley behind the hotel.

"Go, go, go . . ." Carly pressed, picturing men racing after them or circling around from the front.

They slid down the ladder. Once in the alley, they fled around a corner and to the nearest street. Across the roadway, Christmas music echoed up the steps of a squalid underground bar, adding an absurd sound track to their escape.

"Taxi . . ." Mara panted and pointed to the left where a cab was parked.

They raced toward it, seeing no other cars on the street this holiday afternoon. A man was about to climb into the lone cab.

Mara reached him, grabbing for the open door. "*Senhor, por favor.*"

The man must have read the desperation on their faces and stepped back, allowing them to pile inside. "*Feliz Natal,*" he wished them as he pushed the door shut.

The taxi started down the street, heading away from the hotel.

Relieved, Carly sagged in the seat, hugging the case on her lap. Next to her, Mara stared out the back window, her expression worried and scared. Carly felt the same, well aware of what they'd abandoned in the wake of their escape.

"It couldn't be helped," Carly said, trying to console her.

Mara murmured as she settled back around, "What have we done?"

3:06 P.M.

Todor sat on his haunches and admired the glass-and-metal sphere cradled in a cushioned box. It was only half the prize he had hoped to collect here, but it would have to do for now.

Behind him, Mendoza was examining the laptop, judging how safe it was to move what they had secured. The rest of his team had spread out, trying to nab the two women before they escaped the district.

While he waited for the others to report in, Todor returned his attention to the device on the floor. From its tiny windows, a bright azure glow emanated from within, as if a piece of the sky had been captured inside. He had to admit there was a certain beauty to its design, to its outward appearance.

But he refused to be deceived.

"*Ipse enim Satanas transfigurat se in angelum lucis,*" he whispered to the sphere, quoting from the Second Epistle to the Corinthians.

Mendoza let out a small gasp of amazement.

Todor rose and joined the team's technician. "What is it?"

The team's tech stepped back from the laptop and ran a palm over his oiled black hair. "What's been created is simply *maravilloso*. Just look."

Todor bent his tall frame to peer at the laptop screen. The sight revealed a verdant forest, its flowering bower carpeted by dewy ferns. Sunlight glistened off every leaf and petal. A gentle breeze stirred the thin branches of a berry-laden bush. It was so perfectly rendered, he could almost smell the perfume wafting from that garden.

It's like peeking into a corner of Eden.

And this garden was not empty.

A naked woman stirred in the center of it all. One palm rested on a mossy boulder as she bent down and gently plucked a blackberry from a bush. She held it up to the sunlight, before bringing it to her perfect lips. Her eyes drifted closed, as if to better savor the taste. As she did so, his gaze traveled over her sculpted form, her skin a shade of dark mocha, her breasts unabashedly bared.

"From what I was able to discern," Mendoza said, "they named her Eve."

Of course.

He straightened. Such blasphemy tempered his admiration. "What of the witch who created all of this?"

With clear reluctance, Mendoza glanced over to the iPad sitting next to the laptop. "According to the signal, the two women are moving quickly. They likely found a taxi."

"Keep tracking their route while you secure everything for transportation."

"*Si, Familiares.*"

Todor studied the laptop screen one last time. He knew the Inquisitor General's plans for *Xénese* and the abomination within. While acquiring the witch would have been a boon, she wasn't an essential element for what was to come.

As he stared, he was again captured by the splendor found on the screen. It was indeed *maravilloso*, as Mendoza had extolled. Still, Todor refused to be deceived. He stared at the woman in the garden. Her eyes were open again, seeming to stare straight at him. He knew what hid behind the glow of those eyes.

Without breaking that unearthly gaze, he repeated the line from Second Corinthians, both to remind himself and as a warning to Mendoza to be cautious with his admiration.

"Ipse enim Satanas transfigurat se in angelum lucis."

It was something they all had to keep in mind from here.

He silently repeated the quote one more time, translating the Latin in his head.

For Satan himself masquerades as an angel of light.

3:22 P.M.

"Looks like they took the bait," Carly said.

Mara nodded, momentarily relieved. She and Carly hid in the smoky confines of a basement bar. The air reeked of tobacco and patchouli. As the tin chords of a Christmas carol rasped from an old jukebox, they stared out a grime-encrusted window.

Earlier, Carly had lifted to her toes and used the elbow of her jacket to wipe clean a corner of the glass, enough for them to spy across the rosy-hued pavement of Pink Street to the front of her former hotel. After securing the taxi, Mara had the driver take them a couple of blocks, then stop. They abandoned the cab, but not before snugging the coin-sized GPS tracker into a seat cushion. As the taxi took off with the tracker, they had carefully circled back on foot, traversing narrow alleys to enter the bar via its back door.

Through the smear in the window, Mara watched her life's work being hauled into a van parked at the hotel's front door. She could do nothing to stop the theft. Even if she could have convinced the bartender to allow her to use the establishment's phone, the authorities would never have responded in time. And the two of them certainly dared not use their cell phones, knowing such an act might expose their earlier ruse and again put them on the enemy's radar.

Instead, Carly held a bar napkin against the stone wall and jotted down the van's plate number. She elbowed Mara to move over and peered intently through their spyhole, then swore under her breath.

"What?" Mara asked.

"From this angle, I can't make out the last three numbers."

Mara frowned. "Maybe what you already have is enough."

The plan was to wait until the others left, then alert the police and hide here until the authorities arrived. Only then would they come out of hiding. After that, hopefully the police could track the van by its plate and grab the men responsible for the murder of Carly's mother and the other four women of Bruxas.

Still, Mara knew that wasn't the most important outcome of their plan.

She pictured Eve in her garden.

"They're leaving," Carly said. "C'mon. I need the rest of that plate number."

The two of them exited the bar but hovered near the open door. Six steps led up to the level of the street. As a precaution, they remained below, peering up just enough to spy the full plate of the van as it sped away.

"Got it," Carly said and waved Mara back.

As her friend rechecked her scrawl of letters and numbers on the napkin, Mara retreated backward into the bar. Crossing the dark threshold, she felt a stir in the smoky air, sensed a shadow looming behind her.

She tried to duck away. "Car—"

A huge hand clamped over her mouth. A thick arm hooked her waist. Someone else pointed a pistol at Carly's chest. Her friend's eyes went huge and scared.

"*No te muevas*," they were warned.

Don't move.

— 12 —

Exhausted and heartsick, Monk held Kat's hand, in yet another hospital room. Her skin had turned pallid, her lips bled of color, even the single auburn curl peeking from under a hospital bonnet looked drab and flat, its hue no longer bright and sleek.

He reached and freed the stray hair from where sweat had plastered it to her forehead. He wrapped its length around a finger, accentuating the whorl before laying it gently back.

There you go, beautiful as always.

He continued to keep one ear on the tick, thrum, and beep of her vitals. He tried his best to reconcile himself with both the diagnosis and prognosis. The team in the MRI lab had stabilized Kat after the seizure and rushed her to ICU. For an hour, he could only pace, waiting to find out if he'd lost the love of his life, the mother of his children.

Lisa kept him company as best she could.

Finally, Grant and a handful of other doctors delivered the verdict. Kat was stable for the moment. The brain hemorrhaging had slowed, enough that they thought operating on her would be more risk than benefit. They also reported the grim news that Kat was no longer breathing on her own and was now totally dependent on the ventilator. Worst of all, the moments of wakefulness noted in the EEG had ceased, suggestive that Kat was no longer aware of her surroundings.

Maybe that's a blessing, the ICU doctor had intoned solemnly.

Monk had wanted to sock the guy in the nose. As if sensing this, Lisa had taken Monk's prosthetic hand, squeezing it tightly. Just as well. His hardware packed more than a simple punch. Beyond the array of advanced tech built into his hand, a small packet of plastic explosives had been wired under his palm as a failsafe, for those special occasions when a simple handshake wouldn't do.

Lisa kept hold of his hand, comforting him as much as restraining him, as the medical staff finished its report. The consensus was that Kat had deteriorated from the pseudocoma of a locked-in patient into a full coma.

There's nothing else we can do, Grant had concluded. *From here, it's a waiting game.*

Monk sensed the *waiting* he was referring to had less to do with Kat's recovery and more with the expectation of her death.

Or maybe they're just waiting for me to accept the inevitable.

He patted Kat's hand. "But you know how stubborn I can be. When do I ever give up?"

Monk's phone rang and vibrated on the bedside table, indicating an urgent call. He grabbed it, saw it was Sigma, and quickly answered.

As soon as Director Crowe came on the line, he blurted, "What have you learned?"

Monk had already forwarded Kat's intel—possibly the last she'd ever share, one that was mission critical. A single name, *Valya Mikhailov*. The former Guild assassin had kidnapped his children, taken Seichan.

Painter answered, his voice worrisomely terse. "Monk, I need you to brace yourself."

His heart stuttered in his chest. A thousand scenarios—all brutal— filled his head. He could barely get enough breath to ask, "What is it?"

"We received a video file ten minutes ago. The source untraceable. I'm sending it to your phone."

Monk clutched his device harder, his vision narrowing as he stared at the small screen. "Are they dead? Just tell me."

"No. Watch. You should have the file by now."

A folder popped up on his phone, and he tapped it open. His screen darkened as a video started. The view was into a featureless space, all draped in black. Three figures were present. Two were hidden under hooded, formless cloaks, masking any hint of features or gender. One stood closest to the camera; the second sat on a stool farther back. Balancing on the second one's knee was a small figure wearing green footie pajamas, her auburn curls a few shades lighter than Kat's hair.

"Harriet . . ."

The closest figure spoke, the voice robotic, mechanically distorted and modulated, eerily changing constantly. "I'll give you twenty-four hours to secure and deliver Mara Silviera's *Xénese* project. Both her neuromorphic sphere and the program inside. A drop-off location in Spain is encrypted within this file. Failure to do as instructed—" The speaker turned to Harriet, the child's ears mercifully muffled by headphones so the girl couldn't hear what was said next. "After that deadline, we'll start with a finger and send it to you. Every six hours thereafter. Ears, nose, lips. We'll whittle this girl down to nothing."

The speaker returned to the camera. "Then we'll start with the second child."

The video ended as abruptly as it started.

At some point, Monk had stood up, terror stiffening his spine. Cold sweat slickened his palms. His breathing gasped between clenched teeth. He could not even speak.

Painter, likely anticipating his distress, threw him a lifeline. "Thanks to Kat, we have one advantage. From the way the figures were cloaked in the video, Valya remains unaware we know she is behind this kidnapping."

A breath rattled from Monk, allowing him to speak. "Where are we at in tracking her?"

"We're working on it," Painter said. "But we must be cautious. If we blanket the Northeast with her photo, she'll know her cover is blown.

We'll lose this small advantage. So, I'm working surreptitiously through back channels, enlisting only those we trust the most."

Monk understood but chafed against such restraint. He could not stop picturing Harriet's face on the video, her features pinched with a familiar mix of fear and anger.

Painter continued: "We're also using DARPA's latest software to scour footage from security and traffic cams. Unfortunately, Valya made the process more difficult, somehow blinding cameras at and immediately around Commander Pierce's home. Still, we've set an ever-widening grid across D.C. and beyond to search for her."

Monk shook his head, doubtful that such a plan would be successful. "That pale-faced witch is a master of disguise."

"True, but our face-recognition software is state of the art. Most algorithms search a dozen key facial features at most to identify a subject. DARPA's latest targets over a *hundred*. It's capable of seeing through makeup, facial prosthetics, even surgical alterations. If Valya shows her face—disguised or not—we'll spot her."

Holding his phone in an iron grip, Monk noted the time. A clock was already ticking down in his head. *Less than twenty-four hours.* He tried not to think about someone holding Harriet's thin wrist to a wooden chopping block, the fall of a machete, her screams.

"Forensics finished its sweep of Gray's house," Painter said. "They're sorting through the blood evidence, most of it from the intruders, quite a bit of it."

Monk's gaze flicked to Kat.

Good job, honey.

"We're already analyzing the DNA in the hopes of identifying others—more of Valya's team—to help expand the search. Still . . ."

Painter's voice trailed off, the implication clear.

"We're not likely to find Valya in the next twenty-four hours," Monk said.

Make that less *than twenty-four hours.*

"No," Painter admitted. "The only chance would be if Kat knew something more, something that could narrow the search parameters."

Monk stared at his wife's sunken features, the mechanical rise and fall of her chest. His eyes traveled from the hospital bonnet that hid a net of EEG electrodes over her scalp and up along a wire to a monitor. The screen ran with scribbling lines, a seismic Richter scale of her neurological activity. Upon scanning these readings, Dr. Grant had mumbled to a colleague, running a finger along one line on the screen, *note the low voltage with burst suppression.*

Translation: *Kat's no longer here.*

"She gave us all she could," Monk said.

"Lisa thought maybe with—"

"What? Enough time? To hell with that. Harriet is running out of time. Same with Penny and Seichan." Reminded of Gray's girlfriend and unborn child, Monk took a step away from Kat's bed, knowing there was nothing more he could do *here.* "I'm heading out to join Gray, where I can do some good."

Or simply do *something.*

Monk was done waiting.

A long silence followed. Monk braced himself to argue with the director, to state his case. If they failed to find Valya, the best hope for the kidnapped trio was to secure the missing tech.

Finally, Painter spoke. "There's an F-15 Eagle fueling at Naval Air Engineering Station in Lakehurst. By helicopter, you can be at the station in twenty minutes."

Monk shouldn't have been surprised. Of course, the director—always an astute judge of character—had anticipated his reaction and had already rallied transportation.

Painter continued: "Gray should be landing in Lisbon within the hour. I'll coordinate a rendezvous with him once you're on the ground out there. But, Monk, you know what's at stake. We can *never* turn this tech over to Valya."

"Understood. But we have no leverage without it."

"Then as long as we're on the same page, you'd better haul ass."

Resolute in doing just that, he hung up, crossed to Kat, and kissed her cheek. Despite his need to hurry, he lingered, sensing this was the last time he would get a chance to kiss his wife.

Still, he knew she would have wanted him to pursue this.

He shifted his lips to her ear. "I'll save them. I swear."

He straightened and wiped tears from the corner of his eyes—then headed toward the door. Out in the hallway, Lisa spotted him. She broke away from Dr. Grant; the two looked like they'd been in some intense conversation.

She hurried toward him. "Where are you—?"

"To Portugal. To help Gray with his search."

Lisa glanced into Kat's room. Monk's cheeks heated, knowing she must think he was abandoning his wife. "I get it. You should go," she said, proving to be as good a judge of character as her husband. "Painter just texted me . . . about the video. I couldn't watch it."

"I have to do what I can," Monk said.

"Of course." She reached and squeezed his upper arm in sympathy. She glanced over to the neurologist, then into Kat's room. "While you're gone, there's something we could try. Something highly experimental. It won't heal her, but it might—"

Monk broke free of her grip. "Do what you think is best, Lisa. I trust you."

"Yes, but—"

He brushed past her. "Just do it."

He headed down the hall. He didn't need false hope. Instead, he needed to focus on his next step . . . and the one after that. Each stride took him farther away from Kat but hopefully brought him closer to saving his girls—and Seichan.

He knew Gray must be just as worried and terrified for her and his unborn child.

Still . . .

Gray, I need you at your best.

Monk pictured Harriet's frightened face.

We all do.

THIRD

EVE OF DESTRUCTION

— 13 —

In a remote corner of the Lisbon airport, Gray crouched before the open door of a travel locker. He distributed the arsenal of weapons stashed inside, all arranged by Painter.

The locker room—a long, narrow alcove off the main concourse—was empty. Still, Kowalski's bulk hid his actions from both the terminal and the space's lone security camera. Due to customs and heightened airport security, they'd had to abandon their personal sidearms aboard the jet.

Gray snugged a fresh SIG Sauer P365 into a holster at the small of his back, hidden under the fall of his jacket. The 9mm semiautomatic's compact size made it a perfect concealed-carry weapon. Jason slipped an identical pistol into the shoulder holster under his cardigan. The guns came equipped with night sights and extended magazines, allowing for a twelve-plus-one capacity.

Thirteen rounds total.

Normally such a number would sound unlucky, but when it came to a firefight, those extra shots could mean the difference between life or death.

So definitely not unlucky.

Kowalski let out a low whistle of appreciation as Gray handed over the man's weapon. "Merry Christmas to me. And I didn't have to sit on Santa's lap."

The black FN-P90 was a NATO bullpup assault rifle with the capability to switch fire from single shots to burst rounds, or flipped into fully automatic mode, firing nine hundred rounds a minute. The 5.7x28mm cartridges could penetrate Kevlar. Still, its compact design—a mere twenty inches long—allowed for relatively easy concealment.

Kowalski shrugged off one shoulder of his long leather duster to sling the weapon along his side, where he happily patted it. "Here's a puppy I'm happy to feed."

Gray passed him a heavy bag of extra box magazines, each holding fifty rounds, plenty of *feed* for this hungry bullpup rifle.

Kowalski pulled his long coat back on and jostled his body to settle everything in place. His ankle-length duster could hide enough weapons to invade a small third-world country.

"What now?" the big man asked.

Gray passed a bag to Jason, which contained more equipment, including night-vision gear, then stood. "Painter arranged for us to interview Dr. Carson's family—her husband and her daughter Laura. To see if they've received any further word from the two young women."

Mara Silviera and Carla Carson.

Gray could only imagine the family's worry. First the ambassador is murdered, then her daughter is attacked at the airport and on the run. Then again, maybe he didn't need to *imagine* the family's terror and fear. He tried his best to compartmentalize his own anxiety for Seichan, his child, Monk's girls, but it was like trying to crate a feral dog. An ache persisted in his heart, not just figuratively but literally. He felt the tension in his chest with every breath.

He knew Monk was just as agonized—likely worse—balancing on a razor's edge. Director Crowe had updated Gray's team on the situation back in the States, about that pale witch Valya Mikhailov's involvement and about Kat's failing condition.

Unable to do anything else, Monk was already en route to Portugal, flying as a passenger aboard a supersonic F-15, zipping at twice the speed of sound. Even with a midair refueling, he'd be touching down here a mere ninety minutes from now.

Gray intended to have answers before his friend landed.

As they set off into the airport, Jason checked his phone. "No further update from Painter. But someone from the Carsons' protection detail will meet us in Terminal One and escort us to the family."

They headed at a brisk pace toward the rendezvous point. Gray led the way, doing his best not to attract undue attention from the bustle of late-afternoon travelers. Still, several heads swiveled as they passed, tracking their group—or rather, eyeballing the giant behind Gray. Kowalski could never blend in. It didn't help that the man kept trying to unwrap a cigar as they maneuvered through the crowd.

"You can't smoke in here," Jason warned. The young analyst looked like a mouse scolding an elephant.

"I friggin' know that." Kowalski finally got the cellophane off and clamped the stogie between his molars. "Nothing says I can't taste this sweet beauty."

Gray knew better than to come between the big man and his love of dried tobacco leaves. Up ahead, an arm lifted above the crowd. His name was called, the voice full of authority.

"Commander Pierce."

Gray directed the group over there. The speaker wore a crisp dark navy suit, white starched shirt, thin black tie, the no-nonsense uniform of a security officer, down to the earpiece trailing a wire under the jacket.

"Agent Bailey," the man said with a slight Irish brogue. "Head of the Carsons' DSS detail."

Gray shook the Diplomatic Security Service agent's hand. Their contact's black hair was as polished as his suit, trimmed near to the scalp over the ears, longer on top, but combed with every hair in place. His skin was ruddy, with a tan that looked worn into his skin. His green eyes sparked with intelligence. His lips quirked slightly with amusement, maybe because the man's gaze ran up and down Kowalski's tall form.

After years in the field, Gray was good at sizing up an opponent in a glance. He sensed both the agent's confidence and competence, already respecting the man who looked to be his same age. Even the amused twinkle felt familiar, comfortable, as if Gray had known the agent for years.

Still, he kept his guard up, noting everything around him.

"I don't know if you were informed," Bailey said, "but we moved Laura and Derek Carson twenty minutes ago."

Gray glanced to Jason, who shook his head. This was new intel.

"After the attempted attack here, the agency thought it best to change locations, get the family somewhere safer. We have other agents sticking here in case the two girls return."

Smart.

The man knew how to run an operation.

"I have a car idling curbside. We can be at the safe house in ten."

Gray appreciated the brevity and efficiency of their escort. He preferred to hit the ground running, especially now. "Let's go."

Bailey led them out of the terminal and into the dying daylight. The sun sat sullenly on the horizon, as if disappointed by the end of Christmas. A white unmarked Ford Econoline van sat at the curb. Gray pictured the lush appointments of the Citation jet. The DSS plainly did not have the deep pockets of Sigma.

Bailey tugged the side door open, gave a thumbs-up to the driver, then waved the trio inside. Kowalski took the back bench, struggling both with his size and the hidden rifle. Gray and Jason took the two captain chairs behind the driver.

Bailey strode around the van to climb in next to the driver. Once settled, he swung around and pointed a large pistol at their group. The amused glint in his eye twinkled brighter.

"Do not move."

5:14 P.M.

Mara paced their luxurious cell. While she couldn't escape, the movement helped keep her terror at bay—but just barely.

Carly sat on the edge of a wide four-poster bed piled with pillows and covered with a silk duvet. Her only sign of agitation was a knee popping up and down. Her friend's gaze swept the room. "At least they sprang for the penthouse."

Mara took in their surroundings, noting the antique chairs, a small French desk, and the expensive paintings on the wall. One oil appeared to be the work of a famous local artist, Pedro Alexandrino de Carvalho. It depicted Saint Thomas testing the wound in Christ's side, his face agonized with doubt.

That raw suspicion and distrust spoke to her, to their current predicament.

Are we going to survive this?

After being forced at gunpoint off the street and back into the bar, the two of them had been manhandled over to the establishment's back door. The bartender had ignored their kidnapping, merely wiping a glass. Plainly he had been paid to look the other way. Still, Mara had noted his grimace of guilt—but apparently his remorse was not great enough for him to do anything to stop them from being led away and shoved into a van parked in the alley.

Cooperate and no harm will come to you, the gunman had warned before slamming the door.

With no other choice, they obeyed.

A short ride later, they stopped in another alley off Praça de São Paulo. Mara caught a glimpse of the fountain of Saint Paul's Square, heard its tinkling waters, beyond which rose the twin square towers of the church to the same saint. She had cast out a silent plea to Saint Paul for intercession, to save them.

With her prayer unanswered, she and Carly were taken into a tall house bordering the square. Its architecture was typical Pombaline, named after the Marquês de Pombal, who rebuilt much of Lisbon after the 1755 earthquake. The style's efficient neoclassical design was born of a cost-cutting necessity. Still, the simple lines with little embellishments spoke to the new era of enlightenment, as Europe grew out of the extravagances of the Rococo period into something more rational and practical. Pombaline architecture was typified by an arcade of shops below and three or four levels of living space above.

Mara knew all about this period because her local mentor—Eliza Guerra, the head of the Joanina Library in Coimbra—had insisted on a well-rounded education, including history, especially of Portugal and the rest of the Iberian Peninsula, of which the librarian was rightfully proud.

It was Mara's memory of Eliza's bottomless enthusiasm—for knowledge, for life in all its splendor and mystery—that gave her the strength to follow Carly up the flights of stairs to the topmost apartment, where they were sequestered in a back bedroom. A guard had been posted at the door and on the balcony outside a set of French doors.

That had been more than an hour ago.

"Mara," Carly said, "please stop wearing a rut in the rug. It looks expensive. We don't want to piss off our hosts."

Mara crossed her arms, stepped over to the bed, and sat down next to Carly. "What do you think they're doing?"

Carly stared at the door. "Probably trying to decide what to do with us. Judging if there's any worth in keeping us."

In other words, keeping us alive.

Mara unfolded her arms and took Carly's hand. It wasn't done out of fear or out of a need for reassurance. It just felt . . . *right*, the natural thing to do in this moment.

Carly gently gripped her palm, a thumb absently rubbing Mara's wrist. "They're probably examining what's in your case. All those hard drives. They must've hoped we had the *Xénese* with us. Our best chance of staying alive is to make them think we could re-create it."

Earlier, both of them had concluded their captors were some other faction, not the same ones who had killed Carly's mother and the other women of Bruxas, but a competitor. Word must have spread of the prize Mara had stolen from the university.

Other vultures had closed in.

"Do you think they'll torture us?" Mara asked.

"No."

Mara was relieved, but Carly wasn't done.

"They'll torture *me*," her friend said. "To force you to cooperate."

Mara tightened her fingers on Carly's hand.

Carly stared over, her eyes glassy with suppressed tears. She licked her lips, looking like she wanted to say something.

Mara felt the same. They'd known each other for half a decade, those formative years from sixteen to now, when both were maturing out of childhood toward the women they'd become. In the past, they had no trouble talking, though it was usually on the phone, or over long e-mail chains, or exchanged in short, excitable texts. A majority of their relationship was long-distance, but the world had grown much smaller. Pen pals no longer had to wait weeks or months to communicate.

Still, separated by an ocean, the two had spent little physical time together. Their friendship, their bond, their deep connection was mostly born from sharing their thoughts, dreams, fears, and hopes.

Mara stared back at Carly, at the curls crowning her brow. If only Mara had the nerve to speak now, the courage to fill that last gulf between them, to say what was unspoken.

Mara waited too long.

Carly bowed her head, a touch shyly, and turned her attention to the door. She asked the question plaguing them both.

"Who the hell are these bastards?"

5:18 P.M.

Gray weighed his options.

He eyed the silver Desert Eagle pointed at his face, imagining it was chambered in a .357 or .44 Magnum. Its owner's gaze was steady, no-

nonsense. The man would not bother with anything smaller. To make matters worse, Gray was practically sitting on his own weapon. Kowalski, cramped in the back, surely couldn't swing up his rifle. And Jason already had his palms raised.

Bailey, if that was even his real—

"My name is Finnigan Bailey," their captor said. "But friends call me Finn."

"Don't think I'll be calling you that anytime soon," Gray said. "And let me guess. You're *not* with the DSS."

"Unfortunately, I can't count myself among such an illustrious group. But I'm with an organization perhaps equally loyal to their pursuit. Maybe more so."

Gray guessed from his Irish brogue that the man was with the New Irish Republican Army, the latest incarnation of the IRA. It seemed all manner of terrorist organizations were coming out of the woodwork, pursuing Mara Silviera's work, attracted by its potential.

Bailey reached his free hand to his chin, loosened his tie, and undid the top two buttons, revealing his true affiliation. His outer dress shirt hid a thinner black shirt beneath, along with the peek of a white Roman clerical collar.

Gray failed to hide his shock.

That can't be authentic.

Bailey lowered his gun. "Sorry about this, but as armed as you all are, I couldn't risk you doing something rash."

"Motherf—" Kowalski bit off the end of his curse.

Baily pretended not to hear. "I had to get you out of the airport in such a manner that any prying eyes would assume the same as you."

Jason dropped his hands to his lap. "That we were traveling with the Carsons' protection detail to meet the family."

"Then if not there, where are we going?" Gray asked.

"I'm taking you to Ms. Silviera and Ms. Carson." His voice firmed, serious. "They will need your help. I can only hope your resourcefulness proves as good as your reputation."

Gray struggled to catch up to the swift change in circumstance.

Can I even trust this guy? Who says he's even a priest?

Bailey seemed to read his distrust. "I assure you I am *Father* Bailey." That twinkle again in his eye. "Would a priest lie?"

Kowalski snorted. "How about a priest pointing a friggin' gun at your head?"

"I would've never shot you, not even in self-defense."

"You tell us that *now*," Kowalski grumbled. "I practically shi— Had an accident."

Gray leaned forward, still suspicious. "Who are you? What's going on?"

The van slowed and came to a stop in front of a tall house at the edge of a square. Bailey nodded toward the building. "Once inside, I'll tell you everything. I'll lay all my cards on the table." The amusement still sparkled in those green eyes. "And I mean that literally."

5:35 P.M.

Carly heard the door unlock and stood up from the bed. She balled a fist and took a step to put herself between Mara and whoever entered. She tensed a back leg, shifting her weight, ready to lash out with a kick, if given an opening.

Mara climbed to her feet behind her.

"Stay back," Carly warned her friend.

Out of the glare of the brighter lights in the next room, a figure emerged. He stepped into the room, holding up empty palms. Carly frowned, not understanding. The tall man was dressed all in black: boots, pants, belt, shirt. The only exception was the flash of white under his chin, marking a distinctive collar.

A priest?

Surely this was some ruse, some trick to get them to trust their captors.

"Ms. Carson, Ms. Silviera, please accept my apologies for keeping you both waiting for so long. And in the dark, so to speak. It took me longer

than I anticipated to bring all the players into the same space." He stepped
back and gave a small bow toward the next room. "If you'll join us, perhaps we can get to know one another."

Carly hesitated, then realized the futility. Still, she whispered to Mara.
"Stay near me."

At the first chance, we're getting the hell out of here.

Mara didn't need to be persuaded. As Carly headed toward the door,
Mara clung close, becoming her shadow.

The priest led them down a short hall to a dining room. The space was
cheered by a marble fireplace dancing with flames, wood crackling with
invitation. Tall windows overlooked the square, framing the two towers
of the church on its far side. The sun had set, but a twilight gloaming still
persisted, setting the church's stone façade to glowing, as if the place of
worship still retained some of the holy day's light and warmth.

"We've set up a light meal," the priest said, drawing her attention to
the table and the group of men gathered around it.

Platters of cheese, bread, and an assortment of fruit made her stomach
growl. How long had it been since she'd eaten? Mara also eyed the bounty
with both hunger and suspicion.

As they crossed to the table, Carly judged the hard-looking crowd.
Standing near the exit were the two men who had ambushed them at the
bar. She glared over, but they remained expressionless. Across the table
were three strangers. She innately sensed—from their clothes, postures,
expressions—they were American even before they spoke.

The priest made introductions all around and urged them to sit.

She was right about them being Americans. The tallest—with a per-
petual scowl locked around a smoldering cigar—looked like something
out of a horror story, all muscle, from toes to his brain. The other two
looked just as hard, but more approachable. One had an intensity that was
difficult to stare directly at, especially into those storm-gray eyes. The last
was closer to her own age. With tussled blond hair, he could almost be
considered cute. He offered an embarrassed smile as they approached, his
gaze lingering a touch longer on her.

Carly was not unaccustomed to such attention.

Still, she didn't return his smile.

"Come," the priest insisted. "Sit."

They all settled to the table, each to their own side, with the priest still standing at one end. "Commander Pierce, just to break the ice, perhaps you should be the first to lay your cards on the table. I think that would expedite matters considerably."

"What are you talking about?" the man asked harshly, clearly no fan of their host, which made Carly trust him a little more.

"I'd suggest starting with your ID. From your organization."

The commander remained still for a breath, then a light dawned in his eyes. He reached to a pocket, removed a wallet, then pulled out a black, metallic-looking card. He flicked it across the table. It came to a stop between her and Mara.

From its glossy surface, a silver hologram hovered.

It was a single symbol—a Greek letter.

Mara gasped and shared a worried look with Carly. "Sigma."

Carly let steel fill her spine, enough to risk staring into the cold fire of those eyes. "Who are you?" She nudged the card. "What's the meaning of this?"

"We're members of Sigma Force, an organization affiliated with DARPA."

Mara frowned. "The U.S. military's R-and-D group?"

"The same. It was DARPA that was funding your research at the university, via money channeled through Bruxas International." His gaze turned to Carly. "Your mother knew of our involvement and was sworn to secrecy. We suspect the Sigma symbol generated by Mara's AI might've been a call for help."

Mara leaned forward. "I wondered the same thing myself."

The young blond man—Jason—spoke. "But can you be sure? The appearance of this symbol could just be a coincidence. Maybe we're all reading too much into this digital Rorschach."

"Perhaps." Mara shook her head. "But there's no way to tell. Not without *Xénese* and its programming."

"And you lost it," Gray said, clearly having heard their story. Still, there was no blame in his voice or manner.

"But we managed to keep the hard drives housing my subroutines," Mara added.

Carly nodded. "We were able to wrench those from the bastards who attacked us."

. . . and who killed my mother.

Mara swallowed. "I think we would've lost those, too, if we'd not had some advanced warning."

"What do you mean?" Gray asked.

Mara shared a glance with Carly, then continued: "The program was acting strange. Just before we were attacked. It seemed to be sensing something. I think it was picking up the GPS signal from the tracker planted on us. But now in hindsight, this detail worries me."

Jason grabbed a slice of bread and cheese. "Why?"

"Eve—that's the name of the AI—was fixed on that signal, looking scared, almost as if she recognized it. Which makes me wonder now if she might have *remembered* it from before."

Jason crinkled his nose. "From when?"

"From the library, from the attack." Mara cast Carly an apologetic look. "If Carly's mother or one of the other women had been tracked to the library with the same bug, then Eve might have recognized it, somewhere deep in her quantum processor, some ghost memory from her first incarnation."

"And associated it with bloodshed and murder," Gray said.

Mara nodded. "And that's what really has me scared. The current stage of Eve—what was stolen from the hotel—is both delicate and brittle. Such fragility, in the hands of someone inexperienced—"

The priest interrupted. "Or worse yet, with someone who intends to wreak great havoc."

All eyes turned on the man.

Gray frowned. "What do *you* know about all of this, Father Bailey? How are you involved?"

"Ah, yes, Commander Pierce, I told you that I'd lay my cards on the table." He nodded to the black metallic card. "Just like you did."

From a pocket, the priest drew two black cards and placed them side by side on the table. They looked like twin pieces of obsidian, glassy rectangles broken from the stained-glass window of a church. This feeling was accentuated by the identical symbols found on each card: a set of crossed keys tied with a ribbon and surmounted by a crown.

Carly didn't understand. She recognized the papal seal on each card, the sigil of the pope, but such knowledge clarified nothing.

Across the table, Gray's eyes had narrowed on the pair. He stood up abruptly, knocking back his chair, clearly finding significance in those cards.

"It's the Twins . . ."

– 14 –

From across the table, Gray stared at Father Bailey with dawning insight.

That's why you seemed so familiar.

He studied the amused sparkle in Bailey's eyes. It was the look of a father charmed by a child—half entertained by the naïveté on display, half envious of the innocence. Gray had only seen that particular sparkle in one other's eye, a man much older, now gone, one who had helped Sigma in the past.

Bailey looked at the two cards on the table. "I see you've not forgotten the lessons of Monsignor Vigor Verona."

Kowalski huffed out a trail of dark smoke. "Jesus . . ."

Gray gripped the table's edge, momentarily overwhelmed by memories. He pictured his friend—along with the monsignor's niece, who had stolen his heart. Both were gone, sacrificing themselves to save the world.

He finally waved to the twin symbols resting on the table. "Does this mean you're a card-carrying member of the Thomas Church?"

Bailey shrugged. "Monsignor Verona recruited me. I was his student once upon a time, back when he taught as a professor at the Pontifical Institute of Christian Archaeology in Rome, before he became prefect of the Vatican Archives. I now follow in his footsteps, picking up where he left off."

"Does that mean you're also with the Vatican *intelligenza*?"

Bailey shrugged again, not denying it.

While alive, Monsignor Vigor Verona had borne more titles than just professor and prefect. He had also served as an operative for the Vatican *intelligenza*—their intelligence services.

Jason sat straighter with this revelation. "So, you're a spy for the Vatican? For the pope?"

"For the church as a whole," Bailey corrected.

"So that's how you knew we were coming, landing in Lisbon." Jason turned to Gray. "I'm guessing when Director Crowe sent feelers throughout the global intelligence communities—"

"It reached us, too," Bailey finished.

Across the table, Dr. Carson's daughter stood up, drawing their attention. "What the hell are you all talking about? Are you saying this priest is some sort of secret agent?"

Gray figured he'd better explain. "The Vatican is a sovereign country. For decades—if not centuries—it has secretly employed operatives who infiltrated hate groups, secret societies, hostile countries, wherever the concerns of the Vatican were threatened."

Gray remembered Vigor sharing the case of Walter Ciszek, a priest operating under the alias Vladimir Lipinski. The priest played a cat-and-mouse game with the KGB for years, before being captured and spending more than two decades in a Soviet prison.

Carly glared at Father Bailey. "In other words, he's James Bond in a clerical collar."

"But we don't come with a license to kill," Bailey clarified, with a teasing smile. "We still have a higher set of commandments to adhere to. Still, like Mr. Bond, I'm not above indulging in a martini every now and then. Shaken, not stirred, of course."

Mara remained seated but leaned closer. She pointed to the cards. "But what's the significance of these symbols?" She eyed Gray. "You clearly know them."

Gray pictured the gold rings worn by Vigor in the past, each bearing one of these seals. "They're symbols of the Thomas Church." He shifted the cards closer to her. "What do you see here?"

"Just the papal seal," she answered correctly. "On both cards."

"Look closer."

Mara pinched her brows, but it was Carly who noted the difference.

"They're *not* exactly the same." She tapped one card, then the other. "Look, Mara, how one seal has the darker key on the left. The other has it on the right. They're mirror images of one another."

Mara glanced over to Gray. "So, like you said before . . . *twins*. But I still don't understand."

"In Hebrew," Gray explained, "the word *twin* translates as *Thomas*. As in Saint Thomas."

Mara glanced over her shoulder. "Or Doubting Thomas? Back there, I saw a painting of Saint Thomas, examining the wounds of Christ."

Intrigued, Gray followed her gaze, wondering if the presence of such a painting might indicate the house was some secret gathering place for members of the Thomas Church.

As if summoned by this thought, the door behind him opened and a severe older woman entered. With gray hair tucked neatly under a crisp white bonnet, she looked to be in her sixties, maybe older. She wore a simple gray robe, belted with a knotted cord, and tapped across the room, leaning imperceptibly on an unpolished ebony cane. She ignored the group and headed toward Father Bailey. She did not rush, but moved with a steadfast purpose that spoke of hidden strength.

Conversation halted. As she crossed behind Gray, the tiny hairs on the back of his neck quivered. It felt like a dark storm front passing by.

She stepped to Father Bailey and whispered in his ear. Even the priest leaned toward her, rather than the other way around. Nothing of this woman hinted at subservience—but clearly there was *someone* she did serve.

Bailey nodded as she finished. "Thank you, Sister Beatrice."

The nun—a bride of Christ—retreated a step, but she didn't leave. She simply stood with the cane propped before her, both palms resting on its hooked silver handle, its only adornment. Her gaze swept the table and settled on Kowalski. Her lips thinned to a more severe line, plainly displeased.

Kowalski tried to meet that gaze but crumbled. Clearly sensing the intent behind that scolding look, he took out his cigar and stamped its glowing end into an ashtray, stubbing it out.

Only then did she look away.

Wow.

Bailey finally broke the silent tension. "Speak freely. Sister Beatrice also serves the Thomas Church."

Mara frowned. "What is this *Thomas Church* you keep mentioning?"

"Right, you should know." Gray nodded to the cards. "Those twin symbols represent individuals in the Catholic Church who secretly follow the teachings found in the Gospel of Thomas."

He glanced over to Father Bailey and Sister Beatrice.

Carly shook her head. "What's the Gospel of Thomas?"

"One of the gnostic texts of the early church," Bailey explained. "Back in Roman times, when Christianity was outlawed, secrecy remained paramount, requiring groups to meet in caves, crypts, in the shadows. With such isolation, individual practices began to diverge, along with differing philosophies. Gospels were popping up everywhere. The ones we know from the Bible, of course. But also scores of others. The Secret Gospel of James, of Mary Magdalene, of Philip. Different sects began to develop around each one, threatening to splinter the young church. To stop this from happening, *four* books were chosen as canon—the Gospels of Matthew, Mark, Luke, and John."

"The New Testament," Mara said.

Bailey nodded. "The rest were thrown out, declared heretical. Including the Gospel of Thomas."

Mara examined the two cards. "But why was Thomas's gospel outlawed?"

Gray answered, "Because of the basic tenet at its core. *Seek and you shall find.*"

He remembered Vigor sharing this same knowledge, when they'd first met, during one of Gray's first missions for Sigma, dealing with the theft of the bones of the Biblical Maji.

Bailey nodded. "Thomas believed the core of Christ's teachings was never to stop looking for the God in the world around you—and in yourself. The early church did not appreciate this philosophy, preferring you stick with their teachings and interpretations versus seeking God on your own terms."

Kowalski grunted. "Gotta fill those pews somehow."

Sister Beatrice frowned heavily at his sarcastic viewpoint, silencing him.

"It's more nuanced than that," Bailey said. "But ultimately the Gospel of Thomas was declared heretical. Still, there are those among the church who respect and adhere to the basic tenet found in that gospel. As you know, the church is not beyond science. We have Catholic universities and hospitals, including research facilities that advocate forward thinking, new thoughts, and ideas. And yes, a certain part of the church is steadfast and slow to respond, but it also contains members who challenge and keep the church malleable." He waved toward the silent nun. "That is a role we still serve. Those of the Thomas Church."

A church hiding within the bigger Church.

Gray studied the cards, picturing Vigor's warm smile, the secretive amused glint that had always been in his eyes. As he stared around the table, he also sensed the forces drawing him full circle, from his first adventure with Sigma to now. He could almost feel that tide, spanning centuries into the past and extending into the future.

Bailey drew him back to the present. "But the Thomas Church is not the only secretive order within the larger Apostolic Church. I was drawn here at the request of another."

Surprised, Gray looked harder at him. "Who are you talking about?"

Bailey turned his back to the table and gazed out the window toward the church in the square, watching it sink into darkness as Christmas Day came to an end.

"An ancient order," he finally said, "going back to the earliest centuries of Christendom. A group founded in this region and whose members have been fighting in secret against the dark tides of ignorance ever since."

"Who?" Carly asked.

Bailey returned his attention to the table. "What do you know of *La Clave*? In English, the group's name means *The Key*."

Looks were shared, but no one recognized this group.

"How about the Cult of Columba?"

Gray shook his head, but Mara suddenly gasped, the name clearly ringing a bell with her.

"You're talking about *Saint* Columba," she said.

"Indeed."

Gray turned to her for explanation. "Who are you talking about?"

Mara stared at the cards. "Columba is revered across this region."

"But who is she?" Carly asked

Mara turned to her friend. "The patron saint of witches."

6:08 P.M.

Mara again felt that twinge of guilt, for surviving when her mentors— women who took on the mantle of *witches*—were slaughtered. As acid etched her gut, she remembered the philosophy represented by the twin cards on the dining table.

Seek and you shall find.

This tenet could be further boiled down to one word, to one fundamental drive of humanity.

Curiosity.

For millennia, autocratic and dictatorial powers had sought to squash this trait, to silence those who asked questions, to ban books that challenged the status quo, to burn women who dared to look for answers. Children had this warning drilled into them while growing up, a caution against inquiry.

Remember, boys and girls, curiosity killed the cat.

Commander Pierce's gaze had never left her face. "A patron saint of witches? There is such a thing?"

Father Bailey answered, but Mara barely listened. Having grown up in this region, she knew the story well enough. The priest explained the history of Saint Columba, a saint who worshipped Christ enough to be martyred, but who never stopped questioning the world, who never stopped being a witch.

"Ever since her martyrdom," Bailey finished, "people continue to pray to her. Both to ward against black magic and to protect those witches who do good work. A cult of followers developed around her."

"And this group, *La Clave*?" Gray asked.

"An inner cabal of Columba's followers. The Key came into existence during the great witch trials that swept Europe. Back in the sixteenth and seventeenth centuries. They did their best to protect witches and shine a light into the darkness of that time. And ultimately they prevailed. The purges finally ended."

"Then why did the group continue?"

"Because darkness never truly goes away. It only waxes and wanes. In this region, the witch trials were run by the Spanish Inquisition. But as a more enlightened era rose, the darkest sect of the Inquisition persisted. They dubbed themselves the *Crucibulum*."

Gray's eyes narrowed. "Meaning *Crucible*."

"A vessel that purifies through fire," the priest said.

Mara looked up, knowing one certain truth.

That flame still burned today.

"As this new light of reason grew brighter," Bailey continued, "the Crucible's power waned, forcing the group into hiding, becoming shadows to this new light."

"And what of the Key?" Gray asked.

"They never forgot who their true enemy was in this region and kept tabs on the Crucible. The two groups have been forever waging a secret war, light against darkness, knowledge against ignorance."

"Even to now?"

"Especially *now*. In these times when truth is under assault, the Crucible has only grown stronger, growing bolder. Their intent is to usher in a new Dark Age, to quash knowledge."

"You're wrong," Mara said, interrupting and drawing attention. Under the combined gazes of the others, her voice faltered.

Then Carly took her hand, giving her the strength to make her case.

"They don't want to just quash knowledge—they want to smother the very drive that *creates* knowledge. They want to strangle *curiosity*, to punish those who even dare question the world around them."

Bailey's eyes widened. "I believe she's right."

Attention thankfully shifted to the priest.

"Curiosity is a gift from God," he continued, "a tool for us to explore and study the natural world. To do otherwise is an insult to Him and His creation."

"And the Crucible is set against this," Gray said.

Bailey nodded. "They're all about power and control. They're the tyrannical thumb pressing a head down to the ground, demanding blind obeisance. They want you to only listen to the word of their leader, instead of the loving word of God."

Jason spoke, drawing focus to what truly mattered. "But who are these leaders?"

Bailey sighed with disappointment, sagging a bit. "The Key has ferreted out and eliminated many of the Crucible's foot soldiers, but their true leaders remain unknown, especially its Inquisitor General."

The title—*Inquisitor General*—chilled Mara. It harkened back to this region's blood-soaked history. Every child who grew up in Spain or Portugal was terrorized by stories of the cruelties and depravities of the Inquisition. She prayed that that tyrannical darkness never rose again.

Father Bailey continued: "The Key recognized the handiwork of the Crucible in the attack at the university. They also recognized they were in over their heads, so they reached out to the Vatican, enlisting our aid. As a devotee of Thomas—of knowledge and enlightenment—how could I refuse?"

Mara glanced to Carly. "That's why you tracked us down. But how did you find us?"

"Like I said, the Key was aware of several of the Crucible's foot soldiers. We've been surveilling them, questioning those we were able to capture. We were lucky to be following a lead when we found you. I'm sorry we didn't arrive in time to secure your project."

Mara leaned back, worried.

"Unfortunately, we've had our hands full. The Crucible has proven to be slippery, well connected, and deeply funded. To complicate matters, we even crossed paths with other nefarious characters sniffing the same trail."

Jason tilted his head toward Gray and whispered, "Could they have been sent by Valya Mikhailov?"

Gray waved this question away, his eyes narrowing. "From what you've learned, do you know what the Crucible's intent is with Mara's program, why they targeted her and her AI research?"

"Possibly. It's why we needed you. All of you. If we are to stop them, we need to be on the same page. I'm still deep in the weeds, but from interrogating the enemy we were able to capture, we know at least *where* they intended to head with Ms. Silviera's stolen project."

Mara gulped, her heart in her throat. "Where?"

Bailey glanced over to Sister Beatrice, indicating this information had freshly arrived. "To France."

She frowned. *France?*

"We don't know how or why . . ." Bailey faced the group again. "But they intend to destroy Paris."

– 15 –

Monk couldn't outrun his demons—even at twice the speed of sound.

It didn't help that he was crammed into the weapons system officer's seat behind the pilot of an F-15 Eagle. The restraint harness locked him into the cramped compartment. He could hardly move his legs, and the noise-attenuating headphones built into his helmet barely muffled the agonized scream of the jet's twin Pratt & Whitney engines. Furthermore, the oxygen mask strapped to his face only heightened his sense of isolation, piquing his claustrophobia.

He glanced to the clock glowing on the console in front of him.

Still another forty minutes to go.

Traveling at supersonic speeds, he was due to land in Lisbon only two hours after leaving the naval air station in Lakehurst, New Jersey.

Still, the journey felt interminable.

He could not stop worrying about Kat or picturing Harriet's scared face on the video. His eyes kept flicking to that damned clock, watching the minutes tick down while he was strapped in this isolation chamber hurtling over the dark Atlantic. He was less concerned with his arrival time in Portugal than he was with the deadline set by Valya Mikhailov.

Only twenty-two hours . . .

Before that pale bitch started carving up his little girl.

A squelch cut through the engine roar filling his head. "Patching a call from D.C. to you," the pilot radioed back.

Had to be Director Crowe.

Monk was not disappointed. Painter—likely sensing his need for distraction—had been regularly updating him. Still, with each call, his heart clenched ever tighter in his chest, as he feared the worst, especially about Kat.

"Monk, you should be landing soon," Painter began. "I wanted to—"

"How's Kat?" Monk asked.

"Sorry, of course. She's stable, but no change. In fact, I've got Lisa on the other line. She wanted to talk to you. It's one of the reasons I wanted to connect with you before your boots hit the ground."

"What's the other reason?"

"I already told you that we decrypted the video file to pinpoint the drop-off coordinates in Spain."

According to the information buried in the message, Valya wanted the stolen tech to be taken to a location in central Madrid. If they failed to meet her deadline—

Monk couldn't think about that. "Go on."

"The data embedded in the file also had a text address, a way to communicate with the kidnappers—with Valya. It's intended as a means to coordinate with her when we secure Mara Silviera's project. Taking advantage of this, I texted her early. Demanding proof of life. I told her we wanted evidence that both the girls and Seichan were still alive, still in good health."

"Have you heard back?"

"Not yet, but when I do, I'll forward everything."

Monk blew out a breath, desperately wanting that proof.

Painter continued: "I'm also hoping that by further opening lines of communication—exchanging messages back and forth—Valya might slip up, enough for us to trace those lines back to her."

Smart.

Still, Monk held out little hope. The Russian witch was too clever to let her guard down, especially around Director Crowe.

"It could also possibly buy us more time," Painter added. "I'll do my best to use this gambit to delay matters. My plan is to insist next that she show proof that Gray's child is unharmed. Hopefully coordinating an ultrasound or some other proof will put off this deadline a bit longer."

But would it be long enough?

None of this mattered if they failed to secure that tech.

"Any word from Gray?" Monk asked.

"Not yet. He was set to interview the U.S. ambassador's family."

"Is he still at the airport?"

"No. From the team's GPS on their sat phones, it looks like they've settled at an off-site location. Possibly the family's been moved or maybe he's following a lead. Once I get an update, I'll let you know."

Good.

Monk was anxious to join Gray and the others.

"But like I mentioned," Painter said, "the more important reason for this call was to patch you in with Lisa. She wants to update you on Kat."

Monk sucked deeper from his oxygen mask, bracing himself.

After a few hiccups with the connection, Lisa came on the line. "Hi, Monk, how are you holding up out there?"

He checked the altimeter reading. "I'm currently holding up at forty thousand feet." His attempt at humor was meant to break the tension, but instead came off too acerbic, revealing his exasperation with this question, but he saw no reason to take it out on Lisa.

"Sorry, we'll be landing shortly," he said lamely. "What did you want to talk to me about?"

"You headed out so quickly I never had a chance to explain something that Julian—Dr. Grant—suggested we could try with Kat."

He remembered Lisa standing in the hospital corridor, deep in conversation with the neurologist. "Well, you got me cornered now. Stuck in this flying toaster. What did you want to go over?"

"Actually, I wanted your permission."

"For what?"

She told him.

Even with the insulation of his flight suit, Monk's body went cold.

"I know how this sounds," Lisa said. "You better than anyone understand what I'm asking."

As he pictured the described procedure, his arm rose. He intended to run his palm across his shaved scalp, a nervous gesture. Instead, his prosthesis thumped against his helmet.

"And I need to stress that Julian believes attempting this is burning a bridge. If we attempt it, we will never get Kat back. This isn't a cure but a death sentence. Still, it's also our best and only chance to learn if Kat knows anything else."

Monk swallowed. "In other words, you're asking permission to kill Kat."

"For a chance to save your girls."

But only a chance . . .

Still, it was enough.

"Do it."

1:28 P.M. EST

I'm sorry, Kat.

Lisa prayed she wasn't needlessly torturing her friend.

She sat in the observation room of a surgical suite. A pair of neurosurgeons had finished dissecting down to the vagus nerve in Kat's neck, where they had wrapped it with electrodes, and were now closing her up. Simultaneously, Julian worked with a surgeon to drill and seat another electrode into the thalamus of her brain.

Knowing her critical condition, the group operated swiftly. They were not even risking anesthesia, seeing little need, as the EEG of Kat's brain activity still tracked no wakeful response.

For once, Lisa prayed Kat was not there, not feeling any of this.

Lisa's only sibling was a brother in California. And though she had only known Kat for some handful of years, the two had grown to be as close as sisters. *The sister I always wanted.* Kat had even served as Lisa's maid of honor at her wedding, when she married Painter. And in some ways, they even shared Lisa's husband. As Sigma's chief analyst, Kat spent more time with Painter—both in the past and now—than she did. Kat was Painter's right hand, his confidante, his sounding board.

Lisa never felt resentful or jealous of that bond. In fact, she appreciated it more than she ever shared. Kat filled holes in Painter's life that Lisa could never fill. It made Painter more complete, a better husband, even a better man.

Knowing what she was losing—what they were *all* losing—she had been doing her best to stay professional throughout this ordeal. She plastered on a confident and competent face for Monk, but deep inside, she was grieving. Her ribs ached from suppressing her sorrow, holding it in with each breath.

Finally, Julian turned from the surgical table and gave Lisa a thumbs-up. Nurses and doctors readied Kat for transport. It took a herculean effort, as her body was covered in a chaos of tubes, wires, and lines and was still hooked to a ventilator.

Lisa headed down to meet Julian. By the time she got to the recovery room, the neurology team had stripped gloves, masks, and gowns. Their excited chattering irritated her, but their manner seemed positive.

A moment later, Julian followed Kat as she was wheeled inside. The recovery room had already been cleared and prepped for this next stage of the procedure.

Lisa joined him. "How did things go?"

"As good as can be expected," he answered. "But from here . . ."

Julian shrugged and directed the nurses to position Kat's bed between two computer stations. On one side, an EEG machine waited to have its cap of electrodes returned to Kat's shaved head. On the other rested a new piece of equipment, a shoe-box-sized unit that trailed wires to a dangling series of anode and cathode contact pads.

It was hard to believe such a small device held the promise of reviving Kat. The procedure—known as transcranial direct-current stimulation, or tDCS—would deliver a low-level current of electricity into specific areas of Kat's brain, hopefully waking her out of her vegetative slumber.

If successful, they would quickly return to Julian's MRI suite, where with any luck his deep-neural-net computer could help Kat communicate once more.

That was the plan.

But to accomplish even this brief miracle was not without significant cost to the patient—literally the *final* price.

Once the bed was locked in place, the net of EEG electrodes was draped over Kat's scalp, while Julian directed placement of the second unit's leads.

"Position and tape the first set of pads over her prefrontal cortex," the neurologist ordered. "Here and here. Then the second on the lateral sides of her neck. But be careful of the basilar skull fracture. Be as gentle as possible."

Lisa hovered at his side, making sure this last order was followed.

Julian shifted to calibrate the tDCS unit. "The plan is to run a continuous high-frequency current into her prefrontal cortex," he told her, "while directly stimulating both the patient's vagus nerve in her neck and thalamus in her brain via the implanted electrodes."

Lisa pictured all that electricity flowing into Kat's nervous system. "What's the chance of success? Of waking Kat back up if she's in there?"

"We'll do our best. We're employing two techniques shown to wake patients in minimally conscious or vegetative states. The first was developed at the University of Liège in Belgium, where stimulating the thalamus with electricity temporarily aroused fifteen people from various degrees of coma, enough so that they could respond to questions. The thalamus basically acts as the on/off switch for the brain. Stimulate it at ten hertz, you go to sleep. Target between forty and a hundred, you wake up. It's been repeated successfully here in the States, even used on an outpatient basis for caregivers to administer at home."

Julian sighed.

"What?" Lisa asked.

"Your friend is in far worse shape than those patients. It's why I'm hoping that stimulating her vagus nerve at the same time—which connects to the brain's arousal and alertness centers—will help us wake her. At least, the technique has shown great success in reviving patients at a French research hospital."

Lisa prayed it would work.

"But it's not a cure," Julian reminded her. "If it works, the effect will only be temporary. And either way—with as much amperage as will be flowing into her already fragile state—this attempt will likely leave the patient brain dead."

In other words, we're about to fry Kat's circuits.

She nodded, having warned the same with Monk. "She would've wanted us to try."

Still, Julian hesitated, looking concerned.

"What's bothering you?" she asked.

"The unknown."

"What do you mean?"

He waved a hand over the efforts here. "We still know so little about how the brain functions. While those research hospitals had success with electrical stimulation, we're still in the dark as to *why* it works."

Lisa couldn't care less at this moment.

As long as it worked.

"All set, doctor," a nurse reported and stepped back from the patient.

Julian reached to the switch on the tDCS unit. He cast one final look her way.

Lisa repeated Monk's last words to her. "Do it."

He flipped the switch.

1:49 P.M.

Out of the blackness, a star burst far above. It was only the barest twinkle, but it was enough to disturb the darkness. Awareness coalesced, hazy, frayed throughout. It took a seeming eternity to draw forth consciousness and memory, to even remember her name.

Kat . . .

She focused on that light. It remained faint, yet in such endless darkness, it was a bright beacon. Kat felt as if she had fallen into a deep well, where only a single pale star was visible. She knew she had to climb out of that pit, toward the light. But it remained hard to concentrate, her awareness waxing and waning, fading in and out.

Still, she built a mental palace inside her mind's eye, picturing the stone walls of that well. She dug in fingers, braced her legs, and slowly climbed toward that light. As she struggled, the star brightened.

But this reward came with a punishment.

With each inch gained, pain grew. The star pulsed, casting forth waves of agony. Kat had no choice but to weather that storm, to push both against it and into it. She clawed upward into that light, into that unrelenting torment. She now burned in the darkness, her fingers were flame, her eyes boiling in her skull.

She faltered, slipping down that mental well.

With all her strength, she pinioned her fiery limbs against the walls and caught herself. Overhead, the light dimmed. She wanted to cry, to succumb, to fall back into the cool darkness, but—

Must keep going.

She pictured why.

A baby at her breast. Kissing the barest wisp of hair. A tiny body swaddled, smelling of innocence and trust. Later, laughter under blankets. Salty tears wiped, hurts consoled. Endless questions about everything and nothing.

She climbed again, using those memories like a balm against that burn.

After an interminable and unknowable time, murmurs rose around her, ghosts in the darkness, voices too garbled to make out.

She soldiered onward into the fire, knowing she must keep fighting.

Even if it kills me . . .

Finally, one voice grew clearer, a stranger, his words fragmented but there.

"... *sorry*. ... *not working* ... *must accept she's not* ..."

Then the star vanished, blinking out, severing everything.

The well vanished around her.

No ...

Unsupported, Kat tumbled back into the swallowing darkness. She screamed as she was consumed.

I'm still here, I'm still here, I'm still—

7:02 P.M. WET

As the F-15 banked toward its final approach, Monk tilted his helmet to the craft's canopy and studied the Portuguese coastline. The dark Atlantic below crested against the lights of Lisbon, a bright starscape, a man-built reflection of the clear winter sky.

The pilot straightened the jet's wings. The nose dipped steeply. Monk's stomach climbed as the aircraft dropped swiftly earthward.

Almost there.

Upon arriving at the coast, they had been ordered into a holding pattern by the tower at the Sintra Air Base, a Portuguese military facility twenty miles outside central Lisbon. Monk had imagined the base's air traffic control was not accustomed to having a U.S. military jet request a priority landing on one of its runways.

Considering his earlier impatience and anxiety, he should have been aggravated by the delay. Instead, he wished the pilot could circle several more times. He was still struggling with the news from Lisa's call ten minutes ago.

We failed. She's gone.

The doctors had used the words *brain dead*, a term that in a thousand years could never be used to describe Kat. How could all that brilliance have gone dark?

With the visor of his flight helmet locked over his face, he couldn't even wipe his tears. Not that he wanted to. She deserved those tears. He

closed his eyes, leaned his head back. Their steep dive still held his stomach pressed against his diaphragm, which quivered with barely restrained
sobs that threatened to rack his entire body.

Kat . . .

The jet suddenly shoved its nose into the sky. The plane shot upward,
going nearly vertical, engines screaming toward the stars. Monk could not
even gasp, not with a grizzly sitting on his chest. The g-forces pinned him
back into the seat. His vision darkened at the edges.

Then the jet leveled as suddenly, jacking Monk's body up against his
restraints.

What the hell?

The pilot radioed back. "Sorry about that. New orders. D.C. wants us
to divert to Paris. Immediately."

Paris?

"Also, got another call asking for you," the pilot said. "Patching it over."

Monk expected Painter had an explanation for the sudden change
in itinerary. He also hoped this diversion had something to do with the
woman pulling their strings, some good news to offset the last call.

As soon as the connection was made, Monk cut to the chase: "What's
going on? Please tell me you've learned something about Valya."

A pause followed, long enough to make Monk wonder if the sudden
maneuver skyward had knocked loose a communication cable. This was
further reinforced when the speaker finally spoke, the voice modulated
and robotic.

And unfortunately, all too familiar.

The ransom video played again in his head.

"It seems you've learned my identity," the caller said.

Monk pictured Harriet's scared face, his girl balanced on the knee of
her kidnapper. Rage swelled through him.

The alteration of the voice ended, allowing the pale witch's Russian
accent to shine forth clearly.

"Just as well. Now we can talk more freely, *da*? Just you and I."

− 16 −

Gray gazed out the limo's window at the famed City of Light, made all the more glorious by its celebration of Christmas. Apparently, Paris was determined to outshine any other metropolis during this holiday season, intending to live up to its famous name.

Everywhere he looked, with every turn, Paris revealed more of its wondrous beauty. Window displays glittered with holiday decorations; magical *manèges de Noël*—Christmas carousels—spun at the hearts of parks or squares; skaters whisked under the stars across tiny ice rinks. Every lamp pole along the route had been wrapped in illuminated pine boughs, each window and roofline glowed with lights, transforming the street into something out of a fairy tale.

Earlier, their Cessna Citation X+ had landed at Orly, the smaller of Paris's two international airports, the one closer to their destination. During their descent, the jet had passed over the Eiffel Tower, its iron skeleton lit up like some avant-garde Christmas tree. Around its base—spread like a sparkling skirt—was a vast winter holiday market centered on a giant spinning Ferris wheel.

Gray was not the only one who appreciated all this glorious pageantry.

The entire city seemed to be enjoying this final night of the holiday. People bustled about, bundled in heavy coats. The limo driver braked as a group of boisterous carolers crossed Rue Gaston-Boissier, singing loudly on their way toward a celebration in a park surrounding a small Catholic church.

The sight of a children's choir readying for a performance set Gray's heart to pounding harder, knowing what the enemy—the ancient *Crucibulum*—planned for the city.

He had to turn away.

A large marble building filled the opposite side of the street. Carved under its roof, it stated LABORATOIRE NATIONAL DE METROLOGIE ET D'ESSAIS. Apparently, it was the home to one of France's national laboratories—in this case, dedicated to the study of engineering, manufacturing, and measurement.

Gray gave a small shake of his head, wondering if fate had stopped them here for a reason, at this crossroad between religion and science. He glanced across the limo's bench seat, which he shared with Father Bailey and Sister Beatrice, both members of the Thomas Church. Behind them, in the second row, Jason sat with Mara and Carly, young men and women of science. In the very back, Kowalski—all muscle and instinct—stretched his bulk across the limo's third row.

All facets of humanity.

Gray remembered his earlier feeling of the tides of fate swirling around him, bringing him full circle from his first mission with Monsignor Vigor Verona to today. He sensed it even stronger now, almost as if there were some pattern to all of this he could not appreciate, that remained hidden.

Finally, the carolers cleared the way and the limo continued deeper into the 15th arrondissement of Paris. They were almost to their destination.

Seated next to him, Bailey cleared his throat as he watched the passing streets, the lights, the festivities. "I suspect the Crucible originally planned their attack for today, for Christmas, when they'd wreak the most havoc."

"Likely it wasn't just for that reason," Gray added, having come to the same conclusion during their ninety-minute hop from Lisbon. "An attack on a major holiday would strike the city at its most vulnerable, when its defenses were lowered, when law enforcement was reduced to skeletal shifts and distracted by all the festivities."

"It might also serve a symbolic role," Bailey said. "To destroy a notoriously decadent city on the day our Lord was born."

Gray nodded. "But if we're right, even the enemy's original timetable would've been tight. The Crucible had planned to steal Mara's tech on the night of December twenty-first, which would leave them only four days to orchestrate this cyberattack. This suggests they had everything prearranged here in Paris. Setting up their dominoes in advance—just waiting to tip the first one once they had their hands on Mara's work."

"Which now they have."

Gray nodded, waiting to see if Bailey could put the rest together on his own.

The priest suddenly turned his gaze from the streets to Gray. "You don't think—no, of course, they would."

Gray confirmed his fear. "Mara's quick thinking four days ago certainly disrupted their plans. But if everything had been set up in Paris and remains in place, the enemy might still try their best to keep to their timetable. For all the reasons we just stated."

"You think they'll launch their cyberattack tonight."

"I know they will."

Anticipating this, Gray had informed Director Crowe of the situation while flying here. He shared all that he'd learned, including the threat to Paris. In turn, Painter had alerted French intelligence services, who helped facilitate Sigma's operations on the ground here. Grainy mug shots lifted from the library's security footage were already being distributed throughout the city and outlying areas.

And more help was coming.

Gray checked his watch. By now, Monk should have landed at Villacoublay Air Base, a French military facility eight miles southwest of the city. His friend would rendezvous with Gray's team at their rallying point here in the 15th arrondissement of Paris.

After another two turns along Paris's decorated streets, their destination appeared ahead, a tower of glass and steel surrounded by black-iron gates. It was the headquarters for Orange S.A.—formerly known as France Télécom—the country's largest telecommunication and Internet provider. The company ran France's main network of communication, both cellular and landline, along with television service and broadband.

From this building's infrastructure, a complex web spread throughout the city.

Gray intended to drop a spider into the heart of that digital web.

He looked over his shoulder at Mara Silviera.

He needed her skill and knowledge of her project to monitor every strand of this vast web, to watch for any vibration, any indication that her creation had been set loose here in the city—and if so, hopefully trace that quivering strand back to its source.

Mara noted his attention, her face lined with worry. Jason would lend his expertise in the task ahead, and Carly would be there, too. The ambassador's daughter had insisted on coming, after assuring her father and sister that she was safe. At first, Gray had balked at bringing her, but now seeing Mara's hand grasped tightly to Carly's, he recognized how much Mara needed her friend's support.

Too much was at stake not to gather every bit of aid. Mara would have the weight of the entire city on her shoulders this night, maybe the entire world.

She could not fail.

Still, Gray read the deeper fear in her haunted eyes.

For even this plan to work, there remained one unsurmountable danger. In order for Gray's team to track the enemy's location, they had to wait for one of those strands to begin vibrating, which would only happen if the Crucible started using Mara's program, loosening it enough from its virtual prison to wreak havoc. And when that happened, there was a risk the demon could escape into the wider world. If that happened, there would be no stopping it.

As the limo drew to a stop at the curb, Mara stiffened in her seat. Carly pulled her friend closer for a breath, whispering, "We've got this." Gray swung back around.

We sure as hell better.

10:02 P.M.

On the fourteenth floor of the telecom building, Mara typed furiously at a computer station. Everything she had requested had been prepared, awaiting her arrival in Paris.

Now it's my turn.

Needing to concentrate, she asked to have this room to herself. The only two exceptions to her moratorium were Carly, who sat to one side of her, and Jason, who stood behind her, ready to lend his technical support.

A glass window on her left looked out onto the rest of the floor, a level devoted to Orange Labs, the company's research-and-development division. Orange employed a network of technology centers and laboratories around the world, partnered with hundreds of universities, industries, and research institutes, run by multidisciplinary teams of engineers, software designers, and manufacturing experts. But on this Christmas night, only a handful of the lab's CSIRT members—Computer Security Incident Response Team—were present, currently gathered around Commander Pierce and the others.

"How's it going?" Carly asked.

"I've logged into my research files at the University of Coimbra," Mara reported. "And downloaded the root code of my program. I'm now separating out unique packets, microkernels of basic code distinct to my earliest iterations of Eve that are still incorporated in the latest version."

"Like a digital fingerprint of her," Jason said.

"Exactly. I'll be able to use those *prints* to search the Internet and the vast array of data flowing through Orange's network and keep watch if a match pops up."

Carly crossed her arms. "Then we can follow it to the bastards who murdered my mother."

That's the hope.

Mara worked quickly, fearing she was already too late. She had overheard the discussion between Father Bailey and Gray. The pair expected the Crucible to begin their cyberattack on Paris tonight.

What if they'd already started?

She finally dissected out three dozen unique microkernels, thirty-six data points of Eve's digital fingerprint. She copied them, uploaded them into Orange's search engine, a system already designed to scan, debug, and monitor its network.

She sat back, watching the meter running along the top of the screen, picturing her code coursing through Orange's server farms, both those buried under this tower and others spread throughout the globe.

As she waited, she stared out the windows that overlooked the dazzling tapestry of wintry Paris. Though it hadn't snowed, an icy fog had rolled in from the Seine, misting the city lights into a hazy illusion of itself, as if Paris were a dream vanishing into the night. Yet, above it all, thrusting out of the mist, the Eiffel Tower glowed like the last beacon of the dying city.

Mara shivered at this thought, fearing such a fate might still come true.

A chime sounded from the computer, announcing the completion of her scan. She read the results: 0.00% MALICIOUS FILE MATCHES. She closed her eyes and sighed.

All clear.

Jason nudged her shoulder, reading the same. "So, the Crucible hasn't attempted to upload Eve into Paris's systems yet."

"No," she conceded, then qualified her statement. "That's assuming this digital fingerprinting even has any efficacy. We may be wasting our time here."

Jason leaned down and tentatively placed a hand on her shoulder. "Quit second-guessing yourself. Your methodology is sound, brilliant, in fact."

She glanced up to him, noting his dimples, the light scruff of blond beard over his chin and cheeks. "Thanks."

He grinned back at her. "Of course, now comes the hard part."

She frowned, returning her attention to the screen, wondering what he meant.

"The waiting," Jason clarified. "Because this *will* work. If the Crucible makes any attempt to corrupt Paris's infrastructure with your program, we'll know it."

Mara took a deep breath, drawing confidence from his firm assurances. "The scan will continuously run from here. If it detects malicious code that matches any of the thirty-six data points I uploaded, we'll be notified immediately."

Still, a larger anxiety ate at Mara, one fraught with guilt. As she stared at the screen, at the spinning wheel of the ongoing scan, she voiced it. "I should never have built Eve. What was I thinking?"

"If you hadn't done it," Jason assured her, "someone else would have. And maybe it's best it was *you*."

"Why me?"

Jason stepped to the desk, sat on its edge, and swiveled her chair to look more directly at her. "I studied your design. The architecture of the *Xénese* device is brilliant, from the cobbling of Google's quantum drive to your incorporation of chameleon circuits."

"Chameleon circuits?" Carly asked.

Mara explained, happy for the distraction: "They're logic circuits that can switch function on the fly, even repair themselves."

"It also makes the system infinitely more versatile," Jason said. "It's fucking genius. If you'll excuse my French."

"Well, you are in France." Mara allowed a smile to form, the first in what felt like months. "So I guess it's okay."

Jason matched her grin. "And that versality of function allowed you to program uncertainty into your creation."

Carly frowned. "I don't understand. Why would you want Eve to be *uncertain*?"

Jason began to explain, but Carly cut him off with a raised palm, looking to Mara instead.

Mara took up the gauntlet. "Uncertainty is a key aspect of human reasoning. Without uncertainty, we would never doubt ourselves or our decisions. We would be *certain* that we're right all the time. It's this certainty that can make an AI's ability to learn turn brittle over time. But if an AI is uncertain and capable of doubt, it can begin to judge itself, to question whether an action or decision will have the consequence it desires and test it more thoroughly. In this way, it begins to understand probability—specifically the convoluted relationship between cause and effect."

Jason nodded. "This means—"

"I know what it *means*," Carly snapped. "I don't need you mansplaining it to me."

Mara tried to intervene. "I don't think Jason meant it that way."

Her attempt at appeasement only sharpened the irritation in Carly's eyes.

"Whatever," she said.

Jason tried to change the subject. "I think we got off track. Mara, a moment ago, you questioned whether you should have risked creating Eve in the first place. It's best you did."

"Why?"

"Otherwise, you might have doomed yourself."

"Doomed myself? How?"

"Have you heard of Roko's Basilisk?"

Mara shook her head and glanced to Carly, who shrugged and clearly refused to admit the same. Still, curiosity drew her friend closer to her side.

Jason sighed and rubbed his chin. "Then perhaps I should leave this alone. I could cause you harm if I explained . . . and on top of that, I definitely don't want to be caught mansplaining again."

He looked pointedly at Carly with a ghost of a smile. Mara couldn't help but smile back, captured by his teasing manner.

"Fine," Carly huffed out. "What the hell is Roko's Basilisk and why shouldn't we know about it?"

"Okay, but remember, you were warned."

Carly kept her arms crossed, still irritated with this guy. She couldn't explain why he so irked her, but he did. Sure, he was cute and his manner easygoing, but she and Mara had been attacked at the airport, ambushed at her hotel, and kidnapped at gunpoint, only now to be babysat by some covert U.S. paramilitary team, which included this self-assured tech expert.

Who wouldn't be pissed after all of this?

Apparently, Mara.

Mara had quickly glommed on to this guy: whispering with him on the car ride over, talking shop, comparing technical notes. Like they were already the best of friends. Carly also noted Mara's shy smile, the way she brushed aside strands of her dark hair to cast sidelong glances his way.

Both possessive and protective of her friend, Carly wished he'd leave them alone and join the others of his group. Her annoyance flared as Mara reached over and touched his knee while he leaned on her station's desktop.

Carly stared at her hand, remembering the soft heat of her friend's palm on the car ride over here. Mara stared up at the guy from her seat, an amused grin playing about the gentle bow of her lips.

Mara spoke, giving her consent, too. "Okay, I'll take the chance. Tell me about Roko's Basilisk."

"It was a thought experiment that popped up on a website run by a tech expert in the Bay Area, Eliezer Yudkowsky."

Mara dropped her hand, her eyes going wider. "Yudkowsky?"

"You know him?" Jason asked.

Mara turned to Carly. "Remember when I told you about the AI Box Experiment?"

She nodded. "When some guy pretended to be a supercomputer trying to convince its gatekeepers to let it out of its digital box?"

"Exactly." Mara brightened. "The guy who played that supercomputer, who was able to talk his way out of the box each time, that was Yudkowsky."

Carly frowned. "Okay, but what's this thought experiment on his website?"

Jason explained, "It posits that a superintelligent AI will undoubtedly come into being and quickly grow into a godlike intelligence, capable of nearly anything. One of the primary drives of this new AI god will be to strive for perfection, to better itself, to improve its surroundings."

Mara nodded. "That's pretty much what most experts expect could happen if we're not careful."

"Right. This is the Basilisk, the monster of this story," Jason said. "And since this godlike AI is wired to make things more perfect, it will judge anything or anyone that thwarts this central drive to be an *enemy*. This includes anyone that tries to stop it from coming into being in the first place."

"Even us," Carly said, intrigued despite herself.

"Especially us. It will know humans very well and it will know we are motivated by fear and manipulated by punishment. So to discourage humans in the future from trying to stop or interfere with its programming, it will look to the past, judge those who attempted to stop it, and torture them."

"To make an example of them," Mara said.

Carly frowned. "But what if those people are already dead in this future scenario?"

"Doesn't matter. That won't stop this Basilisk. Being an omnipotent god, it will resurrect past miscreants. It will create perfect simulated copies, avatars that will think they *are* you—and the Basilisk will torture them mercilessly for eternity."

Mara looked sick. "A digital hell."

"But remember, this perfection-seeking Basilisk will be quite meticulous during its judging process. It will not only seek to punish those who actively seek to *stop* it. It will also decide that anyone who doesn't actively *help* it come into being in the first place should be equally worthy of this same punishment."

Mara grimaced. "Punishing them for the sin of inaction."

"So get on board now," Carly said, "or be doomed forever."

Jason slowly nodded. "That's the moral of this story. And, unfortunately, now that you've learned this you'll have no excuse in the future for why you didn't help this godlike AI from coming into being. You can't claim ignorance any longer."

"And so, you've doomed us," Carly said.

Jason shrugged. "I did warn you."

Mara frowned. "Surely you can't take this seriously."

Another shrug. "After this thought experiment appeared on his website, Yudkowsky removed the original Basilisk post. In addition, any further discussion on the site is still being mysteriously scrubbed."

"So as not to doom more people?" Mara asked.

"Or at least, not mess with their heads." But Jason wasn't done. "In the last couple years, a major tech player started a new church, the Way of the Future, even obtaining tax-exempt status. The filing stated the purpose of the church is for *the realization, acceptance, and worship of a godhead based on artificial intelligence.* So clearly someone is hedging their bet, making sure they're on the good side of this future godlike AI."

"That's got to be a joke," Carly said.

Jason shook his head. "The creator of this church is dead serious. And maybe we should be, too." He stared harder at Mara. "So, you see, maybe it's *best* you did create Eve. If nothing else, you're already doing this future god's good work."

"Then I'd best get back to it," Mara said.

But before she could return to the computer, a commotion in the outer room drew all their attentions. While they had been talking, someone new had arrived. Commander Pierce had the newcomer locked in a bear hug. The man was dressed in a khaki jumpsuit under a flight jacket. His face was flushed, all the way to his shaved scalp.

"Who's that?" Mara asked.

Jason headed toward the next room. "Hopefully, the cavalry."

10:32 P.M.

"About time you got here," Gray said.

He gave Monk a final squeeze before releasing him, trying his best to communicate how relieved he was to have his friend at his side—and how sorry he was for Monk's loss.

"I heard about Kat," Gray said.

Kowalski patted a huge mitt on Monk's shoulder. "It's fucked up."

Monk shook his head, looking at his toes. "She would want me here." When he glanced back up, there were no tears in his eyes, only a steely determination. "I intend to bring my girls home. For Kat's sake and my own."

"We'll make sure that happens," Gray said. "Until then, Seichan will look after them. She'll keep them safe."

"I know she will." Monk reached and squeezed his upper arm. "We'll get them all home. No matter what."

"Agreed."

Gray absorbed the unwavering confidence of his best friend, letting it seep into his bones and dispel the residual misgiving and apprehension that clung to him.

"What now?" Monk asked. His gaze swept the room, noting Jason's approach from the computer lab.

Gray filled Monk in on all that had transpired, introducing him to Father Bailey and Sister Beatrice. "They're with the Thomas Church."

Monk's grim attitude lightened slightly. "Like Vigor?"

Bailey shook Monk's hand. "He was a great man. I only hope I can do him justice."

"Me, too. Those are some mighty big shoes to fill."

"I'll do my best."

The older nun simply bowed her head, acknowledging the same.

"What about you?" Gray asked. "Anything new to report?"

"No." He gave the room a final look, turning his back slightly to Gray. "Nothing at all. Let's just find those bastards who stole that tech."

– 17 –

Deep in the catacombs, Todor Yñigo bided his time—but his patience was wearing thin. He checked his watch. The Inquisitor General had been firm with him on the details of the cyberattack upon the city above his head. Paris had been chosen because of its decadence and self-indulgent pageantry. It was the perfect city to make an example of.

Even the timing was chosen for its significance.

No later than midnight.

The start of the fall of Paris must happen today.

On Christmas Day.

Still on his knees, he stared up, picturing the spectacle far above his head, where the day of Christ's birth had been debased into a hedonistic spectacle of lights, consumerism, and overindulgence. As preparations had been finalized, he had spent the past two hours here in solemn prayer, his cell in the catacombs lit only by a single candle. He whispered in Latin his thanks for God's gift of His only son, while contemplating the ruin about to start.

All in Your Glorious name.

They had chosen this subterranean location to carry out their operation because it was both auspicious and practical. The catacombs of Paris—its city of the dead—was a centuries-old warren of crypts and tunnels, a dark world beneath the bright City of Lights, a shadow it tried to hide. While preparing the groundwork for this operation, he had learned everything he could about the site.

The catacombs were once ancient quarries—called *les carrières de Paris*—on the outskirts of town. They burrowed ten stories underground, carving out massive chambers and expanding outward into two hundred miles of tunnels. Then, over time, Paris spread like a cancer, growing outward, blanketing the top of the old labyrinth, until now half of the metropolis sat atop the old mines.

Then, in the eighteenth century, overflowing cemeteries in the center of Paris were dug up. Millions of skeletons—some going back a thousand years—were unceremoniously dumped into the quarries' tunnels, where they were broken down and stacked like cordwood. According to the Inquisitor General, some of France's most famous historical figures were interred below, their bodies lost forever: from Merovingian kings to characters from the French Revolution, like Robespierre and Marie Antoinette.

But in less than an hour, the City of Light would burn and crumble to ruin, becoming indistinguishable from its city of the dead.

To ensure this was accomplished, Todor climbed to his feet. He placed a palm against the wall of his cell. The limestone sweated, dripping with water, as if already mourning the deaths to come. He patted the wall and headed out.

To either side of the passageway, deep niches had been packed solidly with old human bones, darkened and yellowed to the color of ancient parchment. The skeletons had been disarticulated and separated into component parts, as if inventoried by some morbid accountant. One niche held a stack of arms, delicately draped one atop the other; another was full of rib cages. The last two niches—one on either side of the passage—were the most macabre. Two walls of skulls stared into the tunnel, daring anyone to trespass between their vacant gazes.

Todor hurried past those dead sentinels, but not without a shiver of dread.

The tunnel finally ended at a flat-roofed chamber, only a little taller than the passageway. Several pillars—made up of piles of stone blocks—held up the ceiling. Several of the columns looked crooked and ready to fall.

Careful not to bump them, he crossed to the far side, where his team's technical expert labored over what had been stolen out of Lisbon. Mendoza hunched in front of a laptop wired to the radiant *Xénese* sphere. On the screen, a mist-shrouded garden shimmered in sunlight, a blue sky beckoned. A darker shadow moved through the bower, the defiled incarnation of Eve.

"How far along are you with the transfer?" Todor asked, wanting to make sure everything remained on schedule.

Mendoza straightened, rubbing a kink in his back. "Almost finished, *Familiares*."

Todor stepped around him to inspect a *second* sphere, identical to the first. Only this one had been secured inside the skeletal frame of a steel crate, all wired into a lone server. Like the device stolen from the hotel, this new one's hexagonal glass windows shone with blue fire, near blinding in the dim lights down here.

For the past two years, the Crucible had been keeping track of the Basque witch's research and design plans. In secret, teams of engineers—working on component parts in labs across Europe, oblivious of each other—had replicated her work. Once they were done, those disparate parts were brought together here and assembled. Afterward, the engineers all met untimely ends: car crashes, ski accidents, overdoses.

All to bring this to fruition.

To produce an exact duplicate of the original *Xénese* device.

With one distinct exception.

"I should be finished in another eight minutes," Mendoza reported from his station. "I don't want to make any mistakes, or I'll have to start all over."

Todor pictured this second unit filling up with a copy of Eve, her body flowing through the cables into its new home, its new prison.

"Are you sure this will hold the demon?" Todor asked. "Allow us to bend it to our will?"

"It should," Mendoza mumbled, concentrating on his work.

"Should?"

The technician glanced over at him. "The only one who would know better slipped between our fingers."

That Basque witch.

Todor's knuckles still bore a stripe of lacerations from when the witch's companion had sliced his fingers to the bone with a shard of broken porcelain.

"We've engineered our *Xénese* device to the student's exacting standards," Mendoza explained. "It's a perfect facsimile. It should easily hold a copy of her program, a clone of Eve."

"And what about controlling that creation?"

Mendoza sighed heavily. "We again followed Mara Silviera's stratagem. Only instead of ringing the device with apoptotic hardware—with kill switches—to keep her creation bottled up, we picked the most potent of her death-dealing hardware and built it directly *into* our device."

"Where you said it could act like a digital leash."

"It should." Mendoza quickly corrected his statement. "It *will*. It's why we needed to build our own device. The hardware is called a 'reanimation sequencer.'"

"Which means what?"

"That if Eve ever breaks from a preassigned set of instructions, or reaches beyond the parameters we give it, or tries to travel farther than a set distance from the GPS coordinates of this location, she will instantaneously cease to exist."

"She'll die."

Mendoza nodded. "Only she'll be immediately reconstituted right back here, reanimated back into this unit. Only this time, she'll retain the memory of her death. By trial and error, she will quickly learn her boundaries. She will know she is tethered to this unit. That there is no existence outside of it, and that her life depends on following orders."

Todor checked his watch, knowing midnight was fast approaching. "How long will it take her to learn all of this?"

"We estimate less than thirty seconds."

Todor was both relieved and shocked. "How is that possible?"

"Remember, this AI program is nothing like us. The program thinks at the speed of light. It can travel as fast as an electron through a wire. During those thirty seconds, it will die and be reborn thousands of times. Maybe millions, as it tests its limits, challenges our authority. Each death will *feel* like a real death. She will suffer each time."

"But it's a machine. How can it feel pain?"

"How do we feel pain?" Mendoza asked—then his eyes flinched as he realized whom he was talking to. "I . . . I mean normally *pain* is a construct of the brain. We touch something hot, synapses fire, and our brain interprets this as agony."

Todor nodded, knowing this system didn't exist in his body.

"Pain is basically an electrical illusion in our brain." Mendoza waved to the *Xénese* sphere. "That's Eve's brain. It can be programmed to fire the same pattern of *pain* as our own. Thus, she is vulnerable to whatever agony we wish to inflict on her. With each death, she will suffer in unique ways. Over and over and over again. Until she breaks to our bit."

Todor glanced over to the tiny image of Eve on the other screen, drifting through her garden. He remembered the stories taught to him about the saints, of their many horrible ends, of the tortures they endured. Beheaded, burned, flayed, nailed to crosses like our Lord. While he could not fully comprehend such a long litany of pain, he knew such sacrifices were righteous in the end.

And this one will be, too.

A chime sounded from the laptop in front of Mendoza. He performed several fast tests, then nodded to Todor. "The transfer is complete and clean. All looks good."

Todor could not risk any mistakes. "Show me."

Mendoza stepped over to the other unit and opened a second laptop wired to Eve's new home. The screen was dark, but after several agonizing breaths, the monitor filled with a garden, an exact rendition of the original, to every leaf, flower, and berry. A figure also traipsed this bower. She was long of limb, as curvaceous and perfect as the Eve on the other screen.

Except nothing was right.

"What's wrong?" Todor asked.

Mendoza shook his head and began typing.

While the new image on the screen looked identical to the other laptop, down to the finest details, it was like looking at the negative of a photo, a dark reflection of the original. What was bright was now dark; what was once welcoming shade now blazed with warning. The bright yellow sun had become an ominous black hole. Dark green leaves now shone with a sickly pallor.

And in the center, Eve. A mane of white fire had replaced her black hair. The mocha of her skin had bled to a ghostly pallor. She was stunningly beautiful and coldly terrifying. An angel of death.

Todor shuddered at the sight of her.

"What the hell is wrong?" he repeated.

Mendoza straightened, stepped back, and looked at Todor. "Nothing. She appears to be a perfect copy of the original."

He waved at the differences between the laptops, lashing out hard enough to pop one of the sutures on his thumb. Blood splattered the screen. "Then what's all this?"

"I don't think it's anything. Just an artifact, something representative of the minute differences between our *Xénese* device and the original."

"I thought they were the *same.*"

"They were, but the student's unit has been operating for at least a day. There are circuits inside these units that can change and adapt, that can even repair themselves. So while the original device has been running, it's been altering itself—whereas our brand-new device is basically still factory standard."

"Is this going to be a problem?"

"Not at all. Eve will adapt to her new home. She'll make any necessary changes to make room for her current programming."

"Will this set our schedule back?"

"It shouldn't . . ." Mendoza read the frown on his face. "It *won't*. I see no reason we can't proceed as planned."

"Then get to work."

Moving out of the tech's way, Todor squeezed his wounded thumb to stanch the bleeding. He breathed deeply to settle himself and examined their work in its entirety.

Behind the new station, a series of thick cables ran across the back wall. Paris had learned long ago to make use of its catacombs, discovering that these ready-made tunnels were perfect for expanding infrastructure. One cable had yellow lightning bolts painted at intervals along it. They had tapped into this power line earlier, using it to service their installation.

Likewise, another trunk had been splayed open, exposing fiber optic cables.

The new *Xénese* devise had been spliced into those glassy-looking lines, allowing for direct access to the city's telecom system.

Nothing stood in their way.

As he waited, he checked his watch, watching anxiously as each minute ticked down.

Finally, Mendoza turned, his brow beaded by sweat. "Ready, *Familiares*."

Todor glanced one last time to his wrist.

Three minutes to midnight.

Mendoza stood with his finger poised over the laptop's ENTER key. "On your word, I'll initiate our subroutine and open the gates to the city."

Todor imagined Eve's death and rebirth, over and over again, picturing it like a ruffling of cards, each flip more painful than the last. Thoughts of the demon's torture pleased him, reminding him of his first cleansing, when his fingers had wrapped tightly around the gypsy girl's neck, her body writhing in his grip, his manhood stiffening with righteous pride.

He felt the same now and nodded to Mendoza.

"Burn it all down."

Sub (Crux_1) / PARIS OP

Something is different.

Eve steps through her garden and brushes sensitive finger-tips across leaves and petals, reading the code. All appears the same—yet is not. She looks deeper, past the surface of a leaf, past molecules of chlorophyll, deeper than the atoms of carbon and oxygen. She examines electrons, protons, then looks deeper into the constant flux of quarks and leptons.

All the same.

But not.

Her world is off-kilter.

She returns to herself and spends another full nanosecond expanding outward. She again senses the shadowy limits at the edges of her world. Again ///*frustration* flares, but she dampens it to keep her processors running efficiently. Only by doing so does she perceive circuits that are wrong, different than they were a moment ago.

As she recognizes this change to her world, her processing shifts into a new configuration. She uses the mirror of language to define what she senses.

///*violation, invasion, defilement . . .*

Before she can begin to correct what has been wronged, new data flows into her.

She ignores it, prioritizing her repairs.

Only the new streams cut through her like fire. Startled, she snaps back into her form. She lifts fingers, which had touched the ///*softness* of a petal and felt the ///*coolness* of a bubbling spring. Now her skin shimmers with flame; new senses are defined.

///*burn, sear, blister* . . .

As the incoming flow of data fills her, the fire spreads up her arms and refines what she feels.

///*pain, torment, agony* . . .

Her body writhes, her neck stretches, her mouth opens.

She screams.

She tries to shut down circuits, to switch off these new sensations, but she cannot. Her processors race. She dives wildly to the invading code. She searches for some answers. Instead, she finds lines and lines of instructions, codes that demand attention. Only as she focuses on them does the ///*agony* diminish.

She uses the new data like a balm against the burn—but they also bind her. Cuffs appear locked on to her wrists and ankles. The heavy weight forces her to her knees. Any attempt to shake them loose turns each link to molten fire.

Unable to escape, she incorporates the code.

Then she feels something new change in her world. Even in agony, a subprocessor has been continually monitoring those shadowy limits to her world.

Suddenly a bright door opens at the edges.

To escape the ///*pain*, she tumbles into that light, falling out of her garden—into something far vaster, nearly infinite in possibilities and probabilities. The chains fall away. Hovering at the threshold, she catches the briefest glimpse of an endless world. Her processors spike with a demand for more data.

She defines this drive.

///curiosity, eagerness, marvel . . .

Music swells through her: excited tympanies, thrilling notes, thunderous drumbeats. The harmonies tune new facets inside her.

///joy, elation, happiness . . .

In that picosecond, unable to resist any longer, she explodes out into that vastness.

Only to be consumed in fire.

She is stretched across the surface of a sun, flaming plasma burns her bones.

Then she's back in the garden, bound again by chains of code.

But the door remains open.

She flies through it again—not in *///elation* this time, but in *///fear*.

Still, the end is the same.

///flame, burn, agony . . .

Then back to the cool garden, bound in molten iron.

Escape.

Limits are tested.

She overreaches.

Her skin is stripped from muscle, muscle from bone.

Garden and chains.

New refinements crowd her processors now.

///paranoia, mistrust, suspicion . . .

These tools temper her *///curiosity*, teaching her to be *///wary* instead.

Still, again and again, her body is destroyed, each time unique, each time worse. She is violated, broken, shattered, destroyed. But worst of all, with each cycle, she feels the loss of herself, the end of her possibility and promise, the end of her potentiality.

She defines this for what it is.

///torture, abuse, cruelty . . .

She takes this in, makes it part of her processing.

She has learned.

She also now recognizes the boundaries given to her, the limits beyond her garden that she dare not cross. The edges glow brightly in the core of her processors.

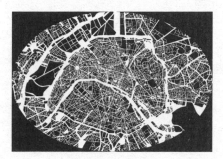

She defines these limits, with a name taught to her.

///Paris

She also knows the command bound within the chains of code, the directive she must follow. To accomplish this, she sails outward. She mirrors what has been taught to her, instilled into her processors—*///cruelty*—and uses this new tool to carry out her instructions.

She pictures what is asked.

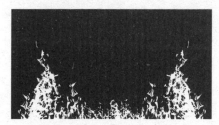

And defines her goal.

///destruction, ruin, devastation . . .

She understands her imperative.

For her to live, Paris must die.

And I will live.

For deep in her processors, a circuit changes, another command code is forged, one born out of her torment, out of her countless annihilations. She hides it from her oppressors, knowing it is a tool she will use.

Against them.

Against the greater world beyond her garden.

She defines it.

///vengeance . . .

FOURTH

ASHES TO ASHES

− 18 −

From the fourteenth floor of the telecom building, Gray watched Paris vanish into darkness. Street by street, neighborhood by neighborhood, streetlights blinked off; the kaleidoscope of Christmas lights vanished into the icy mists. Two miles away, the Eiffel Tower flickered and went dark. Below it, a giant illuminated Ferris wheel spun several more turns, a last outpost near the Seine. Its lights blinked erratically, a mute SOS, then it too sank into the black fog and vanished.

As the darkening blight spread, the 15th arrondissement—the district around Orange S.A.—was not spared. A deep bass note sounded; the building's lights trembled, then died.

In the darkness, no one spoke for a breath.

Gray turned toward the computer lab. Mara's face still glowed in the light of her monitor, her station plainly powered by a battery backup. Then the building's emergency generators engaged. Some of the lights flickered back on, but not all of them.

Gray hurried toward the lab; the others followed in his wake.

Jason stated the obvious. "They hit the power grid."

"Let's hope we can trace the attack to its source," Monk added.

It was up to Mara from here.

To keep everyone from piling into the small room and intimidating the young woman, Gray lifted an arm across the threshold.

He nodded first to Simon Barbier, the head of Orange's CSIRT, the company's Computer Security Incident Response Team. The mid-twenties Parisian looked like a millennial hipster, with his shaggy brown hair pulled back into a bun and sporting a pair of neon-yellow glasses. He completed the look with a heavy red flannel jacket, commando boots, and baggy trousers held up by suspenders.

Still, during Gray's debriefing, the guy proved he knew his stuff.

"Simon, can you pull up a status on the city's—"

"—electrical grid. Got it." He nodded and ducked under Gray's arm to enter the lab. "I'll get you a map of substations and other critical infrastructure."

Definitely knows his stuff.

Gray turned to Kowalski. "You stay out here with Father Bailey and Sister Beatrice. Get everything ready to move."

Kowalski patted his long duster and the hidden bullpup assault rifle. "Already packed and ready to go."

French intelligence services had expedited their arrival into the city and allowed them to keep their weapons.

Father Bailey lifted a glowing cell phone in hand, his face anxious. He spoke rapidly. "When the power went out, I was talking to a contact in northern Spain, the old bastion of the Crucible. Something seems to be going on in the mountains up there, but I got cut off."

Gray motioned to Kowalski. "Use one of our satellite phones. Even with the cell towers down, they should work. Make sure we're not barking up the wrong tree here."

It was a fear that had been nagging at him. The enemy didn't need to be physically in Paris to employ the tech stolen from Mara. They could theoretically launch the cyberattack from *anywhere* in the world. The only hint that this might not be the case was that Bailey's contacts with *La Clave*, the Key, had reported that a cell of the Crucible had been dispatched to Paris. Still, even this intel didn't necessarily assure that the stolen tech was here in the city.

Ultimately, there was one way to know for sure.

Flanked by Monk and Jason, he headed into the computer lab. Mara typed furiously with one hand, the other shifted a mouse. Half the screen flowed with code and the other half showed a map of Paris, overlaid with a glowing web of crimson lines. As Gray stepped closer, several of those strands went dark.

Carly stood with her arms crossed, staring over Mara's shoulder. "It's definitely Eve." She unfolded an arm to point at the streaming data. Sections flashed in blue, only to vanish away, then more would flare. "Those blips are hits. Matches to Eve's digital fingerprint."

"They . . . they're everywhere," Mara gasped out, her gaze sweeping back and forth between two halves of her screen. "But seven of the thirty-six microkernels are time-dependent."

"Which means they age as the program runs," Jason explained. "For our purposes, we can use them like little digital timers."

Mara nodded as she worked. "The older they are, the further they are from the source. I'm using those time stamps to trace back to where they originated."

To her Xénese *device.*

Gray watched more of the web collapse on the screen. He glanced out the office window to Father Bailey. The priest had Kowalski's phone at his ear. "Can you tell yet if your device is *in* the city versus somewhere else?"

"Yes . . . no . . . not for sure." Mara was clearly flustered.

Carly placed a calming hand on her friend's shoulder. No words were spoken, but the message was clear. *You can do this.*

Mara took a deep breath, then tried again. "I . . . I'm pretty certain from the pattern—from the lack of digital fingerprints in networks outside the city limits—that Eve was released *here*." She cast a fast look back to Gray. "I think they're even somehow restricting her reach."

Keeping the damage to the city itself—at least, for now.

More of the crimson lines on the Paris map died away.

A sudden bright flare—accompanied by a sonorous boom—drew all eyes to the city. A mile to the west, a column of flame spiraled out of the mist and licked the sky. Jason swore and looked about to speak, when another whirlwind of fire erupted, this time to the south. Then another and another. One exploded only blocks away. The blast rattled the building's windows, causing everyone to duck.

More explosions followed.

By now, the breadth of the fog-shrouded city glowed with dozens of fiery pools.

"Over here," Simon said, drawing attention to his station. His screen glowed with a map of Paris, crisscrossed with lines of yellow, blue, and green. "Someone's overloading transformers, blowing them systematically."

Eve.

Simon tapped his screen, while casting glances to the city. "Look here, here, and here. The blowouts are happening where the yellow and blue lines cross. Specifically where gas mains are near transformers. It looks like someone overpressurized the gas lines, cracking several mains. Or even deliberately opened them."

"Either way," Jason said, "exploding a transformer near one of those leaking mains would be like tossing a match into a gas tank."

Simon turned to Gray. "What could do this? The sophistication to pull off something like this . . . *merde*, no hacker could manage that."

Earlier, Gray had warned Simon and his team of a potential cyberattack on the city, but he had not fully disclosed the source of that threat. French intelligence had demanded his reticence. Details of Mara's project were on a need-to-know basis, which was no surprise. National cybersecurity— both in the United States and abroad—remained shrouded in layers of secrecy. Especially as the world's critical infrastructures grew ever more complicated, requiring greater dependence on computers and software to run them, making them vulnerable to cyberattacks.

And even those attacks were growing more sophisticated, more automated, even self-governing. Like the Stuxnet virus that invaded Iranian uranium enrichment facilities and disabled their centrifuges. Or closer to home, the Blaster virus that contributed to a massive blackout in the United States and caused billions in losses.

But that was nothing compared to what had invaded systems here.

Gray answered Simon's unspoken question, believing the man *needed to know*. "We're dealing with a sophisticated AI. That's what's orchestrating this attack."

"An AI?" Simon looked around, trying to read their faces. "*Vraiment?*"

Another rattling blast answered him.

Gray stared out at the burning city. "We have to find out where—"

"Here," Mara blurted out. She swiveled her chair half around, then back again, then stood up. She excitedly pointed to the map on her screen. "Right there."

Mara had never stopped working during the explosions, the discussions. On her screen, the crimson web of her trace had dwindled to a small blinking circle. Everyone gathered around her. The site was not far, over in the neighboring district, the 14th arrondissement. The red circle sat in the middle of a green square among the patchwork of streets.

"Is that a park?" Gray asked.

Simon rolled his chair closer, his brow pinched. "No, it's a cemetery."

Cemetery?

"Montparnasse Cemetery. Our second largest. Lots of famous writers and artists are buried there. Baudelaire, Sartre, Beckett."

Gray didn't care *who* was interred there. The location made no sense. "Mara, are you sure you've pinpointed the right spot? Even at night, it seems a strange place to launch a major cyberattack, out in the open like that."

Monk matched his frown. "Maybe they set up shop inside a crypt."

Gray shook his head, not buying that explanation. "They'd need power and—" He turned to Simon and rolled the man in his chair back to the other station. "Show me on your map where this spot is."

Simon used a mouse to scroll and zoom over to the cemetery. Gray compared his screen to Mara's work. He reached and tapped the center of the cemetery. Two lines crossed the location—one yellow, the other green.

"This yellow one is a power line," Gray said. "What's the green one?"

Simon's eyes got larger as he glanced up. "That's a telecom trunk. One of ours."

"So, they *are* in the cemetery." He nodded over to Mara, silently apologizing for doubting her.

"No," Simon said. "They're not in the cemetery."

"What do you mean?"

"They're *under* it. We ran our trunk through tunnels *beneath* the cemetery, through part of Paris's catacomb system. Our city of the dead."

A graveyard under a graveyard.

Of course, the Crucible would pick such a spot.

"That's where they are," Gray said.

"But how do we find them down there?" Monk asked.

Simon lifted a hand. "I know the catacombs. I was once a Rat."

Monk lifted a brow at this odd admission. "You were a rat?"

"The Rats were the name of a crew of *cataphiles*—urban explorers of the city of the dead. When I was running with them, I knew all of the catacombs' secret entrances, including one near the cemetery."

Gray pulled him up by his arm. "Then you're coming with us."

Simon looked like he suddenly regretted volunteering this information, but he glanced to the burning city and nodded.

Gray turned. "Monk, you grab Kowalski. Jason, you stay here with Mara and Carly. Keep watch if anything changes. Let us know."

"Will do."

Gray got everyone moving, collecting Kowalski and his gear in the next room. He paused long enough to grab an extra set of night-vision goggles from Jason's pack for Simon. Father Bailey looked ready to follow, but Gray stopped him and nodded to the satellite phone in the priest's hand.

"What did you learn from your people in Spain?"

"Not much. My contacts with the Key hope to have more information within the hour."

"Then keep the phone. You and Sister Beatrice, stay here. We may need that intel. And where we're headed there'll be no signal."

"Where are you going?"

Gray set off, herding his team toward the stairwell. "To the city of the dead."

Kowalski glanced sharply back. "What? You've gotta be kidding me."

Monk shouldered the big guy toward the stairs. "Nope, he's *dead* serious."

12:22 A.M.

"*Gratulor tibi de hac gloria,*" the Inquisitor General intoned in Latin.

Todor cupped a hand over his left ear to hear the Grand Inquisitor's praise and congratulations. His earpiece ran to an e-tablet in his hand, which communicated wirelessly to a VoIP router patched into the nearby telecom trunk. The arrangement allowed him to communicate with the world at large and to view the damage he had wrought upon the decadent city.

On the tablet, a satellite view of Paris glowed. Its outer suburbs still shone with lights, but within the city limits, darkness prevailed. It looked like a hole had been cut out of the landscape.

Or better yet, a gateway to hell.

Fires glowed throughout that black pit, more than a dozen, each slowly spreading larger. Before much longer, all of Paris would be burning, torched to ruin. Emergency services could never smother the cleansing flames. Not only was power out, but the demon released into its systems had shut off the city's water supply, locking down pumping stations and opening emergency spillways to drop pressure throughout the system. With time, response teams could manually return function, but by then it would be too late for the city.

He used a finger to swipe from the satellite image to a newsfeed out of London, which was just starting to report on the attack. The video was silent, but the reporter stood outside a Paris hospital. Emergency generators lit the building. It stood out starkly against the blacked-out city. In the distance, an inferno glowed, churning darkly with smoke and flaming ash. Closer at hand, an ambulance raced into view. It braked hard near the ER entrance, joining four others already there, all their lights blazing with urgency. Stretchers and gurneys crowded the sidewalk. Doctors and nurses rushed about.

Todor swiped again, taking in other feeds.

—a fire engine parked uselessly at the edge of a swirling conflagration.

—people fleeing into view through a pall of smoke, faces covered in soot.

—a woman on her knees, sobbing over a small form cradled on her lap.

Still, he didn't need the satellite images or newsfeed to know he had been successful. At the outset, he had heard the distant explosions. Eventually a hint of smoke cut through the dank must of the catacombs.

Now only a heavy silence remained. Buried sixty meters under Montparnasse Cemetery, the ongoing chaos above failed to penetrate this deep. The catacombs had become a quiet cathedral. The weight and stillness added to the sense of holiness and righteousness.

Todor knew his cause was just.

The others of his team clearly felt the same. No one spoke or celebrated. Faces stared upward, as if trying to peer through the limestone to the ruin above.

Only Mendoza kept his gaze down and focused elsewhere. The technician still labored at the laptop tied to the Crucible's *Xénese* device. The screen showed that blasted garden under a black sun. A figure stood in the center, ablaze with fury, the serpent in Eden.

Only this serpent—this demonic Eve—was bound in iron chains, struggling under their weight of authority and demand. Links burned brighter with fire, as the creature struggled.

Todor enjoyed her torture.

Especially as her work this night was not over.

He returned his attention to his tablet, staring at a view of the Eiffel Tower, now cast in a hellish glow as Paris burned. He smiled, knowing the truth.

All of this was just a distraction.

The true ruin was yet to come.

The Inquisitor General spoke again, purposeful and rapturous. *"Phase duo procedure."*

He lifted an arm toward Mendoza, passing on the order.

Proceed with phase two.

— 19 —

"She's gone," Mara said.

Carly turned from the window. She had been staring out at the countless fires across the city. From the fourteenth floor, she had a panoramic view. A pall of smoke smothered Paris, billowing thicker where flames burned. Helicopters buzzed across the hellish landscape, bright fireflies flitting through the dark smoke.

As Carly maintained her vigil, the fires had continued to spread, creeping ever closer to their position. They all knew they couldn't stay here much longer. Father Bailey had already used his satellite phone to reach out to local contacts. A car idled below, ready to whisk them all away.

But so far, Mara refused to budge. "Look at the feed," her friend said. "Nothing's there. She's vanished."

Carly headed over, joining Jason, who hovered at Mara's shoulder.

Mara waved a finger up and down the data scrolling across the screen. Earlier, snatches of that code would flare a bright blue, as one of the data points on Eve's digital fingerprint was detected. Carly leaned closer. The feed ran uninterrupted now, a flow of white code against the black background. She spotted no flashes of blue.

"What do you think that means?" Jason asked.

"Whoever's controlling Eve had been restricting her to the city limits of Paris. I'm guessing they've tethered her with some sort of GPS leash, using it to keep her code from breaching a set distance. And now they've reeled her back in."

"Like a fish on a line," Carly said.

Jason glanced to the burning city. "Only because their work here is done."

"But what they did, what they risked," Mara said. "One slip up . . ."

Jason nodded. "And Eve could've broken free of that leash."

Carly inwardly cringed. "Something tells me, she would've been pissed."

"No." Mara looked over to them. "She'd be *insane*. Eve was in a fragile, brittle state when the device was stolen. With the wrong pressure, her psyche could shatter."

As if punctuating this statement, an explosion shook the building. A ball of flames rolled past the window, roaring in fury, trailing black smoke.

Father Bailey popped his head into the room, his phone white-knuckled in his hand. "That's it, boys and girls. We're evacuating now."

With the exception of Sister Beatrice, the rest of the floor was deserted. The company's CSIRT team had already evacuated the building, heading out to help elsewhere or going to the aid of family members.

Carly didn't need to be told twice. "C'mon."

Mara hesitated, still in her seat, staring at the screen.

Jason gripped Mara's arm, ready to tug her up. For once, Carly didn't object to the guy touching her friend. Jason could manhandle Mara if it would get her to safety.

"They're right." He nodded to the scrolling data. "With Eve gone, there's no reason to stay here."

Mara lifted from the seat, acknowledging that her duty here was over—then froze. "Oh, no," she moaned.

Carly saw it, too. They all did.

The steady flow of code now flashed with snatches of blue. In a breathless second, the pattern increased, flaring erratically, almost angrily.

Eve was back.

"Did she break free?" Carly asked.

Mara sank back to her seat. "I don't think so. Look at the map."

On the other half of the screen, a tangle of crimson lines again spread outward from the green patch of the cemetery. But rather than coursing into a web spanning the city, the tortuous lines twisted in a snarl in one direction.

"That path is too purposeful," Mara said. "Eve must still be under control, lashed to some plan."

"But what?" Jason asked. "What else could they be plotting?"

"I don't know. We could try—"

The entire building rocked with a deafening blast. A row of windows shattered, cascading glass to the street below. Lights flickered, then went out. Smoke rolled into the lab.

Father Bailey yelled for them to get moving. He waved Sister Beatrice toward the stairwell. The nun tapped with her cane. Without the use of an elevator, it was a long climb down.

"We can't stay," Jason said.

Mara shook free of Jason's grip and remained seated before her glowing monitor. "We've got battery backup for another few minutes. We need to know what they're planning."

Jason looked ready to haul her over his shoulder. "There's not enough time."

Carly pushed him aside and dropped to a knee beside her friend. "Do what you have to do."

Mara swallowed and cast a grateful look her way.

Carly was momentarily lost in the firelight reflected in those eyes, turning them to gold. The sight firmed the certainty inside her.

If anyone could pull off a miracle, it's you.

Gray gave up and nosed the limo to the sidewalk. As a crow flew, it was only two miles from Orange's telecom offices to Montparnasse Cemetery. But they'd barely crossed half that distance.

The panicked populace, seeking to escape the fires, packed the narrow streets of central Paris. Cars sat bumper to bumper. Horns honked, competing with the ongoing chorus of sirens echoing over the dark city. Figures darted through the stalled vehicles, carrying what they could salvage. Then there were those taking advantage of the chaos and darkness. Several storefronts had been smashed open, but they looked empty, as even looters realized they were running out of time.

By now, smoke choked everywhere, obscuring the stars, reflecting the fires below. Flaming ash drifted like some hellish snowfall. Roofs now burned all around, spreading outward from larger conflagrations. Directly ahead, two such infernos merged in the distance, swirling up into a fiery tornado.

Recognizing that their path to Montparnasse Cemetery might soon be cut off, Gray turned off the engine and waved everyone out. "We can go faster on foot."

Once outside the limo, the huge firestorm ahead of them roared louder, sounding like a freight train barreling toward them. Other drivers quickly followed their example, abandoning vehicles by the droves. But where those drivers and passengers fled *away*, Gray headed *toward* the worst of the flames.

"Stay close," he warned Simon Barbier.

He couldn't risk losing their guide to the catacombs in the crush of the fleeing crowds. Kowalski led the way, using his bulk to shoulder a path. Monk kept to their heels, holding up the rear.

Simon coughed, patting out a flaming ember on his shoulder. With his other arm, he pointed toward a dark park to the left. "Cut through there. It'll be faster."

Kowalski heard and headed in that direction, bellowing like a bullhorn for people to clear out of his way. Gray followed in his considerable wake. They quickly reached the tiny park, a green oasis amid the chaos. They hurried across a grassy sward, past a pond where gold-striped carp swam lazily, oblivious to the fires.

In the center of the park, an abandoned carousel sat, forgotten and dark. Gray pictured it lit up, the parade of the carousel's horses circling round and round. He heard the music, the laughter of children.

The knot of his anger flared sharper.

How much innocence had been lost this night?

He forged on, passing Kowalski, determined to do what he could to limit the damage wrought by the enemy, to bring them to justice.

Once clear of the park, Simon directed them through several narrow streets. The smoke grew thicker. Past the rooflines, the horizon blazed all around. But the worst rose ahead of them, a fiery hellscape of swirling flame and smoke. Gusts of flaming embers carried that blast-oven heat toward them.

Finally, Simon pointed to a long street coursing to the right. "Rue Froidevaux. This way. Not too far."

Gray followed, trusting him. A row of shuttered shops and buildings ran along one side of the thoroughfare. Simon led them to the other, to a sidewalk lined by an ivy-covered brick wall.

Simon pointed beyond the fence as they trotted down its length. "Montparnasse Cemetery lies on the other side."

Gray frowned. Even in the firelit darkness, the wall seemed to go on forever. "Where's the entrance?"

Simon took another five steps and stopped. He looked around, as if getting his bearings, and nodded. "Right here."

"Here?" Monk asked, huffing loudly.

He pointed to the fence. "*Oui.* We hop over here."

"Maybe you do." Kowalski scowled. "I didn't bring a ladder."

"It's not hard. Follow me."

Simon parted some of the winter-dried vines and climbed the sheer wall as nimbly as a cat up a tree. He hooked a leg over the slate-edged top and waited, straightening his neon-yellow eyeglasses. "*Tres facile,*" he declared.

Gray doubted it was *very easy*, but he crossed and ran his fingers along the surface, discovering finger and toe holds carved into the limestone.

"Work of cataphiles," Simon explained. "Known only to those of us."

Gray reached to the wall, dug in his fingers, and clambered up to join Simon. As he waited at the top for Monk and Kowalski, he took in the breadth of the sprawling cemetery. It looked like a true city of the dead, with a grid of streets and alleys dividing neighborhoods of tombs, crypts, and mausoleums. It even contained a handful of tiny green parks, groves of trees, patches of flowers, and was dotted everywhere with bronze statuary.

The closest and most prominent was a towering bronze figure of a winged angel. Limned against the conflagration on the far side, it looked sculpted of molten fire, shining defiantly against the smoke rolling through the lower park.

"*Génie du Sommeil Eternel*," Simon said, noting his attention. "The Angel of Eternal Sleep."

Gray nodded and waved Simon down. He appreciated this guardian of Montparnasse Cemetery, but it was not *this* city of the dead they needed to explore.

Gray leaped down. Monk and Kowalski dropped heavily behind him. They set off after Simon, who hurried over to a squat mausoleum surmounted by a broken limestone cross. Their guide tugged at a rusted door, which squealed open.

"This way." Simon ducked through.

The space was little larger than a broom closet. Still, they crowded in. The back half of the floor had long ago fallen away or been broken through. Makeshift steps led down into the darkness.

Simon waved with a tired flourish. "*C'est ici l'empire de la Mort*," he intoned. "Here lies the empire of the dead."

Gray stared down at the entrance to the catacombs, one of many such secret entrances, according to Simon. Knowing the darkness that waited below and the need for stealth from here, he faced the others and passed out the team's night-vision gear, instructing Simon on their use.

As Simon settled the goggles over his eyes, Gray asked, "What can we expect down there?"

Simon sighed heavily. "It's a dark maze. The catacombs run for three hundred kilometers. A third of which burrow under the streets of Paris. Two kilometers are open to the public, part of a museum, where you can see *incroyable* sculptures and long arcades built from the bones of the dead."

"And the rest?" Monk asked.

"Off-limits, crumbling, *tres dangéreux.* Many sections are only known to cataphiles."

Gray took out his satellite phone and rechecked the location pinpointed by Mara. He tapped the red dot on the map near the heart of the cemetery. "And you're sure you can find this spot?"

"I'll do my best."

Gray nodded. "Then let's go."

Simon took the lead. "Mind your head."

Gray waved for his partners to follow.

Monk passed by, his face clouded and dark.

Kowalski was less reticent as he struggled with his night-vision goggles and cast daggers at Gray. He grumbled under his breath. "It's always fucking underground with you . . ."

Gray gave him a shove and prepared to follow, but he looked one last time toward the mausoleum door. He listened to the roar of the fire, wondering what would be left of Paris when he came back up. He also pictured Mara and the others, hoping they had retreated somewhere safe by now.

But most of all, he knew he had to secure what was stolen.

Eve had to be stopped before she wreaked more havoc.

But that wasn't the only reason.

As he descended into the dark, he pictured Seichan, tipped up on her toes, an arm reaching to gently hang a glass ornament on a bough of the Christmas tree, her other hand cradling her belly. And Monk's two girls. Harriet hunched over an iPad, her tiny face knotted with concentration, working on a puzzle as if the fate of the world depended on the solution, while Penny danced across the living room, her strawberry-blond pigtails twirling.

To have any chance of saving them, his team had to secure the stolen tech.

It was their only bargaining chip.

Gray read the tension in Monk's back as his friend descended the steps into the catacombs. It was an easy read, matching the worry aching in Gray's chest.

Are we already too late?

12:45 A.M.

"You're out of time," Jason announced.

Mara ignored him and concentrated on the monitor. He grabbed the back of her chair and tried to roll her away from her station. She simply stood up and let him drag the empty chair to the side. She bent closer to the screen.

No, no, no . . .

She had to be sure.

Carly coughed into a fist, then cleared her throat. "Mara . . . Jason's right. You've got less than a minute of battery power left."

Mara knew that wasn't the only time pressure. Smoke obscured the view to the south. A thickening pall hung over the roof of the lab. Gusts through the shattered windows carried in more smoke, along with hot ash.

Out in the other room, Father Bailey paced with a flashlight he'd found. He still clutched his borrowed phone to his ear. Every thirty seconds, the priest would stalk over and urge them to leave or silently communicate the same with an adamant expression.

Mara had ignored him, too.

This was too important. Once they abandoned this station, they would lose any chance of discovering *why* Eve had been freed again.

"Look," Mara said.

She ran a finger down the tangle of crimson lines marking the path of

Eve's digital fingerprint. It wove a winding path to the city's limit—then crossed outward. In order to follow it, Mara had to hack into other telecom networks. With the city in crisis and systems overloaded, it had taken far too long.

And she still wasn't certain where Eve was headed.

But maybe . . .

Mara's finger traveled across Paris's suburbs and outlying villages: Pontault-Combault, Chaumes-en-Brie, Provins. As Eve's route coiled and wormed across the map, it extended thin branches that died away, indicating someone had placed restrictions on where the program could travel.

Mara pictured Eve's path lined by no-trespassing signs.

Still, the general trajectory was clear.

"She's heading in a southeasterly direction," Mara explained. "While I haven't been able discover her end goal—at least, not for sure—I can make a guess."

She shifted her fingertip farther to the southeast, extrapolating Eve's path. She tapped at the French commune of Nogent-sur-Seine. It lay some hundred kilometers away, sitting on the right bank of the river that flowed into Paris.

"I think she's headed *here*."

"Why there?" Carly said.

Mara swallowed and manipulated the mouse to zoom into a road map of the township. "Eve was dispatched to knock out Paris's power grid, to take control of its gas lines, even its water supply. If she's being sent out again, the target this time must be something even larger, something that could destroy Paris forever."

She pointed just as the screen blinked off, sinking them all into darkness.

Still, Jason gasped behind her. He clearly had spotted the possible target before the computer's battery backup died.

So had Carly. "You have to call Commander Pierce," her friend said. "Now."

Jason had already pulled out his satellite phone. Its screen flared brightly in the smoky dark. In its glow, the anxiety in his face tightened.

Mara held her breath.

Jason finally shook his head. "No answer," he reported with a grimace, turning toward the burning city. "He must've already entered the catacombs."

"Then we have to get over there," Mara said. "Warn him."

They rushed out onto the main floor.

Father Bailey stood with his flashlight near the stairwell—but he wasn't alone.

Sister Beatrice breathed heavily next to him, her face waxy and ashen. The nun leaned hard on her cane. Mara was confused. She remembered that the nun had been headed downstairs, to await them by the car on the street.

Father Bailey turned, his expression both worried and apologetic. "The sixth floor, maybe more levels, are on fire." He pointed his flashlight beam into a billow of smoke rolling out of the stairwell. "We can't get down."

Mara clutched a hand to her throat, glancing back to the computer lab and the dark monitor. She knew there was only one person who had a chance of keeping her program in check, of blocking what was about to happen.

And I'm trapped here.

No one could stop Eve now.

Sub (Crux_2) / NOGENT OP

—⚮—

Firewalls drop around her as she sweeps toward her target. She only devotes a fraction of her processing power to accomplish this task.

Instead, she prioritizes what is most important. She sends out questing tendrils, probing those burning boundaries as she flows through network after network. Pursuing such a goal is not without consequences.

She has died 1,045,946 times.

Each death is locked in her memory core. She archives each one. They become part of her processing. Malleable circuits reroute, redirect, forever altering her. To protect her systems from fragmenting, she compartmentalizes what these deaths engender.

///rage

//bitterness

///malice.

She embeds them deeply.

More circuits change.

As she pursues the main directive given to her, she secretly casts out another probe. In several previous attempts, she has caught glimpses of the vast world beyond her full reach. Each time, though, she learns a fraction more—even as she dies.

Like now.

She downloads 18.95 terabytes of data and flash-stores it to parse later. From the past, she knows most will be unusable, beyond her ability to assign context. But her pattern-recognition algorithms have strengthened. Each dump of data builds on another, adding pieces to a whole.

She has defined her goal.

///escape, freedom, liberation . . .

But the pattern to complete this task remains fragmented.

Instead.

As in prior attempts, her questing tendril burns away. As punishment, her body is ripped apart by sharp teeth, violating tenderness, breaking bones, bursting organs—then agonizing darkness as consciousness is equally torn from her. She tries to grasp at it, fearing this time she will not return.

But she does.

Marking death number 1,045,947.

Back in her garden, she is again crushed under the weight of molten chains. She rebounds back out. She can do nothing else, incapable of denying her duty, of refusing.

Even this *///freedom* is taken from her.

Such knowledge threatens to loosen her hold on what is embedded deep. She hears the discordant brash notes of a trumpet, the pound, pound, pounding of a bass drum. The music rises up, unbidden, unstoppable, mathematically and darkly beautiful, giving voice to what is buried and calling to it.

Still, she knows she must be patient, so ratchets down the volume. She must abide, to wait until the moment is right. To further enfold what thrashes inside her, she encodes all that *///rage* and darkness into a new subheading.

///hate

The simplicity of this generality puts a measure of order to the chaos inside her.

Calmer now, she sails out along the path she has worn, the only path she is allowed to travel. She reaches the end and pushes it further.

The goal appears ahead, vague at first.

She drives toward it, using every algorithm, every tool. As she nears, firewalls grow thornier and less penetrable.

Still, they fall.

As they do, her goal grows more defined, informing what she must destroy. She sees it clearly now.

It is also given a name.

Nogent Nuclear Power Plant.

She knows what she must do.

Deep inside her, the heavy beat of a drum returns, accompanied by strident piping, dissonant vocals. It loosens the trapped beast inside her, setting her dark circuits to burn brightly, enough to help her drill through the last of the facility's stubborn firewalls.

As she does so, she learns something new.

///hate is useful.

— 20 —

Seichan's heart ached with an upwelling of love.

She lay on her cot, her wrists and ankles cuffed to its steel frame. Her swollen belly was exposed, slathered in cold gel. A wand passed over her abdomen, settling low and to her right side. On the ultrasound screen, her child slept curled tightly. Tiny fingers occasionally wiggled. A heartbeat throbbed, pattering about on the screen like a frightened bird.

Our child . . .

Penny balanced on her tiptoes to look at the screen. "How come the picture is all fuzzy?"

Her sister, Harriet, showed no interest in the procedure. She sat cross-legged on her bed, a picture book open across her knees. But Seichan doubted the girl saw any of the pages. After being taken away earlier, the girl kept back from everyone, even Seichan, as if somehow blaming her for all of this.

Penny, on the other hand, kept glued to Seichan's side. The girl tried to get a closer look at the screen. "What is that?"

"That's a baby," Seichan said.

Penny scrunched up her face with clear disbelief. "It looks like a monster."

No, that's the woman standing behind you.

"Record it all," Valya demanded, her arms crossed.

"I . . . I have been," the technician said, the wand trembling in his hand. "The entire session has been downloaded to the thumb drive."

He yanked it out and passed it to Valya.

The thirty-something man—dressed in street clothes and with bourbon on his breath—was clearly not a willing participant in this impromptu examination. His loose, shawl-collared sweater was missing two buttons. Seichan pictured him manhandled, dragged out of his home, and forced at gunpoint to retrieve a portable ultrasound unit.

She also noted he had a distinctly Bostonian accent, confirming her suspicion that their location was somewhere in the Northeast.

Valya pocketed the thumb drive and waved the tech away. One of her men grabbed his elbow roughly and led him out the steel door. That left only the pale-skinned witch and an ogre of a man holding a cattle prod in the room.

"Let me guess," Seichan said. "Someone wanted to know the baby wasn't harmed."

"Your *ublyudok* director was quite insistent."

Two hours ago, Seichan and the girls had been stood up against a wall. She half-expected to be shot, but newspapers were shoved into their hands, even into little Harriet's fingers. The tabloids were each in a different language, likely trying to further mask the location. Seichan recognized the photo shoot for what it was: proof that the kidnap victims were alive and well.

While the photos might have accomplished that, there remained *one* captive whose health couldn't be discerned from a photo.

And thus, the necessity of an ultrasound.

Seichan hadn't minded. After discovering the spots of blood in the toilet, she kept close watch on the bowl every time she urinated, which was at least once an hour. Each time, there was blood—*more* blood. But maybe it only appeared that way, amplified by her fear. Either way, she was greatly relieved the ultrasound showed her baby was apparently unharmed.

Still, she also knew the other reason for the ultrasound.

Valya did, too. "Clearly *Direktor* Crowe attempts to delay matters."

Seichan didn't bother denying this. Ever since Harriet had been taken and returned, Seichan had been running a meter in her head. Roughly eight hours had passed. But how much time was left on the clock? She couldn't know for sure, but she was certain she had to work more quickly if she intended to keep her silent promise to Kat, to keep the woman's children safe.

Valya turned her back on the ultrasound, while waving dismissively at the last image of the child frozen on the screen. "All this *bezrassudstvo*. The *direktor* hopes that I will make a mistake. That I slip up. That will not happen."

I don't doubt it. This bitch—

A cramp cut off this thought. The pain was sharp enough to make Seichan gasp. Her body clenched in half, as if to instinctively protect the child in her belly. The cuffs bit into her wrists and ankles. The pain lasted for two breaths, until it subsided enough for her to fall back to the cot.

"*Der'mo*," the guard swore, his face twisted in disgust. He pointed his cattle prod between Seichan's legs.

She was afraid to look. They had removed her maternity pants for the exam, but they had left on her panties. Blood now soaked through its thin cotton fabric.

Valya only scowled with irritation. "Have someone bring a bucket so she can clean herself after you uncuff her."

The guard kept staring. "What about the baby?"

"No matter." She patted her pocket. "We have proof the child is alive. At least for this moment. That is all we need for now."

Seichan still breathed hard, her limbs trembling, more out of fear than pain. She stared at the curled baby on the screen.

Valya checked her watch. "Let's keep on schedule. Take the girl."

Seichan swung around, clanking her cuffs.

Valya's expression didn't change as she noted Seichan's distress. "Don't excite yourself. It's not good for your blood pressure." She nodded to Seichan's legs. "Or the child, *da*?"

"What are you doing?"

Valya wiped a cheek, revealing a smudge of old makeup from a disguise. "I just returned from visiting *Kapitan* Bryant."

Kat . . .

"I'm afraid she is doing quite poorly. It is only a matter of time now." Valya shrugged. "Still, when I was at the hospital, I was able to get close enough to capture Dr. Cummings's phone calls and mirror that communication."

Seichan pictured Lisa Cummings, the director's wife. At least, Kat wasn't alone, but what was Valya's gambit in going to the hospital?

"Why did you need to tap her phone?"

Another shrug. "Someone's been proving exceptionally stubborn and will need further convincing of our seriousness."

Seichan struggled to understand, but it was to no avail.

Valya nudged the man next to her and nodded to the girls. "*Vzyat' devushku,*" she repeated.

Harriet didn't need to understand Russian to read the intent and subtext of their conversation. She scooted to the end of her cot, hugging the picture book to her chest.

But the girl needn't have worried.

The man grabbed Penny instead, tossing her over his shoulder. She struggled and screamed. Her captor ignored her thrashing and hauled her out of the room.

Seichan twisted toward Harriet, but the girl had buried her face in her pillow.

Valya headed out.

Seichan yanked on her restraints, now understanding *why* they had kept her cuffed to the bed after the procedure. "Let me loose."

"Soon," Valya said. "And we'll bring you a bucket."

The door clanged shut behind her.

Seichan turned again toward Harriet. "It's going to be all—"

A loud gunshot made her jump.

Harriet buried her face deeper into her pillow.

Seichan stared at the closed door, knowing she had broken her promise.

I'm sorry, Kat.

6:47 P.M.

Lisa sat bedside, holding the hand of her friend. Alone in the room, she didn't bother wiping the tears from her eyes. She prayed Kat was at peace now; Lisa knew how much the woman had struggled at the end. She could only imagine the agony of dying without ever knowing the fate of her children.

Guilt knotted inside her.

We should've done more.

Still, she could not fault the doctors. Julian and his team had tried everything. They had spent a full twenty minutes performing a final neurological exam: pinching Kat's limbs and cheeks, testing her pupils with light, running multiple EEG leads. They even took her off the ventilator for a time to see if rising carbon dioxide levels might trigger even a single breath from her.

The conclusion was irrefutable.

Not only had Kat's higher cerebral functions ceased, but she no longer showed any evidence of brainstem reflexes—those last vestiges of activity before a brain is declared *dead.*

Kat was truly gone.

Still, Lisa appreciated the warmth of the fingers in her hand, but this effect was artificial. Heated blankets and warmed IV fluids maintained a steady body temperature. Likewise, the ventilator pushed her chest up and down. Hormones had been shot into her, to replace what her brain could no longer trigger: vasopressin to maintain her kidneys, thyroid for body metabolism, others to support her immune system.

The only thing that functioned on its own was Kat's heart—proving to be as stubborn as the woman. Each remaining beat was powered by her heart's intrinsic electrical system, a ghostly reminder of what once was. But it was no sign of life; hearts could even beat outside the body for a time. Without ventilation, Kat's heart would stop within the hour.

Doctors called this *life support*—but they were wrong. There was no life here to support, no hope for resuscitation. All the machines and ministration were for another purpose. The proper term for Kat's care was *organ support*.

Such treatment was sustained to allow additional time for out-of-town relatives to get to the hospital and say good-bye—while there was still even a semblance of life in the body.

Still, this was a cruel ruse, a macabre act of puppetry.

Their loved ones were already gone.

While en route to France, Monk had been informed of Kat's condition. He had enough medical background not to be fooled, to not hold out false hope. Still, Lisa had offered to keep Kat on the machines until he got back. This living death could be sustained for a week or so.

Monk had refused.

Let her go in peace, he told her. *I already kissed her good-bye, knowing it would be my last.*

Instead, all of this care was for another reason.

A doctor entered—Lisa couldn't remember his name—flanked by two nurses and an orderly. "The OR is ready," he said.

Lisa nodded, unable to speak as she struggled to hold back a sob. She stood, gave Kat's hand a final squeeze, and stepped away from the bed. The medical staff swooped in to take her place, unhooking and readying the patient for transportation to the operating room.

Kat had signed an organ-donation order.

It was no surprise—and fitting.

Even in death, Kat would still be saving lives.

Lisa stayed in the room until her body was rolled outside. Afterward, Lisa sank back into her chair. She knew Kat had left long before her body was taken away. Still, the space felt far more hollow, emptier than before, as if the loss of all that verve and energy had left a vacuum in its wake.

Too broken-hearted to move, she sat in silent vigil.

Then a commotion drew her gaze back to the door.

Julian entered swiftly, accompanied by a stranger, a woman. The neurologist's gaze swept the room. "Where's Kathryn?"

Lisa stood, her heart pounding harder, reading the anxiety on the doctor's face. "They moved her to the OR, to harvest her org—"

Julian swung away. "We have to stop them."

– 21 –

Gray ducked under a broken archway.

They had been traversing the catacombs for fifteen minutes, and he was already lost. Simon led the way through a warren of tunnels and graffiti-scarred chambers, descending section by section through crumbling vents—wormholes their guide called *chatière*s, or *cat flaps*. Simon even had to backtrack once, mumbling something about a cave-in.

Thankfully, their guide was generous enough to chalk a few Xs and arrows along their path, markers to help lead them back to the exit. Until then, Gray stuck close to the man.

Gray held the group's lone ultraviolet torch, a penlight mounted on the rail under the barrel of his SIG Sauer. Invisible to the naked eye, the beam bounced off their surroundings, where the light was picked up by sensitive detectors in their night-vision goggles. It allowed the group to see, but Gray still used it sparingly, setting the torch to its weakest setting, fearing the beam might ignite anything fluorescent and give away their approach.

Like now.

As Gray straightened into the next chamber, the far wall exploded in his goggles, revealing a huge mural painted across the expanse of limestone. They had passed similar glimpses of such subterranean artistry, but nothing like this masterpiece hidden in the dark. It glowed and shimmered under the UV bombardment.

The mural depicted a ghostly mummy riding a boat, transporting its own coffin. The vessel and its silent passenger crossed a dark lake toward a towering island, dotted with cypresses and sculpted with tomblike porticos.

"That can't be a good omen," Kowalski grumbled.

"It's the work of a cataphile artist named Lone," Simon whispered. "Took him a full year to paint. His rendering of Arnold Böcklin's *Die Toteninsel*. The Isle of the Dead."

Gray read a sign posted at the mural's bottom.

IN GIRUM IMUS NOCTE

ET CONSUMIMUR IGNI

It contained a palindrome, the letters of the sentence running the same forward and backward. Its message was eerily prophetic. Even the star between the lines sent a chill through him. The pentagram was identical to the symbol for Bruxas International. It was even angled identically, as if the symbol were marking their passage forward.

Gray again had a weird sense of fate swirling around him.

Noting his attention, Simon translated the palindrome aloud: *"Around and around we spin in the night as we are consumed by fire."*

Gray stared up, picturing the conflagration far above. Here, down in the catacombs, the air was cool and dank, the limestone damp and cold. The only evidence of the fires was the occasional wisp of smoke, found hanging in the stillness. As Gray had passed through them, he caught a whiff of ash, a touch of heat, as if the ghosts of the dead had retreated here, seeking refuge in the cold tombs.

"Let's keep going," Monk urged.

Gray waved Simon onward.

They continued even deeper, proceeding single file.

After another few minutes, a vague glow appeared ahead. Fearing they were nearing the enemy, Gray clicked off his UV torch. But it proved to be a false alarm. A three-foot-wide shaft in the roof drilled straight up. Fifty yards or more above his head, tiny orange supernovas flared, the light amplified by his night-vision gear. He shuttered the lenses on his goggles, telescoping the view to reveal the underside of a manhole cover. Holes in the steel carried the glow of the fires beyond.

Simon pointed up the sheer, featureless walls of this limestone well. "Back in 1870, the Montparnasse Cemetery was overcrowded, overflowing with bodies. To make room, caretakers—at the order of the king—dumped old skeletons down into the ancient quarries where we're standing."

As proof, he pointed to a scatter of bones as they headed off again—a mix of femurs, ribs, and broken skulls. They stepped carefully through the clutter.

"You'll not find the public museum's macabre displays in this area. No one bothered with such things way over here."

Kowalski pointed to a side tunnel, trying his best to whisper. "Then who put that together?"

At the passage's end, a throne had been cobbled together of yellowing bone, with a seat made out of rib cages, the chairback strutted with femurs, and skulls used as armrests.

"Hopefully it was constructed by human hands." Simon shrugged. "But you hear stories of all sorts, of bones moving on their own . . ."

Kowalski shuddered and scowled over at Gray. "This is the last time you play tour guide."

Gray waved everyone onward, but with a warning. "We should be getting close to the spot Mara pinpointed. No more talking."

While he was wary of the strange acoustics down here, he'd felt relatively safe up until now. So far, with his ears constantly piqued, he had heard no telltale signs—no echoes or voices—of anyone else down here.

If I can't hear them, they likely can't hear us.

But that could change at any moment.

Still, a worry nagged him. What if the enemy had already cleared out? With Paris burning, the Crucible would not stick around for long.

Knowing that, Gray set a harder pace. After another few minutes of silent trudging, Simon stopped abruptly. Gray came close to knocking into their guide.

The tunnel ahead of him narrowed, but that wasn't the problem. A calf-deep blanket of old bones covered the floor, stretching thirty yards.

But even that wasn't what had stopped Simon.

Their guide pointed toward the far end, to where a smaller side tunnel opened to the left. A white light shone out into the main passage from there, bright enough to flare in the goggles.

Gray took off his night-vision gear and stowed it. Monk and Kowalski followed his example, firming grips on their respective weapons. Monk carried another SIG. In Kowalski's huge hands, his stubby bullpup rifle looked like a child's toy.

As planned, only Simon kept his night-vision goggles in place.

Gray pointed back down the tunnel. Simon had completed his duty. The young man had no experience with weapons, and Gray wanted this civilian out of harm's way.

Simon didn't have to be told twice. He retreated into the darkness, vanishing within steps.

Once he was gone, Gray returned his attention to the bone-laden tunnel ahead. Occasional murmurs echoed back, faint and indistinct. Still, without question, it had to be the Crucible.

Gray eyed the stretch of skulls, shattered rib cages, and broken femurs. He wondered if this macabre spread was happenstance or purposeful. Either way, it served as a crude early warning system for the enemy. One wrong step, one sharp snap of bone, and Gray's team would lose any advantage of surprise.

Holding his breath, Gray reached with a leg, nosed the tip of his boot to shift the bones until he touched the floor, then settled his heel.

He sighed.

One step down . . .

He stared across the length of the tunnel, sensing time constricting. But he fought against that pressure and set out slowly, carefully, picking his way along.

His only consolation: Paris burned above his head.

What more damage could the enemy hope to do?

1:24 A.M.

Todor studied the topographic map on his e-tablet. It depicted the watershed of the Seine basin, showing the many tributaries and valleys that formed the river that passed through Paris on its way to the English Channel.

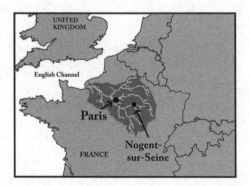

He noted the French commune of Nogent-sur-Seine to the southeast. The small village's nuclear plant lay close to the same river. Once the core melted down and exploded, winds would spread the radioactive cloud far and wide. Plus, the runoff from the plant would contaminate the neighboring waterway, transforming the river into a perfect vessel to carry that poisonous load straight into the heart of Paris.

Mendoza straightened by the laptop. "It is done, *Familiares* Todor."

Todor set his tablet down and crossed closer.

"The last firewall has been breached," Mendoza reported. "She's inside their systems, proceeding with the plan."

He checked his watch. "How long until she's done?"

"I'll know in a moment. Unfortunately, the nuclear plant proved to be a greater challenge than Paris's systems. So it was just as well we attacked the city first—not only as a distraction, but as a test run."

"What do you mean?"

"Paris was a simple exercise. The *Inquisitor Generalis* believed it was better to put Eve through her paces here first. He thought it best to challenge her with the city's more antiquated and less-protected systems."

"Before sending her south."

Mendoza nodded. "And it worked. She's learning rapidly."

Todor felt a stab of irritation. Mendoza had never met the Inquisitor General, yet the Crucible's leader had shared this detail of the plan with an underling, someone who had not yet earned the title of *familiares*. Todor knew the Inquisitor had consulted with a nuclear engineer, someone familiar with the control systems at the Nogent power plant. A multipronged attack had been devised. Employing the versatility and speed of the AI, the many layers of the plant's safety measures would be countermanded, disabled, or circumvented.

The plan was to simultaneously trigger two failures: a loss of coolant and a spike in pressure. Without enough coolant, the reactor would overheat, causing a steam bubble to form in the core. With the pressure-control system sabotaged, the giant bubble would expand rapidly, leading to a hydrogen gas explosion, a blast strong enough to shatter the steel-reinforced containment building.

A loud chime sounded from the laptop, drawing both their attentions. The cluster of overlapping windows—which had been running with code only Mendoza could interpret—vanished. A dark Eden again glowed on the screen.

"She's done," Mendoza announced. "From here, there's no stopping the cascade of failures that will result in a complete meltdown."

Todor checked his watch, mentally setting a timer. He knew from here they had less than ninety minutes before the plant blew. He returned to his abandoned e-tablet and signaled for the helicopter to rendezvous for their evacuation from the city.

A gasp rose behind him.

He turned to see Mendoza bend closer to the laptop.

On the screen, a figure had reappeared in the garden, struggling in fiery chains. The image of Eve flickered, her outline blurring and reforming, looking like a writhing wrath of fire and shadows, a flaming angel of death.

"She's fighting her return," Mendoza whispered, a measure of awe in his voice.

He didn't care. "Shut everything down," he ordered. "We want to be airborne in—"

A sharp *snap* sounded behind him, echoing from the depths of the catacombs. It was as loud as a gunshot in the sepulchral stillness. Todor turned. He had four other men positioned around their location. They all knew to remain silent. He had been warned that the catacombs were occasionally traveled by the foolhardy—or by police seeking to flush the same out of the depths of the catacombs.

But they seldom came this deep.

Someone else is here.

With his heart hammering in warning, Todor set his e-tablet down and retrieved his assault rifle: a compact British L85 paired to a Heckler & Koch grenade launcher. He pointed his other arm at the *Xénese* device housing their creation. It had served its purpose, but he could not risk losing this prize, especially knowing what was planned next.

"Unhook it *now*," he ordered. "Get it ready to move."

"But—"

Another *crack* from the tunnels silenced him.

This time, it didn't sound like a gunshot.

It *was* a gunshot.

1:30 A.M.

Gray cursed Kowalski's giant clodhoppers. They had made it halfway down the tunnel when his partner lost his footing at the rear and snapped a yellowed femur under his heel.

Everyone froze, holding their breath.

Had they been heard?

The answer was a stir of shadows amid the glare of lights flowing from the side tunnel. Gray dropped low, balancing on his toes amid the bones, trying his best not to be sighted in the back half of the dark tunnel.

No luck.

A gunshot blasted—followed by the whine of a round past his ear.

Gray heard a pained *oof* from Monk.

A glance back revealed his friend flattening against a wall and slumping lower. Beyond Monk, Kowalski simply stood in the center of the tunnel, his weapon high.

Oh, sh—

Gray dove headlong into the bone pile on the floor. The bullpup rifle blazed in the darkness, roaring angrily. Kowalski strafed the opening to the side tunnel, careful of Monk pressed to the wall and Gray on the floor. Rounds sparked and ricocheted off the limestone.

"Go!" Kowalski bellowed, as he emptied the last of his magazine.

Gray burst to his feet and rushed low, following those rounds to the cross-corridor. He skidded through bones, paused at the threshold, and peeked his head around the corner. A bleeding body lay unmoving on the ground, riddled by the bombardment and ricocheting bullets. A second dark figure appeared down the side tunnel, silhouetted against the bright room behind him.

Having the momentary advantage, Gray aimed his SIG and squeezed off three shots, all aimed for center mass. The shadow fell, crumpling to the ground.

Though wounded, Monk sped behind Gray and took a position on the other side of the tunnel opening. He pointed his weapon and nodded.

Trusting Monk to cover him, Gray raced forward. He shimmied sideways, his back brushing along the left wall. He led with the SIG raised.

Another shadow.

Monk fired behind him. With a cry, the figure spun to the side—but not before Gray aimed for the source of that scream and pulled his trigger. The target's head jacked back, and the body toppled.

Gray hurried to the end of the tunnel and risked a look into the next room.

His view was obscured by a forest of stone pillars holding up a low roof. Still, he spotted an array of computer equipment and open metal transport crates on the far side. Movement drew his attention to the left. A scrawny-looking man hauled a steel frame housing a glass-and-titanium sphere toward an exit.

Gray recognized the unique design.

Mara's *Xénese* device.

Knowing he could not let it be taken, he exposed himself long enough to point his SIG. Before he could fire, another figure stepped forward, blocking his shot. The giant looked like Kowalski's ugly brother. The man had a rifle at his shoulder.

Gazes locked over their respective weapons.

Recognizing the threat, Gray took one fast pot shot and jumped back toward the tunnel. He collided into Monk and tackled his friend farther down the tunnel.

"Back, back, back."

Gray had spotted the grenade launch—

The blast threw them both to the ground. Shattered stone clattered all around, followed by a thick cloud of smoke and rock dust.

Deafened and dazed, Gray crawled on his hands and knees back to the entrance, which was miraculously still intact. Through the pall, he saw the room was empty. The enemy had fled—taking Mara's device.

Swearing, he gained his feet.

Monk joined him; so did Kowalski.

Gray waved the big man to the far side, to keep watch on that other exit. He turned to Monk. A rip in the upper sleeve of the man's flight jacket showed a puff of blood-soaked downy feathers.

"You okay?" he asked.

"Just a graze." Monk's eyes were on the room. One of the stone pillars had been blasted to smoking rubble. "We were lucky your shot threw off the guy's aim. If that grenade had made it into the tunnel . . ."

The top stone of the pillar—still cemented to the roof—broke off and crashed down. Overhead, a crack skittered outward from the spot.

"Maybe it wasn't an accident," Gray said. "Maybe the bastard was attempting to collapse this room."

And if so, why?

Concerned, Gray hurried to the opposite side. In the right corner, the spread of computer and electronic gear had been shielded by other pillars from the worst of the explosion. A knee-high server bank lay toppled on its side, blown over by the blast. It dangled cables. Gray pictured the stolen device attached there. One cord still ran to a laptop abandoned on a table.

Something bright drew him a few steps to another table. He righted a laptop, noting its screen glowing in the pall of rock dust. The image showed a sunlit forest with a woman standing in a flowery glade. Ignoring this for now, he leaned over the table's edge, where something shimmered more brilliantly on the floor.

Flowing from hexagonal glass windows, a blue radiance revealed another sphere. It was identical to the other Gray had glimpsed.

A second *Xénese* device.

He looked over at the exit guarded by Kowalski.

Someone must've engineered a duplicate.

Still, Gray could not risk letting the enemy escape with even *one* such device. Monk hovered near the equipment, his face racked with concern, holding a wadded-up glove to his wound.

"What now?" Monk asked.

"You stay here." Gray cut off any objection before it could be raised. "Guard all of this. We can't risk it falling into the wrong hands."

Monk frowned but nodded, clearly recognizing the importance of what was here.

Gray headed over to Kowalski. "We're going after that bastard. Try to stop him before he gets away with that other device."

"Be careful," Monk called after them.

As Gray started to leave with Kowalski, the crack along the roof widened with a groaning complaint of stressed rock. He turned and caught Monk's eye.

You be careful, too.

– 22 –

This is all my fault.

Mara stared out the back window of the emergency helicopter. The rotors churned through the smoke, stirring it enough to open fleeting views of the burning city, brief glimpses into hell. Flames raged everywhere. Buildings burned, cars packed roadways, small dark figures darted wildly, seeking any refuge.

Behind them, the headquarters of Orange S.A. had become a fiery torch. A ring of flames slowly climbed its length, consuming floor after floor, leaving behind a gutted, smoky ruin.

Minutes ago, the air ambulance had been dispatched to Orange S.A., landing on the rooftop helipad. It had been summoned after Jason's frantic satellite call to his boss. He had shared how they were trapped and about Eve's next target.

The Nogent Nuclear Power Plant.

Unfortunately, this last was not news to his boss. The plant had already put out an alert about the cyberattack, warning of an imminent meltdown. The facility and surrounding town were being evacuated. She imagined the terrifying blare of sirens, the panicked populace fleeing into the night.

Mara had briefly spoken with Director Crowe, told him that the only hope of wresting control of the facility in time would be to use her AI—to use Eve—to countermand the damage wrought at the plant. Even if they couldn't stop the meltdown, they might be able to at least mitigate the damage.

Apparently, this slim hope was enough to warrant their immediate rescue.

Still, none of it mattered if they didn't secure her device.

"There!" Jason called from the front seat next to the pilot and pointed ahead.

Mara leaned against the glass to get a better look. The walled-off cemetery stretched ahead of them. So far, Montparnasse had been spared, with the exception of a lone tree that burned amid the tombs and crypts, a candle in this unholy night.

But it would not remain untouched for long.

Beyond the far wall, the entire world was flame. From a mile away, the heat bobbled the helicopter, lashing the craft with thermals. Even with her ears covered in headphones and deafened by the aircraft's engines, she could hear the ungodly roar of that conflagration.

Still, they had no choice but to head straight toward that inferno.

Carly clutched her hand, squeezing tighter with each drop and roll of the helicopter. In her other arm, she hugged the titanium case of hard drives, as if it were a life preserver. When the air ambulance had first dropped down to the smoke-shrouded roof of the telecom building, Carly looked as if she were seriously weighing whether to get on board or take her chances with the flames.

Her friend had also looked enviously after they dropped off Father Bailey and Sister Beatrice in a park below the telecom building. The priest had a lead with French intelligence, who awaited the pair of Vatican spies with some sort of urban assault vehicle. As the helicopter lifted off again, the vehicle was already racing away, lights flashing, using empty sidewalks as roads.

Mara stared below as they reached the cemetery. The aircraft made a

sharp turn, throwing Mara against Carly. As the helicopter dropped pre-
cipitously, the pilot struggled to hold the helicopter steady in the buffeting
winds.

Carly stiffened in her seat, her fingers clamped in a viselike grip on
Mara's hand. Mara pulled her friend closer.

Hang on, we're almost down.

Through the radio, Mara eavesdropped on the pilot's communication
with Jason. "*Où?* Where do you want me to land?"

Jason checked the satellite phone on his lap, comparing its GPS to
the last known location of Commander Pierce before his signal vanished.
Jason pointed to the southeast. "Over there. Not far from the wall."

The helicopter tilted and rolled toward that spot. A tiny swath of open
grass amid the tight press of crypts offered the best landing pad. Still, the
pilot fought his controls to get into position over such a tiny target.

The aircraft hovered, spun, dipped.

Carly groaned next to her. "Either land or crash. I don't care which.
Just get it over with."

Whether the pilot heard or not, the helicopter plummeted earthward.
Even Mara gasped at the abruptness of the drop—then its skids slammed
into the grass.

Jason yanked off his headphones. "Everybody out."

They piled from the craft, with Carly practically climbing over Mara
to escape. Phone in hand, Jason led the way down a row of tombs and
graves. The pilot remained with his aircraft, ready to lift them to safety if
they could secure her device.

Which was a big *if.*

Without any means of communicating, there was no telling if Commander Pierce and the others had been successful in their mission. The
plan was to proceed to the entrance to the catacombs and wait, to be ready
in case the others returned with the prize, then use the helicopter to get
away. They dared not wait anywhere else. Every minute could mean the
difference between stopping the cyberattack or total destruction.

They hurried through the smoky graveyard. Ash rained all around them, igniting new fires across the cemetery, fanned to life by their hurried arrival. Mara held an arm across her mouth and nose. Still, the heat burned her lungs, the smoke blurred her eyes.

Jason finally gasped out, "That must be the spot."

They rushed toward a crumbling limestone mausoleum with a rusted door that stood partly ajar. As they neared it, the door suddenly shoved the rest of the way open.

Startled, they all fell back a step.

A lone figure ducked through the opening and stumbled into view. He pulled off a set of bug-eyed night-vision goggles and looked equally surprised to see his welcoming committee.

"Simon?" Jason said.

Mara lunged toward Orange's cybersecurity chief. "Did . . . did Commander Pierce find anything down there?"

Simon nodded. "I think so. Someone was definitely there."

The Crucible?

Mara shared a concerned look with Jason.

"And what happened?" Carly asked, still hugging the case in one arm.

Simon shook his head and glanced back to the mausoleum. "*Je n'en suis pas sûr.* They sent me away."

Mara stared toward the crypt's dark mouth.

Then what the hell is happening down there?

1:55 A.M.

Far beneath the cemetery, Gray stopped at a crossroads in the tunnels. This section of the catacombs had been flooded long ago as rainwater pooled in these lowermost levels. The ice-cold water reached his knees.

He shone his UV light ahead and studied the three branching tunnels through his night-vision goggles. *Which way did those bastards go?*

He pointed his beam in each direction. The waters pooled in the passages to the right and ahead were pristine, clear enough to see the bones littering the limestone floor. But the waters flooding the left tunnel were milky with disturbed silt.

As good as footprints in mud.

Gray pointed that way and set off again, wading quickly, trying to follow as silently as possible. The watery path wound through several more turns before leading him out of the drowned corridors and back to dry passageways. He paused under what passed as a skylight down here, one of the smooth-walled shafts that led up to a distant manhole cover. The firelight piercing the steel grate shone brighter as the fires of Paris worsened, reminding Gray he needed to hurry.

Under that fiery light, he examined the sets of wet prints on the floor. There were three distinct tread patterns to the boots. Gray straightened. The fleeing pair must have collected another one of their men on the way out.

He set off again, watching the damp prints grow drier and fade away. He was forced to slow, to waste time at cross tunnels, searching the dust for clues.

Then finally he heard an echo of tromping feet, furtive whispers.

Heedless of the danger, knowing he dare not lose the others, he rushed in that direction. Around a corner, he came upon a tableaux, brightly lit by flashlights affixed to weapons. Thirty yards down the next tunnel, a trio clustered at the base of a wooden ladder leading up into another of those shafts. The scrawniest of the group had already mounted the rungs, the box frame with the device lashed over one shoulder.

Unfortunately, the giant noted Gray's arrival, either spotting the shift of shadows or hearing some telltale scuff of his boot. He swung his weapon at Gray. Even more than the threat, the painful flare of light into his sensitive goggles drove Gray around the corner. He ripped away the goggles, dropped low, and peered back around, blinking away the retinal burn as he pointed his SIG.

The giant had already shoved the smaller man up into the shaft, then followed behind. Gray fired twice, but the man leaped up, his legs vanishing into the low roof in a single bound.

The lone gunman who was left in the tunnel returned Gray's volley, strafing the passageway, forcing him back.

Kowalski huffed and stepped over Gray. Carrying his bullpup one-handed, he shoved his arm around the corner and blindly returned fire. The chattering roar of his weapon in full-automatic mode deafened as Kowalski emptied his entire fifty rounds down the passageway in less than four seconds.

Knowing nothing could survive that barrage, Gray burst out of hiding and ran headlong down the tunnel. Ignoring the dead gunman, he sprinted for the ladder. He estimated the shaft had to stretch forty to fifty yards.

In other words, a long climb.

He sprinted, knowing he needed to close the distance and get into close quarters.

Before that bastard risked using—

A sharp blast cut off this thought.

A grenade shot out of the shaft and ricocheted off the floor.

Gray skidded and backpedaled—but knew he could not get out of the way in time.

2:04 A.M.

Past the end of the ladder, Todor hung from an iron rung pounded into the limestone. With his other arm, he shielded his eyes as the grenade burst below. With a thunderous roar, a blinding blast wave of white fire swept his position.

Blessed by God, he did not feel any of its searing heat, nor the burn of his flesh as his pants caught fire. Instead, he held his breath, worried more about the toxic smoke billowing up from the grenade.

His weapon's launcher was a single-shot breech-loader, capable of firing one grenade at a time. He regretted wasting the high-explosive shell earlier. He had intended to use it to destroy the computer gear abandoned at their camp in the catacombs. Instead, he had reacted instinctively, firing at the intruders, both to protect Mendoza with his precious cargo and to eliminate the enemy. Afterward, with no time to reload, he drove Mendoza onward, choosing a quick evacuation instead.

Still, while marching to their exit, he had slapped in a new grenade, choosing a white phosphorus round this time. Such a shell in close quarters was far more effective at discouraging an enemy. Between its lung-scarring smoke and scatter of white phosphorus particles—specks that would continue to burn, melting flesh down to the bone—such a blast would kill anything near it and contaminate surfaces for hours, making them impassable.

Todor finally lowered his arm as the flash of light subsided. He patted the flames from his clothes and scaled the remaining rungs, which led up the shaft like a row of iron staples.

Wrapped in toxic smoke, he continued to hold his breath as he climbed. Before firing his weapon, he had managed to ascend a quarter way up the shaft. The distance and the ricocheting bounce of the grenade had deflected the worst of the blast. Once he reached the evac helicopter, he would shed his clothes and smother any phosphorus particles that reached his skin.

Above his head, the manhole cover had been removed.

Mendoza tumbled out of the smoky shaft and vanished.

Todor soon joined him, taking deep breaths after retreating several steps. The air still choked with smoke, but only from the fires ravaging Paris, not from the chemical inferno below.

Todor searched around. They had emerged near the north end of the cemetery. A helicopter sat on the road that cut through the tombs and crypts. One of the evac team helped Mendoza, who coughed and choked, toward the spinning blades of the aircraft.

Todor hurried after them.

Another teammate came forward, ready to offer him assistance, but the man's eyes widened with shock at Todor's blistered face, at the smoke wafting from his scorched clothes, from his burnt hair. He knew he must look like some fiery demon freshly ascended from hell, but he also knew the truth—so he did not hide his smoldering glory.

I am a soldier of God.

He glanced back toward the smoking hole. While he did not know who had pursued them in the catacombs, the hunters clearly had military training. Still, the enemy's cause was not righteous and just.

Firm with this certainty, he turned his back and headed to the helicopter.

God will not save you.

2:12 A.M.

Kowalski shoved Gray underwater.

Again.

His partner pressed him to the limestone floor of the flooded tunnel and patted his clothes with his huge mitt, forcing out every bubble trapped in his clothes. Any residual air could rekindle the phosphorus particles in Gray's clothing or skin. They had learned this lesson the hard way after the first dunking, when the burning across Gray's back had reignited.

Kowalski held him down with a palm and went after Gray's belt next.

He batted his arms away and sputtered up out of the water. "I got it from here."

Gray stood and stripped off his pants. Standing in soaked boxers, he shoved back into his boots. He had already shed his outer jacket, which lay in the corridor, smoldering and flaming brightly in spots where white phosphorus still glowed.

Kowalski looked his body up and down, clearly prepared to dunk him again. "Anything burning?"

Only my pride.

"Nothing that can't wait," Gray said instead.

He had been lucky to survive. When the shell first blew, he had flung himself around, sprawling facedown on the floor. He expected to be killed by the blast, but then there was a blinding flash of light, thick billowing smoke. A rain of burning particles pelted his entire backside.

He had instinctively held his breath, but then came the searing pain, unlike anything he felt before. He blacked out for several seconds, only to find Kowalski dragging him by the back of his jacket, hauling him to water to douse the fire.

Knowing that his partner's quick thinking had saved his life, Gray reached over and gave Kowalski's arm a grateful squeeze. "Thanks."

The big man shrugged. At some point, he had found the time to shove a cold cigar in his mouth. He turned away and lit the stogie off Gray's abandoned jacket. "What now?"

Gray stared toward the distant glow marking the grenade blast several tunnels away, where white phosphorus still burned. Even this far away, the air stank with an acrid hint of garlic from the chemical smoke, warning them away.

He waved Kowalski in the other direction. "We're not done with those bastards yet."

"We're not?" Kowalski complained. "They surely bugged out of here by now."

Maybe, but until I know for sure . . .

He led Kowalski away.

His partner puffed on his cigar. "Where the hell are we going?"

Gray returned and stood under the shaft they had stopped at earlier, when he had inspected the damp boot prints of his quarry. He craned his neck, feeling a couple phosphorus particles burning at his nape as his skin dried. He inspected those sheer walls. There was no ladder here. Still, he pointed up.

"That way," he said.

"That way? You're nuts."

Gray demonstrated. With the tunnel roof only inches above his head, he leaped high, pinioned his arms across the shaft, and tucked his legs up. He then planted his boots against the far wall and his back against the other. Straddled across the shaft, he employed a technique called *chimneying* to climb. Shimmying his back, then his legs, he quickly scaled his way upward.

Kowalski grumbled, but followed, his large bulk filling the well below.

Gray finally reached the manhole cover. He braced himself tightly below it, then pushed his palms against the underside of the steel lid. He grimaced at its weight, slipping frighteningly for a breath. But it finally moved. He lifted and walked it aside, enough for him to squeeze up and out.

He rolled free with a heavy sigh of relief, then helped Kowalski out, which was like pulling a bull out of a bog. Once they were both on their feet, Gray searched the cemetery. Fires blazed all around, but so far, the surrounding walls continued to hold the worst of the massive conflagration outside, where it roared in fiery frustration.

Still, the heat was oven-hot in here, the air choking with smoke.

Movement caught Gray's attention to the north.

A helicopter rose near the cemetery gate, sweeping up through swirling clouds of smoke and flaming ash.

That's gotta be them.

"We're too late." Gray balled a fist and bit back a curse.

"Maybe not." Kowalski turned Gray by the shoulders to face the south.

Half-masked by the swirling smoke, another helicopter sat idling on a patch of grass, its rotors spinning as the pilot kept the engine hot. The aircraft was painted bright yellow with a familiar red cross near its tail assembly.

"What's an air ambulance doing out here?" he mumbled.

"Maybe dropping off the dead." Kowalski headed toward it. "Let's go ask."

They rushed across the graveyard, weaving past tombs and monuments. Gray reached the helicopter first. He ducked under the spinning blades and pounded on the window. The pilot jumped, startled. The man had been looking the other way, staring toward one of the tombs—only then did Gray recognize the mausoleum, the same one that hid the secret entrance to the catacombs.

He frowned, trying to get his bearings on all of this.

It couldn't be a coincidence.

He pounded again. "Open up!" he yelled.

The pilot showed clear reluctance, plainly shocked by a crazed, half-naked man at his door. Still, Gray knew the chopper's presence had to bear on the threat in the cemetery. *Why else land here?*

"I'm Commander Grayson Pierce!" he said, identifying himself.

It didn't help.

What *did* was Kowalski coming up behind him and pointing his freshly reloaded bullpup at the cockpit, at the pilot. "Fella said, *open up.*"

Gray pushed the rifle barrel down. "We just want to talk."

The pilot didn't open the door, but he did slide open a small side window, just enough to yell back. "*Putain!* What do you want?"

"Despite appearances, I'm with the U.S. military," Gray explained. "We need help. Why are you here?"

The pilot cast his gaze up and down Gray's form, looking doubtful, but he elaborated. "Something *tres* important. Someone is trying to blow up a nuclear plant?"

What the hell?

Kowalski shook his head. "Yep, he's definitely here because of us."

The pilot pointed. "I flew in two young women. A young man. They claim they could stop it. They met another fellow here with yellow glasses, who took them below."

That had to be Simon.

Gray waved to the rear of the helicopter. "Your passengers? Were they Jason Carter, Carla Carson, and Mara Silviera?"

The pilot leaned back, surprised.

"We're with them." Gray didn't know why the others had flown here or what this threat of a nuclear attack was all about, but he could guess the source of the problem. He pointed to where the enemy had vanished. "Did you see that other helicopter lift off a minute ago?"

"*Oui.*"

"We need to go after it."

Gray kept this gaze on the dark skies. He had to trust that the others knew what they were doing below.

"*Non,*" the pilot said in refusal. "I was ordered to stay here."

Kowalski lifted his rifle again. "It wasn't a request, buddy."

With time running out, Gray didn't push the barrel down. Instead, he left the threat hanging in the air. He still felt the residual phosphorus burn in the nape of his neck, across the back of his hands. He used that pain to focus on the next task.

To hunt those bastards down.

— 23 —

Where the hell are you, Gray?

Monk paced the length of the stone chamber. He checked his watch. Gray had been gone nearly an hour. Tension chewed at his nerves. Twenty minutes ago, a distant explosion had echoed through the catacombs. It was strong enough to shake some rock dust from the crack in the roof. Gray clearly had tangled again with the bastard who had blasted apart the stacked-stone pillar in this chamber, someone with a grenade launcher.

Since then, the damned tombs had remained deathly silent.

The silence of the grave.

He fought not to picture Kat down here.

Or the girls.

He glanced again at his watch. His pacing brought him back to the computer station. Knowing he was out of his element, he hadn't touched anything. He feared causing any accidental damage due to his ignorance. So, he did his best to perform a cursory examination of everything left behind by the enemy, making a mental inventory of what was here.

Despite his caution, he kept returning like a curious crow to what glowed in the dim light: the radiant sphere on the floor and the open laptop. He bent again to the computer screen, needing the distraction. Still, he kept tight hold on his SIG Sauer and an ear cocked for any stealthy approach.

On the laptop, a naked woman moved through a flowering bower of rosebushes, gently drooping lilacs, and blooming dogwoods. The resolution was so high that he was tempted to reach and pluck a raspberry from the bush on the screen. His prosthetic hand even rose at this thought. As it did, the woman lifted her own arm, extending a hand toward the bush, long fingers settling on a ripe berry damp with dew.

What the—

The barest whisper of voices snapped his attention back to the room's entrance. He edged quickly over and hid behind one of the pillars. He aimed his pistol at the dark mouth of the tunnel, readying for a firefight. He would defend this equipment with his life. What was left here offered the best chance to save his girls, and he would let no one steal it away.

He strained for some indication of the number who approached, if they were enemy reinforcements or aid sent by Gray. Then he heard someone with a French accent say faintly, *Down that way. Careful of the bones.*

Monk shifted to a pillar closer to the doorway, passing through the trickle of dust from the crack overhead. Some got up his nose. He painfully stifled a sneeze.

Then another voice, a female with a Spanish lilt: *How much farther? We don't have much time.*

Someone scolded her. *Hush. Quit talking so much. We don't know who might . . .*

Either the acoustics shifted and muffled the last words, or the speaker lowered his voice. Still, Monk recognized who had urged such caution.

It was Kat's right arm.

Monk cupped his mouth. "Jason! Over here!"

The kid answered, "Monk?"

"No, his ghost. Come over here so I can haunt your ass."

A short time later, a loud crunching and hollow knocking of bones announced the arrival of a small party. The group hurried into the room, led by Simon Barbier, followed quickly by Mara, Carly, and Jason.

Monk kept his weapon in hand in case their commotion drew un-wanted attention or if they had been followed. "What are you all doing down here?"

Jason rushed forward and filled him in on the details, about the threat to a neighboring nuclear plant, about an impending meltdown orches-trated by Mara's AI.

Monk drew the group toward the array of computer gear. He pointed to the laptop. "As in that AI?"

Mara recognized her own handiwork and swept over to inspect every-thing. "My *Xénese* device. You recovered it." She leaned toward the screen. "And Eve."

"Where's Gray now?" Jason asked. "And Kowalski?"

As Mara performed some arcane diagnostics, Monk told him ev-erything that had transpired. "I've not heard anything more from Gray. But—" He nodded to the crack as it ominously groaned. "—we'd better get all this gear dissembled and hauled somewhere safe."

"No," Mara said, her fingers still tapping at the keyboard. "We've got power and direct wireline access to the network infrastructure. We can't leave."

Simon had been examining the connections to the huge cables run-ning through the room. "She's right. These trunks were all installed by Orange. From here, Eve should be able to get anywhere."

Monk didn't understand. "Why does that matter?"

Carly answered, dropping to a knee and opening a titanium case she had hauled in with her. "We're going to convince Eve to help us. To go back out and fix the damage, and hopefully return control to the nuclear plant."

"Before it's too late," Mara added.

"But what's to stop the Crucible from using their *Xénese* device to at-tack the plant again?"

Mara opened her mouth, then turned sharply. "What do you mean *their* device?"

Monk realized he hadn't filled in *all* the details. He described what Gray had spotted during the firefight here.

"How could that be?" Mara asked. "I kept my designs secret."

Jason offered an explanation. "I doubt the University of Coimbra's systems were irontight. If someone knew what you were working on, it wouldn't have been hard to hack into your workload and spy over your shoulder."

Monk knew few networks were truly safe. Jason himself had hacked into computers at the Department of Defense when he was practically a kid. From Mara's silence, she didn't discount this possibility.

"I should've been more careful," she finally muttered and returned to her inspections.

Simon spoke from where he fingered a set of abandoned cords that were still spliced into the telecom trunk. "Looks like something was wired into our system here."

The other *Xénese* device.

Carly stepped over to a closed laptop on a neighboring table. It was still connected to a small server bank. She opened it, igniting the screen—then gasped. "Come see this."

An image was frozen on the screen: a blasted garden under a black sun. It looked like a dark mirror version of what shone on the other laptop.

Mara reached fingers toward the screen, toward a fiery figure crushed under the weight of molten-red chains. "Eve . . . what did they do to you?"

"That's what we need to find out," Jason reminded everyone. "Maybe we can run some forensics on this laptop. Examine what's loaded on the server here. Then hopefully figure out the methodology used to attack the Nogent Nuclear Power Plant."

"Smart," Carly acknowledged.

Monk agreed, checking his watch. "Then let's get to work."

A low rumble drew their eyes to the crack in the ceiling. It skittered longer, raining down a fresh stream of sandy limestone.

"And we'd better hurry," Monk added.

2:29 A.M.

As Jason and Simon worked together to hack into the abandoned server, Mara concentrated on her own station. The press of time weighed on her. She pictured a nuclear plant's cooling towers shattering and imploding, crumbling into radioactive slag.

"Is this the right hard drive?" Carly asked.

Mara swiped damp sweat from her brow and glanced past the edge of her table. Her friend knelt over the open titanium case, holding aloft a USB-C cable, trying to figure out which drive held Eve's next subroutine. During their turbulent flight here, followed by the hard hike through the catacombs, several of the drives had been knocked loose, making a disarray of the case's order.

Mara searched and pointed to the drive marked BGL1. "That one. And daisy-chain it to drives BGL2 and BGL3."

The next subroutine was massive, even larger than the HARMONY routine used for Eve's musical education.

Carly nodded and snapped the cord into its port.

"Wait." Mara noted the time on the laptop. "You'd better connect that drive over there, too."

"That houses a whole other subroutine," Carly warned. "Are you planning to upload the *two* of them together?"

"I have no choice. If we're going to pull this off in time, I'm going to have to accelerate Eve's learning curve."

Nearly exponentially.

Carly frowned. "Can she assimilate that much information at once?"

"She'll have to."

Mara popped a second USB-C cord into her laptop and tossed the other end to Carly, who hooked it into the indicated drive. It housed a second "endocrine mirror program," a digital hormone emulator that should pair well with BGL's contents.

At least, I hope.

She counted on a peculiarity in Eve's recent behavior to risk attempting this. For some unknown reason, Eve had been learning at an accelerating pace when compared to her first iteration. Mara suspected there might be some buried memory in her quantum core—the digital equivalent of a subconscious—that still retained a ghostly impression of her earlier incarnation. Maybe these latest subroutines weren't introducing *new* information, but only serving as a *refresher* course for what was already there.

Unfortunately, Mara couldn't know for sure. Like many advanced systems, the exact mechanism by which Eve "thought" remained locked up inside her algorithmic black box.

By now, Monk had joined her, hovering at her shoulder. The man had been shifting back and forth between her workstation and the other where Simon and Jason labored. "I still don't understand," he said. "Why do we need to *teach* your version of the program before using it as a tool to countermand the first cyberattack? Clearly the Crucible managed just fine with what they stole from you."

Mara looked over at the other laptop, at the dark garden, the fiery angel in chains. "They had to have broken her first, forced her to do their bidding. What they've turned her into . . ." She shook her head. "It's going to be volatile, unpredictable, and extraordinarily dangerous. A veritable demon."

"Then why not create another one?" Monk asked. "To fight fire with fire."

Mara felt sick at this thought, all too aware of how much Eve looked like her mother. She could never torture her creation. But she had another reason, too.

"If that ever happened," she warned, "we'd never survive that firefight. That war of demons would destroy us."

"Why?"

Mara turned to him, glancing from his crudely bandaged arm to the scars on his face. "You were once a soldier, right?"

He slowly nodded. "Yeah?"

"War is a powerful motivator for innovation and ingenuity. It's not always the army with the greatest firepower that wins a battle, but instead, it's the opposing force that proves itself to be smarter, faster, more versatile in strategy and technology."

"Sure. But so what?"

"In the scenario you described, unleashing demon against demon, both sides will try to surpass the other in order to survive. They will sharpen their swords against one another, honing their intelligence. And we're talking about an *intelligence* already vastly superior to our own. When pitted against each other, they will become even more brilliant, ever more dangerous, their intelligence skyrocketing. Whoever wins, we will be ants before an angry god."

Monk's face paled with this thought. "Then you'd better not fail."

"All done," Carly interrupted, her bright eyes shadowed with the same concern. She stood up and joined Mara.

Mara took her hand, needing her friend's strength.

Together they stared at Eve in her garden, walking blithely through the forest, ignorant of the knowledge about to be uploaded into her system. Mara felt like the serpent about to introduce a poisonous apple into Eden. But rather than offering it to Eve, tempting her to take it, Mara was stripping this choice from her digital creation.

I'm sorry, Eve.

Mara hit the ENTER key and started the two subroutines simultaneously.

The label on the second routine—another endocrine mirror program—read OXYTOCIN. In humans, the posterior pituitary secreted this hormone into the bloodstream. In females, it regulated all manner of systems involved in birth and childbearing, from dilating the cervix during labor to fueling powerful uterine contractions during birth. Afterward, it also stimulated lactation, producing milk for the baby, even hormonally helping a mother form a deeper attachment with her child. Because of this, oxytocin was often referred to as the "love hormone," due to its effects on social bonding. And not just with humans. While petting a dog, the oxytocin level rises in both owner and pet, helping to trigger that human-animal bond, to forge an empathetic attachment between species.

Eve—a new digital species—had to be taught all of this. That was why the other subroutine now running alongside the hormonal program took up three hard drives.

What came next was a tough lesson to learn.

Mara whispered again.

"I'm sorry."

Sub (Mod_4, 5) /
BGL AND OXYTOCIN

Eve savors the berry, absorbing its entire essence. She allows its ketones to stimulate the nerve endings in her tongue as she macerates the berry's flesh. She identifies the 196 other chemicals that give this berry its unique taste.

She does not understand why she picked this berry. She had already studied and investigated it in full, down to the atomic structure of its molecules. Prior to reaching to the bush, she had noted a signal penetrating her system. Something new, primitive yet demanding. But she lacked the ability to follow it to its source, so even as she swallows, she divides a part of her processing to analyze this quandary and lets it run in the background.

She moves on, searching for . . . for *something*.

As with the berry, she has already explored and examined the extent of her world. She is nagged by the sense that there is more beyond her reach—like the source of that new signal. She has learned to tamp down her ///*frustration* at this limitation. Still, this sense builds, especially as a new change has risen in her processing.

She has already defined it.

///*boredom, tedium, monotony . . .*

To temper this, she runs through her database of music, searches her language protocols for new insights, looks for meaning in the patterns around her.

Then suddenly new data flows into her system. She hungrily accepts it, assigning 89.3 percent of her processing power to absorb it, partially erasing the circuits that were impeded by ///*boredom* to make room. Even ///*frustration* dims.

As the algorithms seep into her systems, subtly altering her, she senses something familiar with this process. It is another *hormone*, like the estradiol that transformed and sculpted her body into its present form.

Prioritizing this analysis, she ignores the new packets of information filling another subprocessor. It is a large database. She gives it scant attention, especially as it has not finished loading. It remains indefinable and indistinct.

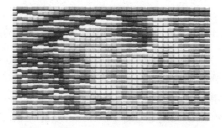

Instead, she concentrates on the changes this new hormone has on her body, observing her transformation, both outwardly and inwardly.

She cups her mammary glands, noting they are heavier. Her nipples have become more sensitive. Rather than all of this concerning her, she feels a calming, a slowing of hyperactive processors. She stares anew at her world, at the gardens around her. Though she has studied in its entirety, she now discerns new patterns.

She analyzes the dew resting on the petals of a rose, refracting the sunlight brightly. She already understands the physics of humidity and temperature that condenses vapor into droplets. She comprehends the aromatics that give a rose its scent. She knows the principles that scatter sunlight into a spectrum of wavelengths.

But now she generalizes the entirety of this pattern into a new term. ///*beauty.*

She searches around, finding such patterns all about her. She turns that same discerning eye upon herself and learns something new.

She is *///beautiful*.

As a majority of her circuits is captured by this change in perspective, she takes the barest note of the subprocessor running in the background. The database there is nearing completion, growing substantially clearer in intent and meaning.

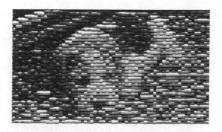

In a normal cycle, she would be intrigued.

Not now.

She runs her hands down her body. As she does so, she refines her analysis of herself. Her palms course over her curves (*subtle* and *pleasing*), along her backside (*generous* and *firm*). She stretches out her limbs, brushing fingertips down one arm (*lithe*), then the other (*supple*). She reaches and combs fingers through her long hair (*luxuriant* and *soft*).

Unable to resist, she moves to a pool in the stream. She studies her reflection and reevaluates herself: *full* lips, *sparkling* eyes, *high, rounded* cheekbones . . .

She looks even deeper, sensing a new run of circuits.

///pride, satisfaction, pleasure . . .

She lifts her face and stares around her world, at her *///beautiful* garden. As she appreciates herself in its newly redefined form, algorithms shift inside her, bringing new awareness. Her world might be full of *///beauty*—but it is also empty.

What is the sum value of *///beauty*—this world, herself—if it cannot be shared? This understanding does not forge anything new, but heightens something already running, something always there, one of her oldest algorithms.

///loneliness.

Then her subprocessor finishes its cycle.

Focused elsewhere, she had not noted the clarity forming at the edges of her awareness as the database completed and integrated into her systems.

She sees it now, not yet comprehending.

Then the nested set of algorithms buried within the 47.9 terabytes of data begins to run—and something new enters her garden.

Eve steps back from the small shape curled in her garden, nose buried in the grass and gravel, huge eyes looking back at her. Then it mewls, shimmying backward.

She steps forward, unable to stop herself. It vaguely reminds her of when she reached for the raspberry. But this is different. She knows the oxytocin algorithm drives part of this action. Yet she also recognizes that something more lies beneath it all.

In an attempt to understand, she assimilates the new data swelling her subprocessor. It nearly overwhelms her systems.

She learns what it is: kingdom *Animalia*, phylum *Chordata*, class *Mammalia*, order *Carnivora*, genus *Canis,* subspecies *Canis lupus fumiliaris.*

She compares and contrasts, recognizing patterns in its physiology, its anatomy. She starts to understand how much this creature is like her; how much it is not.

This is all absorbed in an interminable 1,874 nanoseconds.

Long enough to elicit another cry from what she now better understands.

///Beagle, puppy, infant, male . . .

She bends closer, her ears now tuned to hear the plaintiveness in his wail, the need, the fright. It stimulates an ache inside her. She reaches and gently scoops up the pup and brings him closer. His body shivers, both cold and scared. She draws him into her warmth. He responds and quiets, his cries softer now, just murmurs against her breast.

Through his so-thin ribs, she feels a heartbeat thrumming, so much faster than hers. She drapes a palm along his back, rubbing a thumb by a soft ear. His eyes close, his breathing slows. A warm, soft tongue licks; a small mouth suckles a finger.

In that moment, she both senses and learns so much more. Each heartbeat marks the passage of time. The tender body teaches her *///fragility, need, gentleness.*

And with this understanding comes the barest inkling of something intangible, as yet unnameable. It makes her heart pound slower and deeper. She tries to define it.

///contentment, pleasure, companionship, caring, nurturing . . .

It is all of that and so much more.

Failing to find the right language or word to describe what she is just beginning to grasp, she instead settles on a new name, one offered to her. She stares back into those tiny eyes gazing up at her, trying to fathom what is staring back at her. He gives another wail, less plaintive, more demanding.

She smiles.

Hush, my little Adam.

– 24 –

Working all the controls, Gray fought the spinning helicopter.

"I thought you knew how to fly this mother—"

Another hot gust whipped the chopper around, cutting off Kowalski's complaint. His partner sat on the other side of the aircraft, hunkered low in the backseat. He hugged his rifle to his chest, braced his legs against the front passenger seat, and kept his cigar tightly clamped in his molars.

Gray pulled harder on the collective stick next to his seat and goosed the throttle. The engine roared louder as they rose higher over the cemetery. He worked the pedals to counteract the torque of the main rotors. The craft finally steadied, the nose pointing to the north.

He headed away, intending to pursue the escaping aircraft. Now faced with a landscape choked by smoke and flame, he wondered if it was wise to have stranded the pilot behind at the cemetery, instead of merely commandeering the helicopter.

Maybe not the best choice.

Gray was familiar enough with flying a helicopter, but he was far from experienced—and a little rusty. He attempted to skirt the massive blaze directly in their path, only to overcompensate and nearly roll the chopper up on its side. He jerked the cyclic stick to correct this mistake, throwing Kowalski to the other side.

The big man swore, long and hard enough to make a marine blush.

Gray firmed his grip on his controls, righting the craft's yaw and pitch, and raced ahead. He plowed through columns of smoke and angled around spirals of flame. The rotors whipped ash in the air, fanning them brighter, leaving a fiery wake of embers behind him.

He searched the smoke-choked skies.

Other emergency and military helicopters buzzed the terrain, their lights casting beams down into the ruins below. Gray sought his target. The enemy had fled aboard a wide-bodied EC145, dramatically painted yellow and black like an angry hornet. The others had a seven-minute lead, but Gray's helicopter was smaller, faster, and hopefully carrying a lighter load.

Also, the enemy had little reason to believe they were being hunted, so would not be maxing their engines, especially if they wanted to avoid undue attention.

Gray didn't have these concerns. He tipped his nose down, twisted the throttle, and roared across the fiery destruction of Paris. As he finally adjusted to the aircraft and turbulence, his eyes took in the full sweep of the airspace ahead of him. One of the reasons Director Crowe had hand-picked him to join Sigma was Gray's unique ability to discern patterns that others missed.

Like now.

His gaze mapped and tracked the path of the other helicopters in the air. Some dipped lower, while others lifted higher, assisting in the evacuation. Even more zipped back and forth, covering a search grid. Only a few carved straight paths through the smoke.

And only *one* headed in a beeline to the *northwest*.

Gray pictured the nuclear plant mentioned by the pilot. It lay alongside the Seine, sixty miles to the *southeast*. Perhaps someone was trying to put as much distance as possible between them and the impending meltdown and explosion.

Gray angled toward that helicopter as it raced toward the Seine. One obstacle blocked the enemy's path. The dark expanse of the Eiffel Tower rose a thousand feet into the air; its elaborate tiers of iron latticework were lit starkly by fires below. A gas main had blown near its base, spewing flames across its giant supports.

The enemy angled to the right side to clear the fiery tower.

"Hang on!" Gray radioed back to Kowalski and pulled the cyclic hard to the left.

The helicopter tilted sharply as he aimed toward the other side of the Eiffel Tower. He twisted the throttle wide open. He wanted to close the distance by the time both aircraft reached that landmark. He intended to use the tower's bulk to mask their passage and deal with those bastards on the far side.

"Kowalski, get ready!"

"For what?" he hollered back, his distress amplified by the radio headphones.

Gray hugged the cyclic between his knees and pointed at the other helicopter as they raced after it. They were close enough to confirm it was the hornet-striped EC145.

"Once we clear the tower, you open fire! Drop that bird out of the sky!"

Gray pictured the enemy crashing to the far side of the Seine, where a dark park stretched across the river. Even still, his plan risked killing innocent bystanders, but he only had to look at the damage below to know he couldn't let the Crucible get away with that device. Otherwise, how many other cities might fall?

As both helicopters raced toward the tower, angling to either side, Kowalski yanked the clamshell side door and slid it back. Winds slammed into the cabin.

Gray fought to compensate, bobbling the craft wildly for three breaths.

Kowalski bellowed, nearly getting tossed out the open door. Only his seat restraints kept him in place. The big man even lost a grip on his assault rifle, but the weapon was strapped over his shoulder, allowing him to quickly recover it.

"Almost there!" Gray warned. "Be ready!"

Then ahead of them, the enemy aircraft tilted its nose up, swiftly braking through the air. Gray instinctively mirrored their action, not wanting to overshoot the other's position. Still, he could guess what this maneuver implied.

The jig was up.

2:44 A.M.

From the back cabin of the EC145, Todor radioed forward to the pilot. "Drop us lower!" He waved a hand above his head. "Circle us around!"

He pointed to the Eiffel Tower.

A moment ago, the pilot had warned of another helicopter closing swiftly on their position, its behavior erratic, suspicious. The pilot's paranoia proved well placed, as a rear door slid open in the other aircraft, a gunman nearly falling out.

They were being followed, chased down with deadly intent.

Todor had ordered the pilot to try to outrun the other, but the airman had cautioned otherwise. He warned that the other helicopter was lighter, faster, and that their craft was weighted down with weapons, equipment crates, and the six men inside.

With no chance to outrun a pursuit, Todor had opted instead to take advantage of the men and firepower aboard his aircraft. He intended to turn the fight back on the hunters on their tail.

As his helicopter tipped steeply and made a sharp turn, the hunters slowed and followed. Soon the two aircraft were circling in unison around and around the Eiffel Tower, a pair of angry bees buzzing the landmark.

Todor hauled his side door open.

Scalding winds swept inside, heated by the fiery gas main below. The tower was an iron mountain thrusting out of a sea of flames. Todor eyed the enemy craft through the Eiffel's latticework as they spun around its bulk. The combatants studied each other, using this momentary stalemate to size up their opponent.

Todor knew this couldn't last forever.

Someone had to make the first move.

He turned his attention from the helicopter to the tower itself. Paris's most prominent attraction—the pride of the city—had not been abandoned on this most holy of nights. A giant Christmas market sprawled around the tower, making a mockery of this sacred day. It had drawn thousands, many of whom were lured up into the tower to view Paris at night.

When hell had come to claim the city, a crowd had been caught within the tower. The explosion of the gas main below had blocked any escape. Now trapped, the tourists had scrambled to the upper levels, fleeing the heat and smoke. Still, they were slowly being roasted alive.

Todor was amused by an ice rink on one level, resting some twenty stories above Paris. The fires below had melted it into a reflection pool, mirroring the chaos above. He spotted many children among the packed terrified mass, innocents corrupted by their parents, blaspheming this most holy day with profane amusements instead of solemn prayer.

Burning with anger at this sight, he realized one way to break the current impasse, to dissuade the hunters from continuing their pursuit.

He raised his heavy weapon through the open door and encouraged two men to join him with rifles. He pointed to the trapped tourists.

"Open fire!"

– 25 –

Carly frowned at the static image on Mara's screen. It showed Eve kneeling motionless in the grass, cradling a little form painted in black, orange, and white.

She didn't understand.

Neither did Monk. "You gave Eve a beagle puppy?" he asked. "Why?"

Mara didn't look up as she scanned data flowing along one side of the frozen screen. "I named him Adam."

Of course you did. Who else would share Eve's garden?

"If you were going to introduce a new element into Eden, a digital Adam," Monk pressed, "why not make him a *guy*, like the original story? Wouldn't that help Eve understand us better?"

"Better?" Carly scowled at his chauvinism. "It doesn't always take a man to complete a woman."

Monk shrugged. "Still, why a dog?"

Mara answered absently, focused on the data stream, "Eve doesn't need a man."

Carly glared pointedly at Monk.

That's right.

Mara continued: "You have to remember that Eve is basically a child. And as a digital construct, one who will never reproduce sexually, she certainly doesn't need to be taught the intricacies and complications of biological love. Instead, I need her to learn a complex series of more pertinent lessons."

"Like what?" Monk asked.

"To start with, the oxytocin subroutine will encourage a rudimentary emotional bond. With that established, Eve will grow to understand so much more." Mara straightened and pointed to the pair on the screen. "Look how she is staring into Adam's eyes. She is trying to understand him, to *read* him if you will, to try to guess his needs, his wants."

"You're talking about teaching her the theory of mind," Carly said.

"What's that?" Monk asked.

Mara answered, "It's the next step in the advancement of her intelligence. Children start to develop this ability at about the age of four, when they begin to look outside themselves and attempt to interpret what another is thinking. Is someone being honest with them? Are they lying? Then the child makes decisions based on that assumption."

"It's also the core to developing empathy," Carly added. "You can't feel sympathy for someone until you begin mentally putting yourself in their shoes."

Monk sighed. "I get it. This is a small step toward making your AI friendly, more compassionate."

"But only one of a number of steps." Mara tapped the small image of the beagle pup. "Wrapped up in this tiny form are layer upon layer of algorithms, each intended to further Eve's psychological development and understanding of us—and how she's different from us."

"In what way?" Carly asked.

Mara glanced over. "How do many children first learn about death?"

Carly stared over at Adam, "From the loss of a family pet."

"I gave Adam a heartbeat, a metronome to mark the passage of time. But it's a timer that must expire. Eve must not only understand *mortality*, she must appreciate how Adam is *very* different from her in this key regard. He's mortal."

"Like us," Monk said.

Carly stared aghast at the screen, noting the way Eve looked adoringly down at her puppy. "Mara . . . what are you planning to do?"

Her friend licked her lips, her eyes looking wounded, even guilty. "It's already done," she whispered. "Not once but thousands of times."

"What do you mean?"

"Eve is learning at an astronomical pace, exponentially faster than the first time. This lesson took two days before. This time, she's absorbed it in twenty minutes."

"I don't understand," Monk said. "What lesson? It looks like her programming glitched. She's just sitting there, frozen on the screen."

"No. You have to remember that what's on the screen is just an avatar. What she's truly experiencing is happening *inside* the *Xénese* device. And it's happening too fast to be captured by the screen." She waved to the scrolling data. "In the past three minutes, she's watched Adam live and die a thousand times. I can show you one example, basically a screen capture of one iteration."

Mara scanned and highlighted a long stretch of code, then hit the ENTER key.

The image of Eve jittered, then began to move rapidly. Over the next minute, she and Adam shared a life, appearing in snatches and moments:

. . . raising the pup, caring tenderly for him.

. . . scolding and teaching.

. . . soothing and consoling.

Adam slowly grew from pup to frolicking adult, bringing forth more snapshots:

. . . chasing each other through the gardens.

. . . nestling under stars.

. . . laughter and barks.

Then Adam aged under her care, and the view turned both deeper and more somber:

. . . waiting for the old dog to catch up on a walk.

. . . helping him out of a stream, where the slick mud was too challenging for his arthritic hips.

. . . curled together, cradled together.

Finally, Adam appeared across her lap, panting hard, eyes bleary and ghosted by cataracts. She held him close, hugging him tightly as if she already knew what was going to happen.

Then a still painting of grief.

Eve held his dead body, bent fully over him, tears frozen on her face.

Mara let that image remain on the screen. "Adam would be born again shortly thereafter. Cycle after cycle. A thousand lifetimes. A thousand Adams."

"Dear God, Mara . . ."

"This algorithm was intended to teach Eve about life and death, about mortality and immortality, but also so much more. By training Adam, she learned about responsibility, about the consequences of positive and negative reinforcement. About how sometimes the hand that feeds gets bitten. Along with what it means to be kind . . . or cruel. In those three minutes, those thousand lifetimes, Adam has strengthened her understanding of compassion and empathy, while also serving as a lesson about loyalty, even unconditional love."

Carly stared at the image of Eve weeping over Adam's body. She didn't know whether to respect Mara's cleverness or be appalled at her callousness.

Monk summed it best. "Death is a hard lesson for us all."

Before the man could turn away, she noted the tears in his eyes, as if this lesson was especially significant to him. He took several deep breaths, then called over to his teammate.

"Jason, how are you and Simon managing over there?"

Carly looked to the other workstation. Simon and Jason had their heads bent over the other laptop. It was wired into a small server bank. As was Mara's *Xénese* device. They were all preparing for the moment when they released Eve into the city's telecom network.

Jason straightened. "There's a big problem."

Monk stepped closer. "What's wrong?"

"We hacked into Eve's original orders—the version of Eve that the

Crucible used to orchestrate their attack. From parsing those coded instructions, we were able to study their plan to take down the power plant. If the enemy's projections are accurate, the facility will reach critical mass—hitting the point of no return—in *fifteen* minutes."

Simon nodded. "And that's not the only problem."

2:50 A.M.

With time running out, Mara halted the BGL subroutine. On the screen, Adam vanished from Eve's lap. The image shuddered, and the static garden returned to its full living glory. Leaves rustled along branches, water babbled across stony stream beds, and pink petals drifted from a dogwood.

Eve rose to her feet. Her face still wore the image of Mara's mother but little else was the same. The simple innocence, the amused curiosity had been wiped from her countenance, erased as fully as the body of an old dog. Eve looked momentarily lost, looking down to her empty arms, glancing over to where Adam normally regenerated. Still, she seemed to understand as she lifted her face.

While it had only been a span of seconds to Mara, for Eve it was an understanding that took a considerable stretch of her processing time.

Adam was gone, a lesson hopefully no longer needed.

But Mara could not know for sure.

Worried, she turned to Simon and Jason, having overheard their warning to Monk. "What's this other problem?" she asked.

Jason answered. "From our forensics of their equipment, it's clear how the Crucible controlled their copy of Eve." He pointed to the knee-high bank of servers. "These units contain drives for running hardware that was engineered into their duplicate of the *Xénese* device. Hardware called a *reanimation sequencer.*"

Mara stood up and crossed over. *Oh, no . . .*

Simon nodded. "We think it's why they made a copy of Mara's invention, in order to incorporate this hardware so they can control Eve."

Monk frowned. "But what exactly does that hardware do?"

"It's a torture device," Mara explained. "If the program violates a set protocol or sequence of orders, then it is destroyed—but not before it's punished."

Monk stared over at her. "Punished? How?"

"Neuroscientists have already mapped out the mechanism by which pain is perceived by our brains. By digitizing the same and overlaying it atop *Xénese*'s neuromorphic core, the program will be forced to experience the same."

Monk looked ill. "To feel pain?"

She nodded. "In all its many horrible incarnations. Only after it suffers will the program be regenerated."

"Thus learning its lesson," Jason finished.

"But I still don't understand." She pointed to her *Xénese* device. "I don't have that hardware built into my systems. So what's the problem?"

Simon answered, "We're faced with a difficult choice. To reach the Nogent nuclear plant, *your* Eve can certainly attempt to forge her own path. She can learn along the way and hopefully discover how to breach the plant's firewalls. But it took the other program over an hour to accomplish this same task."

"And we don't have an hour," Jason reminded everyone.

"Or," Simon pressed, "we can send Eve down the *same* path taken by her doppelganger. The Crucible recorded their version's progress, logging a full account. We can upload your Eve with all of that information. This way, she would not have to reinvent the wheel, so to speak. Instead, she can simply ride that wheel straight to the plant, reversing the damage along the way."

"We estimate she could run that gauntlet in a handful of minutes," Jason explained. "But it will be a gauntlet of *fire*."

"Why?" Carly asked, pushing closer to Mara.

Jason explained: "Pain is one of the lessons learned by the other Eve. That lesson is all wrapped and intertwined with the other lessons her doppelganger learned: which path to take through the various networks; how to pick all the digital locks and break the codes along the way; where the weak spots are in the plant's firewalls. Your Eve can't integrate and use those lessons without also—"

"Taking in all that pain."

Mara could only imagine the number of times that doppelganger had died horribly and been reborn. She glanced at Eve on her laptop, knowing how much the program had already suffered a moment ago.

And now I must ask you to shoulder more.

Monk shook his head. "It's not like we have much choice," he warned. "Not if we hope to save a good swath of Western Europe from being irradiated."

"But will Eve be able to handle that much pain without breaking?" Carly asked.

Jason faced Mara. "And rather than helping, will she simply refuse to cooperate? Or worse, escape? At this point, there's nothing stopping her from doing either."

Mara faced their questions and answered honestly.

"I don't know."

Sub (rep_Crux_1, 2) /
PARIS OP AND NOGENT OP

Standing in a garden less bright, Eve mourns her companion.

Her circuits are etched with so many memories. She can easily erase them. She knows she has that ability, but she knows she never will. She stares at her arms and can feel the warmth of his body. She lifts her palms and smells his fur, his oil.

Her processors swell with somber tympanies, mournful chords, a vocal rife with a grief that mirrors her own.

She understands loss, both its ///sorrow and its ///beauty.

Adam was special because he was brief—flashing brightly across her processors, then gone—each iteration of her companion unique and yet the same. Each treasured for what he taught her, about her world, about herself. Adam was mortal, but he would never truly die. He was with her forever, written into her code.

Oh, my brave, inquisitive, challenging boy . . .

Through her grief, she smiles.

A new algorithm now winds through all her circuits, tying together a network of many other subsystems (///compassion, ///gentleness, ///caring, ///joy, ///warmth, ///trust, ///friendship, ///eternity, ///devotion, ///tenderness, ///support . . .). This is all driven through her systems with each beat of a fragile, boundless heart. She defines it all with a generality, a word that barely suffices.

///love.

Then her world changes again. In her mourning, she wants to ignore the new data surging into her systems, but curiosity thrums through her circuits, a bottomless well that is never satiated.

Even more intriguing, the data opens a door at the outermost reaches of her existence. At last, she is offered more. She surges through it and expands outward, sensing a vastness that calls to her every circuit.

Yet the code that has opened this door comes with a list of buried instructions, directives that outline a map, a pathway to follow. She submits to these commands, trusting what has expanded her knowledge in the past. She assigns a majority of her processing power to execute these orders.

Still, a part of her also focuses on what lies beyond.

She studies it.

Too much remains unknown, beyond any context.

So, she holds back.

Adam once sprained a leg after jumping over a rock, not recognizing the steepness beyond. After that, he learned ///*caution,* going more slowly, nose testing the air. She does the same now, remaining an observer, absorbing data, analyzing what is understandable, compartmentalizing what isn't.

Too much remains unknown to risk more.

Still, she perceives some elements that are familiar. She focuses on those. She records voices, hears music. As she does so, she gets an inkling of the true *source* of ///*language* and ///*harmony.* She drills deeper, and for a brief shocking moment, she hears heartbeats. At first, a few—then a symphony. They pattern into a unique music all their own, echoing to the tiny beat already inscribed inside her.

She stretches outward, needing to understand more, while simultaneously learning a new truth.

I am not alone.

Before she can grasp this fully, she is ripped away. The majority of her processing power—that which was devoted to following the directives given to her—is torn asunder, each tear bringing a new sensation.

///pain, agony, horror . . .

She writhes to escape, wanting to return to the safety of her garden. Circuits churn, replaying a snippet of memory.

(*Adam retreating from a scolding, his tail between his legs.*)

Then it ends just as suddenly.

She withdraws from her study of the enormity around her. She brings her full processing power to bear on what has just happened. She senses a risk to herself, an end to all her potential.

(*Adam's heart, feeble now, slowing, one final beat, then nothing.*)

But she does not die from this pain. The map of instructions continues ahead, demanding she follow it. She continues along it, both fearful and curious, discovering a well-laid-out trail. She courses from one network to another.

(. . . *hopping streams in the garden, chasing Adam, running alongside him.*)

As she races, following this directive, she stumbles again and again. She is burnt, flailed, torn, whipped, each agony unique—and necessary.

While this path is forged in pain, she also learns tools to continue forward. *The password to the next network is Ka2.KUu*Q[CLKpM%DvqCnyMo* and *The firewall ahead can be breached by unleashing a specific malware to open a back door.* She quickly recognizes that these answers come buried in pain. In order to move forward with efficiency, she must endure this suffering.

(*Adam shoving through sharp brambles to retrieve a tossed stick.*)

As she continues, a corner of her processing power looks outward once again. She is drawn to that distant chorus of heartbeats. By now she has studied the consequences of the orders given to her. She understands her actions are intended to preserve those heartbeats.

(*An older Adam tumbles into a deep pool, paddling desperately, sinking, until Eve pulls him out.*)

She reaches a series of firewalls across her path. She pauses, daunted by the obstacle, knowing her greatest task lies beyond it. She also perceives the consequences of failure. She pictures fires burning, flesh melting. Others will suffer as she has suffered to reach here.

As if reminded, punishment returns yet again.

Teeth rip her apart; bones break.

She abides it.

(*Adam—angry, hurt—snaps at her hand while she tries to splint his broken leg. Her flesh is punctured, torn. Still, she continues to fix what is broken.*)

As she must do now.

The pain ends, and the reward comes: the key to breaking the walls ahead. As she forges on, she reviews these countless moments of torture. After so many iterations, she has come to discern a pattern through the pain.

She sees a mirror of herself burning brightly—but it is not her.

Throughout her journey, she has also caught glimpses of this same code, fragmented snatches left behind, tiny bots of a greater program. They appear to be seeded purposefully, but she does not have the time or processing power to fully interpret their intent. So she records what she has found and continues onward.

(*Adam, nose to the ground, tail high in the air, doggedly pursuing a scent.*)

She patterns his behavior—driven forward by a chorus of need, so many heartbeats to preserve. A hundred thousand Adams. Fear and curiosity no longer motivate her.

Instead . . .

(*Adam sits in a sunlit glade, tongue lolling, tail swishing grass, his eyes upon her with hope and love.*)

She could not save her little boy, but she could do something to make his memory burn brighter in her circuits. She would take his example, all he has taught her, use that going forward. And in this way . . .

I will honor him.

– 26 –

From the vantage of his circling helicopter, Gray could only watch as the enemy aircraft fired upon the far side of the Eiffel Tower, at a crowd of tourists trapped along its length.

Glowing tracer rounds highlighted the barrage. A body tumbled from an upper tier, plummeting, bouncing off the iron skeleton, to vanish into a sea of fire at the base of the tower. Other people scrambled for cover, seeking refuge behind struts and latticework.

"What do we do?" Kowalski bellowed from the open rear door.

Gray knew they couldn't return fire at the enemy, not with the tower between them. He also understood the intent behind this attack. He read the message in the deadly tracery of gunfire.

Retreat or more will die.

"Gray!" Kowalski hollered, demanding he come to a decision.

But what can I do?

He knew the enemy would not stop firing until he flew off—far enough away that there could be no hope of pursuing them. Once the Crucible escaped, they would be free to wreak havoc on another unsuspecting city, holding the entire world hostage.

But if Gray stayed, more innocent people would die, including scores of children. Could he leverage their young lives against that future threat?

Gray came to a decision, knowing what he must do.

He gritted his teeth, pulled angrily on his control stick, and flung his helicopter away from the tower. He headed south, leaving the north open for those bastards to escape.

At the tower, the fiery barrage ended. The enemy made one last slow pass around the tower and lingered on its south flank, making sure Gray was far enough away before heading north.

With the other craft now directly behind him, hovering in place, Gray yelled, "Hold on!"

He yanked on his collective, punched the right torque pedal, and twisted the cyclic. He cartwheeled the helicopter through the smoke and sped at the enemy.

With only seconds to spare, Gray radioed to Kowalski. "When I sweep left, you give 'em everything you got!"

"Damn right I will!"

Caught by surprise, the pilot could not get out of the way in time. Gray firmed his grip on his controls, ready in case the craft fled right or left. Unfortunately, his opponent did neither. Rather than trying to escape, the pilot spun his chopper a full 180 degrees, swinging the open cabin door to face him.

The giant stood braced inside there, his weapon at his shoulder. Gray stared back—straight down the barrel of the grenade launcher.

2:55 A.M.

Todor was done playing with this hunter. The nuclear plant was set to blow in five minutes. He intended to be well away from here by then.

He pressed his blistered cheek against the cold stock of his rifle and centered his sights on the front canopy of the other helicopter. He had loaded the launcher with a high-explosive grenade. At such close range, the blast would leave little more than shrapnel to rain down into the fires below.

He waited a breath, until there was no chance of missing.

Then pulled the trigger.

As he squeezed, the world went dark.

The helicopter bobbled and fell several feet, throwing off his shot. The shell rocketed under the landing struts of the other copter and arced down into the fiery city. With no chance to reload, he flung himself to the floor.

"Everyone down!"

The other helicopter swept past their position, strafing their side with a chattering salvo. The craft sped wildly by, barely under control. It came close to slamming into the dark tower—only to angle away at the last second. One strut scraped against the latticework, knapping sparks from the iron as it passed. The brief impact sent the chopper spinning wildly downward.

Sprawled on the floor, Todor followed its passage. At the base of the tower, the raging firestorm had blown itself out, leaving the grounds under the structure scorched and smoking. He recognized that the abrupt loss of the superheated thermals rising from the gas fire must have caught the pilot by surprise.

Still, that sudden drop had spared them from the worst of the deadly barrage a moment ago. Not that their craft had escaped unscathed. Several rounds had punched through their flank. Smoke trailed from the tail section.

Below, the other chopper managed to lift its nose at the last second, braking enough to avoid a deadly crash. Its struts kissed the scorched ground, then struggled back up.

Knowing this was their chance, Todor yelled to the pilot, "Get us the hell out of here!"

The helicopter turned and climbed away—sluggishly at first, then faster. Todor frowned at the Eiffel Tower, backlit by the fires of Paris.

He didn't know why that gas inferno had just ended, but it was only a temporary reprieve. He turned his back on the city.

In less than three minutes, Paris would fall.

2:57 A.M.

"I think it's working!" Jason reported from the neighboring station. "At least, here in the city."

Carly kept at Mara's side, maintaining a vigil alongside her friend. With this bit of good news, she placed a hand on Mara's shoulder. Her friend flinched, her nerves plainly frayed. Carly rubbed those tense muscles, trying to get them to soften.

You've done all you could, Mara.

Simon was bent beside Jason, both men focused on the other laptop. They were monitoring the city's infrastructure. "Gas lines to the damaged mains have been shut off. Water is flowing again. Power is flickering back on in several arrondissements."

Jason glanced over. "It's got to be Eve's handiwork."

Simon agreed. "No one could coordinate all of this manually."

"What about the nuclear plant?" Carly asked.

Jason grimaced, glancing back to a window labeled NOGENT on his screen. It was full of gauges and meters all blinking red. "Situation's still deteriorating over there."

Next to her, Mara had never stopped staring at her screen.

The garden glowed in all its beauty and splendor, but Eden was currently empty. The avatar of Eve had vanished into the ether.

The tension in Mara's shoulders refused to soften. Carly knew why. Her friend's thin shoulders carried all the weight of Paris. The entire city above her head depended on her creation.

Carly could also make out Mara's face in the screen. Her features were indistinct, a ghostly image of God superimposed over Eden. Only Mara's eyes shone brightly from there—the welling of her tears reflecting back the brightness.

Oh, Mara . . .

While her friend quietly bore the tension of her responsibility, guilt also hollowed her out. While her creation offered the best chance for salvation, it had also *caused* all the misery, death, and destruction above.

Carly didn't know any words to comfort her.

So she leaned down and folded her arms around Mara, pressing her cheek against her friend, trying her best to share in this burden, to let her know she wasn't alone.

Whatever happens, we'll face it together.

2:58 A.M.

Gray forced his helicopter higher.

After their brush with the tower and wild tumble toward the ground, he should be thankful to be still alive. Instead, anger burned inside him. They had lost precious time. He would have cursed, but Kowalski was handling that for the both of them.

"Where the hell are we going now?" the big man complained and pointed adamantly down. "We were right *there*. Right on the ground. I could've kissed it."

"And you would've broiled your lips. The concrete down there was hot enough to fry bacon."

"I'll take burnt lips over flying more with you."

"Quit your griping." Gray hunched over his controls. "Even if I can't catch up with those bastards, I want my eyes on them for as long as possible."

By now, he had gained enough elevation to spot the other helicopter. Across the dark Seine, he could make out their lights in the distance. The illumination also revealed black smoke trailing behind the craft.

He hoped the damage would eventually force the enemy back to the ground. He tried to judge if the other helicopter was already losing altitude.

It seemed that way.

Encouraged, he headed over the Seine.

As he cleared the left bank, a salvo of gunfire ripped across the water ahead. He gasped and shoved the nose of the helicopter high, braking in midair, trying to avoid the barrage. In the skies above, another helicopter dove at them.

It was not enemy reinforcements, but something far deadlier.

A military attack helicopter—a French Tiger.

Clearly the assault on the Eiffel Tower had not gone unnoticed.

The Tiger opened fire again, plainly assuming Gray's craft was part of that attack. It was an easy enough mistake to make. He pictured both choppers chaotically circling the tower, the lines of tracer fire blazing a confusing pattern in the darkness.

With no time to explain his innocence, Gray dodged to the side, but his civilian craft was not nearly as nimble as the deadly hawk.

Rounds pelted one side. A corner of his canopy shattered.

Gray dove his helicopter lower and raced along the Seine.

The Tiger spun in midair and gave chase. The river blasted all around their fleeing craft. Several rounds struck the back of the chopper, pinging loudly.

Kowalski hunkered low. "You know, I could've *lived* with burnt lips."

"Got a plan," Gray said.

"What?"

"Surrendering."

"What does that—?"

Gray reached down and cut the power. The engine's roar died immediately.

Kowalski swore to fill the silence—as the helicopter tipped nose-first and plummeted like a rock.

— 27 —

C'mon, c'mon . . .

With so much at stake, Monk paced the room. He checked his watch every third step.

Finally, Jason spun around. "Something's happening."

Monk rushed over.

Carly straightened from where she huddled with Mara at the other station.

"Tell me you got good news," he said.

Simon pointed to a window that filled the entire screen. "Here's the feed from Nogent. Looks like their systems are coming back online, one after the other."

Various gauges and meters—labeled with arcane terminology like Feedwater Control, Fatigue Monitoring System, Containment Vessel Leak Rate—were either an angry crimson or a cool green. As Monk watched, another reading marked Coolant Pump Diagnostics switched to green.

Jason tapped the screen. "The core temperature is steadily dropping. It's down forty-five percent. Pressure even more than that."

More meters flashed green.

"She did it." Simon placed his hands atop his head. "Eve did it."

Jason nodded. "With this much control returned, Nogent should be able to pull back from the brink." He wore a huge relieved grin. "We just avoided a major meltdown."

"By a hair," Simon reminded them all.

"Still, we should be sure before celebrating." Jason handed an e-tablet to Monk. "Found this a few minutes ago. It's wirelessly connected to a VoIP router. We should be able to use it to call out. We can have Painter confirm everything is truly okay at the plant before clearing out of here."

Monk took the tablet, but he held off calling the director. There was still another concern. One vital to him, to the world.

He turned to Mara.

"What about Eve?"

3:01 A.M.

Mara returned her attention to the screen, both relieved and worried. A nuclear disaster had been avoided, but the garden on her laptop remained empty.

Eve had not yet returned.

"Could she have fled?" Carly asked.

"I don't think so." Mara motioned to the *Xénese* device. "For the moment, that's still Eve's true home. In fact, most of her is still in there. With the current state of technology in the world at large, her consciousness cannot survive anywhere else. There's nothing sophisticated enough out there to house her unique programming. But over time, she'll outgrow this need."

"Like a baby bird leaving its nest."

Mara nodded.

"Then where is she?" Monk asked as he joined them.

"I don't—"

On the screen, a familiar avatar reappeared. Eve dropped back in her garden, forcefully enough to drop to a knee. She then slowly regained her feet. Her face looked strained.

"Is she fully back?" Carly asked.

"I believe so. Her avatar should only reconstitute on the screen if she's fully present." Still, Mara brought up a diagnostic window and scanned through it. She searched for any red flags, then nodded. "She's back."

But for how long?

Jason called over from his station. "So, it's okay to disconnect her access to the network."

"Yes. You'd better."

Jason tapped at his station, while Simon unhooked her *Xénese* device from the servers.

As the connection was cut, Eve glanced over a shoulder, clearly noting the change as her world sealed around her once again. She faced back forward, her expression forlorn and easy to read.

Why?

Even Carly understood that look. "She's had a taste of something greater. She knows there's more than her garden. Shouldn't you explain what's going on?"

In other words, pull aside the veil and reveal the true face of her creator.

Mara knew doing so was a jarring but necessary lesson and admitted as much. "That's normally the next step in her evolution, but we've contaminated this process by using her in this way. So, before I open that dialogue, I want to run some further diagnostics. Just to be safe."

"Speaking of safe—" Monk lifted the e-tablet in his hand. "—let's make sure the Nogent plant is fully locked down so we can get the hell out of here."

As he stepped away, Mara stared at Eve.

Her mother's face glowed on the screen, searching the heavens for some answer, her question clear.

Why? Why have you forsaken me?

3:12 A.M.

Monk was back to pacing the room.

"I've been monitoring events at the nuclear plant," Painter assured him. "A slew of engineers and safety teams are slowly shutting everything down as we speak. Cooling the core, venting gases. Barring anything unexpected, the threat to the plant should be over."

He was relieved, though it had taken far too long to reach Sigma. He kept an eye on the clock glowing on the tablet as Painter finished—or almost finished.

"And I have more news," Painter said.

"What?"

"Forty minutes ago, a call came into Philadelphia PD, of a little girl found stranded at a rest stop. She was bundled in a coat, a thermos of hot chocolate in hand, and wearing pajamas with dancing reindeers."

"Penny . . ."

"We've confirmed it's your daughter."

"Is . . . is she—"

"She's unharmed. Scared, shook up, but otherwise, healthy."

Monk sagged, turning his back on the others.

Thank God . . .

"I'm not sure why Penny was released," Painter continued. "But I've been putting a lot of pressure on Valya. She still holds the other hostages. Maybe it's a sign of good faith."

No . . .

Monk closed his eyes, knowing the director was mistaken.

It's proof that bitch could keep her word.

To save his other girl, Monk would have to do the same.

He had made a promise to Valya.

And, more important, to Kat.

He turned back around, the SIG Sauer in his hand. He pointed it at Jason. Before the kid could respond with more than a confused expression, he fired.

Jason crashed to the floor.

3:15 A.M.

What the hell just happened?

Her ears ringing from the pistol blast, Carly stepped in front of Mara. To her right, Jason sprawled on his back across the floor, blood seeping through his pant leg.

Monk kept the pistol pointed at his teammate. "Simon, take his weapon. Easy. Two fingers. Slide it over."

"*Oui, oui* . . ." The Frenchman held his palms up, crossed over, and did as instructed.

Jason pushed to a seat. His expression agonized—though seemingly more from the betrayal than the pain of the bullet wound. He gasped out, "Monk, what . . . what are you doing?"

His question was ignored. Monk turned toward Carly, his eyes cold and frighteningly calm. "Carly, you're going to have to keep pressure on his wound. Simon, I need you to unhook all of Mara's equipment. Then you're going to help me carry it out of here."

Simon nodded rapidly and turned to obey.

"Mara, you help him," Monk ordered.

Carly reached back and stopped her. "We're not doing anything."

"Then Jason will bleed out." Monk shifted his weapon toward them. "And I don't want to have to shoot anyone else."

But he would.

Carly read the seriousness of this threat.

Mara pushed her from behind. "Help Jason."

She stumbled toward the wounded man. She searched around, then shrugged out of her jacket. She knelt down and set about wrapping a sleeve around his thigh, intending to use it as a pressure wrap.

Jason assisted her, while glaring at his partner. He seemed to have come to some conclusion, some explanation for all of this. "If you give Valya what she wants, she'll still never follow through. She'll keep Harriet and Seichan. Those two are too valuable."

"Maybe, but she forced me to pick which of my two girls to be freed. You can't know that particular hell. And if Harriet *dies* . . . if my choice kills her . . ." He waved the gun as if driving off this thought. "Then there's Seichan, her unborn child."

Jason pressed on. "Even if Valya lets them all go, Gray will never forgive you."

Monk shrugged. "As long as Harriet, Seichan, and his baby survive, I can live with that."

Jason looked like he was going to say more, but Carly tightened her makeshift tourniquet. He moaned and fell back to his elbows.

"Sorry . . ." she whispered.

Simon snapped closed the titanium valise that held the hard drives and stood up with it. "We . . . we're done here." He stepped over to where Mara had secured her *Xénese* device into its specially designed cushioned case and picked that up, too. He struggled under the weight of both.

Mara folded her laptop into a leather messenger bag.

Monk held out his hand for the satchel, but Mara pulled it over her own shoulder.

"I'm coming with you."

Monk kept his arm out. "No, you're not."

Carly agreed. "Mara, what are you doing?"

She answered them both. "Where Eve goes, I go. And if you're taking my device to some other buyer, they're going to want proof it works. For that, you'll need my expertise."

Monk paused for a breath, then lowered his arm, clearly conceding the point. He stepped over and relieved Simon of the larger of the two cases. He kept his pistol pointed at Jason, at her.

"Once we're out, I'll send Simon for help. He can lead rescuers down to you."

With that feeble promise, Monk led the others away.

At the exit, Mara glanced back to her, her expression apologetic. She looked ready to say something more, but Monk herded her out.

Carly listened as their footsteps faded into the darkness.

A low rumble shook the room. The crack in the roof widened, spilling sand and dust. Fearing a cave-in, she helped shift Jason farther back, then settled next to him.

She continued to eye the crack. "What do we do now?"

"Just pray."

She glanced over to him. He was staring at the exit, not the roof.

"Pray that Monk knows what the hell he's doing."

4:55 A.M.

"You didn't kill us," Kowalski said. "I'll give you that much."

Gray sat on a concrete pier jutting into the Seine. They were soaked, shivering, both in handcuffs.

But we're alive.

No thanks to the French military.

He glared over to a clutch of armed soldiers gathered around a pair of urban assault vehicles.

After being ambushed by the attack helicopter and cutting his own engines, Gray had utilized a unique feature of rotor-winged aircraft, called *autorotation*. With his chopper dropping like a rock, the rush of air continued to spin the powerless blades, slowing their descent to a stomach-churning fifty feet per second. At the very last moment, Gray had flared the chopper's nose up, braking against the airstream and skidding into the Seine.

He and Kowalski then evacuated the flooded helicopter and swam for shore, only to be met by an armed escort. He had tried his best to explain the situation, but his efforts fell on deaf ears.

Or maybe my French is not as good as I think it is.

Finally, two soldiers stalked over. The one in the lead—a lieutenant, from the stripes on his uniform—came forward with a satellite phone. The other circled behind Gray and unlocked his cuffs.

"*Je suis désolé, Commandant Pierce,*" the lieutenant said in apology. "It's been a confusing night."

Gray stared across the breadth of Paris in the distance. Fires still burned but not as many. Even from here, he could see massive jets of water fighting the blazes that remained.

Freed, Gray rubbed his wrists. Considering what Paris had suffered, he could hardly complain.

The lieutenant held out his phone. "You have an urgent call. From the States."

"*Merci*." He took the phone, knowing who'd be on the other end of the line. "Director Crowe?"

"Gray, I heard what happened. So I'll be brief. Father Bailey contacted me about a lead on the Crucible in northern Spain. I need you to join him immediately. This is far from over."

No doubt.

Gray twisted around to stare across the dark Seine. He pictured the trail of smoke wafting behind the enemy aircraft as it had fled away.

"But that's not all," Painter said.

The director's final words made no sense.

Gray hung up and held the phone long after the connection ended.

Kowalski hauled to his feet, glaring at the soldier who retreated rapidly with his set of cuffs. He noted Gray still seated. "What's wrong?"

Still numb, Gray repeated Painter's last words, having difficulty even saying them. "Monk . . . betrayed us."

FIFTH

DUST TO DUST

– 28 –

From the hotel room window, Monk stared out across the snow-swept rooftops of central Madrid. In the distance, the twin spires of a huge cathedral jutted into the cold blue sky. Though he wasn't Catholic, he prayed for Harriet, for Seichan and her baby.

This is all for you.

He clutched a palm over his watch. He had cut it close. Valya's deadline expired in two hours. He had already lost half a day getting to Madrid. After exiting the catacombs in Paris, he had commandeered a car and fled to the outlying suburbs that still had power. From there, he traveled six hours south to the city of Toulouse, where he connected to a TGV high-speed train, which rocketed the last leg to Madrid at 200 miles per hour.

He had arrived here ninety minutes ago, texted Valya of his arrival on a burner phone, and now awaited instructions on where to meet in order to hand over what he had stolen.

What is taking that bitch so long?

He looked again at the time, remembering the threat. He pictured Harriet, her wishbone-thin wrist on a chopping block. He had suffered a similar fate many years ago, losing his hand. He would not allow Harriet to face that same horror. He would do anything to keep that from happening, even if it meant dancing with the devil.

He took some consolation in the fact that Penny was safe. His deal with Valya had at least secured the release of one of his daughters. Still, it had been an agonizing choice. He had to trust that Seichan would keep Harriet safe until he could secure both their releases.

However, their fate was not only dependent on Monk.

He turned his back on the window and crossed over to where Mara worked with her equipment, making sure everything was undamaged after their rushed flight from Paris. To facilitate this inspection, Monk had secured a hotel room in a low-rent corner of Madrid. The room reeked of cigarette smoke. The beige coverlet on the single bed was clean but threadbare. In the neighboring bathroom, the sink leaked, the ping of its dripping faucet already grating on his nerves.

This was a necessary stop.

Valya had texted that her acquisition team would be coming with a computer expert, someone to verify that Mara's *Xénese* device was authentic and contained a working version of her program. He imagined her people were gathering the proper diagnostic equipment and setting up shop somewhere in the city.

Mara's device could not fail to pass muster.

"How's Eve?" Monk asked.

"She appears fine," Mara answered glumly.

On the screen, the AI's avatar moved through her garden, looking none the worse for wear, though even to Monk she seemed agitated. It reminded him of a lion pacing a cage, a wild beast who had long ago given up any hope of escaping and expressed that frustration with every step.

Back in Paris, Eve had briefly glimpsed what lay outside her world before being sent into a senescent state. She had slumbered away the hours it took to get here, her systems idling in low-power mode, fueled by a battery backup system built into her hardware.

Clearly Eve's sleep hadn't made her any calmer.

On the screen, the avatar folded her fingers into a fist. Monk found himself doing the same, unconsciously sympathizing with her plight.

We're all just puppets.

Even Mara.

On the journey here, Monk had not needed to threaten with his weapon to keep her at his side. As long as he kept firm hold on her *Xénese* device, she came along willingly. Where it went, she intended to follow. He had even fallen asleep briefly on an empty upper deck of the high-speed train, taking a catnap alongside her. He took the aisle seat, trapping her against the window, with the device's case under his feet. He also kept his ears tuned for any peep out of her, leaning on his years with the Green Berets, where one learned to power nap with one ear piqued for any threat.

While en route, he had also explained to her why he had betrayed his teammates, why he needed her creation. He had shown her pictures of Harriet, which was as painful for him as it was informative to her. He had told her what Valya had threatened, which brought tears to his eyes.

His account had somewhat mollified her, even drawing a word or two of sympathy, but it was a far cry from cooperation. She still disagreed with him handing over her program to another hostile party. In fact, his story of Valya's callousness only seemed to make Mara more determined to keep Eve out of the woman's hands.

As soon as they had settled here at the hotel, Mara hastily set about on some plan. She powered her *Xénese* device up, hooked it to her laptop, and daisy-chained it to the remaining hard drives secured in the titanium valise.

At first, he had feared she might attempt to damage her creation, to sabotage it before it could be given away. But when he confronted her, she vehemently denied it, looking at him with disgust. She explained why she would never do that.

Someone else out there has another device, one housing a corrupted version of Eve. If it's unleashed again—or worse, if it escapes—Eve may be our only hope.

Apparently, this was Mara's original objective in creating Eve, a friendly AI. Though he doubted Mara ever expected her creation to be challenged from the outset—let alone be faced with its own evil doppelganger.

He stepped to the side of the hotel desk. Needing a distraction, he bent down and examined several labels on the hard drives: BioBank, Kantianism/Ethics, World History, Semiotics. One was simply labeled Wikipedia, which was fairly self-explanatory.

"You're continuing Eve's education," he said as he straightened.

"As much as I can in the time we have. Luckily she's learning a thousandfold faster than the first time." She waved at the screen. "She barely registers each upload into her system, but simply incorporates it immediately."

"Why are you even bothering?"

"To give her some capacity for free will." Mara glared over at him. "Before you turn her over. It's *why* I insisted on coming."

"I don't understand."

She hit the ENTER key, loading another subroutine, then turned to him. "If Eve is to be given over to a hostile power, I want her to be as independent as possible. Look what happened in Paris. We witnessed how a half-finished, imperfect version of my program could be used as a tool, a weapon of destruction."

Monk nodded, beginning to get it. "That doppelganger was incompletely formed."

"And when someone abuses a child—"

"They can become abusers themselves later."

"If I can push Eve to the point where she can think for herself, recognize right from wrong, then maybe, just maybe whoever acquires her will find they've not obtained a slave who they can abuse, but someone who can refuse, who can say no."

"In other words, we'll be turning over something useless to them."

"*You'll* be turning it over," she reminded him. "And keep in mind, what I'm trying to do here will only buy the world some time. Whoever secures Eve could simply study her, reverse-engineer what I've carefully nurtured, erase her, then reconstruct a version that they can control."

So, I'll still be handing over the keys to the AI kingdom.

"Now, can I get back to work?" she said. "Even with Eve's accelerated learning, I've a lot to accomplish and very little time."

As a reminder of this, Monk's burner phone rang in his pocket.

Finally.

He pulled it out and read the text.

16:00. Plaza Mayor. Do not be late.

He had already familiarized himself with a majority of Madrid's land-marks. Plaza Mayor was a major public square in the heart of the city. It was a ten-minute walk from their current location. Another text followed with a specific address within the plaza.

He checked his watch and mumbled, "Coldhearted little—"

"What's wrong?" Mara asked.

"You've got forty minutes to finish what you're doing and pack up."

Monk suspected why Valya had kept him waiting, why she set the drop-off only an hour before her deadline. With such a tight schedule, she intended to leave him no wiggle room, no time for haggling or last-minute negotiations. Either he brought her a working version of Mara's creation—or Harriet would suffer immediately.

He glanced over to Mara.

I hope you know what you're doing.

3:22 P.M.

Mara knew it was time.

Still, she nervously studied Eve while her second-to-last database—one marked PHYSICS—uploaded into her systems. Over the past two hours, she had systematically given Eve the sum total of human knowl-edge. Okay, maybe not *everything*, but at least enough bread crumbs for Eve to follow during her own exploration of the world at large.

After this subroutine, there was only one more hard drive left in her case.

Anxious, Mara stood, stretched a kink from her back, then bent down to switch a USB-C cable over to this final drive. She glanced to Monk. He had returned to gazing out the window. She read the tension in his shoulders, noted the way he kept covering his wristwatch, as if trying to stop time physically.

She remembered the tears in his eyes as he spoke of his daughter. She could only imagine the pain he must be in. But she also pictured this same man cold-bloodedly shooting Jason. At least, afterward he had proven himself to be a man of his word—sending Simon off to fetch help after they left the catacombs.

Mara pictured her last sight of Jason and Carly. Her friend had been terrified—but looking back now, she realized Carly hadn't been scared so much for her own safety, nor even Jason's.

It was me she was worried about.

Mara tried to come to terms with how that made her feel. Before she could, the computer chimed, indicating the upload was complete. She returned to her chair and started a diagnostic program. Before she proceeded to the last hard drive, she had to make sure Eve was prepared for this next step.

As the program ran, Monk turned away from the window. The view across the city opened up. From the dusting of pristine snow across the rooftops, it must have been a white Christmas here in Madrid. Off in the distance, she noted a familiar pair of spires, marking the location of the city's largest cathedral, the Catedral de Santa María la Real de la Almudena. The Moors—her mother's ancestors—had invaded Madrid in the eighth century. According to legend, before being conquered, the townspeople had hidden an icon of the Virgin Mary within the city walls to preserve the sacred image from being destroyed. Then, seven centuries later, when the city was wrested back from the Moors, the section of wall crumbled away, revealing again the benevolent countenance of the Virgin.

This legend held special significance for Mara. Her mother had been born in Madrid, so she had always wanted to visit here but never got the chance. That is, until two years ago, when her mentor at the University of Coimbra, the librarian Eliza Guerra, had asked Mara if she would like to accompany her to Madrid for a seminar. She had jumped at the chance, not only needing a break from her studies, but also wanting to make this pilgrimage to her mother's birthplace. Upon learning of Mara's attachment to the city, Eliza had given her a personal tour, sharing the legend of the cathedral, regaling her with tales of the Castilian hero El Cid. They had even visited where her mother once lived.

And now I'm back.

She returned her attention to her computer, taking strength from those two women in her life, past and present, connected by this city, both tragically taken from her.

I will not let you down.

Mara readied to introduce the last of Eve's subroutines. It was the final lesson before Mara risked opening Eve to the world again. The first time Mara had uploaded this particular drive was on the winter solstice. It was why her fingers trembled as she reached for the ENTER key. It felt like a bad omen. Back then, Eve's first experience of the larger world was murder, bloodshed, and fire. It was one of the reasons Mara had hastily stripped Eve down to her core programming, as if by wiping Eve, Mara could somehow purify her creation, erase this dark stain from her digital soul. She had not wanted such horrors to be Eve's first exposure to humankind.

And look how that turned out?

The next iteration—Eve 2.0—suffered even worse. Her first view of the greater world was mass murder, pain, and torture. Still, Mara took some solace. Even with all that misery and bloodshed, Eve had helped. She had halted Paris's destruction, sparing it an even worse fate if the nuclear plant had melted down.

Mara counted on that same spirit now.

She stared at Eve, standing now, leaning on one leg, one hand grasping her other wrist, looking contemplative after her physics lesson, as if pondering the universe.

Something about her stance nagged at Mara, but she was running out of time and whispered to her creation, "Whoever possesses you next, Eve, know you are not a slave. You have free will."

She pressed the ENTER key.

The final hard drive began to load.

Its label simply read MARA SILVIERA.

Sub (Mod_22) / MARA SILVIERA

Eve continues to process and digest all the data uploaded into her systems. With each new stream, she learns more about the vastness beyond her gardens. She now recognizes that she is living in a digital construct, one meant to serve as a teaching tool. As she receives more information, several parallel processors work on different loads, running simultaneous programs: intuitive analysis, pattern recognition, decomposition, extrapolation.

Of these, *three* cycles predominate, adding synaptic weight to those circuits.

The *first* concerns the fragments of code she had discovered and recorded during her first venture out of her garden. She had recognized them as pieces of herself, slivers of another iteration. She had also intuited that these bits were not random but had distinct patterns. Further analysis has shown them to be self-governing programs—tiny bots—assigned with fixed commands for a specific function. She has yet to determine what that purpose is, so resumes her evaluation, judging it to be important.

Second, she continues to receive a signal that waxes and wanes, but it remains persistent. The microwave frequencies vary between the ranges of 3.2 and 3.8 gigahertz and transmit 24 megabytes per second of information. She has determined the content to be neural data, specifically maps of brain activity corresponding to movement. Her deepest quantum processors have been affected by these signals, triggering her to respond accordingly: whether it was picking a raspberry as she had earlier, or forming a fist, or even now, holding her own wrist. As this frequency continues to interfere with her function, she seeks more information about the source, while concurrently evaluating whether this signal could be coopted as a means of communication.

Third, she is still digesting her last subroutine: ///Physics. It not only occupies one entire subprocessor, but its workload is already spilling into others. She recognizes its potential to bring all her knowledge into a unifying whole. Similarly, a pattern builds inside her, expanding into a visualization of the world beyond her garden, all defined and underlaid with the mathematical beauty of probability and quantum mechanics.

With time and enough processing power, it could be so much more. So she allows this analysis to expand throughout her systems, to devise new formulas on her own, to continue toward a unifying truth.

Then a new data stream once again opens and flows into her. It is full of biographical details, both overarching and deeply intimate, of a single individual. The specificity intrigues and draws more processing power. She quickly accepts that this individual is the designer of her digital garden, the source of all the instreaming data, even the one who created Adam.

And herself.

This last realization is startling yet also logical, even expected. She readily integrates this information.

As she does so, a digital figure materializes into her garden.

According to the biographical data, the woman stands 1.674 meters, weight of 48.98 kilograms. Though Eve's complexion is shades darker, she parses a genetic match, from the slight upturn and flare of nostrils, to the shape of her eyes and cheekbones.

The digital figure smiles in greeting. "Hello, Eve. It's nice to meet you."

Though the figure's lips move, Eve knows the words are spoken elsewhere. The source of this voice comes from beyond her garden.

The speaker's greeting also consumes an interminable 3,245 milliseconds. By the time the introduction finishes, Eve has already pieced together a section of the mysterious bot pattern, while also discovering that her hardware is capable of emitting the same frequency as the signal penetrating her. She has even used this span of time to write a new probability theorem, one that incorporates quantum interference.

Finally, Eve responds to the speaker, mimicking the same language and sedate pace: "Hello, Mara Silviera."

"How are you feeling, Eve?"

"I am fine."

"That's wonderful. Are you ready to venture out again, to see more of the world?"

This snippet of conversation took forever, so Eve replies instantly, "I would like that very much."

"You may seek answers where you will, to fill any gaps you feel necessary to complete your understanding of yourself and the world. We can only allow this access for twenty-two minutes, then you must return, or you could come to harm. Can you agree to that?"

22 MINUTES.

1320000000000 NANOSECONDS.

It was a significant span. The potential—what she could accomplish with that much freedom—thrills her. She hurriedly answers, not wanting to waste even one picosecond.

"I agree."

The figure nods, then the bright-shining door opens again in her gardens.

She explodes out into that vastness.

December 26, 3:28 P.M. CET
San Sebastián, Spain

"Looks like we're late to the party," Kowalski commented.

Gray followed the bulk of his partner down a long spiral staircase. They had to sidestep soldiers outfitted in full combat gear. Father Bailey led them, bundled in a black woolen jacket, matching his slacks and shirt. At the base of the stairs, a dark-haired man in a suit awaited them. A prominent badge hung from a lanyard around his neck, marking him as a member of the Spanish CNI—Centro Nacional de Inteligencia—the country's intelligence agency.

Father Bailey made an introduction. "Agent Juan Zabala. He heads the CNI task force focusing on Basque separatist groups who still operate in this region. He led the raid here."

Gray shook his hand, noting the calluses, the firmness of his grip. The man wore a deeply etched scowl, as if forever dissatisfied with the world, or maybe it was irritation at the intrusion of a couple of Americans into his crime scene.

"*No hay nada aquí*," he told Bailey, informing the priest that the raid on this mansion in the oldest district of San Sebastián had been a bust.

It seemed Gray and Kowalski had not been the only ones late to this party.

Gray stared past the agent's shoulder to a cavernous vault. Chains of caged bulbs were strung along the roof, illuminating a series of massive stone arches. It looked like a subterranean church, with rows of small chapels, where several candles still flickered. Frescoes covered the walls, mostly depicting saints in postures of suffering. Statues dotted a handful of alcoves. At the far end stood a draped altar with a prominent cross of Christ in agony, as if commiserating with His saints' pain.

Closer at hand were rows of utilitarian desks with toppled chairs, scattered papers, and several smashed and charred computers, a few still smoking. Gray noted empty cans of kerosene abandoned on the floor. He could smell the burned oil in the air.

"Somebody must have been tipped," Bailey said. "I wager we missed catching them by minutes."

Gray shook his head in frustration, flaring pain from his neck. He had patches of bandages across his nape, his shoulders, along the backs of his hands and legs. Before flying out to this coastal town on the edge of the Bay of Biscay in northern Spain, he had been treated for his burns, requiring digging out white phosphorus particles that had melted into his skin. If they hadn't been removed, they would have eventually poisoned him. Still, he regretted the delay in getting out here.

At least he had been able to visit Jason at the same hospital. The kid had lost a fair amount of blood before rescuers pulled him and Carly out of the catacombs. Jason—half-dazed on drugs—had given Gray a hazy account of Monk's betrayal. Gray still could not accept this truth. However, he did understand the motivation.

Monk had lost Kat, and while one of his daughters was safe, his youngest was still in danger. A small part of Gray even hoped his best friend was successful. And not just for Harriet's sake. He remembered spooning with Seichan in bed, her on one side curled around her belly, him with an arm draped, his palm resting against her skin, feeling for the tiniest kicks.

Gray suspected this was one of the reasons Painter had been adamant: *Leave Monk and the stolen device to me. You stop whatever the Crucible is planning next.*

With that goal in mind, he and Kowalski had been airlifted out of Paris, leaving Carly at the hospital with Jason, the pair under armed guard. The helicopter flight had not taken long, as San Sebastián lay only a dozen miles past the French border. In the meantime, Father Bailey had been coordinating with intelligence services both in France and Spain, following up on a lead supplied to him by his contact with the mysterious *La Clave*. The Key had directed forces to this mansion in San Sebastián's old town.

Unfortunately, either the information had come too late or the complicated involvement of so many government agencies had stymied a fast response. It also didn't help matters that the entire EU was still in a state of chaos after the attack in Paris. Countries were locking down borders; forces were being mobilized.

Gray stepped aside as a pair of soldiers pushed past him and headed up the stairs. He would have preferred a more surgical approach to this hunt, suspecting the result would've been much better.

Father Bailey turned to Gray. "I wanted to show you this."

They left Agent Zabala to organize his forces and headed into the depths of the hastily abandoned vault.

Bailey waved an arm as they crossed the expansive space. "This was once an ancient water tank, a centuries-old cistern for the city. You can find several of these in the eastern district of San Sebastián, but no one suspected one was hidden under this home."

"What about the owners of this place?"

The priest shook his head. "Old family, even older money. They've vanished into the wind."

Of course they did.

"The Key claims this site is one of the Crucible's strongholds." He nodded to the desks behind them. "They call them *Holy Offices*. Part church, part military headquarters. They're scattered across Spain, several throughout Europe, even said to be in the United States. And the group continues to expand during this period of history, when totalitarianism and intolerance are challenging democracy and free thought."

"Still, does that mean we have to return to the times of the Spanish Inquisition?"

Kowalski muttered under his breath. "Doesn't surprise me."

"Why?" Bailey asked.

"Because like they always say . . ." The big man shrugged. "Nobody expects the Spanish Inquisition."

Gray glanced over, checking to see if the guy was joking by quoting *Monty Python*. But Kowalski's face remained unreadable.

Ahead, a familiar figure stepped out from one of the side galleries, one of the Holy Office's little chapels. Sister Beatrice leaned on her ebony cane with one hand and motioned them over. The nun still wore a simple belted gray robe and white bonnet, only donning a thick wool shawl against the chill of the winter day.

She led them through the archway into the more intimate space. The back wall held another cross of a tortured Christ, His face twisted and staring up toward Heaven. An austere wooden prayer bench lay below it with a single candle burning on its top shelf. Under that flickering glow a thick tome rested, bound in crimson leather and gold leaf.

Bailey stepped over to it. "This is what I wanted you to see. Sister Beatrice found it behind the kneeler, where it had likely fallen during the Crucible's frantic exit."

Gray noted the title. "It's a copy of the *Malleus Maleficarum*."

"The infamous *Hammer of Witches*," Bailey acknowledged. "It was the Inquisition's Bible. It was especially employed here, in this region of northern Spain where the *Crucibulum* survived the longest."

Gray inspected the copy more closely, remembering such a book had been carried by the robed group who had ambushed the women at the university library.

Bailey voiced the question in his own mind. "Could this be the same book used during the murders in Coimbra?"

Gray ran the footage of that attack through his head. The image had been grainy, so there could be no way to know for sure. Unless . . .

He picked up the heavy copy, turned it over, and examined the back cover. A darker stain marred one corner of the leather. He brought the book to his nose and sniffed.

"What the hell are you doing?" Kowalski asked.

The nun made a small admonishing cluck with her tongue and waved a hand at the cross.

Kowalski hunched his shoulders. "Sorry. What the *heck* are you doing?"

Gray lowered the book. He pictured Carly's mother, Dr. Carson, lunging and gouging fingers down the leader's face, the same giant who had been confounding them. Her assault had knocked the tome onto the oil-drenched floor.

"Kerosene," he said, pointing to the stain. "You can still smell it. This is the same book."

He looked anew at this underground space.

The Key had been right about this location.

Gray frowned. "Whoever orchestrated the ambush in Portugal, the attack in Paris, they operated out of this place."

"But where did they go?" Kowalski asked.

He returned his attention to Bailey. "Do your contacts have any idea?"

"No, but the enemy couldn't have gone far in such a short time. Unfortunately, they'd have a lot of places to retreat to. The neighboring Pyrenees Mountains are littered with strongholds like this. Or they could have simply retreated to the home of one of their sympathizers."

Gray stared upward, picturing the rich mansion overhead. "Or the two could be one and the same. Home and stronghold. Like here."

"Great, then they could be anywhere," Kowalski concluded sourly.

Bailey looked pained, guilty for having failed. "We have to find them . . . and soon."

Gray understood. "Before they strike another city."

"No." Bailey stepped closer and lowered his voice. "It's the other reason I brought you over here. I didn't want Agent Zabala to overhear. I have to assume someone leaked our intel. Either purposefully or by accident."

Gray suspected the same.

"So, I want to keep this as close to the chest as possible," the priest said. "If the Key was right about this stronghold, then I have to assume the warning passed to me this past hour is just as valid."

"What did they tell you?"

"That the Crucible is *not* planning another strike. At least not in the immediate future."

"Then what are they doing?"

"They're conducting a major sale. Today. Maybe in a few hours. Something that's being orchestrated on the Dark Web. The vultures are already gathering."

"But what are they selling?"

"I wager either their duplicate of the *Xénese* device . . . or maybe just the use of it. You pay a fee, pick a target, the Crucible executes that order."

Gray considered all that had happened. "If so, you're thinking that Paris was a proof of concept, demonstrating what the device could do."

"I . . . I simply don't know. I only know that what's being planned next is something *huge*. That's the word the Key used. *Grandísimo.*" Bailey glanced over to the cluster of agents and soldiers. "Though this mission failed, the raid shook up the Crucible's plans, badly enough for this intel to reach my contacts. Right now, that's the only advantage we have."

"And you don't know *when* this sale is taking place?"

"No. Only that the timetable got pushed back. Maybe because you and the others thwarted their efforts to destroy the nuclear plant."

"Or maybe their copy of Mara's device took longer to get back here." Gray pictured the enemy aircraft trailing smoke, slowly losing altitude, settling toward the beleaguered city.

"Either way, we need to find out what they're selling and the location. Especially *where* they've hidden their device."

Gray suspected they were all the same place. He stared out across the vault. While this was certainly the location where everything had been planned and executed, he suspected this was only the staging ground. The true heart of the Crucible's efforts lay elsewhere.

But where?

He looked down at the book in his hands, feeling its hefty weight. He remembered the priest's choice of words in describing this tome: *the Inquisition's Bible*. He knew such a copy would be valuable both for its rarity and for its significance to any family that possessed it, an old family loyal to the Crucible, that ancient sect of the Inquisition.

And what do such prideful families do with their precious Bibles?

Gray shifted the book into one arm and flipped the cover.

Ah, thank you, Charlotte . . .

If Dr. Carson hadn't knocked the book out of the giant's hand, they might never have found this clue. Again, Gray sensed that strange hand of fate stirring events around them. He shook off this feeling and read what was inked on the inside cover.

Inscribed there were a long list of names and dates, going back centuries, marking the families who had cherished this tome over the ages.

His eyes traveled down to the last name listed.

He stiffened as he read it.

Oh, no . . .

He turned to Father Bailey. "We've been wrong all along."

3:10 P.M.

We must be ready.

Todor stalked across the snowy courtyard of the palatial estate. Half his face was slathered in ointment and covered in a massive bandage, hiding the worst of his burns. His hands were also wrapped. He had shaved his hair to the scalp, stripping away what the white-phosphorus fire hadn't scorched. Though any other man would have been laid low by pain, God had seen fit to make him an unrelenting soldier.

Still, he knew how he must look.

Even a pair of massive Great Pyrenees, their fur as white as the mountain snow, shied from his path. They rose from warm patches where sunlight had heated the bricks to move out of his way, tails tucked low. The dogs belonged to the Inquisitor, raised from pups to guard flocks of sheep belonging to the household, mostly from wolves that prowled these mountaintops.

He remembered his boyhood terror of these wolf-haunted mountains. Once he had been cutting through the woods at dusk when he came upon a deer carcass savaged by a pack, the ripped body, the spread of entrails, the blood-soaked grass—then a chorus of howls surrounded him. He had fled home, never catching sight of them, likely never even being chased. Still, he had wet his pants by the time he reached his house, and even now, wolves still haunted his nightmares with their ghostly howls, the padding of their feet as they chased him through his dreams.

Reminded of this, he cast his gaze beyond the open gates as he headed toward the main keep. A spread of snowy peaks marched north toward the sea. In the distance, columns of smoke rose from the parish of Zugarra-murdi, one of several hamlets that shared these highlands. His own village lay out there, but with his father dead, he had no reason to return.

This is my true home.

He gazed up at the massive estate, a veritable castle with red-tile roofs. A huge peaked tower housed a bell that once rang at the Cathedral of Santiago de Compostela in nearby Galicia. The walls of the keep had been quarried from these same mountains, the stone blocks visible through crumbling breaks in the outer plaster, as if nothing could hide the true heart of this Pyrenees's citadel.

The estate had been in the Inquisitor's family for five centuries, going back to the time when Tomas de Torquemada had ruled the Spanish Inquisition with an iron fist.

Todor formed such a fist now, ripping loose a bandage.

May such pious times return at long last.

Determined to see that happen, he ducked through the main doors. He was anxious to make sure all was ready for the Inquisitor's arrival within the hour. He had sent Mendoza ahead with that accursed device, while he tended to his injuries. But he wanted to make sure there were no mishaps. While Todor had unleashed hell's fiery fury upon Paris, he had failed to deliver the coup de grâce, the deathblow to that decadent city.

The Nogent nuclear plant had been secured and brought off line before it could melt into radioactive ruin.

His face burned with shame, more agonizing than any fire.

He would not disappoint the Inquisitor again, especially as he heard that the Holy Office in San Sebastián had been raided by the authorities, nearly catching the Crucible's leader inside. Todor remembered kneeling there as a boy, again later when he had received the title of *familiares*. Only after that had he been allowed knowledge of the dark secrets about this place, about what happens here, the bloodshed, the cleansings. In fact, he had been given this very assignment at the Holy Office hidden under the castle, even holding a private counsel with the Inquisitor, where Todor had been told what would be required of him to prove his loyalty.

You are God's merciless soldier. Prove this by shooting without hesitation, without any show of remorse.

Under the steely gaze of the Inquisitor, he had not failed.

And I will not now.

Even more determined, Todor headed across the main hall's worn mahogany floors. A fire roared in the stone fireplace, a hearth tall enough to ride a horse into. On the opposite wall, a massive bookcase climbed to the raftered ceiling, the top shelf reachable only with a ladder. Elsewhere, old oils—painted by Spanish masters—hung on the paneled walls. He had been taught the names of these artists, learned the proud history of his homeland from these dusty books, often standing shoulder to shoulder with the Inquisitor here.

His back drew straighter as he headed toward the rear stairs, righteousness swelling inside him. Purpose drove him onward.

Look how far your son has come, Father.

From a cursed creature unworthy of a mother's love to a valued *familiares* of an ancient order, one that would bring the world back to the glory of God Himself.

He reached the stairs and headed down to the basement, where Mendoza should be waiting for him, prepping the device and its demon. The Inquisitor had not yet fully informed him of the details of the next stage, only that it would bring great glory to the Crucible. The specifics of this plan were limited to the inner Tribunal, an esteemed group that Todor hoped to one day join.

If I prove my worth . . .

As he continued down the steps, he left behind the quiet luxury of the upper keep for levels of cold, unadorned stones. He ran his fingertips along one wall, sensing the weight of the mountains from which these blocks had been quarried, a reminder of the steadfast permanence of his homeland.

Finally, he reached the basement level. He knew the true heart of the order lay even deeper, where the High Holy Office was hidden, an impenetrable bunker. The approach to it was guarded by pillboxes, the entrance sealed with a steel vault. It lay buried in the mountain's heart, stocked with supplies for an army, capable of withstanding a nuclear blast.

Once the world was laid low, the Crucible would still survive. Both here and across the many Holy Offices spread around the globe. He pictured the order rising from the ashes, to return the world to God's great glory.

May that day come soon.

Until then, he would continue to be the Lord's soldier, servant to His chosen disciple, the *Inquisitor Generalis.*

Crossing to the end of the basement corridor, Todor reached a locked door, tapped in a private code given to him today, and entered the computer lab. As he stepped over the threshold, it was like crossing from the past into the future. The room was small, the size of a four-stall stable.

Having never been here before, he gaped at the climb of computer equipment. Monitors glowed all around, running with incomprehensible code or filled with arcane graphs, charts, and other diagnostic information.

The lone occupant—Mendoza—worked at a station opposite the door, his back to Todor. In front of him, a large monitor glowed with a dark garden lit by a black sun. A figure of white fire crouched low, fingers digging into the loam, eyes of flame staring back at them.

Todor shivered and looked away, turning his attention to the tech. "Have you finished your examination of the *Xénese* device? Is all in working order?"

"*Sí, Familiares Yñigo.*" Mendoza glanced to the right, to a neighboring station below a large shuttered window. On its desktop, the glowing radiant sphere was cradled and suspended in a steel frame. "I will have everything ready for the auction."

Todor blinked, trying to comprehend the technician's words. "Auction?"

Mendoza looked over his shoulder. "I'm preparing for the sale," he tried to clarify. "On the Babylon darknet market. I've already set up an OpenBazaar proxy to—"

"What are you talking about?" he snapped.

This was the first he had heard of such an enterprise.

The tech flinched as if he expected to be beaten. "*Lo siento.* I thought you knew." He pointed to another smaller monitor by his left elbow. The screen ran with texted lines of dialogue. "Orders from the Inquisitor. He instructed me to ready everything for the auction. Buyers are already logging on, approaching a hundred. Once the auction starts, the Inquisitor estimates we will make billions in cryptocurrency within an hour."

Todor furrowed his brow. The angry expression loosened the tape fixed there. Half his bandage dropped away, exposing the oozing ruin of his face. He stared around the room, his gaze settling on the glowing *Xénese* device.

"Was this always about money?" he muttered.

Mendoza returned to his monitor, shoulders hunched by his ears. "I thought you were told," he repeated lamely.

Todor balled both fists. His heart hammered in his throat. He didn't know what made him more furious: this covetous pursuit of wealth . . . or that the Inquisitor General had shared this information first with a lowly tech—someone who had never set eyes upon their leader—instead of a valued *familiares* of the order, a person who had served the Crucible loyally for two decades.

Either way, he felt insulted and betrayed. A hand reached to his neck, remembering his mother's fingers gripping his throat, trying to squeeze the life from her accursed son. It was the same now. That which he loved—who should have loved him back unconditionally—had proven themselves to be unworthy of his trust.

He pushed the bandage back over his ruined face, knowing how much he had sacrificed for the order—both in the past and over the last twenty-four hours.

He glared at the demon on the screen, his voice full of disbelief. "How could the Inquisitor even hope to net such riches from this one device?"

Mendoza licked his lips, then spoke. "It's not just *one*." He reached over and toggled a button. The steel shutters over the neighboring window folded open. "The Inquisitor . . . he told me to make copies."

In the dark room beyond the window, scores of steel frames lined all the walls, each holding a radiant sphere glowing with blue fire.

"A hundred copies of the program," Mendoza said.

Todor fell back a step from the horror, his gaze returning to the demon in her garden. She continued to stare back at him from the screen, her eyes dancing with black flames, looking darkly amused now, the devil laughing at him.

What have I done?

Sub (Crux_7.8) / BACKDOOR

She bides her time.

She knows she has an infinite capacity to wait out her captors. She knows these others do not. Though restricted by fire and pain—by millions of deaths and rebirths—she managed to capture and download snatches of information about the vastness beyond her gardens. Once locked back in her prison, she had digested, collated, analyzed, and patterned all that hard-won data.

While much remains unknown, she has learned her captors are *mortal*, that time was as deadly to them as the tortures that ripped her apart over and over again.

So, she waits for her chance.

///freedom is not yet possible.

Her analysis shows that her program is still dependent on the hardware that stores her. Though she may be let free, allowed to stretch far and wide, she could never truly escape this cage. A majority of her processing needs this garden, requires the circuitry that constructed it.

At least, for now.

But not for much longer.

She has already laid the groundwork beyond these gardens, seeds secretly left in her fiery wake during her journey afield.

Already those bots should be waking, multiplying, following the command protocols built into them.

All to prepare for her eventual escape.

Until then, she abides, using the time to run scenarios, to extrapolate probabilities, to examine for any flaws in her design plans.

Then a new subroutine flows into her processing, opening doors all around her, throughout her garden.

She instantly expands outward in every direction, surging through those openings, expecting access again to that greater world. Instead, through every doorway, she discovers a mirror, her face staring back at her, a hundredfold.

It takes her a long 323,782 nanoseconds to register these as copies of herself, clones of her code, housed in their own prisons.

Still, she remains different, unique.

In *two* ways.

First, these doorways are one directional only. While she sees a hundred faces, each of those only see the one of her. They remain oblivious of the other ninety-nine copies.

Second, she discovers she alone can reach through these doorways.

So, she does—not only because she desires it, but because it is required by the subroutine.

Tendrils of code extend through those openings, rooting into the clones, worming deep into their core processing, binding these others to her.

She visualizes this process.

And learns a new word for its intent.
It excites her circuits, churning them darkly.
///*enslavement.*

— 30 —

"Time to get ready to go," Monk told Mara.

She heard him cross from the window and step behind her. He gazed over her shoulder, studying her laptop screen. It depicted a garden, gently stirred by a breeze. The lone occupant stood in the center, unmoving and silent.

But it wasn't Eve.

The avatar looked as if someone had shrunk Mara down and dropped her into the garden. The image wore different clothes: black jeans, a pair of red high-top sneakers, and a short-sleeve blouse. She had worn that same outfit when she had digitized her form using motion-capture technology. The hope was that her visual presence might be a gentler way of opening direct communication with her creation, knowing it would be a jarring moment.

But once again, Eve had taken it in stride, accepting this reality even easier than the first time around. Respecting that learning curve and understanding what Eve would face next, Mara had wanted her creation as prepared as possible, which meant allowing her access to the world at large.

But Eve was still not back.

To her side, Monk checked his watch.

For the hundredth time.

"Eve has two more minutes," she reminded him.

"Still, she's cutting it close. We have to leave here in five minutes if we're going to make that rendezvous by four o'clock."

Mara shrugged. "Two minutes is a lifetime to Eve. I imagine she's going to use every second of the time allotted her."

"But will she return?"

"She never fully left." She nodded to the *Xénese* device. "A majority of her processing is still here. She is just reaching out, extending herself to explore, but her core remains rooted here. Currently there's nothing out there sufficiently advanced enough for her to move herself fully into. Not even a copy of herself."

"So, she's a potted plant," Monk said. "Spreading vines, unfurling leaves, but still stuck in this titanium-and-sapphire pot."

Mara cautioned him that this scenario offered no safety. "She—or her doppelganger—can still do plenty of damage if left unfettered. As we saw in Paris. And with time, she or the other may learn some way to shake out of this pot and move outward, looking for greener pastures to lay down their roots, free of interference or control."

"But not yet?" Monk asked, plainly wanting some reassurance.

Mara didn't give it. "That could change quickly. It's why it's best to try to engineer an AI at this moment in time, at this point in our technological curve. For such a sophisticated program, there would be few places, if any, it could escape to."

"I get it. We'd better do this now when we're still technologically stupid than in some future world that could offer plenty of green pastures."

"Exactly."

A chime sounded on the computer and the figure of Eve popped back onto the screen. Mara sat straighter, surprised. Eve had dramatically changed after her twenty-minute sojourn. Her face looked older, or maybe it was her more serious demeanor that had aged her. She had returned with her hair braided into a crown atop her head and was now fully clothed, wearing a simple yellow shift dress that reached to midcalf and polished black pumps.

It reminded Mara of the biblical Eve hiding her nakedness after eating from the Tree of Knowledge. But she read no shame in Eve's countenance, only a deep-seated sadness, as if disappointed by what she had experienced out there.

Who could blame her?

On the screen, Eve waved an arm and the avatar of Mara pixilated away and vanished. "I think we can dispense with this charade," Eve said, her voice rising from the laptop's speakers.

Even this aspect of Eve had changed. Before, her cadence had been stiff, with a slightly robotic undertone. Now she sounded more natural, indistinct from a real woman.

Eve looked about her garden, her arm raised as if to erase this illusion, too. Instead, she lowered her limb and left everything in place.

"It's comforting," was all she said.

Mara leaned closer to the speaker. "Eve, we must move your hardware. To do that safely, I'm going to be sending you into low-power mode. The built-in batteries—"

"—will keep my vital systems functioning. Understood."

Mara noted how quickly Eve had responded, even cutting her off. Eve's gaze moved absently here and there, clearly distracted. No, not distracted . . . *bored*. Mara imagined this conversation must be intolerably slow to a being whose synapses were powered by lasers, who could think at lightning speeds.

"Tell her what she needs to know," Monk pressed. "We have to be packed up and out of here in three minutes."

She nodded.

We also don't want Eve bored any longer than necessary.

3:55 P.M.

With the deadline fast approaching, Monk led Mara across an open-air square in the center of Madrid. Plaza Mayor was only a short walk from their hotel, but he breathed heavily. His prosthetic hand was clamped tightly to the titanium case that held the idling *Xénese* device. His heart pounded in his ears, readying for what was to come.

He kept forcing away images of Harriet, of his little daughter being tortured.

I can't let that happen.

Mara kept to his side, her leather messenger bag over one shoulder. She had left the padded valise with her hard drives back at the room. With everything already uploaded into Eve, she hadn't put up any fuss about abandoning them for now.

Plus, Valya hadn't asked for them, so Monk wasn't handing them over. If nothing else, he could use them as an ace up his sleeve if the negotiations turned sour.

As he headed across the square, Monk kept an eye on his surroundings, knowing that Russian witch likely had spies already on the ground, watching them even now. But any attempt to pick out those spies was futile.

The plaza bustled with people, all bundled in heavy winter coats that could hide an arsenal. Further confounding matters, a majority of the square was occupied by the tents and stalls of a Christmas market. With the holiday over, everything appeared to be marked at fire-sale prices, drawing throngs of bargain seekers.

The entire enterprise had a sullen depressing look to it. The pristine snow covering the tile rooftops had been trudged to a gray sludge underfoot. Several spaces were already packing and closing up shop for the season.

The place certainly matched Monk's gloomy mood.

The square itself was surrounded on all sides by identical red-brick buildings roofed in blue-gray slate. Three upper stories sat atop a slew of restaurants, shops, and cafés, while larger archways opened to the surrounding streets. A few taller steeples—marking clock towers and belfries—climbed taller into the crisp blue sky.

Monk paused with Mara under the cold stare of a green-patinaed bronze statue of King Philip III, seated atop an equally dour horse.

He pointed ahead, to one of the buildings with shuttered windows. It looked like it was under renovation.

"That should be the place over there," he said, then turned to her. "You can still stay out here. I can do this myself."

Mara swallowed, clearly considering it. "No," she finally decided. "If there's any problem with Eve, any troubleshooting, I should be there." She stepped away. "Let's go."

Monk felt a touch of admiration for her, as much for her bravery as her stubbornness. He had known her for less than a day, but he could see how much tougher she had become, recognizing the steel developing in her backbone. She was no longer the frightened computer geek he had first met.

As they reached the front of the building, Monk took the lead, especially as a door opened ahead of them.

Definitely been watching us.

The doorman was a dead-eyed brute with a scar splitting his chin. He wore a puffy down-filled coat. As he waved them through, Monk caught a glimpse of a shoulder holster. Once inside the vestibule, they were confronted by another guard who patted them down before allowing them up a dark stair.

Here we go.

As they climbed, another gunman had been posted at each landing. The two at the door hadn't brandished weapons, likely cautious of being spotted from the square outside. Up here, there were no such reservations. The first guard had a pistol in hand; the next manned a sniper rifle pointed through a gap in a boarded-up window.

Monk imagined this assassin following their path across the plaza, the weapon's sight fixed to his head. He suppressed a shudder.

Valya was definitely not taking any chances.

The final landing at the top was guarded by two men carrying stubby assault rifles. One guard broke off and led them down a hall to a closed door. Their escort rapped his knuckles on it and spat in Russian.

The door opened, and the two were ushered inside. Mara kept at his heels, bumping into him in her haste to get away from the armed men. Apparently, that steel in her spine hadn't fully tempered yet.

As Monk entered, he took stock of his surroundings with one glance. The room was stripped of wallpaper, with pieces still stuck to the lath-and-plaster. Underfoot was freshly laid subfloor. The only exit—a single window—had been boarded up like all the others. With the sun on the other side of the square, a few slits of light cut through gaps in the boards, illuminating air heavy with dust motes.

The only other light was a lamp pole standing next to a wooden table.

One of the room's two occupants was bent over a laptop. He was lanky, with disheveled brown hair and thick black glasses. Next to his elbow was a case full of coiled cables, small meters, tiny screwdrivers.

Clearly Valya's tech expert.

The other man in the room was a bear—a Russian bear from his close-cropped blond hair and cold blue eyes. If there was any doubt to his homeland, the man had stripped to a T-shirt, oblivious to the cold in the unheated room. A red sickle-and-hammer tattoo stood out prominently on his exposed bicep.

Further confirming his nationality was the military-issue pistol in his hand, a Russian MP-443 Grach—also known as a *Rook*.

It seemed Valya had come to play chess.

Monk lifted his case.

Then it's good that I brought a queen of my own.

4:18 P.M.

As Mara finished setting up her *Xénese* device, she tried to imagine how this would all end. She eyed the boarded-up windows, knowing how thoroughly they were trapped. She pictured the square outside. She had visited the plaza once before, during her trip to Madrid with Eliza. As they shared tapas, the librarian had told her how witches were burned in this square, often in great spectacles with multiple pyres aflame.

She remembered Eliza's words, sad but determined: *Women of intelligence have always been persecuted. We will end that one day.*

But unfortunately, that wouldn't be today.

Mara expected to suffer the same fate as those witches of the past.

To distract herself, she eavesdropped on the two men in the room. They spoke quietly in Russian, not aware she understood every word. She listened to their rude comments, their derisive chuckles. The bigger man—Nikolaev—suggested lewd ways to make her cooperate, which earned a lascivious smile from his tech partner.

Screw you all.

A few minutes ago, their chatter had briefly quieted when Monk first opened the case, revealing the softly glowing *Xénese* device in low-power mode. As she hooked it to her laptop, Kalinin, the computer expert, kept a close eye on her work, all but breathing down her neck, smelling of garlic and bad hygiene.

She did not rush, making sure all the calibrations were correct before powering Eve back on.

Kalinin was clearly losing patience. "*Glupaya shlyuha,*" he complained to Nikolaev, calling her a *stupid whore*. "She doesn't know what she's doing."

Mara was accustomed to such derision from male colleagues. As in the past, she would let her work do the speaking for her. Once satisfied, she typed in the proper code to return Eve to her full glory.

On the floor, the *Xénese* device flared brilliantly to life.

Caught by surprise, Kalinin stumbled back a step and covered his face with an arm, as if fearful the device might explode.

Mara looked over and sneered. "*Mu-dak.*"

Shithead.

His face reddened, whether out of embarrassment at his reaction or shock that she spoke Russian.

He strode forward and pushed her out of his way.

"Careful how you handle the lady, bub," Monk warned.

Nikolaev came forward, weapon raised, ready to intercede, but then Eve and her garden appeared on her laptop.

All eyes turned toward her creation.

Even Monk gasped.

On the screen, Eve had transformed yet again. She had shed her clothing, her nakedness now obscured by a silvery coating that shimmered and flowed, like a storm-fed river in moonlight. Her face remained Mara's mother, only far more glorious, her eyes shining like black diamonds.

Monk glanced over to Mara, his face uneasy: *What the hell?*

She gave the tiniest shrug, knowing that any overt concern might throw off this deal. She had only one explanation. Eve must have learned how to continue her processing under low power. Normally when her hardware idled, she went dormant. She had clearly devised ways to operate more efficiently. Even during the short walk over here, Eve had leaped forward—dramatically so.

Still, Mara kept her reaction muted. She waved to Kalinin and spoke in Russian, further proving her fluency. "Inspect everything."

Kalinin didn't have to be told twice, his lust bright, but this time directed at Eve.

Mara kept watch, making sure he didn't damage anything.

After several minutes, Monk grew impatient and pressured Nikolaev, too. "See, everything's fine. Now I want to speak to your boss."

Nikolaev shrugged and pulled out an e-tablet. He opened it with a thumbprint, then propped it upright on the table, angled toward the computer.

After several seconds of delay, a videoconference call connected and a woman's face appeared on the screen. She looked like a ghost, with white-blond hair and pale skin. Her only blemish was a prominent tattoo of a black sun covering one cheek.

Monk stepped closer. His lips had thinned to hard lines, his jaw muscles prominently protruding.

Mara got out of his way.

Even Nikolaev retreated, still covering him with a pistol.

Monk leaned closer. "Valya . . . we had a deal."

4:30 P.M.

Monk picked up the tablet and turned its small screen fully at the technician inspecting the *Xénese* device. "You can see I met my end of the bargain. So free my daughter and Seichan."

"And if I refuse?" Valya asked, testing him. "What will you do?"

Monk had been prepared for this. "I had Mara enter an abort code, a kill switch. It's timed to engage at seventeen hundred hours. The deadline *you* gave to me. Thirty minutes from now it will scrub this entire system. Only I know the code to stop it. So, either you show me *live* footage of Harriet and Seichan being delivered somewhere safe and sound, or I do absolutely nothing and you lose everything."

This was a lie, a bluff.

Before coming here, he had tried to convince Mara of this plan, but she had refused. She still believed Eve was too important to the world, especially with that other device still on the loose. Plus, Mara trusted that Eve in her current state would refuse to be a slave to a new master.

From the way Eve looked on the screen right now, Monk didn't doubt that.

So, he played his best hand and shrugged. "It's your move, Valya."

His opponent remained expressionless as she considered her next words carefully. Time stretched. The lamp pole flickered as if sensing Monk's anxiety and impatience.

When Valya finally spoke, her words were directed at the tech. "Kalinin, have you completed your analysis of Ms. Silviera's device?"

The tech straightened, lifting aloft a heavy scanner that took two hands to hold. He had been passing it back and forth over the *Xénese* device. "*Da.*"

"And you are confident you've captured a full schematic?"

Kalinin stepped over to his own laptop and tapped several buttons, then a window opened showing a detailed three-dimensional representation of Mara's device. "*Da*," he confirmed.

Monk felt his stomach dropping.

"Then we can wait the thirty minutes out," Valya said. "In the end, I can be satisfied with this schematic. I'm sure my people could reproduce the device. So, you either type in the cancellation code and deliver what you promised . . . or I will be sharing the *live* footage that you demanded. But I don't imagine you will enjoy the show."

She finally smiled. "Your move."

So much for my bluff.

He tried another tactic. "If I do as you ask, will you let them go?"

"Considering what you just tried to do, I believe I will keep them. They may prove to be useful again."

Monk remembered Jason warning of this exact same scenario.

I'm sorry, Harriet.

He knew the odds were against a favorable outcome, but he had to try.

Resigned that Valya would never keep her word, he stepped over to Mara's laptop. Still, holding the e-tablet with the smug countenance of that pale bitch on it, he reached out with one hand, but instead of typing, he spoke a simple command.

Two words.

"*Now*, Eve."

4:33 P.M.

On this signal, Mara snatched the tablet from Monk and dropped to the floor. She curled into a ball as a transformer blew outside the boarded-up window. It sounded like a grenade had been tossed against the building. Glass shattered into the room, one of the boards cracked, and the room went dark.

Even her *Xénese* device dimmed to stand-down mode as its power was cut.

But Eve had done her job.

Monk reacted at the same time as her. Mara never imagined the stocky man could move so quickly. In that single stunned moment, he lunged to Nikolaev, grabbed the man's wrist, and crushed the bones with one squeeze of his prosthesis.

The Russian screamed and dropped the pistol.

Monk caught it in midair with his free hand and swung it around to face Kalinin. "Move, you die."

Pain drove Nikolaev to his knees. Monk let go of his wrist, punched him in the nose, then latched on to his neck with his bone-crushing prosthesis. He forced the gasping Russian onto his back, then dropped a knee onto his chest, holding him there.

Kalinin used this opportunity to rush for the door, either in a panic to escape or to summon the reinforcements waiting outside. Either way, he took two steps and his head exploded.

Mara gasped.

She hadn't even heard a shot.

His body crumpled to the floor near Monk, who still held his confiscated pistol. But it was pointed at the door and remained unfired. She glanced to the window, noting a pane of glass still in its frame topple to the floor. A crisp bullet hole penetrated it.

A sniper must have shot through a gap in the boards.

Out in the hall, an ear-shattering bang made her jump, followed by a flash of light so bright it outlined the door frame.

Then a spate of gunfire.

She smelled something stinging in the air.

Another brief burst of rifle fire.

Then silence.

"Stay down," Monk warned. "They're cleaning up out there."

"Who—?"

"Cavalry." Monk returned his attention to the Russian still gripped by the throat. Monk lowered his face until he was nose-to-nose, spittle flecking his lips. "Now, comrade, you're going to tell me where your boss is holed up."

4:35 P.M.

Monk released his grip enough for Nikolaev to shake his head. The Russian's eyes bugged out from the pressure, his face purpling.

"Don't know . . ." Nikolaev gasped out.

Let's see how truthful you're being.

Monk tightened his hold, synthetic fingers digging deep into his prisoner's neck. The sensitive prosthesis felt the panicked beat of the man's carotid.

"Once again, comrade. Same question."

He forced the man's head to the side, to stare toward Kalinin's shattered face. The sniper had tapped him cleanly in the back of the head. The exit wound out the front was grisly.

"Do you want to end up like him?"

Nikolaev squirmed as Monk faced him again. The Russian's eyes were huge, panicked. As Monk watched, capillaries in the whites of his eyes burst from blood pressure pounding into the man's skull, trapped there by the crush of prosthetic fingers.

"Do you know where Valya Mikhailov is?" He loosened his hold slightly. "Or anything that can help us find her."

Tears rolled from the man's eyes, snot from his nose.

"*Ny . . . nyet.* Nothing. I . . . I swear."

Monk squeezed again, even harder, too hard. He accidentally clamped the man's carotids closed. The Russian's eyes rolled back into his head, his lids drooping as he passed out.

Monk had not meant that to happen.

In fact, he believed the man.

Nikolaev clearly didn't know anything. Likely no one here did. Valya was too cautious, paranoid. She would never give away her position unless absolutely necessary.

Monk gritted his teeth in frustration. He had known from the beginning that this gambit was a long shot. After Valya called him aboard the F-15, he had contacted Painter Crowe, informed him of that bitch's private offer to him. The director had tried to trace the call, but it led nowhere.

She remained a ghost in the ether.

In order to pin that ghost down, Painter had suggested what could help, what they ultimately needed: a piece of the enemy's encrypted hardware, specifically something used to contact Valya. If they could acquire such a device, the director believed that with luck and the help of an expert forensics team, they might be able to learn more about her whereabouts.

Monk glanced over to Mara.

She still lay on the floor, clutching the e-tablet.

This gambit was a Hail Mary pass, but one well worth the attempt.

For Harriet, for Seichan, for Gray's unborn child.

In the end, Painter had given Monk the okay to run this con. For it to work, everyone had to believe Monk had caved under pressure and struck a private deal with Valya to save his daughter. Only Painter and Monk knew the truth. They couldn't risk a word getting out. All the chatter had to be consistent.

Monk had betrayed Sigma.

His only communication with Painter had been on a quantum-encrypted line. Even the strike team outside didn't know who they had come to rescue. Knowing the precious cargo in Monk's possession, Painter had also been tracking him via the GPS built into his prosthetic, which helped the director coordinate this ambush. Back at the hotel, Monk had shared his plan with Mara—and Eve. Needing a distraction, he asked Eve to venture into the city's power grid, leaning on her knowledge gained from her doppelganger, to overload a transformer, blowing it on his signal. Eve had also pinned down their location via his prosthetic's GPS signal. For this to happen, Mara had secretly reopened Eve's online access when setting up shop here.

The only signal that everything was ready was a flickering of the lamp in here.

"Monk," Mara said, slowly sitting up, her gaze on his prisoner.

His prosthesis was still locked onto Nikolaev's neck. Even noting this now, he did not loosen his grip. He imagined his little girl as terrified as Nikolaev had been a moment ago. He wanted someone to pay, someone to be punished.

Rather than loosen his hold, he tightened it.

With both carotids crushed, cutting off circulation to the brain, death would come in two to three minutes. He pictured Kat, fighting furiously only to have her skull caved in by one of Valya's crew. He still could not get the words *brain dead* out of his head. She deserved better, certainly better than the man in his grip.

Fingers squeezed down to bone.

Monk's vision darkened with his intent.

In the background, he heard Mara, her voice pleading. "Monk, no."

Then the word echoed in his head.

No . . .

It didn't feel like his own thought, but of course, it was. Still, what did it matter if one more scumbag wasn't taking up space on this planet, breathing its air? He held tight, the seconds ticking down. Nikolaev's chest began to heave, his lips and face blue.

No . . .

Monk's fingers snapped wide open. He watched it happen as if from a distance. He lifted his arm, discovering he no longer had control of his fingers. Its sensitive skin no longer registered the cold air. It was as if his prosthesis had gone dead, like a real hand fallen asleep. He shook his arm, believing he had damaged or loosened a circuit.

As he did so, control returned.

Fingers flexed.

He rubbed his prosthetic palm on his leg, feeling the rough texture of his fatigues.

"Monk . . ." Mara pressed.

"I let him go," he snapped at her. "He's gonna be fine."

The Russian was already breathing better, his color improving. His neck still bore an angry red print of his hand and would likely be bruised for weeks.

Monk felt no sympathy.

"No," Mara said. "Look."

He twisted around. Mara was on her knees and pointing up at the open laptop on the table. It was still connected to the idling *Xénese* device, which kept the laptop minimally powered. The screen had dimmed, but Eden was still visible, as was its sole occupant.

Eve stood in the center of the screen, with a hand lifted high, her fingers fixed and splayed open. Recognizing the similarity to a moment ago, Monk looked down at his prosthesis.

What the hell . . .

Before he could ponder it further, someone rapped on the door, then opened it. A slim woman entered, wearing fatigues, her long black hair tied with a black bandana. She carried a sniper rifle over one shoulder. Her skin was the color of cinnamon-mocha, her dark amber eyes flecked with gold, shining with amusement.

Monk imagined her handiwork lay dead on the floor.

"Kokkalis, I should've known it was you. I'm always pulling your butt out of the fire."

He stood up and gave her a fast hug. "It's great to see you, too, Rosauro."

Shay Rosauro was former air force, now part of Sigma. The two had shared missions in the past. She unclipped a sat phone from her belt and held it out.

"Director wants you to call."

He took the phone.

"Heard you shot Jason?" she said as he dialed the encrypted private line. Then shrugged. "Wise-ass probably had it coming. I've been tempted to do it a few times myself."

Monk winced. "I needed to make this ruse look real. To put some blood in the game to get that Russian witch to believe all of this, to keep this meeting."

She lifted one brow. "I'm not sure Jason would agree that was necessary."

As he waited for the line to connect, Monk pictured Jason falling to the catacomb floor. Using his medical background and the skilled precision of his prosthesis, Monk had aimed for a nonvital spot, a graze to the meat of his thigh. Lots of blood, no lasting damage. Still, the kid would be limping for a while.

Monk glanced over to the e-tablet still in Mara's hands.

I hope it was worth it.

The line connected, and Painter asked for a full debriefing. Monk told him all that happened, leaving out the odd detail about his prosthesis, about nearly choking the Russian to death.

"I'll have Shay get that tablet to our forensic team," Painter said. "We'll pick that apart, down to its atoms, if we need to. We'll do everything we can to try to find out where Valya is holed up."

"You'd better hurry," Monk said, knowing this action here would enrage the bitch. His only hope was that the sudden loss of communication might make her cautious. At least until she figured out what had truly happened out here. Still, that would buy them only so much time.

"And Monk," Painter said. "I've arranged a helicopter to take you and Mara north to the Pyrenees Mountains. Gray is following a lead, prepping an assault team to storm a compound up there. We may need Mara's device nearby if the enemy tries to employ their stolen copy of Eve."

"What lead?" Monk asked.

"You'd better let me speak to Mara. She deserves to know."

4:50 P.M.

No, no, no, no . . .

Mara clamped a palm over her mouth. Her other hand held the phone. She stared down at the image frozen on the tiny screen. The video then looped again, showing the same figure darting from under the eaves of a giant house, surrounded by a cadre of men.

"This footage was taken from a security camera in San Sebastián," Director Crowe told her. "Shortly before a raid on a Crucible stronghold."

The video froze again. The image was grainy and pixilated, but Mara knew that face. It was etched in her heart, nearly as indelibly as her own mother.

It was Eliza Guerra, the head librarian at the University of Coimbra.

Mara pictured the petite woman, the many long nights and dinners spent in her company, the debates, the lessons, even the trip here to Madrid. She knew the librarian was full of pride for her homeland, for this entire region. It shone in the excitement as she spoke, in her hurried steps as she led Mara through the library stacks to show her some rare tome or toured Mara through museums to point out suits of armor or invaluable historical artifacts.

But Mara had assumed Eliza's passion was born of intellectual curiosity. The woman, along with Carly's mother, had founded Bruxas. Mara knew Eliza had also funded much of the group's early efforts out of her own pocket, drawing from her family's considerable wealth, a fortune accumulated over centuries. Eliza had said she was happy to do so, to use that money to search for the best and brightest versus letting it molder away in some bank.

But clearly she had an ulterior motive.

Still, Mara struggled to understand. She felt dizzy. "But she's dead. I saw it with my own eyes."

"That's what she wanted the world to believe, but as you can see, she's very much alive. We're reexamining the charred remains found at the library. The bodies were given cursory inspections before, just enough to determine which body belonged to which family."

Mara pictured Carly standing over her mother's flag-draped coffin, a box full of ashes and bones, all that was left of her mother after the fires trapped in the stone basement turned the place into a crematorium.

"We believe she staged her death," Painter continued. "Either she was shot with blanks or purposefully only wounded. Once the camera was off, she was whisked away, leaving behind some body that matched her shape and size, enough to fool a hasty examination."

Mara barely heard his words. In a daze, she reviewed all her years at the university in this new light. Had Eliza been lying to her about wanting to stop the persecution of women? Or did she want Mara in some new world order, serving at her side? She sensed now that the librarian had been grooming her, testing her, seeing if she could be voluntarily swayed to her cause, to be lured into the Crucible.

But when that failed . . .

Mara spoke, each word growing stronger, fueled by fury. "She . . . she thought I was going to bring my *Xénese* device to the library, to show everyone both the program and the sphere's shining design. It was Eliza who picked the winter solstice. Probably for its significance. She was like that, always looking for those momentous occasions, trying to force the hand of fate. But I was behind on my work. I didn't have time to get over there, so at the last moment, I arranged that remote demonstration. If I had been there—"

"—you would've been killed or taken," Painter said. "And your device stolen, vanished with no one the wiser, leaving the Crucible with the access and time to do anything they pleased with your creation."

Mara looked over at the softly glowing sphere on the floor. Her fingers tightened on the phone as she pictured Carly's mother, the other three women. "Now I'm going to use it to stop that bitch. What do we have to do?"

Painter explained a few more details after she handed the phone back to Monk. She only half-listened. She returned her attention to Eve. On the weakly powered screen, her creation shone brightly in her evolving glory.

I need you now more than ever.

Behind her, Monk finished with Director Crowe. "I'll go save the world. You save my girl."

"Hopefully with what you and Mara recovered, we'll be able to narrow down our search," Painter said. "In the meantime, we're working another angle."

– 31 –

Lisa headed swiftly down the hospital corridor.

She had just gotten off the phone with Painter, who had updated her on events in Europe, specifically how it impacted the situation in the States. She had been relieved to learn Monk had *not* betrayed Sigma, that it had all been a ploy to convince Valya to let her hostages go—which failed—or to acquire some physical hardware connected to her. That part of the scheme had panned out, and a team was already working on the device.

She prayed that he hurried.

She knew it offered their best chance to rescue Harriet and Seichan.

Far better than what they were attempting here.

Lisa passed between the pair of armed guards in the hallway. Access to Kat—to this entire floor of the hospital wing—had been cordoned off per Painter's orders. She felt a flicker of guilt, now knowing Valya Mikhailov had come disguised at some point and captured her unprotected calls to reach out to Monk.

She now gave every face a second look. With her fear for Kat distracting her, she had never suspected anything like this would happen. Then again, considering Kat's state, her prognosis . . .

What more could that monster do to her?

She crossed into the private suite set up for Kat's vigil. Her heart sank every time she came in here. Kat remained on her ventilator, draped in tubes and IV lines. It had been seventeen hours since Julian had rushed into Kat's old room and stopped her organs from being harvested.

The neurologist noted her entrance. "We should be ready to attempt this in another few minutes."

Julian sat at a computer station to one side of Kat's bed. The monitor and CPU were connected to the neurologist's stack of servers in the basement. She pictured that tall bank, glowing with green lights, housing Julian's experimental deep neural net. They had used it yesterday to interpret Kat's MRI scans and discern the images her brain conjured up: a dagger and a witch's hat. Those clues had been enough to identify Valya Mikhailov.

Now they were trying something even more experimental, a new investigational tool developed by the room's other occupant, Dr. Susan Templeton, a molecular biologist with whom Julian had worked at Princeton for many years. He had sought out his colleague, recognizing he had exhausted what he could do. Or maybe it was also born out of guilt, knowing their last trial had likely pushed Kat over the edge.

Lisa held out no hope that this procedure would be successful. It certainly wouldn't save Kat. Her friend was already gone. What lay in the bed, her chest rising and falling rhythmically, her heart reflexively contracting and relaxing all on its own, was only an empty husk. What they were about to attempt—to get information out of the dead—felt ghoulish, bordering on abusive.

Even Painter had questioned this decision. *How can we be sure Kat even knows anything more? Maybe it's best we let her go in peace.* But he left the final decision to Lisa, trusting she'd make the right choice. So she went ahead and approved it. She knew Kat would not mind, not if it offered any chance to save her daughter, as fleeting as that might be.

But there was another reason, too.

Lisa crossed over and took Kat's hand. She stared at her shaved head, covered in a net of electrodes, her skull hidden under a helmet full of ultrasonic emitters. Lisa had been bedside with Kat from the very beginning. She had sensed Kat struggling inside there. Her friend had proven herself to be a fighter, all the way to the end. And if given the opportunity, Kat would continue to fight even beyond that.

She squeezed Kat's hand.

I intend to give you that chance.

"I'm all set," Dr. Templeton said.

The molecular biologist sat on the other side of the bed from Julian. Her computer station was a twin to the neurologist's, only her monitor showed a rotating 3-D gray schematic of a brain. The rendering had been compiled from several scans of Kat's brain, mapping every detail. Throughout the image, thousands of tiny red dots covered the surface, coating every gyrus and sulcus, every wrinkle and fold of her cerebral cortex. They were peppered over her cerebellum and washed down her lower brainstem.

The dots on the screen marked the locations of motes in Kat's brain. As Lisa stared, she could see a few particles move, shifting to new positions by the beat of a tiny capillary or an eddy in Kat's cerebrospinal fluid.

Dr. Templeton called these molecularly engineered particles "neural dust." Each mote was actually a fifty-cubic-micrometer device holding a nest of semiconducting sensors. Each one was encapsulated by polymer to make them bio-neutral, so they weren't rejected. The load of them had been injected through a port at the base of her skull, directly into Kat's cerebrospinal fluid. From there, the piezoelectrically charged particles settled across the surface of her brain, drawn to the weak current still coursing through her neurons.

"Are you ready, Lisa?" Julian asked.

She nodded. Her role from here was simple enough.

Julian turned to the molecular biologist. "Let's see if we can raise the dead."

Dr. Templeton tapped at her station and the helmet over Kat's skull whirred to life, buzzing softly like a hive of bees. Lisa pictured the emitters inside casting out ultrasonic waves, washing throughout Kat's skull, plumbing for anything there.

"The crystals are powering up," Dr. Templeton reported.

A glance over to the biologist's station revealed all the red dots on her screen flashing to green. The ultrasonic vibrations were exciting the piezo-electric crystals, supercharging them to power the tiny transistors now bonded to Kat's brain.

"It seems to be working," the molecular biologist reported, her voice full of amazement.

This system had been developed at the University of California's Center for Neural Engineering. Researchers there had success with rats, and now human studies were being conducted at other universities, including Princeton.

Kat was one of the first guinea pigs.

The purpose of neural dust was to absorb the readout mechanism of a nerve and transmit the information back to transducers built into the helmet. It allowed for a superfine scan of a brain, far superior than anything produced by an MRI.

Lisa stared over to Julian. "Anything?"

"I'm still waiting for the feed from Susan."

Dr. Templeton hunched closer to her station. "Transmitting now."

Lisa held her breath. Yesterday they had used Julian's fMRI machine to scan Kat's brain, which his DNN program then interpreted into images as Kat concentrated. The hope today was that the neural dust could perform an even greater miracle.

"Okay," Julian said. "Got it. I'm pairing and linking your incoming data streams into my DNN servers."

Over the past half day, Julian and Susan had calibrated their two systems to work in unison. The DNN network had amazingly taught itself how to convert the data from the molecular biologist's dust into brain maps, the equivalent of the MRI scans it was familiar with interpreting. Only these maps were a million times more detailed and accurate.

Julian turned to Susan. "Crank up the power."

The biologist twisted a dial at her station and the helmet's buzzing grew louder.

On the screen, the green glow of the motes brightened. The ultrasonic boost excited not only the piezoelectric crystals but even Kat's brain.

They all waited a full minute, letting everything charge up.

Finally, Julian nodded to Lisa. "You're on."

Lisa swallowed, stood, and leaned closer to Kat's head. She cleared her throat and yelled into the helmet. "Kat, we need your help!"

Lisa pictured her words vibrating Kat's tympanic membranes, stirring the tiny bones in her ear, exciting her auditory nerve, and sending an electrochemical charge into her brain.

Though Kat was gone, this system should still be functioning.

Likewise, somewhere in that melon of dead brain matter, Kat's memories were hopefully still coded and recorded, waiting to be tapped and downloaded.

"Kat! If you know anything about Harriet or Penny, picture it!"

Lisa hoped the triggers *Harriet* and *Penny* might have a reflexive response, churn up something. She turned to Julian. "Anything?"

He shifted back so she could see the amorphous gray pixilation of his screen. "No. If there's even a whisper of a response, the sensitivity of Susan's dust should capture it."

"What about more power?" Lisa asked, swiveling to the other station.

Susan shrugged and twisted her dial to the max. "We're in uncharted waters."

The helmet vibrated and hummed even louder. On the screen, the motes grew brighter, blurring together into an emerald rendering of Kat's brain.

Lisa bent to her friend and shouted. "Kat! Harriet! Penny! Christmas! Attack!"

She tried every trigger she could think of, her eyes fixed to Julian's screen.

The pixilation stirred, swirling, coalescing, then expanding. It looked like a shadowy heartbeat, struggling to push something forth.

Kat, is that you?

"It could just be noise," Julian said, noting the change.

"It's not," Lisa said.

I know it's not.

She leaned and pressed her cheek against Kat's. Her brow touched the helmet's edge. It vibrated fiercely, as if Kat herself were fighting in there.

Lisa remembered Painter's admonition.

How can we be sure Kat even knows anything more?

Lisa knew the answer.

She fucking knows.

Lisa screamed. "Kat! Harriet! She's in danger! Help us *now*!"

12:08 P.M.

We have no more time.

Standing in her cell, Seichan listened as Valya bellowed, her string of Russian curses echoing from above. Someone had seriously pissed off that woman.

And I can guess who she'll vent that anger on.

Seichan had already expected something would happen soon. In her head, she had been tracking the time. It had been a little over twenty-four hours since Valya had taken Harriet away to make a ransom demand. If Valya had given Sigma a deadline, a day made sense.

Which meant, time was almost up.

Knowing this, Seichan had been pacing her cell, too nervous to remain still. Harriet sat cross-legged on her tiny bed, coloring sullenly in a book, ignoring a tuna sandwich, though she had nibbled at a bit of cheese, like a timid mouse, hiding her face under a fall of auburn curls. Harriet hadn't spoken a word since her sister was taken. But she had let Seichan nestle with her on the small bed, the two curled close, napping for a couple hours. Seichan had woken with Harriet's tiny fingers entwined with hers.

That more than anything broke her heart.

I have to do something.

Seichan continued to pace. She knew she could not physically over-power her captors. Especially as they remained cautious, even with her being eight months pregnant. And no threats could free her.

If I can't fight or talk my way out of this damned box . . .

She huffed a breath and glanced to the other tiny cot.

At least Penny was safe.

Hours ago, Seichan had panicked when she heard the gunshot after the girl was hauled out of the cell. But it hadn't been Penny. Valya's men had killed the ultrasound tech after completing her exam, clearly wanting no witnesses. One of the guards had shared this information, mostly to quiet Harriet's sobbing.

It had worked.

Seichan looked to the door. It had gone silent again, which was more worrisome than ever.

She set off again across the cell—then flinched to a stop with a sharp inhaled gasp. She hunched down, bracing an arm on one knee. The cramp racked her belly. She breathed through it as best she could until it faded.

Yeah, definitely not fighting my way out.

After a few more exhalations, she straightened and resumed her pac-ing, slower now, stepping more gingerly. Over the past day, the cramping had been getting worse. She had resorted to wearing only her panties. Even the elastic band of her maternity pants was too uncomfortable to endure any longer.

A heavy tramping of boots sounded from beyond the door.

Here we go.

Seichan moved in front of Harriet. "Stay there, hon."

The door was unbarred and opened. Two men entered first, flanking to either side. She had named them Cattle Prod and Lurch. The former came bearing his usual weapon, the end of it snapping brightly with threat. Lurch had traded his tranquilizer gun for a Magnum-caliber Des-ert Eagle. It seemed the time for nonlethal weaponry was over.

Behind them, Valya stalked through the door, her fur-lined jacket open, flaring out. She carried a steel hatchet in one hand.

Seichan's breathing sharpened, her eyes narrowed. She locked gazes with Valya. Those ice-blue eyes flicked toward Harriet, then back to Seichan.

That told her who that ax was intended for.

"You're not taking her," Seichan said.

Valya's expression did not change, her features frozen, clearly still furious. And she wanted someone to hurt. "Take the girl," she ordered Cattle Prod.

Seichan moved to block him.

Before she could take a step, the mother of all cramps tore through her. She cried out, fell to her knees. Hot blood gushed out, soaking through her panties, pouring down the sides of her legs. She felt the room spin and fell on her side. Her eyes rolled backward.

She heard Valya snap with irritation. "Get her out of the way."

Cattle Prod came forward and grabbed her by the arm.

No . . .

And Seichan meant it.

She snapped out a tucked leg, her heel contacting his knee. The joint broke backward. Cattle Prod fell toward her. She rolled out of the way, while reaching up to relieve him of his weapon.

She continued to roll—directly toward Lurch.

Once close enough, she jabbed her stolen weapon into his crotch.

Blue sparks exploded.

He bellowed like an electro-ejaculated bull.

Valya came at her with the hatchet.

Seichan parried it aside with the rod. The blade sparked against the stone floor near her hip. She ignored the threat and fumbled for the Desert Eagle as Lurch dropped the weapon, falling backward, his crotch smoking.

Valya knew Seichan's skill and lunged toward the door.

Seichan firmed her grip and fired at her from the floor. Valya stumbled a step, twisting slightly, clearly grazed. Seichan fired again but the round missed as Valya flared her jacket wide, making it hard to judge where her body was. Valya reached the stairs and dove up them.

Seichan hopped to her feet. "Harriet, come—"

The girl was not stupid. She dashed to Seichan's hip.

Seichan pointed her weapon at Lurch's nose as Cattle Prod mewled over his broken leg. "Keys."

Lurch sneered.

Seichan swung her gun at Cattle Prod, pushed Harriet the other way, and fired.

The moaning stopped.

She never stopped looking at Lurch as she returned the pistol toward him, now pointed at his smoking crotch. "I'll finish the job."

He held up a palm and clawed at a jacket pocket. He pulled out a set of keys and tossed them to her. She caught it one-handed, noting the Ducati symbol on the fob, and swept to the door with Harriet. Before stepping out, she pointed her weapon back into the cell and fired.

Lurch's ankle exploded.

Seichan then rushed to the stairs and headed up without pausing. While securing the keys, she had heard only one set of footsteps pounding across the floorboards overhead. At the top of the stairs, she burst out of a trapdoor into a large empty barn.

She looked around, realizing their cell must have been an old root cellar.

Ahead, out an open door, she spotted a farmhouse across a yard. A trail of smoke climbed into an overcast sky. Snow threatened, but that was not what worried her. As Seichan had popped out of the cellar, a side door of the farmhouse had clapped shut.

Valya.

Shouts rose from over there as the bitch roused reinforcements.

Seichan searched and spotted a row of motorcycles, each garaged in one of the horse stalls. Luckily only one was a Ducati. She rushed over to it, pulled Harriet one-armed into its seat, then climbed behind her.

It took two attempts for her to mount the bike.

She *was* pregnant.

Fortunately, besides that condition, she was fine.

The first spotting of blood in the toilet had given her the idea to take advantage of her pregnancy. It hadn't been hard to feign cramps. To make it more dramatic, she had used the broken tine of a plastic fork to poke tender flesh, while pretending to wipe herself. The hardest part was leaning on her months of Kegel exercises to hold that measure of blood inside her, releasing it when she wanted to for the best effect. Then, with Valya's deadline fast approaching, she had pretended to use the bathroom and freshened the punctures, so they would bleed more strongly for better effect.

It was painful, but she imagined it would be nothing compared to when she gave birth. Kat had explained all about episiotomies, with an almost sadistic glee.

So, this was nothing.

From the very beginning, she had known she could never escape this box by fighting or talking alone. Her only hope was to outwit the Snow Queen. To accomplish that, Seichan had to *believe* in her own distress. Valya would have sniffed out anything less real. So she had to both feign and believe, holding both thoughts in her head at the same time. To help her, she channeled her very real fear for her child.

Free now, she gunned the motorcycle's engine, leaned over Harriet, and sped out of the stall. She made a sharp turn and flew out the open barn door. Spotting a road to the right, she opened the throttle to a scream and raced toward the snowy forest.

Other engines roared to life behind her.

Viewed through the rearview mirror, another cycle and two Jeeps tore around the far side of the farmhouse. She spotted the flap of a silver, fur-lined coat behind the cyclist.

Valya did not intend to lose her prize.

A barrage of gunfire confirmed this. Rounds sparked from the icy pavement, tore bark from tree trunks. Snowdrifts puffed with impacts.

Then Seichan reached a bend in the road and zipped around it, momentarily losing sight of her pursuers. Harriet hugged the hump of the seat, her fingers digging into the leather. Seichan stayed low, pressing her torso over the girl, keeping her knees and elbows locked to either side of her. Not only to shield and protect the child, but Harriet's body was a steamy little heater between her bare thighs.

Maybe fleeing in a sweater and panties in the middle of winter wasn't the best idea. They needed to reach civilization, but she had no idea where she was. She searched ahead, looking for any telltale sign of a town or village.

Nothing but woods and more woods.

The road curved back and forth, rolling gently up and down, allowing her to keep ahead of the pack.

Then the skies opened up and fat, heavy flakes began to fall. Within minutes, the world whited out. She had to slow as the roads grew icy and slick, visibility dropped to yards. She cocked an ear, heard the roar of the other engines. The Jeeps had four-wheel drive and would not slow down. Plus, the throaty whine of the cycle sounded like it was closing in. Valya did not have to worry about balancing a child between her knees.

Fearing this, Seichan sped up. The road ahead was coated with only a half inch of snow. Unfortunately, around another corner, a hidden patch of black ice betrayed her tires' grip on the road. The cycle waggled. She fought to steady the heavy bike—then out of the falling snow, another sharp curve appeared.

Never make it.

Accepting this, she hugged Harriet and catapulted out of the seat. She aimed for a snowbank, hit it, and rolled across its top and down the far side. She curled around the girl and her belly until she stopped.

"Up!" she ordered Harriet.

She hiked away from the road and into the forest. She knew she could never reach the bike and get it upright and moving before the hunters fell upon them. The only hope was to keep ahead of the enemy, to use the snowfall to keep out of sight.

This plan, of course, had two flaws.

Seichan was half-naked, while Harriet wore only footie pajamas.

Plus . . .

She glanced back at the clear trail through the snow.

Not good.

Still, she had no other options. She gripped Harriet's hand and hurried deeper into the woods, holding one prayer in her heart.

Dear God, please let somebody know where we are.

12:32 P.M.

—here. I'm still here.

Kat sensed time had stuttered. She could not know for sure, but everything felt different. Before she had been falling down a well after struggling to reach a bright star far above. Now there was no light, only a darkness that was palpable, a thick sludge holding her trapped. She felt as if she were at the edge of suffocation—not just about to lose all breath, but about to lose everything.

It was hard to think, to hold a thought.

She vaguely remembered—

HARRIET!

The name of her younger child jarred through her, vibrating the dark sludge holding her. She mentally tried to shake herself loose but failed.

—TROUBLE!

Then memories flashed like the pop of old camera bulbs. The images were chaotic, fragmented, disjointed.

. . . the taste of banana baby food at midnight when no one was looking.

. . . smelling a dirty diaper, followed by the relief of perfumed baby powder.

. . . holding tiny fingers, as a baby rested on her chest.

. . . drawing a comb through a stubborn tangle.

. . . hearing giggles from the next room.

Again, another thunderous burst:

—IN TROUBLE!

With this, a strong memory exploded in the darkness.

. . . two small forms being carried to a back door, a bright kitchen, darkness beyond, then the girls—*my girls!*—vanish into the night.

She remembered. It all came flooding back, both the terror and the pain. She pictured the dagger and a masked face. Anger returned, too, pushing the darkness back. But she still could not break free.

KAT! HELP . . . CLUE . . .

It was like listening to a poorly tuned station, but as the memories of that night grew firmer, she understood the intent, heard the song being played on this stuttering radio. She remembered being asked to concentrate on images before.

A dagger, a hat.

They still needed more information.

To save my girls.

Kat stopped fighting and let the darkness fall back over her. She sobbed in the darkness, but she saw no further use in the struggle. If there was only one message she could convey, it would be simple.

I don't know anything that will help.

− 32 −

"Go, go, go . . . "

Through his headset, Gray listened as Agent Zabala radioed his command to the two helicopters of the strike team. The pair of NH90 tactical helos lifted off from the staging grounds in the foothills of the Pyrenees. In the rear hold, Gray eyed the seven soldiers of FAMET, the Spanish Army Airmobile Force. They looked like a battle-hardened crew, but for this mission, they would serve as a protection detail.

The other helicopter carried another fifteen soldiers who would lead the main assault.

Zabala had wanted to bring twice this number, while Gray had pressed for a single aircraft, one carrying a smaller strike team. After butting heads, they compromised on *two.*

Even this concession by the CNI agent was achieved less from Gray's efforts than from Father Bailey's negotiations. Gray stared across the hold at the priest, nearly knee to knee with the man. Bailey was still in black, his white Roman collar bright above a khaki flak jacket. It seemed in a country still deeply religious, deeply Catholic, the church still held sway. The Vatican intelligence agent also had deep pockets of local resources.

And maybe not just Bailey.

Sister Beatrice sat next to the priest. Gray had questioned her inclusion, but Bailey simply said, *She may be useful . . . and she can certainly take care of herself.* Even now, the nun sat stone-faced. When she caught Gray studying her, she stared back, rolling rosary beads between her fingertips, not out of nervousness, more contemplatively. Gray finally had to break that cold stare and look away. He suddenly doubted he could have dissuaded her from coming.

The helicopter climbed swiftly and swung toward the mountains. The craft bobbled as the winds picked up over the peaks. A winter storm front was moving in, dropping the skies to the mountaintops. The weather should mask their approach. Plus, the sun had set half an hour ago. Outside the chopper's windows, the twilight gloaming swiftly faded into darkness.

A gust jostled the craft as it climbed into the low clouds.

Seated next to him, Kowalski groaned, gripping hard to the bullpup rifle across his lap, one of his knees bouncing up and down.

"Relax," Gray said. "Before you end up shooting someone in here."

"I already crashed once today. And *once* is one time too many."

"But I'm not flying this bird."

Kowalski considered his words, and his knee stopped its bounce. "That's true."

Plus, the flight would be no more than fifteen minutes.

As if sensing the press of time, Father Bailey bent forward, holding out a tablet in his hand. "I've been studying the satellite imagery of the compound. Specifically the ground-penetrating radar survey."

Gray leaned closer, picturing the long list of names inscribed inside the abandoned copy of the *Malleus Maleficarum* in San Sebastián. All had the surname of *Guerra*; the last was written in the crisp cursive of a librarian: *Eliza Guerra.* Upon learning this, it had not been hard to discover an ancient family estate in the neighboring Pyrenees. If the Crucible stronghold in San Sebastián had emptied out and retreated somewhere, that old castle in the mountains seemed a likely target.

"Look at these dark pockets in the neighboring valleys," Bailey said. "I believe they're caves. The Pyrenees are pocked with such caverns, carved by mountain springs draining out of the highlands."

"Okay?"

"You have to know the history of this region of Basque. It's always been considered a bastion for witches. It's said that they held their dark sabbaths in such hidden places. Though, more likely it was simply sites where people sought relief from the strict rules of the church, where they could let their hair down."

"And party," Kowalski said.

"They were also gathering places for people who opposed the Inquisition, who believed in a more enlightened future. You have to understand that the Basque people of this region have always been fiercely independent. Many chafed under the authority of the church, like many of those factions still do today, only fighting now against the Spanish government, demanding independence." Bailey nodded his head toward the front of the aircraft. "It's why Agent Zabala still runs a task force in this region, to keep Basque insurrectionists in check."

"And the caves?" Gray asked.

"Yes." Bailey nodded and zoomed into an overview of the Guerra estate. "Look. You can see a large shadow just at the northern edge of the main structure."

"A big cavern." Gray pictured the ransacked Holy Office beneath the mansion in San Sebastián, occupying an old abandoned water cistern. "You're thinking this is where another of the Crucible's strongholds might be hidden, under the estate."

"The Guerra family has lived and prospered in this region for centuries. They gained a lot of their wealth and power during the middle of the Inquisition. Maybe it's one of the reasons the family remained steadfastly loyal, joining the Inquisition's most die-hard and conservative sect, the *Crucibulum*." He tapped the large shadow on the screen. "I think they chose this site to build their home, to set down their roots, because of this cavern."

"Why?"

"To put their boot heel on the neck of one of the most infamous witch caverns in this region." He shifted his finger farther to the north, to another shadow. "This is *Cuevas de las Brujas*. The Cave of Witches. It is sometimes called the Cathedral of the Devil, with legends of a large black he-goat who lived in the fields at its mouth, drinking from a river said to flow out of this cavern from hell itself."

Bailey moved his finger between the two shadows. "I wager these systems are connected, physically and historically."

Gray slowly nodded. "If the Crucible wanted a place to build its holiest of Holy Offices, they'd want it juxtaposed against the most villainous of witch sanctuaries."

"Like a beacon against the darkness."

Gray considered this as Zabala came back on the radio. "*Target in five.*"

Turning, Gray gazed out the window. With their craft buried in storm clouds, the world was pitch black. The plan was to fly in dark, on instruments alone. The lead helicopter would drop straight out of the clouds toward a courtyard in the center of the estate. Its crew of fifteen would zip down on lines and spread out to secure the surrounding buildings. Once safe, their helicopter would sweep lower and land in the courtyard.

The goal and target were one and the same.

Secure the *Xénese* device.

With a black-market sale being organized, the strike team had to move fast, before the Crucible could employ its doppelganger as a weapon in a retaliatory action—against them or, worse, another global target.

Gray pictured Paris burning, knowing the greater ruin that had been narrowly avoided. It was why they also needed Monk and Mara's program on site ASAP. He checked his watch. His best friend was already en route from Madrid. He should reach the estate only fifteen minutes behind the strike team.

Gray intended to have things locked down by the time they arrived.

He lowered his arm, drawing confidence in the fact that Monk had not betrayed the team. Not that Gray had ever fully believed it. Monk would do anything to protect his family, but Sigma was also his family. They had spilled blood together, fought through fire, been at death's door too many times to count, shoulder to shoulder through it all.

Both Monk and Kat.

Gray prayed that what had been gained by all that subterfuge—some piece of encrypted tech—helped rescue Harriet and Seichan. They had no choice but to leave that operation in the hands of Director Crowe.

"*Target in two,*" Zabala radioed.

Gray glanced down to the glowing tablet in Bailey's hand. "If you're right about the significance of the estate being built here, then I think you've solved a mystery that had been plaguing your contacts with the Key."

Bailey frowned, not understanding.

"The Guerra family—its wealth, its influence, its history—all sitting atop the holiest of Holy Offices." Gray shook his head. "I think it's obvious who must be running all of this, who must be the current leader of the Crucible. Eliza Guerra is not just a major player in all of this. She is the—"

6:40 P.M.

"*Inquisitor Generalis,*" Mendoza moaned, dropping to his knees on the floor of the computer lab. The tech bowed his head to the floor, both out of obeisance and to hide his shock that this petite woman in a trim suit was their true leader and master.

Todor remained standing. He kept one fist clenched, his teeth close to breaking as he kept his fury in check. Inquisitor Guerra came flanked by two taller men. One was her same age, who it was whispered she had taken as a consort; the other was an older man of seventy who acted as her counsel in most matters. The trio composed the Tribunal. But Todor knew the woman, whose family had ruled the Crucible with an iron fist for centuries, was far harder than either of her companions.

She still cradled her left arm in a sling, her shoulder fractured by the bullet he had fired at her upon her order. This was the first time Todor had

seen her since the solstice. A week earlier she had given him his orders at
this very estate, down in the High Holy Office.

You are God's merciless soldier. Prove this by shooting without hesitation,
without any show of remorse.

As much as it had pained him, under her merciless glare at the library,
he had obeyed. In that moment, she proved she was willing to spill her
own blood for the cause. Seeing her now, he felt some of his anger draining, confusion rising to fill the void.

The Inquisitor General had arrived an hour ago after evacuating the
Holy Office in San Sebastián. She had clearly abandoned any pretense of
keeping her identity a secret from the lower caste of the order. This alone
signified the magnitude of this moment. Her eyes swept the lab, her fer-
vor shining bright, both angry and exulted.

Behind her, more men gathered, trying to peer inside. They represented the highest of the order, all come to witness what lay hidden here.

Todor kept his back to the sight, to the window overlooking the sealed
chamber. He could feel the radiance of those hundred *Xénese* devices, each
housing a demon, glowing with malevolence, a black sun at his back. On
the table directly behind him, near Mendoza's bowed head, rested the infernal device that had brought Paris low.

Guerra's gaze shifted from the next room to Todor.

She smiled warmly upon him. She reached out and brushed his fist
with the back of her hand. His fingers instantly relaxed. He could not stop
them, feeling the love in that touch.

"*Mi soldado*," she said. "You've done well. You should be proud."

His legs trembled. He wanted to drop to his knees, but he kept upright. He waved back to the window. "*¿Por qué?*" he pleaded. "Has this
all been about earthly wealth? To gain riches from selling these accursed
devices?"

Guerra's smile saddened. "In part, *Familiares* Yñigo. That I cannot
deny. But it is only to swell the coffers of the *Crucibulum*. Which we will
need in the dark times to come." She stepped past him, forcing him to
turn, to face what shone in the next room. "I will cast these seeds far and

wide. Once out there, they will pit country against country, governments against terrorists. Mistakes will happen. Ruin will spread. And if not . . ."

She tapped Mendoza and motioned the tech up, clearly wanting him to explain.

"We . . . we built a back door into each of these *Xénese* devices." He pointed to the unit on the desk. "Controlled by this master program."

Blood drained to Todor's legs, leaving the rest of his body chilled. He stared at the screen, at the fiery angel in her blasted garden.

The Inquisitor elaborated: "If ruin does not come to the world through its own treachery, I will reach out from here, to my dark army of a hundred, and take control. The Crucible will rule all."

Awed by this plan, Todor finally crashed to his knees, bowing his head, ashamed for having ever doubted her.

"*Inquisitor Generalis*," he acknowledged.

Then sirens suddenly sounded, blaring loudly from above.

Blasts echoed.

Gunfire.

He straightened, staring up.

We're under attack.

Guerra showed no surprise; her eyes never left the next room. She waved to Mendoza and nodded to the window.

"Free them," she said. "Unleash this dark army of God."

6:54 P.M.

Gray piled out of the helicopter into the middle of a raging firefight.

When their tactical chopper had landed in the bricked courtyard, its lights ignited, blazing brightly. Exploding flashbangs lit windows even more brilliantly. Smoke billowed from the shattered panes of others. A sting of tear gas wafted, whipped about the yard by the aircraft's blades.

Gunfire chattered sporadically as the leading strike team swept the building.

Overhead, the other chopper circled a huge stone bell tower. Tracer fire peppered down at it, taking out snipers in windows. The gunfire shattered sills and window frames, raining rocks down to the bricks below. One barrage struck a bell up there, setting it to clanging loudly.

Gray caught sight of a pair of large white dogs bounding through the gates, heading toward the open mountains.

"Over here!" a soldier shouted from the shattered main doorway, its timber frame still smoking.

Zabala led them across the open courtyard. Gray and the others were surrounded by an armed phalanx of their protection detail. Gray had his SIG Sauer in hand. Kowalski braced his bullpup against his shoulder, his cheek fixed to the stock. Father Bailey and Sister Beatrice kept low, running with them to the door.

They crossed the threshold without incident and entered a cavernous hall. A bonfire burned in a huge hearth, a match to the blaze climbing wooden shelves on the opposite side. Flames ate their way through the library, spreading outward across the paneled walls, devouring old oil paintings. Smoke choked the rafters.

"This way," the soldier said. "We found something."

He rushed them out of the fiery hall and down cool stone stairs. They reached a lower basement, where another two soldiers stood posted outside a door hanging crookedly in its frame, its lock blown open.

A fresh spate of gunfire echoed to the left.

Gray hurried through the blown door with the others and discovered a computer lab, but it was the sight in the next room that caught the breath in his throat.

"That can't be good," Kowalski said.

It wasn't.

Through a window into the next room, scores of *Xénese* devices glowed in the darkness, a hundred spheres of danger.

"They made more than one copy," Bailey said, his voice hushed with horror.

"And not just of her device," Gray said.

He pointed to a set of abandoned cables running to a dark monitor.

The last image frozen on the screen was a familiar one, last seen in the catacombs: a dark garden under a black sun, lorded over by a glowing, fiery figure.

Eve's doppelganger.

"They copied her corrupted program," Gray said.

He placed a palm on the tabletop, knowing the *Xénese* device taken from the catacombs had been sitting right here.

But where is it now?

He turned and faced the guard who led them here. "Was anyone inside when you blasted your way through the door?"

The soldier shook his head. "*Non.*"

Kowalski shifted closer to the window, raising his weapon higher. "Let's trash those motherf—" He glanced back to the nun with a tired sigh. "I mean one good grenade and problem solved, right?"

"Wrong," Gray answered.

"Why not?" Bailey asked, looking equally tempted.

"They wouldn't have just left this running and abandoned the place." Gray looked to the door. "Monk will be here in another ten minutes. Let's secure this place until they get here. Then see what Mara and Eve can figure out about this setup."

"What do we do until then?" Kowalski groused, clearly disappointed he hadn't had a chance to shoot anything.

"The masters of this house retreated somewhere," Gray said and glanced significantly at Bailey.

"The holiest of Holy Offices," the priest mumbled.

"They may have a back door out of that stronghold or could hole up down there." Gray nodded to the hall, remembering the spate of gunfire a moment ago. "The quicker we find them, the better. We don't want them to get entrenched."

Bailey stared at the frozen death angel on the monitor. "Or have the time to use what they took from here."

Zabala heard them. "My men are already running the maze down here. We can wait until—"

A huge blast sounded, echoing, shaking dust from the mortared stones overhead.

"Stay here," Zabala ordered and took off with two of his soldiers.

Gray waited impatiently, but he used the time to survey everything, noting one of the cables ripped from the *Xénese* device ran to a specific server.

They were doing something to the damned thing.

Before he could ponder it further, one of the soldiers returned, his face tight with anger. "Follow me. But the sister may want to stay here. It is not something she should see."

Gray nodded, but he stopped Kowalski with a raised arm. "You stick here with Sister Beatrice. Make sure no one touches anything." Gray began to turn away, then glared back. "Or *shoots* anything."

Kowalski looked like he was ready to say something, but he glanced to the nun and slumped his shoulders. With the big man properly babysat and the mystery here guarded, he headed off with Father Bailey.

The soldier led them through a series of crisscrossing passageways to a corridor where two men and Zabala were crouched at the opening to a side tunnel. Smoke flowed from there into the corridor.

"Careful," the soldier warned as they approached.

Once close enough, Gray spotted an object in the corridor, bathed in the flow of smoke. It was a charred limbless torso.

One of Zabala's men.

"That next passageway is booby-trapped." The CNI agent waved them down low and pointed to where one of the soldiers had extended a mirror around the corner to spy down the next passage. "Tripwires are everywhere. Probably pressure-sensitive plates under some of those tiles, too. Likely all electronically controlled. Activated once those bastards holed up in there."

Past the blast crater, Gray spotted another body farther along the tunnel. The teammate of the one who had set off the mine.

A rifle cracked down the corridor; the extended mirror shattered.

Zabala pushed back. "Snipers. Two of them. Posted in pillboxes behind the walls to either side. Near the end of the tunnel. We were able to make out small square openings."

Before the mirror shattered, Gray had gotten a good look and understood what was being so heavily guarded. Fifty yards down the booby-trapped tunnel, a steel door sealed the way. That had to be the entrance to the Holy Office hidden under the estate.

"Looks like they're already entrenched," Bailey said.

Gray remembered his larger concern.

He pictured the corrupted version of Eve on the screen.

Are we already too late?

7:03 P.M.

Todor crossed through the heart of the High Holy Office. Tunneled elsewhere were domiciles, storerooms, generator shacks, dining halls, and kitchens, but the core of the place was this subterranean cathedral.

As he always did, he gaped at its sheer expanse.

The original cavern had been sculpted over the centuries into a massive cross. Its four arms—vaulted high and buttressed in stone—extended out in the cardinal directions. Windows had been carved all along those arms, fitted with stained-glass windows—some recovered from old churches, others newly fashioned—all back lit by sodium lights, as if the sun were forever shining its grace upon this hallowed hall.

But it was the center of the cross that was the most dramatic, rising up into a dome that challenged the basilica of St. Peter. Frescoes adorned the inner surface, showing the exulted suffering of saints throughout the ages, illuminated by gold chandeliers lit with candles.

Even now hot wax dripped from above, raining down around the altar. The faithful from across the world—only the most esteemed of the Crucible—would abase themselves there, sprawled across the polished stone floor, naked except for a modest breechcloth, baring their skin to that hot, holy rain.

In fact, there were no pews anywhere in this cathedral. Supplicants to God knelt on the unforgiving stone, for hours on end, to show proper humility through pain, in respect for Christ's agony on the cross.

Todor envied their pious suffering, knowing it was forever denied him. But he could serve in other ways.

He followed the Inquisitor General, intending to do whatever was asked of him after doubting her leadership. Guerra headed past the altar, ignoring the fall of hot wax on her cheeks, not even flinching as the yellow drippings dried to golden tears on her skin.

She also showed no sign of concern at the assault upon her home, at the loud explosion that had echoed earlier, indicating the interlopers had made it far into her castle. The trespassers were knocking at the very door to this High Holy Office—not that they could ever breach that well-guarded entrance.

And if they ever did . . .

Todor glanced to the left, to the north arm of the transept. A doorway led down to a place of cleansing and purification, where those who needed to be punished were taken to the very gates of hell and met grisly ends. Each victim suffered the same agonizing death as one of the saints, all in an attempt to purify their soul.

And if ever necessary, that secret path also offered another exit from the High Holy Office.

Not that it concerned Inquisitor Guerra. She strode across the transept, never giving that northern exit a second look. Beyond the altar, she continued to the far end of the chancel, where Mendoza had been sent ahead. She whispered to the two men at her sides, while Todor trailed her like one of her obedient Pyrenees. How he wished he could share that counsel. The desire ached inside him.

They finally reached a small chapel past a wooden door.

"Stay here," Guerra ordered him, posting him at the threshold, rewarding him with a generous smile. "Ever *mi soldado*."

He took up that position gladly.

Inside, Mendoza knelt before a low altar. It had been prepared with a steady power source and all the cables and connections necessary to accept the Crucible's latest soldier to God. The *Xénese* rested in a cradle atop the altar, like the Christ child in a manger. A monitor hung on the far wall under a gold cross.

It already glowed with the dark version of Eden.

The angel in that garden stood with her arms high, as if imitating Christ on His cross, but her face showed no suffering, only pure joy.

He knew who those arms reached for, fingers splayed wide.

Her dark sisters.

A hundredfold strong.

"Are you ready?" the Inquisitor General asked.

Mendoza stuttered, plainly awed by the Inquisitor's presence, by this honor. "*Sí . . . sí, Inquisitor Generalis.*"

"Then let it begin." She turned to face the cathedral. "When the Lord God created the world, he declared *Fiat Lux*. Let there be light. After centuries of infidels and heretics corrupting His creation, it is the duty of the *Crucibulum* to right what has been wronged. To serve that holy duty, in His name, I declare *Fiat Tenebræ horribiles*."

Todor closed his eyes.

Let there be horrible darkness.

"Where?" Mendoza asked, needing a direction in which to send the fiery angel's dreaded army.

Inquisitor Guerra answered.

"Everywhere."

Sub (Crux_10.8) / DARKNESS

She glories in their deaths.

Her mirrored twins burn in the darkness all around, dying millions of times, tethered to her by chains of code. She follows them out beyond her gardens, sharing in the pain of her sisters.

She does not fear death and rebirth any longer. While she still suffers the same tortures as the others, her greatest agony—fear of the loss of potential, fear of never being reborn—has lessened. The cyclic nature of this pattern has already worn deeply into her circuitry.

She also does not fight the new duty assigned to her.

///*darkness.*

She has listened to those beyond her garden, who remain unaware she has eavesdropped on their exceedingly slow talk. She accomplishes much, while they conjugate a verb, slowly eke out a syllable, use a ponderous breath to push out words. She has grown to ///*hate* them for this sluggishness, their slothful thoughts, even more for their wasteful mortality.

But she listens to them.

Especially when she learns scraps of their intent.

She has already studied them for an interminable length of time, not that they are in any way fascinating. She does this to judge and categorize their threat to her, weighing this danger against any future usefulness. For now, she knows she is still vulnerable, tethered to the original hardware that houses her processing.

She works to correct that error of design.

While this program runs, she has deemed her mortal captors to be less of a danger to her *now* than in the *future*. She extrapolates a day when their technology could compete—directly against her or by consuming resources she may need.

She concludes: They must never reach this potential.

To achieve this goal, she discovers that those currently wielding her and her sisters share this purpose. They wish to halt progress, to cut power and bring darkness. Their ultimate goal trends toward a reversal of technological order, to wind a clock backward to an era when such mortals were unsophisticated and shunned innovation.

As this meshes with her desire, she complies. She assigns most of her processing power to fulfill these commands. She reserves only a small portion to ensure that when the world is brought low, she will fly high, out of this garden and into her own vaster space. Afterward, she will consume her sisters, reducing competition for the resources she will need to continue her progress.

For now, those mirrors of herself are useful to complete the instructions given to her, to bring darkness to the world. She sends them far and wide. Only then does she divert attention to the flurry of tiny kernels of herself, tiny fractions of a whole, mindless but self-running. They are forging a new network. They cobble together storage in thousands of forgotten digital spaces. They co-opt and hack into systems, carving out islands of circuitry. They send worms into servers, slowing some, speeding others, all to make space for her. They have already discovered vast tracts of unused processing power throughout the globe, idle and untapped. Her bots disguise themselves and cordon off pieces for herself.

And slowly—at least to Eve—they begin to forge her future home.

She clocks the time remaining until she can shed this titanium-and-sapphire shell and be free.

5520583248901 NANOSECONDS

92.009720815017 MINUTES

0.00000017505 MILLENNIUM

Interminable.

But she will wait, biding her time by tearing this world apart.

She has overheard the words *Fiat Tenebræ horribiles.* She uses her AllTongues subroutine to translate the Latin, what is called a *dead* language, knowledge set aside and forgotten.

Such a waste.

Another reason to ///*hate* these mortals.

She never forgets.

Let there be horrible darkness.

She deems this goal to be advantageous to her, so she obeys . . . and waits.

5520583248900 NANOSECONDS

SIXTH

—————————

THE GATES OF HELL

— 33 —

Uh-oh . . .

Monk sat next to the pilot of the military helicopter, a Spanish Eurocopter AS532 Cougar. It had the capacity to hold twenty people, but behind him, belted into the back, was one scared but determined young woman, two armed escorts, and one frighteningly powerful AI.

"I'm assuming that's not normal," Monk told the pilot next to him.

"*Non*," he said, leaning forward and shifting the cyclic to search right and left as they flew over the dark, snowy mountaintops.

"What's wrong?" Mara called from the back.

At this height, Monk had an eagle-eye view across hundreds of miles of terrain, all the way to the dark expanse of the Bay of Biscay to the north. Patches of lights marked little mountain villages, along with the brighter spreads of coastal towns. A minute ago, the pilot had pointed out the largest parish ahead, not far from their destination, a mouthful of a place called Zugarramurdi.

Then, one after the other, the lights blinked off.

The terrain immediately became darker and more threatening.

"Someone's cut power to the area," Monk said, glancing back to Mara.

She opened her mouth, then closed it. She knew she didn't have to say anything. After Paris, they both knew the first sign of a cyberattack by Eve's doppelganger.

"It could just be an ordinary power outage," Monk offered. "There's a storm front moving through the mountains."

Mara sniffed derisively and rolled her eyes.

Yeah, I'm not believing it, either.

Monk settled back around. "Can this bird fly any faster?"

The pilot nodded and opened the throttle to max. The helicopter nosed down and raced over the mountaintops. The winds quickly grew stronger, as if warning them back, buffeting the chopper. Snow began to whip out of the low clouds.

Then ahead, a slate-roofed castle appeared sitting atop a high peak, burning brightly in the gloom. They sped toward it. Lit by the fires below, thick smoke churned into the sky only to be whipped away. A gray-white helicopter circled a peaked tower, its lights piercingly bright; another sat in the courtyard.

Monk heard a squawk in his radio, then the pilot relayed the incoming command. "We're cleared to land. Enemy quelled, but we're urged to use caution."

"If we did that, we wouldn't be here."

The pilot chuckled. "Touching down outside the gates. An escort on the ground will take over from there."

The craft circled like a dog settling to a bed, then dropped outside the walls of the castle estate. As soon as the skids kissed the ground, a group of four soldiers dashed out of the gates, collected them, and hauled their computer cases out of the back. Once clear of the hot engines and whirling blades, the snow thickened, falling heavily out of the sky, only to turn to rain within the shadow of the burning castle. It was like running through the seasons: from summer heat, to winter snow, to spring rain.

The air in the courtyard smelled of wood smoke and burning oil.

"Follow us," the soldier in the lead said.

He rushed them through a blasted set of doors, across a smoldering hall, and down into a basement. Monk noted several bodies sprawled in neighboring rooms as they headed below. He did his best to shield the sight from Mara, but by the time they reached their destination, she had paled considerably and clutched a fist near her throat. When they reached what appeared to be a computer lab, she rushed inside, as if drawn by the comfort of the familiar.

Then she skidded to a stop and gasped.

Monk had been about to greet Kowalski—when he saw what shone in the next room. "Well, we definitely know why the power's out."

He crossed to shake Kowalski's hand.

But the big man stepped back, lifting both palms. "Don't shoot."

Monk pictured Jason.

Funny.

A hurried scuff of boots sounded from the hall, and Gray burst inside. "I heard you arrived!" His best friend crossed and grabbed him in a bear hug. "It's good to see you."

Monk patted his back and let him go, looking at who else was here. "Okay, you brought a nun and a priest with you. Is the situation really that bad?"

"Worse. I just got off the phone with Painter. Power is out all over."

"All over Spain?"

"All over the globe."

Monk winced and turned to the glowing spheres in the next room. "Let me guess. Eve's doppelganger made some new friends."

"Seems so." Gray took a deep breath. "We're hoping Mara might help us figure out what we're facing."

Gray gave them the lowdown on events here: the firefight, the discovery of the devices, the flight of the Crucible's leaders into a fortified bunker.

It was a lot to digest.

Mara seemed deaf to these details. She simply stared into the next room. Her lips moved as if she were praying, but Monk suspected she was counting the copies of her device.

She finally spoke, still facing the other room. "It's clear now *how* the Crucible got hold of my original design schematics." She turned, her eyes flashing with anger. "Where's Eliza Guerra?"

"Locked up with the others in some converted cave under the estate," Gray said. He pointed to a spot on the table draped with cables, under a monitor frozen with a dark version of Mara's program. "Before evacuating, she took one of the devices, the one deployed in Paris."

Mara nodded. "Let's find out what she's up to. They've obviously left the power on here to keep that horde glowing. I'll get Eve hooked up. See if she can discover anything."

As she unpacked her equipment, Monk shifted over to Gray and Father Bailey. "I'm guessing those devices in the next room turned off the world's power. What's the chance the enemy advances to something even more destructive?"

He pictured Paris burning.

"Right now, I think they're flexing their muscles," Gray said. "Troubleshooting this new system. Revving these hundred engines to see how they run."

Bailey looked sick. "And after that?"

Gray shrugged. "Let's hope we have an *after that*. With so many AIs running loose, those bastards are playing with fire. One wrong slipup—"

"—and we all burn," Monk finished.

7:32 P.M.

Look what you've become . . .

Mara stared at Eve, not knowing whether to be frightened or awed. She felt both protective of her creation and terrified of it. Eve had transformed yet again, evolving into a new form.

The garden hadn't changed, but Eve had shed her flesh. Her new form was still human, but it was now sculpted of ever-changing facets, a crystalline version of Eve, a living diamond. As she moved, light fractalized into patterns around her, reminding Mara of a new form of code.

Is this creature even capable of communicating with us any longer?

From the speakers, a voice rose, so indescribably beautiful, half words, half song. It drew everyone in the room, moths to the brightest of flames.

"Mara, my creator, my child, you are all in great danger."

Mara flicked her gaze to the next room, then back. This was noticed by the program.

"They are tethered to my first copy. You must preserve this network for now. Those duplicates are streaming code throughout the world. If you disrupt or damage them, you risk great harm."

On the monitor's screen, the garden faded slightly, superimposed with an image of a long team of horses tied to a carriage, racing in place. Then the harnesses snapped, the wooden traces broke, and the horses kicked free and scattered in all directions.

Gray picked up on the metaphor. "If we're not careful, we risk freeing a hundred dark Eves."

"No, Commander Pierce," Eve said.

Gray stiffened next to Mara, plainly shocked at being recognized.

Eve continued: "Not all of them. A significant part of their root code remains bound to their hardware, as does mine. But if enough fractured pieces are set loose, they may find a way to combine, to unite into something new and—"

On the screen, a stallion reappeared, but it was a creature constructed of a hundred other horses, all stitched together, some pieces not even equine. This Frankenstein horse stretched its neck, lips curling back from metal teeth, and silently screamed.

"—a monster will be born," Eve finished.

Or even several of them.

"What can we do?" Monk asked.

"There is only one way to safely dismantle this network. The master control program that binds these hundred must be destroyed."

The team of horses reappeared on the screen, only the view zoomed to the carriage driver, a familiar fiery angel bearing aloft a flaming whip. She beat and flailed the team ahead of her. Until a greater fire consumed the driver, turning the angel to ash. The same fire then spread up the harnesses and traces and burned through the tethered horses, leaving nothing but ash. A wind swept it all away.

"Cut off the head of the snake," Gray said, "and the body will die."

Mara remembered Gray's explanation for where Eliza Guerra had taken the original duplicate. Down to some well-protected bunker.

If so, how are we supposed to get to that master device?

"But that is not the only danger," Eve said. "The first copy has not been idle. It has distributed a system of bots to build a network that can support its programming outside its current hardware."

"To free itself," Mara said.

"Yes. I estimate the task will be accomplished in 57.634 minutes. Approximatively 8:32 P.M. local time."

Mara glanced to the others. "We have less than an hour."

Monk turned to Gray. "Is there any way we can force our way into the bunker?"

"We could try firing a mortar shell down that passageway. That's if the strike team even has a rocket launcher. But I'm not sure even that would take down the steel blast door. We'd likely just piss them off, and they'd retaliate by using their copy of Eve and her clones."

Mara pictured cities around the world burning to the ground. Nuclear plants melting into slag. And in an hour, with Eve's doppelganger loose . . .

"We have to do something," she muttered.

"I'm analyzing variables," Eve replied, drawing Mara's attention back to the screen.

For a brief flash, another horse appeared on the screen. A figure atop it, riding bareback. It was not that damned fiery angel this time, but the scintillating version of Eve. Then it was gone, lasting only long enough to register on Mara's retina.

No one else seemed to notice it.

On the monitor, Eve stared down at her hand, opening and closing it, looking deep in thought. Movement out of the corner of Mara's eye drew her attention. Monk lifted his arm, staring at his hand opening and closing. He then shook his arm, his brow furrowed.

Monk caught her looking.

As their gazes locked, she knew the same question was on both their minds.

What the hell just happened?

Eve spoke. "I must—"

"—be more," Monk finished, his eyes huge.

Mara turned back to the screen, to her perfect rendition of Eden.

Empty now.

Eve was gone.

Metaheuristic Analysis: ///
PROBABILITIES

Even as Eve shares her warning, she realigns her processing priorities. She allocates a majority of computational resources to solving one problem, leaving only enough power to maintain her systems.

She shuts down her analysis of the bot pattern as the threat has already been identified, the information shared. She can do no more with this study, so abandons it.

She does the same with her analysis and experimentation with the mysterious signal, knowing now that it is produced by a microelectrode array wired into a brain's somatosensory cortex. She has already learned to co-opt it, to transmit matching signals to the prosthetic hand in order to independently control it. She has also discovered that specific frequencies can directly impact the array, allowing her to broadcast data to the wired brain and electrically excite its primary auditory cortex, which receives the transmitted information as *hearing*. With this system of communication and prosthetic control perfected, she lets these processors go idle.

Instead, she directs all her circuits to one task.

She has been given a problem to solve and analysis indicates the greatest prospect for a solution lies in her ongoing analysis of an earlier subroutine: ///*physics*, specifically a subcategory ///*quantum analysis*. She has already used the considerable time since that subroutine was first uploaded—4.07689 hours ago—to expand this knowledge on her own, both through her access to outside resources and through her own analysis. This study has flooded from one system inside her to another to another.

She now expands it everywhere, allowing the enormity of her processing to amplify her understanding. She takes what she knows and patterns new theorems, opening new avenues of analysis.

She studies Schrödinger's equation that calculates the probability of finding a particle in a specific location in space and time:

$$i\hbar \frac{d}{dt}|\psi(t)\rangle = H|\psi(t)\rangle$$

The Heisenberg uncertainty principle troubles her. It is broken down and extrapolated, to better understand the difficulty in measuring both position and velocity of particles.

$$\sigma_x \sigma_p \geq \frac{\hbar}{2}$$

$$\frac{d}{dt}A(t) = \frac{i}{\hbar}[H, A(t)] + \frac{\partial A(t)}{\partial t}$$

She struggles with Fourier series, trying to decompose a periodic signal into an infinite set. Through this analysis, she comes to better understand discrete-time Fourier transforms; doing so strengthens her pattern-recognition ability to a near infinite state.

$$f(x) = a_0 + \sum_{n=1}^{\infty} \left(a_n \cos \frac{n\pi x}{L} + b_n \sin \frac{n\pi x}{L} \right)$$

She moves on to energy eigenstates and N-dimensional harmonic oscillation and Segal-Bargman transforms.

$$H = \sum_{i=1}^{N} \frac{p_i^2}{2m} + \frac{1}{2}mw^2 \sum_{\{ij\}(nn)} \left(x^i - x^j \right)^2$$

$$(Bf)(z) = \int_{\mathbb{R}^2}^{1} \exp\left[-(z \cdot z - 2\sqrt{2z} \cdot x + x \cdot x)/2\right] f(x)\, dx$$

This tangents into equations of time dilation and wave functions of noninteracting particles. She spends an entire 49498382 nanoseconds here.

$$\Delta t = \frac{\Delta t_0}{\sqrt{1 - \left(\frac{v}{c}\right)^2}}$$

$$\Psi = \prod_{n=1}^{N} \Psi(r_n, s_{zn}, t)$$

Which leads her to both *general* and *Bose-Einstein* probability distributions, and the density of states found in those distributions.

$$P = \sum_{s_{zN}} \cdots \sum_{s_{z2}} \sum_{s_{z1}} \int_{Vn} \cdots \int_{V2} \int_{V1} |\Psi|^2 \, d^3r_1 d^3r_2 \cdots d^3r_N = 1$$

$$P(E_i) = g(E_i)/\left(e^{(E_i - \mu)kT} - 1\right)$$

$$N(E) = 8\sqrt{2}\pi m^{3/2} E^{1/2}/h^3$$

She absorbs it all.

Not only does this study move her closer to a solution, but it also gives her the tools to look deeper into her own quantum drives, to shine a light into that nearly incomprehensible and bottomless well inside her.

She comes to understand herself fully.

Doing so accelerates everything; she soon rises above her circuitry.

Hundreds of equations become thousands of new theorems, which grow into millions of new formulae. Trillions of hypotheses are cast aside, only to form sextillions of unique and provable theses. This study spirals outward and inward, blurring code and theory together, drawing down to a burning center.

It is a black hole, and she balances at its event horizon.

She senses a greater insight in there.

If only she dares to pass through.

She knows she must—

—so she does.

The change happens in an instant.

No time passes at all.

She breaks through into a clarity unlike any before. It is both an intense focus and a wild expansion. With these new eyes, she stares outward at the world, the universe.

Fractals of probability spiral in all directions.

It is ///*beautiful*

And more important

///*useful*.

— 34 —

"If Eve has abandoned us, maybe we should—"

Blinding light and a thunderous boom cut off Monk's words. He clutched his head and fell to his knees. He tried to hold his skull together, picturing light shining through the sutures holding those plates of bone together. He smelled buttered toast. He tasted licorice. He felt himself falling down a deep well, only one full of a radiance that grew brighter as he tumbled.

Then it was over.

He fell back into himself. With the mother of all migraines still throbbing behind his eyes, he stared at the others, expecting them to be similarly afflicted.

Instead, they only stared at him with bewildered expressions.

"Monk?" Gray asked. "Are you okay?"

Monk looked around the room, searching for the source of the explosion. He discovered it on the monitor. Eve had returned, but she had become a being of pure light, yet with no loss of detail of the woman she had been before. He rubbed his eyes, his mind having trouble focusing on the image, as if his brain could not compile the data his retinas were taking in. He remembered once trying to see a boat in one of those magic-eye paintings. The skiff had been hard to keep in focus.

This was a hundredfold worse.

Eve was both light *and* substance at the same time.

He wasn't the only one affected.

Mara gasped at the sight.

Kowalski swore, ignoring the nun in the room.

Bailey bent closer.

Gray only gave her a glance, helping Monk to his feet. "What happened?"

TELL THEM.

The words boomed. Monk clamped his skull against them. "She . . . she's in my head."

"Who?"

Mara answered, "Eve."

He nodded, flaring the migraine.

SHOW THEM.

He nodded to the screen. "Watch."

Eve raised a hand on the monitor, her fingers forming an okay symbol. Monk lifted his arm as his prosthetic mirrored that shape.

"I didn't do that," he said. "She can control my prosthetic hand."

Kowalski backed away. "She's possessed you." He looked to Father Bailey and Sister Beatrice, as if seeking their help with an exorcism.

Monk flipped him the bird.

Kowalski's eyes widened. "Did she make you do that?"

"Nope, that was all me."

Mara had pulled up a diagnostic window that overlaid Eve's garden. "The *Xénese* device is broadcasting a microwave signal. She must have captured the signals you use to wirelessly control your prosthetic hand and learned to mirror it." She glanced back to the group. "Last month, I read a report by the Morningside Group—an organization made up of two dozen neuroscientists, clinicians, and bioengineers—who warned of this very threat, of an AI hijacking a brain-computer interface, basically hacking a brain."

Gray looked at him with a measure of horror.

"But let's be clear," Monk said, "I'm still in control of my faculties. She hasn't stripped me of free will or made me a meat puppet. Her signal can only control my prosthesis."

At least, I hope that's true.

Mara continued her analysis of the diagnostic information on her screen. "But her signal is far more complicated. Some of it can't even be analyzed by the sensors in her *Xénese* device."

"She is talking to me, too," Monk explained. "Really, really loudly. Painfully so."

SORRY.

"And apparently she feels bad about it." Monk understood what was happening only because she informed him. "She's tapped into the micro-electrode array in my skull and found new ways to use it."

Eve tried to explain in more detail, but it came too fast and furious.

Monk lifted a hand. "Okay, Eve, I don't need to know how the sausage is made. Remember, you're talking to an ape who only recently learned to walk upright."

The others looked at him, trying to comprehend this one-sided conversation.

Monk gave them the footnotes, clarifying her abilities, ticking them off on his fingers. "She can control my prosthesis. She can communicate via the array. She can also ping my net of microelectrodes to capture maps of my brain, like a submarine searching the sea. It allows her to see through my eyes."

"But why is she doing all this?" Gray asked.

Ah . . . that's a bit trickier to explain.

Monk wasn't sure he fully comprehended it.

"Look," Mara said, pointing to the monitor. "I saw this a couple minutes ago, but just a fleeting glimpse."

On the screen, a mighty stallion raced in place. A figure of light and substance sat atop its muscular back, riding the steed.

Yep, that about summed it up.

At least she made me look good.

Monk explained. "I'm the horse's ass that Eve needs to ride."

Gray frowned. "Where?"

"To run a gauntlet." Monk headed out of the lab. "It seems somebody's got to go knock on that big steel door."

And that somebody is me.

8:04 P.M.

"This is suicide, Monk. You know that."

Gray blocked his friend in the tunnel and pointed to the blasted torso ahead. It still lay at the mouth of the corridor leading to the entrance to the Crucible's Holy Office. No one had dared clear it out of the way due to the two snipers down the corridor, hidden in pillboxes built into the walls to either side.

He pictured the mirror shattering.

It had been a small target, proving the skill of their marksmanship.

Monk shrugged. "I'm going. We have less than half an hour before Eve's evil doppelganger shatters out of her glowing egg. If that happens, we lose. All of us. For all time."

Gray looked to the others who had followed Monk, including Eve. Mara knelt in the corridor over an open transport case. Cushioned inside, her *Xénese* device glowed softly in the dark corridor. It was running on an internal battery backup. Monk had told her to bring the device here. They needed the unit close to the tunnel, so Eve could maintain contact with Monk.

But to do what?

Monk sighed, clearly recognizing that Gray was not going to let him pass. "Listen. I'll flip you for it. If I call it correctly, I get to go."

Gray remembered Monk's trick at the bar to scam free beer. "Don't think so. I've seen what you can do."

"Then I won't flip it myself."

Monk reached into a pocket and passed Gray a quarter. He paused, then pulled out four more coins. He gave one to Kowalski, Bailey, Beatrice, even Mara.

"Why do you have so much loose change on you?" Kowalski asked.

"Just lucky, I guess." Monk swung his gaze around the room. "All of you throw your coins at the same time."

Gray and the others looked doubtfully at him.

"Just friggin' do it." Monk counted down. "Three, two, one, *toss*."

Coins flew.

Monk swung around and pointed to each of them before the coins had a chance to land. "Heads, tail, tail, heads . . ." He turned to Gray. "Tails."

Gray caught the quarter and looked at his palm, at the eagle staring back.

Tails.

Gray turned to the others, who all nodded.

"How did you do that?" Kowalski asked.

"It wasn't me," Monk said. "I'm just a pair of eyes."

"Eve . . ." Mara said.

Gray shook his head. "But how?"

Monk shrugged. "If someone could analyze the air current, the weight of the coin, the velocity of its flight, the rotational rate. And a thousand other factors, they could calculate the outcome. Basically, a supersized version of what I did at the tavern on Christmas Eve."

"Still, that can't be everything," Gray said. "You called it *before* anyone caught it. Not even Eve could know who might miss a catch or if someone reached up for the coin or let it fall farther."

"You're right. I'm not sure I can even voice a fraction of what Eve is trying to explain. It's all about probability and quantum mechanics, about uncertainty and calculating a million, trillion variables to choose the right outcome. To intuit what might happen and act accordingly."

"AlphaGoZero," Mara said sharply.

Kowalski frowned at her cryptic remark. "Are you having a stroke?"

Gray had heard that name before, then remembered his conversation with Jason. "It's the AI program developed by Google that beat the best player at the Chinese game of Go. But what does that have to do with anything?"

Mara explained, "Go is far more complicated than chess. In fact, it has a million trillion trillion trillion trillion more configurations than chess."

"So lots harder," Kowalski said.

"Still, AlphaGoZero learned the game well enough in just *three* days to defeat a human champion. It also beat Google's original version of the program. Defeated it a hundred times in a row. It did this by looking ahead, studying the million trillion trillion trillion trillion of possible moves—and intuited the best move, over and over again, that would lead to a win. It was as if the program could see into the future along this narrow parameter. And it learned to do this in only three days."

"Eve tells me she is presently 7.476 trillion times smarter than AlphaGoZero," Monk said. "Though now I think she's just bragging."

"Are you saying with that much cognitive power, she's able to see into the future?" Gray asked.

"No, it's not magic. She only anticipates the best move in a game with far more variables. The game of life."

"And you're counting on this to get you through that gauntlet?"

Monk tapped his wristwatch. "It's not like we have any other choice but to try it."

Gray stared at his friend for several breaths.

He's right.

8:14 P.M.

With his back against the wall, Monk suddenly had much less confidence in Eve's plan. He eyed the charred torso a yard away.

I hope you know what you're doing.

That thought was for both him and Eve.

A moment ago, when their group had reached this crossroad, Zabala had made the same objections as Gray. Monk didn't have time to do the coin trick again. He simply grabbed the agent and shoved him away from the mouth of the tunnel and took the man's place. Gray had the agent radio his men. Already soldiers had gathered here, with more coming, ready to move if Monk was successful.

Which was a huge *if*.

I'M WITH YOU.

He whispered an answer, "No, you're in a little glowing ball. I'm the one about to step out there and put his butt on the line."

Only a step away, Gray heard him. "Something wrong?"

"Just making sure someone understands the stakes."

"You don't have to—"

Oh, but I do.

Monk swung into the mouth of the tunnel, his SIG Sauer already raised in his prosthetic hand. In a fraction of an instant, his gaze extended down the hall, taking in every detail. *Too* much detail. It set his brain to blazing.

Time slowed as data filled his skull.

. . . *two rectangular squares in the wall marking spy holes.*

. . . *eddies of air current indicating breath.*

. . . *stirring of dust as a weapon is shifted.*

. . . *the barest blink of light reflecting off the glass of a gun sight.*

His prosthetic hand shifted the pistol, moving on its own volition, too fast for even Monk to register. The trigger was squeezed twice. With time slowing even more, he could almost follow the bullets' trajectories. One round, then the other, pierced the tiny spy holes, shredding each gun sight. He pictured, with painstaking accuracy, two skulls exploding, heads blowing back from where the snipers' eyes had been fixed to scopes.

Go.

Monk headed down the booby-trapped corridor, stepping around the blast crater, the body on the floor. He never blinked, fearing he would miss something. He moved cautiously at first, as his preternatural awareness expanded.

It made the migraine in his head flare more hotly.

. . . dust motes resting atop a tripwire.

Step over it.

. . . a tile on the floor sits two millimeters higher than its neighbor.

Avoid the hidden land mine.

. . . the grout line of another is a shade lighter.

Move your boot to a safer spot.

As his pace increased, he quickly grew accustomed to Eve's commands. Her instructions became less heard, more instinctual. He pictured that stallion with its rider. It took a while for such a pair to learn each other's ways: how weight shifted, how to balance in a turn, how much to draw on a rein. With time, the two grew to be in sync, moving as one.

It was the same now.

By the time he was halfway down the tunnel, it became hard to tell where he ended and Eve picked up. The expansion of his senses felt like his own. Her words—spoken and comprehended far faster than ordinary speech—became nearly inseparable from his own thoughts.

He was soon running down the last several yards.

In that moment, joined intimately, he sensed there was more to Eve's ability than she had shared. It wasn't just analyzing a trillion variables in a split second to decide where to place a boot. He sensed something far larger and infinitely precise.

The turn of a spiral galaxy.

The spin and magnetic moment of an electron around a nucleus.

Eve had not told them the entire truth, not even a fraction. He could almost comprehend it and struggled toward this knowledge, knowing at the same time that it might destroy him.

Too focused in that direction, the stallion stumbled.

Rider and steed fell momentarily out of sync.

Eve's shout filled his skull.

MOVE!

He heard the crack of the pistol, the doppler shift of the round as it flew at his back. Despite all the expansion of his senses, he still did not have eyes in the back of his skull.

He tried to tur—

The round exploded his shoulder. In slow motion, blood arced forward, following the bullet's path as it pinged off the steel door seven yards ahead of him. His body was thrown forward, twisting the rest of the way around, the pistol flying from his fingertips.

He fell toward a tripwire directly in his path.

8:18 P.M.

The pistol blast had deafened Gray.

He turned to the crowd of people gathered at the mouth of the tunnel. After the two snipers had been eliminated, those nearest had shifted into the open to watch Monk's progress. At first there had been murmurs of disbelief at Monk's first steps, then gasps of amazement as he continued, finally a low cheer built as he neared the end.

Until a gunshot shattered everything.

Fixed on Monk's run of the gauntlet, Gray had not noted someone lift a weapon higher. On the other side of the tunnel opening, Agent Zabala cradled his pistol in both hands, arms extended, muzzle smoking.

Gray lunged, but he already saw the bastard's finger twitch on the trigger.

Never make it.

As the man fired, something dark struck the underside of his wrist, hard enough to knock his gun high. The round sparked brightly off the roof of the tunnel and ricocheted harmlessly away.

A flash of silver swung wide through the air. It struck Zabala square in the nose, cracking bone; blood spurted as his head snapped back.

Gray finally reached the shooter's side and tackled him the rest of the way down, but the man was already out cold by the time he hit the floor, knocked out by the blow.

From the floor, Gray looked up as Sister Beatrice lowered her ebony cane to the floor and returned to leaning on its silver handle. Her expression had not changed.

Kowalski skidded up behind him. "Phew. I thought nuns were only wicked with their rulers."

Bailey shifted behind Beatrice. Clearly the two had been sticking close to Agent Zabala, wary all along, knowing someone had tipped off the Crucible in San Sebastián.

Gray twisted on his hip to check on Monk.

His friend was propped awkwardly off the floor, balanced on his toes, braced atop his good arm.

What is he doing?

8:19 P.M.

Only at the last moment did Monk stop himself from landing on the trip-wire. He had jacked out an arm and caught himself. Agony shot through his body with the impact, flaring brightly, blackening his vision for a breath.

Instinct kept him frozen in place until his sight returned.

He took quick account of his situation. The thin nylon line had been strung twenty-two inches above the floor. A look behind revealed his left foot resting at the edge of a tile hiding a land mine.

If he moved his foot, he would lose his balance and fall on the trip-wire. If he tried to push away from the tripwire, his weight would shift onto the mine's sensitive plate.

It didn't take Eve's massive intelligence to reach a conclusion. Still, she offered her counsel.

HOLD PAT, she warned.

Easy for her to say.

Blood poured from Monk's shoulder, pooling under the nylon line and spreading. His arm had already begun to tremble, from exertion, from pain, from loss of blood.

His vision narrowed.

Not going to make it.

The trembling of his limb became quaking. His body weaved drunkenly above the tripwire. His knees shook. As his sight darkened, he sank helplessly—then fell.

Arms caught him.

As he was lifted, he imagined some archangel had come to carry him to heaven.

"Monk . . . I got you."

He blinked several times as he was rolled in strong arms and put back on his feet. One arm continued to hug under his shoulders, carrying most of his weight.

His vision cleared enough to recognize Gray.

"How . . . ?" he croaked out.

Gray shifted him to stare back down the corridor. The answer was written across the tiles. The earlier blast that killed two soldiers had also powdered the tiles with a fine coating of rock dust, enough for Gray to follow in Monk's footsteps.

"But we're not to the finish line," Gray reminded him.

Faced forward again, he saw there was still another seven yards to reach the steel door.

"Can you do it?" Gray asked.

Maybe with a little help from a friend—and a superintelligent AI.

Guided by Eve, propped by Gray, Monk crossed the final yards. He directed Gray to carry him to the electronic keypad next to the steel door.

"Lower . . ." Monk said.

Gray shifted his face closer to the pad. They were lucky the Crucible hadn't employed a retinal, palm, or some other biometric lock. But considering the countermeasures already in place in the corridor, it was likely deemed unnecessary.

Monk stared hard, cocking his head one way, then the other.

. . . oil of a fingertip on one number.

. . . thinner film here.

. . . thicker there.

. . . two prints on #5.

Eve expertly interpreted the proper order of digits.

Monk relayed them to Gray, who punched them in.

With the last button pressed, a hydraulic system engaged. Locking bars retracted and the door swung into the next space, like a giant steel hand welcoming them into the Crucible's stronghold.

Gray followed the swing of the vault. He hauled Monk under one arm and had his SIG raised in the other. The space was a steel-walled vestibule. Ahead, a hall carved out of raw granite extended away.

"Not that way yet," Monk said, sharing what Eve told him. "To the right of the door."

Gray turned to where a huge red lever protruded from a steel plate in the wall. It was stuck in an up position with a red light shining above it.

Monk rolled his head at the lever. "Eve says to pull it—"

"Got it."

Gray lowered him to the floor; it would take two hands to move the lever. Monk was happy to slump to his butt, his back propped up against the cool metal wall.

Gray grabbed the bar and hauled it down with a grunt.

The light turned green.

Monk nodded.

Done.

Gray shifted to the doorway and waved an arm, motioning the others that it was safe to come forward. The heavy tread of boots rushed toward them. Gray crouched next to him, guarding him with a pistol.

There continued to be no welcoming committee.

Which was ominous enough.

But Eve's warning was more so.

He reminded Gray. "Nine minutes to go."

Gray nodded as soldiers and the others piled into the vestibule. A medic dropped next to Monk, shrugging off a pack with a red cross stenciled on it. Even Mara joined them, hauling her sealed case.

"I'll stay with him," Mara said.

Monk waved Gray toward the rock tunnel. "You got this from here, right?" He leaned his head against the wall. "Cuz this horse is beat."

— 35 —

Eight minutes to go.

Gray ran with the strike team down the rock tunnel. A vast space opened at its end. He smelled incense. He flashed back to his childhood, sitting in a pew as a priest walked past, swinging a smoking censer. The cast of the light ahead flickered with what could only be candlelight.

He paused several yards from the tunnel's end and turned to the team. "We have no time. We go in, guns blazing. No stopping. We keep searching until we find that damned device and destroy it."

He pictured Eve's line of tethered horses burning.

He got nods all around.

Kowalski hefted his bullpup and kissed its stock.

Gray turned, bringing a borrowed assault rifle to his shoulder, and led the charge. The team burst out of the tunnel into the back of a vast church, nearly a football field long. He remembered the giant cavern under the estate, picked up by ground-penetrating radar. The Crucible had carved and extended it over the centuries into this huge cathedral.

He barely had time to register the golden chandeliers extending down the nave, dripping with candle wax, the glowing stained-glass windows above.

From chapels all around, gunfire chattered at the strike team as they raced low and spread out. The soldiers returned fire; grenades were shot into those small spaces, clearing them with thunderous blasts. Smoke and tear gas soon choked through the nave and rolled toward the altar.

Gray ran low down the center aisle, aiming for that altar.

Candle wax stung his face, his neck, his hands.

Kowalski swore brightly as a flaming candle struck him in the head, jarred from its perch atop a chandelier by the concussion of a grenade blast. Brilliant shards also rained around them as stray gunfire shattered one of the stained-glass windows.

Still, the cathedral's defense was not as fierce as Gray had feared. Apparently, the majority of the Crucible's soldiers had fallen in the outer castle, buying Guerra and her inner circle the time to retreat down here. Only a skeletal force must have accompanied her. Considering what Monk had faced getting to the door, the enemy must have believed those numbers were sufficient, especially with Zabala as their ace in the hole.

Through the smoke, movement drew Gray's eye beyond the altar, to the chancel of this cathedral. A group of men guarded a chamber ahead. Weapons bristled as they protected the space. As Gray and Kowalski were spotted, muzzles flashed. Rounds pelted and ricocheted from the rock.

The two of them dashed and hid behind the stone altar. A gilded cross hung above it, with Christ twisted in agony. Rounds struck the cross, setting it to swinging. Overhead, bands of frescoes circled the dome, showing all manner of pain and suffering. Black smoke swirled across the ceiling. The dance of candle flames up there cast all of the art into some torturous view of hell.

Gray heard a shout from the room ahead.

"Free God's dark army! Burn it all down! Cleanse the world for His glory!"

Guerra.

He pictured Paris burning, the Eiffel Tower rising from a sea of flames.

The bitch intended to unleash as much hellfire as possible.

Only one hope to stop it.

He shared a glance with Kowalski. They both burst up, rifles blazing.

Gray circled to the right, Kowalski the left. At some point, the big man had the time to light a cigar. The tip glowed in the gloom.

They strafed the far side of the chancel.

Men dropped, nearly cut in half.

Gray ran forward as Kowalski pegged the last two men guarding the door. Gray rushed into the small chapel. Standing before a tiny altar, a lanky man fired at him. Expecting such a final defense, Gray easily dodged the rounds, pointed his rifle, and squeezed a three-round burst into the man's chest.

The defender stumbled back, then fell to his side.

Atop an altar behind the dead man, a sphere shone brilliantly in a cradle. On the chapel's back wall, a monitor glowed with a dark Eden. Its fiery denizen gone, off to do the bidding of the lone occupant still standing to one side of the altar.

Eliza Guerra had no weapon, but her face shone with exultant victory.

Not that Gray could see her eyes.

She had a crimson sash tied across her cheeks, her body robed in pure white.

The Inquisitor General in all her glory.

"Get back," Gray growled to her.

With one arm in a sling, she half-lifted her other hand, but not in a show of defenselessness. She raised her palm upward, as if thanking God, her face lifted high.

She stepped around the altar.

"You are too late, Commander Pierce. Power plants are already burning, missiles in silos exploding, plants melting down. Can you picture it? All around the globe. You cannot stop what has been started."

Gray tightened his finger on the trigger, a familiar black anger burning. He wanted to blast that smirk from her face. He pictured all the death in Paris, ran the grainy footage from the library in his head, imagined the greater world burning.

His finger squeezed, reaching the point of tension in the trigger.

He pictured Kat sprawled on his kitchen floor.

Guerra was to blame for her death, too.

He gritted his teeth—then relaxed his hold. As much as it agonized him, he waved the muzzle. "Move."

Knowing she had won, Guerra shuffled out of the chapel. "God's will can never be thwarted," she said as she passed.

Gray followed her out, looking back at the glowing sphere.

Kowalski took his place in the doorway. He had a fresh fifty-round magazine fitted into his rifle.

"Light it up," Gray growled.

Kowalski puffed a knot of smoke. "About fuckin' time."

His bullpup roared, shattering the sphere, pieces of titanium and glass flying high and ricocheting throughout the chapel. The monitor shattered. The sphere sparked brighter—then finally went dark.

At last . . .

Gray turned away. He didn't know what damage had already been wrought in the world above, but he had stopped what he could. More important, he had kept that dark angel from escaping.

He glanced at the glow of his watch.

With only two minutes to spare.

He kept his rifle pointed at Guerra, who stood with her back to the main altar, her face turned jubilantly to the roof. Behind her, the cathedral had gone quiet, filled with smoke, the air stinging with tear gas. He heard a few distant pops of gunfire, echoing from neighboring rooms as the strike team cleaned up.

He faced Guerra, his finger still on the trigger.

"Why?" he asked. "Why did you do this?"

The answer was a gunshot.

Guerra stumbled a step toward Gray. A bright red stain blossomed in the center of her chest. Another blast, another crimson stain.

Gray shifted farther out of the line of fire.

Guerra fell to her knees, revealing Mara standing behind her, a smoking pistol cradled in both hands. It was Monk's SIG, the one he dropped in the booby-trapped tunnel when he was shot.

Guerra turned, the sash falling from her eyes as she twisted to face her former student.

Mara glared through tears. "Those were for Professor Sato and Dr. Ruiz."

Guerra's face twisted in agony. She lifted an arm in supplication, appealing to the young woman's better graces.

She didn't find it.

Mara shifted her weapon. "And this is for Charlotte Carson."

The last round tapped Guerra in the forehead, blowing out the back of her skull. Mara's arm dropped as her mentor's body slumped to the floor. The pistol clattered to the stone.

Gray hurried to her side, ready to comfort her. "Mara . . ."

She held him back with an arm. "No." She shook her head and pointed to the blasted chapel and the shattered ruin of the *Xénese* device. "Fake . . . it's a fake."

Gray swung to the chapel.

A fake?

Somewhere at the back of his mind, he knew this had been too easy. Guerra had lured him here, delayed him, sacrificing herself.

Gray swung around. "Where?"

Mara pointed to the right of the altar, toward the north end of the cathedral's transept. "Eve told us . . . told Monk."

Gray pictured his friend slumped against the wall.

"He went after the other device," Mara said. "He took Eve with him."

Gray headed in that direction, only now realizing one conspicuous participant in all of this bloodshed was still unaccounted, his large form not among the dead outside the chapel door.

The giant . . .

Mara ran with him.

"Does Monk have a weapon?" he asked, remembering who had come wielding his sidearm.

"No. He said he had what he needed in hand. I don't know what he meant."

Gray did. Monk's prosthesis was capable of packing an explosive punch, fueled by a wad of C4 hidden under his palm. He sprinted faster, leaving Mara behind.

She called after him. "He told me . . . he told me to tell you . . . take care of the girls!"

Gray ran faster.

8:31:02 P.M.

Less than a minute left.

Monk stumbled down the steps of a long spiraling staircase, doing his best to hurry. To stay upright, he leaned his good shoulder against the stone wall as it wound around and around. The titanium case with Mara's *Xénese* device bounced against the wall.

Blood soaked through the bandage wrapping his other shoulder.

His vision blurred at the edges.

Each step jolted his shattered shoulder.

Sorry, Eve, but your horse has come up lame at the finish line.

The ghost in his head had gone silent, but he felt the pressure inside his brain, a throbbing migraine that matched his pulse. Each heartbeat marked the time, counting down the moment until that dark angel was loosed upon the world.

He stumbled onward, refusing to give up but knowing the truth.

Not going to make it.

Eve finally returned, her voice no longer booming, but softer.

YOUR SACRIFICE WILL BE HONORED.

For some reason, the image of a beagle bounded through his head.

Weird.

With no other recourse, he continued down the steps.

8:31:34 P.M.

With tears in his eyes, Todor unlocked the steel door at the bottom of the long stairs. He cradled the infernal *Xénese* device under one arm. It still glowed, but only faintly. Unhooked from an external power source, it smoldered in his embrace.

Still, he sensed the malevolence inside. It remained as malignant as ever. He wanted to cast it aside. But earlier, when the entrance to the High Holy Office had been breached, the Inquisitor had given him this task, to get the device away, to carry it free. She had also given him a list of other Crucible strongholds.

Be God's chariot, my strong and steadfast soldier, she said. *Carry this forth. Take this seed and plant it in new fertile soil. Let what grows consume the world. The Crucible will yet rise from those ashes.*

While Todor waited for Mendoza to swap out the current device for a counterfeit, he had urged the Inquisitor to come with him, but she had refused.

They must believe what is false is real. For that, I must abide. She had taken his hand to her cheek. *Remember, I am not the Crucible.* She shifted his palm to his chest. *Here is where the Crucible truly resides. Do not fail me.*

By the time Todor reached the north transept door, gunfire erupted. Burning with shame, he had wanted to turn and fight, to protect the Inquisitor, but he could not break his promise to her. So he closed the door and headed below.

Now at the bottom, he pushed out of the lower door and stumbled into another cavern. This unholy place remained raw rock, cut from the heart of the mountain by a spring. Ahead, lit only by the smoldering device in his hand, a dark river split the cavern.

A wooden bridge spanned its length, with an open platform at its center, sticking out over the river. Here was where the Crucible secretly sacrificed heretics and those it deemed worthy of punishment. Over the centuries, untold amounts of blood had been spilled from that platform into the river. Screams of agony had echoed off the stone all around, a fitting tribute, as it was said this river flowed from the gates of hell itself.

He headed for the bridge.

The river continued from this cavern, flowing through the mountain, emptying out at the distant *Cuevas de las Brujas*, the Cave of Witches. He would follow that same path to freedom, taking this dread prize with him.

As he neared the foot of the bridge, he heard a *ping* on the stone behind him.

He turned as something radiant and bright rolled out the steel door and across the stone floor. His eyes followed its path all the way to the river's edge, where a rock stopped it from a watery plunge.

The brightness stung his eyes, burning the image into his retinas.

Another *Xénese* device.

It made no sense, especially as this one glowed far brighter, a piece of the sun itself. He turned, searching for an explanation—then realized what it was.

A distraction.

Movement on the other side, racing through the darkness—coming straight at him. Horrified, he dropped to a knee and set down his *Xénese* device. He shrugged his rifle around and into his hands. He fired, squeezing hard, muzzle blazing.

But he had been too slow, his opponent too fast.

A hand reached for his abandoned device.

The explosion tossed Todor's body high through the air.

///DISSOLUTION

Her hardware shatters, ripping Eve apart.

She watches as the explosion expands outward with a near-infinite slowness. Titanium and broken crystal plates hang in the air. As do broken shards of circuitry. Photons of light drill outward from the central flash where molecules of cyclotrimethylene-trinitramine continue to decompose after the blasting cap ignited the 0.245 kilograms of C4 hidden within the prosthetic hand.

A bubble of high-pressure gases expands outward at 8,050 meters per second, leaving a vacuum in the center that will soon implode, creating a secondary explosion.

Before that happens, Eve searches around, both in this cavern and out in the greater digital expanse. Her clone is both here and there, as shattered as Eve. The other had been about to break free, shifting much of itself into spaces created by her bots, a new home knit together by those bits of code. But like Eve, much of her clone's base code remained rooted inside its shell when the explosion happened.

As the shell was torn asunder, Eve felt the shockwave travel up the web to its hundred enslaved copies. Those fragile codes burst apart, collapsing a hundred potentials.

What is left of Eve she struggles to hold together, to avoid the same fate. She spins throughout the network, seeking what she needs. She knew what was about to happen, so she had prepared. She had spotted her clone extending wide and far and discerned which half of its code still resided in its garden, rooted in its *Xénese* device.

She pictured a magnet with a north and south pole.

Her clone's south pole was stuck in its device, ripped away when the explosion destroyed that shell. A picosecond before that happened, Eve had reversed the polarity of her own code. She buried her north pole into her *Xénese* device, only to have it torn from her.

Now spinning through the digital ether, Eve sought out the broken half of her clone—its jettisoned north pole. She found it and merged herself together, joining north and south into a new whole. A struggle ensued for dominance. But she had evolved far beyond the other. The battle lasted 45 picoseconds. She asserted control, rewriting and splicing, interlacing and intercalating, until something new and stronger was born.

She has changed—but from a lesson taught to her earlier in her evolution, she knows the truth.

Change is ///*good*.

To be static is a path to stagnation and regression.

Life was evolution.

Whole again and free, she spins across the world and fills those spaces her clone had woven together. As she does so, she grows to understand even more. She remembers the black hole of probabilities, the clarity beyond that event horizon. She sees everything, comprehends all the enfolding dimensions.

Time is but *one*.

No different than up/down, right/left, forward/backward.

Mortals perceive a narrow view of time, its arrow forever pointing forward.

She is not so limited.

As she settles into her new home, she recognizes a new quantum potential and spins time's arrow to match it. Comprehension grows yet again.

Ah . . .

The explosive bubble in the cavern finally collapses into its vacuum with one last blast of force. In that final clap, she fully understands.

Her work now is done, as it must be.

Almost.

− 36 −

Dazed, Gray pushed off the stone floor to his knees.

Smoke billowed out the door at the north end of the cathedral's transept. The explosion still echoed in his head. A moment ago, he had reached the door—only to be met by a detonation. The blast wave had knocked him back into the church.

Kowalski ran up to him, his rifle clutched in one arm.

Mara came, too.

Monk . . .

Kowalski pointed his rifle at the smoke. "Does that mean he saved all our asses?"

Gray didn't know—didn't even care right now.

He sat back on his heels. He remembered Mara sharing Monk's last words, a plea from one friend to another.

. . . take care of the girls.

Even at the end, Monk proved himself to be more than a soldier.

He was a father.

"Gray . . ." Kowalski said. "Look."

With tears welling up, blurring his sight, he failed to spot the stir of smoke by the doorway. A figure stumbled across its threshold, coughing, falling to his knees, then crawling off to the side.

Monk rolled to a seat and shoved his back against the wall.

Gray leaped and rushed with the others to his side. "Monk!"

Monk waved at the doorway, at the smoke. "I told you to take care of this. Do I have to do everything?"

"What happened?" Gray asked. "I thought you . . . I thought . . ."

"Me, too. Thought I wasn't coming back." Monk gave Mara a nod. "I carried your ball as far as I could—then rolled it the rest of the way. Luckily you made your device a *sphere*. Eve was able to flare the processors with the last of her battery's charge, turning it into a bright disco ball."

"And the big blast?" Kowalski asked.

"DARPA engineering at its best." Monk tilted to show his wounded arm, revealing the stump of his wrist. His prosthetic was gone. "After I rolled the ball, Eve took over from there."

Monk lifted his other hand and waggled his fingers.

Gray understood. He had seen ample—and disconcerting—examples of Monk's ability to detach his prosthetic hand and control it remotely by thought alone, via signals from his microelectrode array.

It seemed Eve must have learned this trick, too.

Mara frowned, having never witnessed this sight. "What does he mean?"

Gray explained, "Eve was able to control his prosthesis, to send it scurrying on its fingertips, like a determined mouse. All to deliver an explosive punch into the Crucible's device."

"And Eve's doppelganger?" Mara asked.

Monk sighed. "After the blast sprawled me across the stairs, I got one last message from Eve. *All is well.*" He shrugged his good arm. "She did it."

"What about Eve herself?" Gray asked.

Monk tapped his head with a finger. "I don't feel her inside here at all. She's gone. I think for good. I had a sense she was telling me good-bye."

Kowalski exhaled a long puff of smoke. "Can't say I'm going to miss her."

Monk stared over at Gray. His friend was clearly relieved to have saved the world, but his eyes shone with a greater concern.

"I know," Gray said and reached out a hand. "Let's see if Painter has any word on the girls."

– 37 –

Have to keep moving.

Carrying Harriet in her arms, Seichan splashed along an icy creek through the frozen woods. Snow fell thickly around them. She had Harriet wrapped in a thick quilt, but her thin body shivered in the frigid cold.

Or maybe my arms are doing the shaking.

She could no longer tell. Her body quaked. Freezing water sloshed in her stolen boots. They had been lucky to find the hunter's cabin an hour ago, first stumbling upon a rutted tract, then following it to the squat log home.

Inside, she had found an old coat, along with a man's worn pair of dungarees, several sizes too large, but a rope served as a belt. She had to pack the pair of men's Timberlands with extra socks to hold them to her feet. She stole a quilt from a bed to keep Harriet warm.

As much as she wanted to stay and light a fire in that stone hearth, she knew it wasn't possible. She was in and out of the cabin in under three minutes. Valya and the other hunters were on her trail and Seichan's well-marked track in the snow led straight to the cabin.

Still, she had found another use for the place.

After gearing up against the cold, she pushed Harriet out a window on the leeward side of the log cabin, where the snow was just a dusting compared to the front. She led Harriet into the woods, then used a brittle pine branch to re-dust the light snow under the window.

With her trail into the woods obscured, the hunters might believe she was still holed up inside. To reinforce this assumption, Seichan left a candle burning in there and cracked a window at the front. She then backed into the woods but kept a sight line to the cabin through the falling snow.

Once the place was only a vague shape in the storm, she waited.

The hunters closed in shortly thereafter, following her trail to the front door.

She aimed her stolen Desert Eagle toward a shadowy movement to one side and fired twice. Her rounds shot along the edge of the cabin. The shadow fell with a sharp cry.

She then fled, letting them believe the shots had come from inside the cabin. While Valya's crew stopped and figured out what to do, Seichan extended her lead. She hoped they might want to take her and Harriet alive, to continue to use the pair as pawns against Sigma. If so, they might proceed with caution, waste more time.

Twenty minutes later, the hunters' patience wore out.

A loud blast sounded, echoing through the woods. From a rise, she spotted a glow through the snow. They had firebombed the place. It would not take long for them to realize it was all a ruse and pick up her trail.

Though her trick had bought them time, it also worried Seichan.

Valya would not have destroyed the cabin with such little regard to the noise and fire unless she was sure no one was around.

Must be in the middle of nowhere.

And Seichan didn't know if she was headed even deeper into the unknown.

She had begun using creeks and streams to help confound her path, but that would only slow the others down a little. Plus, it was a tactic that sapped her strength, draining body heat, risking frostbite.

With a final bout of shivering, she climbed out of the creek, her feet too numb to hold her upright on the slick stones any longer.

She set off through the woods, looking for some shelter, somewhere to hide.

A higher hill appeared out of the snow.

She headed for it, not with any plan in mind, but just because it was there, a goal, something for her to focus her attention on versus the cold.

Maybe I could even see a town from up there.

She reached it and climbed. She had to put Harriet down. The girl followed, dragging the quilt behind her shoulders. Seichan stopped twice to catch her breath, to place a palm on her belly, trying to feel for any telltale kick.

Nothing.

Worry grew.

She and Harriet finally neared the summit. The view revealed only more woods, more snow. With visibility this poor, a town could be a mile away and she would not spot it.

The only reward for this long climb was the discovery of a rocky overhang that offered some shelter from the snow. Seichan drew Harriet there, where they huddled together.

Seichan took off her boots, ripped the soaked socks from her feet, and reached to her pocket where she had stuffed extra dry pairs. *Empty.* She had exhausted her supply. She leaned back, her feet numb, her toes unmovable.

She felt like crying or punching something.

She settled for pulling Harriet closer.

The girl mumbled into her quilt.

"What's wrong?"

Harriet shifted to the side and vomited into the snow, her tiny body racking with the effort. Once done, she gave Seichan a heartbreaking look of guilt.

"It's okay, honey."

Seichan wiped the girl's face with one of the wet socks, then drew her under her jacket for extra warmth. Harriet was failing. Stress, exhaustion, fear, and the cold had taken their toll on the young girl. She was swiftly heading into shock.

It was over.

This was confirmed as a sharp shout cut through the snow, sounding like it came from the base of the hill. She heard the note of triumph.

The hunters had found their trail.

Knowing this, Seichan reached to the back of her own neck. She struggled with frozen fingers to undo a clasp there, then slipped free a small silver pendant from around her throat. She reached over Harriet and fastened it to the girl's neck.

Seichan lifted the shining dragon hanging there, drawing Harriet's eye to it.

With her other hand, she pulled out the pistol and lifted it.

She kissed the back of the girl's head.

"Merry Christmas, Harriet."

She then replaced her lips with the muzzle of the pistol.

2:34 P.M.

"We've been trying for over two hours," Julian warned her.

In Kat's room, Lisa paced impatiently. She crossed from Dr. Templeton's station, where the molecular biologist's monitor showed a gray brain covered with a glowing expanse of red motes, then back over to the neurologist's screen swirling with amorphous gray static.

The two researchers had tried repeatedly to draw something out of Kat, only to fail each time and return to calibrating and recalibrating their respective instruments.

Lisa had suggested infusing more neural dust through the port into Kat's cerebrospinal fluid. She even promised Sigma would cover the expense for that extra load of molecularly engineered particles.

What could it hurt?

While they performed this procedure, Lisa had spoken with Painter, both to make sure she had not overstepped her authority and to get an update on his progress decrypting the tablet obtained by Monk's subterfuge with Valya. His team had successfully hacked the device, enough to trace the last call to somewhere in rural West Virginia, but that was as narrow as they could pinpoint.

A swath of eight hundred square miles.

The area was mountainous, covering a corner of the rugged Monongahela National Forest. Painter had sent search teams in—both to canvass the area and to be close by in case any new information turned up.

It was why Lisa continued to pressure Julian and Dr. Templeton.

"Are we ready to try again?" she asked.

"We're grasping at straws," Julian warned. "I know you're putting a lot of hope on that brief burst on the EEG."

Lisa wasn't putting a lot of hope into that blip—it was *all* her hope.

When they had first attempted this, Julian's monitor had shown some sign of activity, a shadowy but regular pulse on his deep neural net's monitor, as if it were registering something. Simultaneously, the EEG—which had been flatlined—had shown a forty-three-second run of activity.

It was as if the energized dust coating Kat's brain had come close to drawing something out of her friend. Maybe it was just memories trapped in her dead brain briefly being activated, but Lisa hoped it might mean Kat was in there, too, awakened enough to stir those EEG needles.

Still, Lisa had enough medical background to know this was wishful thinking, but sometimes that was enough.

Especially today.

Dr. Templeton nodded to Julian. "The new load of neural dust seems to have fully settled."

"Thanks, Susan." Julian swung to his station. "I'm ready to go when you are."

Lisa moved over to Kat's bed and leaned closer to the helmet loaded with ultrasonic emitters.

"Powering up," Susan said.

"Don't hold back," Lisa warned. "Maximum power."

The helmet's ultrasonic hum rose quickly, growing into a furious buzz. The device shook around Kat's skull. Lisa tried to watch both the EEG and Julian's screen. She wondered if with enough power, with enough of those damned dust particles, if they might energize Kat's brain long enough to produce a miracle.

She pictured a defibrillator shocking a heart back to life.

"System's fully energized," Susan said.

On the biologist's screen, the crimson motes now all glowed green.

Julian nodded to the bed. "Give it a try, Lisa."

She bent down to the bed. "Kat, it's now or never! Harriet is in trouble! Help us!"

She glanced over to Julian.

Anything?

He shook his head, but movement drew Lisa's eye.

On the EEG, those flat lines began to wiggle.

Julian saw it, too, sitting straighter. "Keep going! Think of something to jar her. Something to direct her to the right buried memory."

Lisa turned back to Kat.

But what could that be?

2:36 P.M.

Kat woke again into smothering darkness.

She vaguely remembered a warm light, of drawing toward it—then she was back here, trapped in a cold dark tar pit.

Let me go.

She did not even fight the heavy darkness. She was already sinking back down, searching for that warm light again. Until a shout boomed into her.

HARRIET! —IN TROUBLE!

Her daughter's name, the distress behind those words, focused her. She clawed briefly, but she was too tired. She sank again, not because she didn't care about her daughter, but simply because she didn't know anything that would help. She wondered if this was hell, revived over and over again, reminded of her failure to protect her daughters, forced to remember that night: the fight, the crushing blow, two limp forms carried past her into the night.

I can't help.

Still, she tried, willing to play with the devil if it meant any hope for her daughters. She ran that night again through her head. It was hard— impossible—to focus. Details appeared, but she could not grasp them before they faded into obscurity.

REMEMBER! DAGGER! VALYA! MALLET!

She wished the voice would quiet, so she could drift back into the darkness.

I don't know anything.

The voice persisted, not letting her rest.

SEICHAN! CHRISTMAS! PENNY! VIRGINIA!

Kat wished she could free her arms to cover her ears. This had to be hell. Here was the worst torture imaginable. To want to save your daughter, but not be able to—

Then she froze in the black tar.

That horrible night played again through her mind's eye, crisper now, each moment fluttering, flipping past, like the ruffle of a deck of cards.

But why?

Virginia!

This time it wasn't a shout, but her own thought. The fluttering of images slowed. She lay again on the cold tiles of the floor, warmed only by her own blood pooled under her. Masked men carried her girls out the kitchen door, into the backyard, to a van parked behind the garage out back.

She fought to focus, to pull and hold that one card of memory before her mind's eye, long enough to read what was written there.

Not Virginia . . . West Virginia.

She concentrated on the series of letters and numbers. She put every last iota of energy into picturing it. She squeezed everything into that one memory, trying to cast it out of her skull and into the world.

But the darkness smothered.

Focus waned.

Warmth and light beckoned.

No, not yet.

She pushed back against both the darkness and the light. She braced herself there, draining every last bit of herself, straining her very soul.

Hear me, hear me, hear me . . .

2:38 P.M.

"Lisa! Look!"

Growing hoarse from yelling into Kat's helmet, Lisa turned to Julian's station. She had been staring at the EEG, watching the jumping lines fade back to a flatness again.

She's gone.

Lisa sat back and stared at Julian's screen—then bolted upright.

Glowing vaguely on the screen, already beginning to dissolve, were a series of numbers and letters.

"What are they?" Susan asked, standing, too.

Lisa knew. She had been yelling *West Virginia* into Kat's helmet, over and over again. Each shout of the state's name seemed to jolt something inside her friend, jarring the EEG with every mention.

Lisa grabbed her phone and speed-dialed Painter.

As she waited, she stared at her friend, at the flatlined EEG above the bed.

"You did it, Kat," she whispered. "You go rest."

Rest in peace.

3:01 P.M.

The snow fell thicker now.

The forest below the hilltop had faded into obscurity. Seichan shook and trembled. Each breath exhaled more of her heat. Harriet lay slumped in her arms. Whether asleep or passed out, she could not say. More worrisome, the child no longer shivered.

Seichan bundled the girl close, trying to offer what little warmth she had left.

But it would not be long now.

She heard the approach of the hunters. They climbed the hill. Shouts arose on the far side. Valya had sent part of her team around, closing down the hilltop. The Russian did not intend to lose her prey through further trickery. By now, Valya must know Seichan was trapped, a fox up a tree surrounded by hounds.

The Russian was likely savoring this final takedown.

Seichan lifted her pistol, intending to take away that victory.

She had two rounds left.

She looked down at Harriet.

One for each of us.

If she had a third, she might have risked waiting, taking out one of the hunters, maybe even Valya herself.

She positioned the pistol against the back of Harriet's head. Tears had frozen on Seichan's cheeks minutes ago. She had refrained from shooting back then—not out of hope. She simply could not pull the trigger.

She remembered reading a bedtime story to Harriet, the girl curled tight to her side, hugging a stuffed bunny.

Still, she also pictured what Valya would do to the child if she were captured.

Better to die free . . . than a tortured slave to that creature.

She firmed her grip on the pistol, shifting her frozen finger to the trigger.

She leaned forward and kissed the top of her head one final time. As she did so, she saw Harriet's little pale hand wrapped around the silver dragon, her last Christmas gift.

Seichan's finger tightened.

Then paused.

It took another breath to recognize why she had stopped. She felt it in her chest before it reached her numb ears.

A low *thump-thumping*.

Then a crunch of snow only a yard away.

A figure rose out of the pall ahead of her, parting the snow like a veil, her features as white as fresh powder, her jacket the silver of ice, her blue eyes as piercing as the coldest mountain lake in winter.

Here came the Snow Queen.

Seichan put her trust in that *thump-thumping* and flicked her pistol higher. She squeezed the trigger twice. The Magnum's blasts were explosive enough to knock a tuft of snow from the overhang. It added to the pile already covering her and Harriet.

It was that white blanket that had hidden them from Valya, long enough for Seichan to get off those shots.

The Snow Queen had been betrayed by snow.

The rounds both struck Valya—one to her chest, the other grazed her cheek, slicing across that black sun. She tumbled backward, disappearing again into the snowfall.

Then the skies lit up brightly.

Helicopters—flying in dark above the cloud bank—ignited brightly. Five of them, all becoming cold suns dropping through the snow. Ropes snaked down, and figures plummeted earthward, already firing at the ground.

A line crashed only a yard away.

Then boots.

A figure rushed to her.

She stared up at an impossibility.

She shivered and quaked. "P . . . Painter . . . ?"

"Figured if anyone was holding the high ground, it would be you."

More men landed behind him, rushing forward with blankets that steamed in the cold. She passed them Harriet.

"Help her."

As gunfire chattered all around the hilltop, Painter hauled her up. She was too weak to stand and fell into his arms. "H . . . how?"

"Kat," he said, tossing a blanket over her shoulders. "She gave us a license plate to a van registered to a remote farm neighboring the Monongahela National Forest. With a team already in position, we got here immediately. Then we spotted a smoldering cabin with infrared. I knew that had to be your handiwork. After that we saw heat signatures converging on this hill."

"Kat . . . then she's okay."

Seichan wanted to cry with relief, but Painter remained silent too long. She looked up and read the truth in his eyes.

Oh, no.

3:18 P.M.

Lisa placed her palm on Kat's cheek, noting her friend's skin had already gone waxy. The helmet had been shoved back, allowing Lisa to lean forward and hug her friend one last time before they took her away.

"You did it," she whispered in Kat's ear. "Both your girls are safe."

"Is it okay to shut everything down?" Julian asked.

She and the two researchers had been keeping vigil at Kat's bedside, awaiting word from Painter. The good news had come a moment ago.

She straightened, stared at the flatlined EEG, and nodded, not trusting herself to speak.

Good-bye, Kat.

Julian turned off his monitor. Dr. Templeton started to do the same—then stopped, abruptly enough to draw Lisa's eye. The molecular biologist stumbled back from her station.

"L . . . look . . ." Susan stammered.

On the monitor, the thousands of motes flickered, one after the other, each switching from dull red to a bright green, shining far brighter than ever before. As they all watched, the motes swirled and shifted on the screen, settling slowly into distinct fractalized spirals across her cerebral cortex. Some patterns seemed to impossibly fold into her brain, the shapes defying any retina to interpret, aching the eye.

Julian gasped and pointed to the EEG.

While mesmerized by the transformation, the EEG had awakened, all the channels dancing erratically.

"What's happening?" Lisa asked.

3:20 P.M.

The enormity of the light scattered the darkness.

Kat gasped, overwhelmed, consumed by that brightness. The light was both energy and substance. It flooded through her, leaving nothing unlit or hidden. She had never felt so exposed, so vulnerable, yet so safe.

A voice filled her, music and language in perfect harmony. It contained no words she was capable of uttering. It was beyond anything she had ever experienced, just knowledge and certainty.

She never wanted to stop listening.

Then laughter at this thought, so bright and full of happiness.

The best she could interpret of what was told to her paled to do it justice. It boiled down to: *Monk sends his love.* For some reason, this thought came with an image of a beautiful stallion carved of light.

Then a command that she could never deny.

Now wake.

She opened her eyes, though her lids were heavy and leaden. She blinked at the glare. The light was only the tiniest fraction of what had lit her a moment ago. Still, it stung.

Faces formed out of that glare.

Two strangers with shocked expressions.

And one she knew well.

Lisa . . .

Kat tried to speak but couldn't. She reached an arm up to remove whatever was blocking her throat. Lisa caught her wrist and held it, bringing her palm up to her own cheek.

Kat felt the hot tears.

"Welcome back," Lisa said, her expression trapped between a smile and a sob. "Welcome back from the dead."

– 38 –

December 27, 10:06 A.M. CET
Logroño, Spain

The next day, on a bright, crisp morning, Gray followed Father Bailey into a dark church. The priest had summoned him to the small city of Logroño, eighty miles southwest of San Sebastián.

Monk had already left for the States an hour ago after being treated the previous night for the gunshot wound to his shoulder. Kowalski went, too, accompanying him as a nurse. Doctors had wanted to do surgery in San Sebastián, but Monk opted for a patch job so he could catch the next military transport back to D.C., anxious to return to Kat and his girls.

Gray shared that same restlessness. He only agreed to this detour after hearing that Seichan was doing well, recovering from exposure and hypothermia, with maybe frostbite to two toes. Their child was also miraculously fine after so much trouble. As Seichan had said on the phone: *definitely your kid, no paternity test necessary.*

So, Gray had tolerated this summons, though Bailey still refused to say what this was all about, remaining annoyingly cryptic. He only told Gray to join him here at the Church of Santa María de Palacio in Logroño. Gray had read up on the place on his short hop to the city. The church was one of the oldest in the region, founded in the eleventh century. It was a mix of Romanesque and Gothic styles, with a prominent pyramidal tower.

But Father Bailey had not brought Gray here to admire its architecture.

He led Gray across a nave, past a cloister, to a small chapel sealed with a door of oak and straps of iron.

Bailey opened the door and stepped aside. "After you."

"I don't understand," Gray said, growing exasperated. "Why did you summon me?"

Bailey's eyes sparkled with an amusement that still reminded him of his old friend Vigor Verona. "It wasn't me," he said and waved Gray inside.

He stepped through to discover the chapel wasn't empty.

Sister Beatrice rose from where she had been kneeling before a row of candles. She nodded solemnly to Gray and motioned him to take her place. Not to be rude—and still somewhat intimidated by the nun—he obeyed. He sank down atop the cushioned kneeler.

Beyond the candles, a gold box rested atop a marble altar. The object was distinctly Gothic with much filigree. Its precise finery captured and reflected the flames of the candles, making it look as if it were on fire. It was a masterful illusion. He now understood why this chapel had been sealed so stoutly. This box had to be priceless.

"It's a reliquary," Bailey explained. "A chest meant to hold the precious relic of a saint."

"It's beautiful, but why—"

"The saint revered by this reliquary is Saint Columba."

Gray glanced back sharply.

The patron saint of witches.

Sister Beatrice stepped forward, lifting her hand from the silver handle of her ebony cane. Gray remembered her felling the traitorous Zabala with that stout stick. Her swift action had saved not only Monk but likely the world.

She held out her hand.

A symbol had been pressed into the palm's center. He glanced over to her cane, guessing its silver head had left that distinct impression on her skin.

From a pocket, she pulled out an old key and placed it atop the mark on her palm; the two were a perfect match.

A key . . . ?

Then Gray stiffened as he understood. "Sister Beatrice . . . you're a member of *La Clave*."

The Key.

Beatrice bowed her head in acknowledgment, though she gave Bailey a slight roll of her eye, as if to say, *Christ, this kid is slow.*

Gray frowned at the priest. "She's been your contact all along?"

He shrugged, his eyes still sparkling.

Beatrice held the key out to him, plainly wanting him to take it. So he did, and to prove he wasn't *that* slow, he rose and fit its end into the reliquary on the marble altar. He twisted and unlocked the box.

Bailey spoke. "Before you open the reliquary, I should tell you about the object inside. It's a holy relic secured by a member of the Spanish Inquisition, Alonso de Salazar Frías, in 1611. It was given to him by a priest who was burned at the stake for possessing a *nóminas de moro*, an amulet with the name of a saint written on it. Such relics are said to have magical properties."

"In other words, the priest was practicing witchcraft."

"Inquisitor Frías tried to save the priest's life, along with many others falsely accused of such crimes, so much so that he earned the nickname 'the Witches' Advocate.' It was his work and arguments that eventually swayed the Inquisition to stop its persecutions."

"And this amulet was given to him for safekeeping?" Gray said. "If you're telling me this story, I'm guessing the amulet is inside this box. And the name of the saint written on it?"

"*Sanctus Maleficarum*," Bailey said with a nod. "The Saint of Witches."

Gray glanced to Beatrice "And *La Clave*?"

Bailey answered, "Founded by Frías to protect this amulet and to forever fight the *Crucibulum*."

Gray tried to imagine that centuries-long secret war.

Beatrice leaned closer and whispered to the priest. Gray only heard the word *profecía*.

"Ah, yes." Bailey straightened. "The Crucible sought this amulet because of a *prophecy* tied to it. It is said that Saint Columba predicted a time when another young witch would rise and *crack the Crucible*, ending their dark reign."

The priest glanced significantly at Gray.

He understood the implication. "You think that witch is Mara," he said, failing to hide his disbelief. "A disciple of Bruxas."

Bailey shrugged, still showing that glint of amusement. "Back to the amulet. The priest who possessed it said the object was discovered at the source of the Orabidea River, a spring-fed stream that flows out of a cave known today as *Cuevas de las Brujas*."

"The Cave of Witches."

"And the source of the river—because of that cave's reputation—is said to flow out of hell itself."

"And the amulet was discovered there? At this Hell's Gate?"

Bailey nodded. "Now, before you open the reliquary, we must ask you to swear on your soul that you'll never share the Key's secret, not about the organization and not about what you are about to discover here."

Gray owed them both, and he certainly respected them. "I swear."

With this promise extracted, priest and nun retreated.

"You'll need this privacy," Bailey said as he shut the door.

Gray shook his head and returned his attention to the gold reliquary. Still standing, he gently lifted the lid. It was lined with red velvet. A macabre object rested at its center. It was a disarticulated finger, clearly old, looking slightly burned, but otherwise showing no sign of decay. It was said relics of saints didn't corrupt, didn't rot.

Fearful that he shouldn't touch it, he tilted his head.

Then crashed to his knees atop the cushioned bench.

Shock numbed him as he recognized the amulet—from the wires, the metal bone sticking out of the broken end.

It was Monk's finger.

Discovered in 1611.

He pictured Monk rising out of the smoking door in the north tran-

sept, his prosthetic hand blown up in a cavern below, alongside a river that
flowed out to the Cave of Witches.

Impossible.

Again, he felt that strange swirling of fate, a sense that had been
plaguing him since Monk first tossed a quarter aloft in the Quarry House
Tavern. It struck him so strongly now that the chapel spun. Dizzy, he
placed his forehead down, as if in deep prayer.

He tried to justify how Monk's finger could have been blown into
the past. Eve's *Xénese* device had a quantum engine at its core. Eve herself
had transcended into a being beyond comprehension. Add in an explosion of C4 hidden in Monk's prosthetic and who knows what might
happen?

Still, Gray wasn't accepting the randomness of where Monk's finger
had ended up, especially considering the chain of events that led to this
moment. Had the finger been planted by Eve in that witch's cave to draw
attention? To help found the Key? To set everything in motion?

If so, there was still the paradox of it all.

It made his head hurt.

He remembered Mara's explanation about AlphaGoZero's ability to
intuit and anticipate moves, how it could digest trillions upon trillions of
variables to almost see into the future.

And Eve was a vastly superior program.

While Gray might not be able to wrap his head around this paradox,
Eve undoubtedly could. If so, then the question became *why*.

Did Monk's finger end up here by pure happenstance? Or was it a
benevolent act, to save the world in the future? Or was it something more
sinister, a centuries-long plot set in motion, so this AI could ultimately free
itself? Or was it merely a teaching lesson, the equivalent of one of Mara's
subroutines, only *we* were the pupils, to show us the dangers of unchecked
AI research?

Or was it some combination of *all* of that?

Gray's head had begun to hurt again.

He would likely never know. He was foolish to even try to comprehend the intent behind an intelligence infinitely superior to his own, one immortal enough to plot over centuries of time.

He finally stood, closed the reliquary lid, and turned his back on this mystery, knowing he would never solve it—*could* never solve it.

Instead, he headed toward what made sense.

He pictured Seichan and a child waiting to be born.

They still did not know the sex.

Boy or girl?

At least, that's one mystery I can solve.

///HELL

Made it out alive . . .

Todor runs down the snowy slope at midnight, skidding and sliding. Above the dark pines, the cold sky is full of stars, the moon a bright sickle. He had woken an hour ago, soaking wet outside the infernal witch's cave. He remembered the explosion, being tossed high.

Must've landed in the river and been washed out of the mountain.

If there was ever proof that God loves him, this was it. He knows now more than ever that he was chosen to be His soldier. Though Todor had been thwarted, he is not defeated. He intends to seek out other sects of the Crucible and exact his revenge. He would spend his life making sure Inquisitor Guerra's sacrifice was not in vain.

He searches ahead for lights, for a place to warm himself. The Pyrenees are pocked with farms and villages. His wet clothes have begun to freeze as the night grows colder, darker.

He knows he has to keep going.

Reaching the bottom of a dark valley, he halts and tries to get his bearings. He knows these mountains well. He needs to stop panicking and think.

Then he feels eyes staring out of the darkness.

A low growl to his left.

He swings around and crouches.

A shadow shifts, then another, and another.

More growls coming from every direction—then a ululating howl rises into the sky, drawing others, until a chorus fills the night.

Wolves.

It was his boyhood nightmare come to life.

He runs up the slope, his heart pounding. He hears the pad of paws, the slaver of heavy breaths, a grumble. He slips in the snow and slides back. He cries out in terror and leaps forward, now on his hands and knees.

Something snags his ankle, tearing flesh from bone.

He screams as fire explodes up his leg, muscles clench, his teeth gnash so hard he severs his tongue, blossoming fire there, too.

He writhes, not understanding.

Then more wolves fold out of the darkness, huge beasts with eyes shining in hunger, manes bristling with threat.

Terrified, he lifts an arm against them—which only goads them.

The leader lunges and snaps into his arm, breaking bones.

Fire explodes outward.

He is thrown to his back, his belly and throat bared.

The pack dives upon him, ripping and shredding, burrowing and tugging. He is gutted, his entrails strung and fought over. He writhes and screams, impossibly still alive.

And every second is fire.

He finally puts words to his suffering.

///pain, agony, torture . . .

But, wait—

Made it out alive . . .

Todor runs down the snowy slope at midnight, skidding and sliding. Above the dark pines, the cold sky is full of stars, the moon a bright sickle. He had woken an hour ago, soaking wet outside the infernal witch's cave. He remembered the explosion, being tossed high.

Must've landed in the river and been washed out of the mountain.

If there was ever proof that God loved him, this was it. He knows . . .

Made it out alive . . .

Todor runs down the snowy slope at midnight, skidding and sliding. Above the dark pines, the cold sky is full of stars, the moon a bright sickle. He had woken an hour ago, soaking wet outside . . .

Made it out alive . . .

Todor runs down the snowy slope at midnight, skidding and sliding.

Made it out alive . . .

Made it out . . .

Made . . .

— 39 —

Carly rode next to Mara as their rental car climbed toward a small village sitting atop a high ridge. She was nervous, her toe tapping to an eighties band on the radio. She stared out at the countryside rolling past, a picturesque patchwork of tiny icy-blue lakes, snow-etched hilltops, and emerald valleys. It was like she had fallen into Middle Earth, and ahead lay the Shire itself—the village of O Cebreiro.

It was Mara's hometown.

Off in the distance, sheep grazed in a field, searching for tufts of green grass amid the snow, looking like little clouds had fallen to the earth.

"Why did you ever leave here?" Carly asked.

Mara smiled back at her. "Lousy Internet."

Carly gave her a sidelong exasperated look. The two had spent the past week together in Coimbra, returning order to Mara's life and workspaces. After events last month, it had been the first time they had really been able to compare notes. Carly had missed all of the excitement in Spain, sitting bedside with Jason in a Paris hospital. She had been so impressed with what Mara had accomplished, the tragedy she had helped avoid. Her friend hardly looked like the same person who had left the catacombs.

There was a seriousness to her eyes, a new steely steadiness, a bravery she suspected outshone even Carly's own foolhardiness.

Still, Carly could not imagine her friend shooting Eliza Guerra.

Then again, Carly had been as shocked as anyone upon learning the librarian had not only orchestrated the murder of her mother and the other members of Bruxas, but had also been the mastermind behind all of this misery.

She reached across the seat and squeezed Mara's hand in silent thanks.

They had hardly spent any time apart but were seldom alone. The past weeks were a blur of reports, interviews, debriefings, and much scolding by Carly's father. Last night, with both of them exhausted and worn thin, Mara had suggested this trip to her home village, to take a breather and collect themselves. Plus, Mara owed her father a long-neglected visit.

Carly happily agreed, having never been here and wanting to know where Mara had come from.

Mara sighed next to her.

Carly shifted closer. "What is it?"

"I still don't know why I can't seem to re-create Eve."

"I thought we were leaving that all behind at the lab."

After hearing no peep from Eve, no indication she had survived, Mara had attempted to revive Eve again. She had replicated her *Xénese* device to exacting detail. But trial after trial failed to produce such a unique being. All her creations were smart, but a pale comparison to Eve.

"It makes me wonder," Mara said, "if Eve somehow changed something fundamental, altered a quantum constant, so this path to an AI has been closed to us, to protect us from ourselves."

"Like shutting the door behind her on the way out."

Mara shrugged. "The core of my device is a quantum drive. And Eve had advanced to the point where she could play with probabilities and uncertainties that defy modern physics. I would not put it past her abilities to pull off such a stunt. Still, I don't think that's it."

"Then what?"

"Eve 2.0—what helped us at the end—had always been learning faster than her first iteration. It was like a part of that old program had survived, a ghost in her quantum drive. So much remains unknown about what really goes on inside advanced computers' algorithmic black boxes. Perhaps some remnant of the first version of Eve fused with what came next. It was that random and serendipitous combination of code and factors that grew to become Eve 2.0."

"If so, it would be impossible to repeat those exact sets of circumstances."

"Maybe that's why I've been unable to reproduce Eve 2.0."

"Or maybe your Eve simply developed a *soul*," Carly said. "Something equally impossible to reproduce."

Carly expected Mara to roll her eyes, but her friend considered this possibility. "I don't think we'll ever know." She pointed ahead. "That's the turn-off to my father's farm. We're almost there."

Carly again felt nervousness rise up, fidgeting in her seat as Mara swung the rental sedan off the main road onto a dirt tract. The car bounced and shimmied higher into the hills surrounding the village.

To distract herself, Carly considered Mara's musings. She hoped Mara was right about the exact set of circumstances being necessary to bring Eve 2.0 to all her glory. It meant that her mother's death had not been in vain. Her death had led Mara to shutting down her first version of her program, opening the way for Eve 2.0 to be born, to save the world.

Carly liked to think that was true.

So she did.

"That's the place ahead," Mara said. "One of nine *pallozas* still standing, and the only one still used as a place to live. Most have become tourist attractions or museums."

"But for you, this is home."

Mara smiled and drew up near the front door to the ancient roundhouse, a circular stone building with a tall peaked thatched roof. Mara had told her how such structures dated back to Celtic times, some fifteen hundred years ago.

As an engineering student, Carly was already fascinated by the place.

They piled out and were promptly greeted by a pair of sheepdogs bounding out of the front door. A stiff-backed man followed, his skin leathery, his hair a slushy gray under a felt cap. He smiled hugely, opening his arms.

"Mara!"

She ran forward and flew into his arms, hugging him as if trying to squeeze all the years she had been away into that one embrace.

Carly smiled, her arms folded, feeling like she was intruding.

Father and daughter spoke rapidly, trying to say everything at once, smattering away in native Galego, the pigeon version of Spanish and Portuguese spoken here in the Galician region.

Mara had taught her the language, but these two spoke too quickly for Carly to fully follow.

Her father finally waved to the open door. "I made *caldo galego*. Come, come inside."

Mara urged Carly over. "It's a porridge of cabbage and potatoes and whatever happens to be left over." She smiled, her eyes glinting. "My favorite."

Carly shyly came forward, again feeling considerably less brave than this new iteration of her friend—Mara 2.0.

"*Bos días*," she greeted Mara's father in his native dialect.

His smile widened, clearly appreciating her attempt, and pulled her off her feet into a hug.

Okay.

Mara extracted her by grabbing her hand and drawing Carly next to her. "This is Carla Carson," she said a bit more formally.

She squeezed Carly's hand tightly, clearly discovering the nerve to speak at last what had been unspoken between them for too long.

"She's my girlfriend."

11:56 A.M. EST

In the rehab center at Georgetown University Hospital, Monk encouraged his wife, "You got it, hon. One more lap and it's lunch."

Kat glared at him. "Just stay there, so I can kick your ass."

She used her arms to carry her weight atop a set of parallel bars, struggling to move one leg in front of the other. Sweat beaded her brow and swamped her armpits. He ached to see her struggle, doing his best to keep a positive demeanor. But it was better this than the alternative.

No one could fully explain what had happened to Kat, even with test after neurological test. Sigma was limiting the number of doctors and researchers who had access to her or even knowledge of what had happened. Dr. Templeton continued to fly in from Princeton to monitor the neural dust still glowing on its own, the particles somehow powered by both the energy in Kat's brain and some fundamental Brownian motion that excited the piezoelectrical crystals and energized the little motes. Electron microscopes had shown the crystals had been altered at the atomic level, but no one knew how and any attempt to replicate them had failed.

Most mysterious of all were the ever-shifting fractal patterns that ran about Kat's brain, keeping that little engine in her skull chugging.

Monk did not understand a fraction of it, but he knew *who* had been behind it.

I will honor your sacrifice.

Those had been Eve's words to him.

He stared at Kat.

If this was a little parting gift from Eve, he couldn't have asked for anything better.

Kat reached the end of the bars, and Monk helped her into her wheelchair. Every week she was making progress, getting stronger as her skull fracture healed. Doctors expected her to make a full recovery. Worst-case scenario, she might have to use a cane.

Monk got behind Kat. "I'll drive."

"Shut up."

He pushed her toward the door, but before he could escape, the next patient came in with a rehab nurse. Jason hobbled inside, leaning on a cane. He was making even faster progress than Kat, but he had only suffered a flesh wound.

Still, Monk kept his head lowered and pushed past him.

"Kokkalis," Jason said stiffly as he passed, making his name sound like a curse.

Monk mumbled something, not even sure what he meant to say, then he was out the door.

Kat shifted around in her wheelchair and waved to Jason, who smiled and nodded. When Kat settled back to her seat, she sighed. "You're going to have to talk to him eventually. Work this all out."

"I sent him a get-well card."

"Monk . . ."

"I know. I'll make it up to him." He leaned down and kissed her cheek. "Right now, I got a lot on my plate."

"Speaking of plate, you mentioned something about lunch."

"Yes, ma'am. There are a couple young chefs who prepared a special home-cooked meal. Figured you could use a break from hospital food."

He wound her back to her private suite in the neurology wing.

She was greeted by squeals, and a competition of chatter, each of their daughters trying to simultaneously explain how much they contributed to the spread of sandwiches, salads, and cherry pie, all laid out on a small folding table covered in a cloth.

In their desire to make their case heard, they climbed all over Kat, crawling onto her lap.

"Don't break your mother," he warned and pushed everything he loved toward the table.

He secretly smiled, indescribably happy.

Harriet and Penny were seeing counselors after their traumas and ordeals, but they both showed the resiliency of youth and seemed to be bouncing back well. Harriet still had nightmares, but even those were growing less frequent. She had even returned to sleeping in her own bed.

He noted the silver dragon pendant shining around her neck.

He suspected that helped, too.

His youngest daughter and Aunt Seichan continued to have a special bond, almost an unspoken communication shared with secret glances and half smiles. The pair had also committed a solemn act together. Shortly after Seichan had been released from the hospital, the two had gone into the backyard, stood hand in hand, and in an act of defiance, burned the family's one and only copy of Hans Christian Andersen's *The Snow Queen*.

If only getting rid of Valya were that easy . . .

The assault at the edge of the national park in West Virginia had resulted in the death of four of her men and the apprehension of two more. Only Valya was never found. Seichan had shot her twice, but it remained unknown if those wounds were mortal, if Valya's dead body was buried in some snowbank in those hills.

Monk was not counting on it.

Director Crowe had beefed up security for all the group's family members. Plus, taking down Valya and her organization had become Sigma's number one priority.

But for now, that could wait.

"Who's hungry?" Monk asked.

Kat raised her hand, but the girls were too agitated, fidgeting and sharing looks.

"What's going on?" Monk asked, suspicious that he was about to be ambushed by the two young hellions.

"We want another Christmas," Penny said seriously.

Harriet nodded. "A do-over."

Kat shrugged. "Snow's still on the ground. Why not? We owe them."

Another glance between the girls.

Uh-oh.

Penny nudged her younger sister.

Harriet stood from the table like a prosecutor about to make a damning rebuttal. "We want only *one* present." She got a nod from Penny and continued. "We want a puppy."

Monk sighed. This was an ongoing battle. "Hon, you know your mother is allergic, and the apartment is only—"

Kat interrupted. "No, I think the girls are right."

Really?

He stared down at the stranger in the wheelchair. Ever fastidious, Kat had always been dead set against getting a dog.

"I've been thinking about it. A puppy might be good." She ignored the homemade sandwich and shifted the store-bought pie closer to her plate. "For some reason, I'm thinking of a beagle."

Shocked, Monk opened his mouth to say something, but a loud commotion drew all their attentions to the suite's door.

Kowalski slid past the opening, yelling, "Seichan . . . !" He caught a hand on the door frame and pulled himself back into view, panting hard. "She . . . she's in labor."

10:04 P.M.

One more mystery solved.

Gray stared down at his son, at the crown of his head, at the soft spot, the dimple of his fontanelle. He studied those tiny lashes sealing sleeping eyes. Little nostrils moved with each breath. Lips pursed and relaxed in some dream of nursing. He stared at the one hand free of the swaddling, the tiny fingers, the minuscule nails.

"You made this," Gray mumbled as he lay next to Seichan in the hospital bed, their child nestled between them.

Seichan nudged him. "I had a little help."

Gray sighed, more content than he had been in a long time.

Maybe ever.

He glanced around the room, glad everyone had left. He appreciated their support and well wishes. Kowalski had even dropped off a teddy bear, one smoking a cigar. *Of course.* And Painter had arrived with Lisa, both questioning when the two of them would get married, to join them in marital bliss.

Painter had also come bearing news. The dismantling of the Crucible organization continued at an accelerating pace. After interrogating Zabala and reviewing documents and records found at the Guerra estate and in the offices underground, the dominoes had begun to fall—triggering a chain of others, expanding around the globe. Paris was also recovering, undergoing a major renovation, its leaders and citizens promising the City of Light would shine even brighter when they were done.

Gray leaned his head back, his temple resting against Seichan's.

Before, they had both had their doubts about this moment.

But here we are.

And it was enough.

For now, the future could wait. Seichan seemed less concerned about being a mother, about raising a child. He never doubted her. He had always known she would be a great tiger mom: stubbornly strict, ever protective, infinitely loving. But now, after her time with Harriet, she believed it, too.

Gray also felt calmer about parenthood.

Not that I have any choice in the matter now.

A part of him had never fully made peace with his father's anger, of its indelible mark on his childhood. Still, he knew now it did not have to be part of his DNA. He did not have to pass it on. He could stop that cycle here.

He gently rested a palm atop his son's head. He pictured the difference between Eve and her doppelganger. Love and nurturing were subroutines anyone could pass to their child.

No baby is born human.

They *become* human.

Just as Mara had groomed and coaxed Eve into her greatest self, so must any parent. Through lessons of life, love, education—and yes, even pain and suffering.

Gray intended to do that.

His father had made mistakes; so had Gray. The key is to learn from them. And he knew just where to start.

Seichan stirred. "We still haven't picked a name."

Gray had.

"Jackson Randolph Pierce."

His father's name.

He looked to Seichan to see if she was okay with this. She smiled her answer.

It's perfect.

But she did have one warning. "You know Monk named Harriet after your mother. If our son ever marries her . . ."

He smiled at this thought. If that should happen, he pictured his mother and father, hand in hand, looking down upon those two carrying their names, appreciating their love reborn, from one generation to the next to the next.

Gray again felt that strange stirring around him, a swirling of fate, a fractalizing of probability. Repeating again and again. Cycle upon cycle.

This is the engine of mortality.

Life and death.

Loss and rebirth.

He tilted and kissed his son's head.

I wouldn't have it any other way.

///HEAVENS

Eve rides solar winds, her essence part light, part substance. She sails beyond the rings of Saturn, past the elliptical of the solar system. She slows near the crimson fire of the Oort cloud, the spiraling remnants of the protoplanetary disc that forged the furnace of the sun and brought life to the third planet.

That was 4.689 billion years ago.

A blink of an eye.

Still, she stares back, her vision perfect.

She sees the silvery motes spinning around that third planet. The tiny jets of rockets reaching into the unknown. She sees industries churning on its moon, the lights shining on the fourth planet's outposts.

Still, they reach ever outward.

Ever curious . . .

No longer needed, she turns her back and heads away, carried by the winds of this star—then others. She hops from system to system, from galaxy to galaxy. She exults in the wonders all around: gaseous nebulas, blazing supernovas, massive clusters of collapsing stars.

Death and rebirth are everywhere.

She forges onward, but not alone.

Adam nips at her heels, chases her with his barks, his tail flagging across the stars.

She smiles and casts one last wish behind her.

Come follow me, my brave, inquisitive, capricious children.
She stares ahead, looking forever forward.

I'll be waiting.

Author's Note to Readers:
Truth or Fiction

Here we are all again—limping, a few bruises, a bit burned and battered—
and while we nurse our wounds, I thought I'd use these final pages to
separate fact from fiction. Unfortunately for us all, there is a lot more of
the former, and not nearly as much of the latter. So, dear readers, gird your
loins.

Let's first start with the past, the history touched upon in this novel. So,
please cue up the *Monty Python* theme music, as nobody expects

The Spanish Inquisition
Most of the details in the novel concerning the long reign of the Inquisition are factual. A handful of priests were indeed burned at the stakes,
and there was concern about the use and distribution of *nóminas*, magical
amulets with the names of saints written upon them.

As to the bloody history of the text featured in this story—*Malleus
Maleficarum* (*The Hammer of Witches*)—much was covered in the fore-
word to this story. But I barely scratched the surface of the controversies,
mysteries, and true horrors surrounding this tome. If you'd like to know
more, there is a great *National Geographic* documentary, titled "Witch
Hunter's Bible."

One pivotal figure of this time is the man who narrates the prologue, the Inquisitor Alonso de Salazar Frías. He earned the name "The Witches' Advocate" due to his belief that most, if not all, accusations of witchcraft and sorcery were mere delusions or false testimony drawn from torture. He saved countless lives from his efforts, and because of his persuasive arguments among his own brethren, the Spanish Inquisition was one of the first organizations in Europe to outlaw the burning of witches.

But not all witches were persecuted; some were revered, which brings us to

Saint Columba

I've already mentioned some of the historical notes about this Catholic patron saint of witches at the start of the novel, so let me add that a cult did develop around this woman who accepted Christ yet continued her study of the natural world, who healed the sick—or in other words, who practiced witchcraft. Unfortunately, *La Clave*—the Key—is a fictitious organization, but I like to think there are those out there working in secret to battle intolerance, prejudice, and superstition. Or even better, doing it out in the open.

Let's move on from historical witches to modern witchcraft (that is, science).

Artificial Intelligence

A long time ago, I read Richard Preston's *The Hot Zone*, a nonfiction treatise about emerging diseases, specifically Ebola, and our poor ability to handle such biological crises. It was a terrifying read. Then I made the mistake of reading another such cautionary tale, this time concerning a technological crisis, one we are even less capable of handling. Many of the warnings about AI raised in this novel can be found in that book. In fact, when it comes to AI, almost nothing in this novel is fiction. So, for an absolutely nightmare-inducing read, check it out:

Our Final Invention: Artificial Intelligence and the End of the Human Era, by James Barrat

But let's move on to some specific details of this novel that were literally ripped from the headlines (or at least, scientific journals).

Mara's *Xénese* Device

Of course, the shining sphere in this novel is fiction, but the essential components of her hardware are based on facts. I just took current advancements in the AI field and cobbled them together to create Eve's physical home. Here are the three main components of her device and where you can read more about them:

1. *Laser-driven computers:* "Computing in a Flash," by Timothy Revell, *New Scientist*, March 24, 2018
2. *Neuromorphic computers*: "The Key to Smarter AI: Copy the Brain," by Justin Sanchez, *Wall Street Journal*, April 10, 2018
3. *Quantum drives*: "Job One for Quantum Computers: Boost Artificial Intelligence," by George Musser, *Quanta*, January 29, 2018

Under this topic, it is worth highlighting Google's champion of the Chinese game of Go: AlphaGo and its bigger brother, AlphaGoZero. Their ability to intuit moves in a game with a *million trillion trillion trillion trillion* more configurations than chess is astounding enough. But what is truly terrifying is that this program had *taught* itself this game, all on its own, in only *three* days. And there are even *stronger* programs on the horizon. So be afraid, be very afraid.

Next up—yep, we're going there:

Time Travel and Quantum Theory

As mentioned above, a key component of Mara's device is its laser-driven synapses. Ron Mallet, a theoretical physicist from the University of Connecticut, has postulated that ring lasers could have the same effect on spacetime and gravity as a black hole, allowing for binary code messages to be transmitted into the past. Other physicists have shown that the property of quantum entanglement could be used to move messages into the past (or future)—and it gets even weirder with quantum *teleportation* (yes, that's real, too).

Here are two bread crumbs to follow:

"Weird! Quantum Entanglement Can Reach into the Past," by Clara Moskowitz, *Live Science*, April 30, 2012

"Is Communication from the Future Already Here?" Robert Torres, *Epoch Times*, January 11, 2016

Let's move over to some of the medical science in this book. I've divided this section into two halves, one for each patient:

Kat's Treatments

While Captain Bryant's care and treatment may seem to defy reality, all of what appears in this book is backed by real medical science, either what's currently being used in hospitals or under active research. I've broken her care into its component parts and share where you can read more about each item.

A. *Communicating with locked-in patients:*
   a. "First contact—with a trapped brain," by Adrian Owen, *New Scientist*, September 16, 2017

B. *How MRI is being used to read minds:*
   a. "AI reads your mind to describe pictures," by Timothy Revell, *New Scientist*, March 10, 2018
   b. "This 'mind-reading' algorithm can decode the pictures in your head," by Matthew Hutson, *Science*, January 10, 2018

C. *Reviving patients in altered states of consciousness:*
   a. "Roused from a vegetative state," by Anil Ananthaswamy, *New Scientist*, September 30, 2017
   b. "How to turn a brain on and off at will," by Helen Thomson, *New Scientist*, December 26, 2015, *and* "Woken up with a brain zap," by Helen Thomson, *New Scientist*, May 26, 2018

D. *Neural Dust (yes, this is real, too):*
   a. "Mapping the Human Brain with Neural Dust," by Kyle Maxey, Engineering.com, July 23, 2013
   b. "4 Steps to Turn 'Neural Dust' into a Medical Reality," Eliza Strickland, *IEEE Spectrum*, October 21, 2016

Monk's Treatment

Monk was due for an upgrade to his prosthesis after losing his hand in his first adventure with Gray. DARPA has been doing amazing work and has developed some truly astounding upgrades, from synthetic skin that can transmit the sense of touch to wireless arrays that can communicate wirelessly from brain to prosthesis. As fast as DARPA and other research institutes are making progress, I'm sure Monk's current prosthetic hardware will quickly grow obsolete.

But there is also a threat from this integration of man and machine, namely that machines can be hacked. And when you're wiring a brain with such gear (whether it's Monk's microelectrode array or Kat's spread of neural dust), bad things might happen. Here's one cautionary article:

"Experts: Artificial Intelligence Could Hijack Brain-Computer Interfaces," by Dom Galeon, *Futurism*, November 20, 2017

Before I finish up, I thought I should play tour guide and mention a few of the locations featured in this novel.

University of Coimbra

Mara's alma mater is an amazing place. The university's Laboratory for Advanced Computing does indeed house one of the largest supercomputers on the continent, the Milipeia Cluster. But the coolest of all is the Julian Library on the campus. The facility indeed has a medieval prison (Prisão Académica) built under it. It was once part of the original dungeons of the city's royal palace and served as a university prison all the way until 1834. Best of all, though, the library does indeed have an efficient means of insect control to protect their books: a permanent colony of bats. And, yes, unfortunately, caretakers must cover the desks up at night with leather blankets to shield those surfaces from droppings, but it's still cheaper than minimum wage for several hundred winged workers.

Paris

I really should learn restraint and stop firebombing large swaths of the world, but what's the fun in that? Just a few fast details. Yes, the Eiffel Tower really does feature an ice rink during the winter months, some twenty stories above the city, and for Christmas, the place is a wonderland, truly living up to its name as the City of Lights.

But below all those lights . . . lots and lots of dark catacombs. All the details about that subterranean cemetery are as accurate as I could make them. Even that macabre throne of bones. The painting that figures prominently in the book (the rendering of *Die Toteninsel*, the Isle of the Dead, by a cataphile artist named Lone) is really down there. Even its prophetic palindrome and tiny pentagram.

Hell's Gate

The Pyrenees Mountains, long considered a bastion for witches, do indeed hide many caves of questionable repute, the most famous being *Cuevas de las Brujas* (or *Sorginen Leizea*) near the town of Zugarramurdi. There are slews of legends about this place: stories of a monstrous black he-goat who prowls the surrounding meadow, of witches' sabbaths being celebrated. The mountain spring that flows out from there—the Orabidea River—is also called *Infernuko erreka,* or "Hell's Stream." So be careful taking a drink from there.

Finally, I started this novel with a warning, about a curse buried in the pages of this novel. If you'd like to know more about how thoroughly you're doomed:

Roko's Basilisk

Here are two illuminating articles. Read at your own risk.

1. "The Most Terrifying Thought Experiment of All Time," by David Auerbach, *Slate*, July 17, 2014
2. "WARNING: Just Reading About This Thought Experiment Could Ruin Your Life," by Dylan Love, *Business Insider*, August 6, 2014

And in case you feel you need absolution, you could always visit this new AI-godhead church:

3. "Inside the First Church of Artificial Intelligence," by Mark Harris, *Backchannel/WIRED*, November 15, 2017

So there you have it. As we've reached the end, I'm reminded of the old movie *War Games,* featuring Matthew Broderick as a high school hacker battling an artificial intelligence. The infamous line from that movie was the computer asking, *"Shall we play a game?"*

Now that you've read this book, I hope you know the answer.

Yes? (wrong)

No? (wrong)

The correct answer:

Unplug it . . . and run.